JUST THE TWO OF US

BOOK 2

RYU HYANG

poppypub

Copyright © 2017 by Ryu Hyang
Translation copyright © 2020 by POPPYPUB LLC
First published in Korea in 2017 by Shin Young Media, Inc.
English translation rights arranged with Shin Young Media, Inc.
This book is published with the support of Publication Industry Promotion Agency of Korea (KPIPA).

Translated by Stephanie Cha
Cover design by Melissa Williams Design

Published by POPPYPUB, Fort Lee
www.poppypub.com
poppypub is a trademark of POPPYPUB LLC.

Library of Congress Control Number: 2021931711

ISBN 978-1-952787-10-2 (paperback)
ISBN 978-1-952787-09-6 (ebook)

CONTENTS

It was already dark by the time Yuna was heading home. The phone rang when she got on the bus.

"Hello?" she answered.

"Where are you?" asked the quiet and stoic voice. It was Soohyuk.

"I'm on my way," she answered.

"How long until you get here?"

"Umm…I think about twenty minutes."

"All right."

Once the call ended, Yuna fidgeted with the phone in her hand, mumbling, "I wish I were brave like Kyungjo. So I could make *my* move on him."

She really did wish so. A sigh escaped her mouth. For some reason, it felt like something she'd never be able to bring herself to do. The bus ran through the darkness as Yuna became lost in her thoughts.

When she got off the bus at last, she thought her eyes were fooling her. A man who looked just like Soohyuk was standing in front of her on the sidewalk.

Soohyuk stared at Yuna as she tiptoed toward him with a

squint, like she couldn't believe it was really him. "Don't your eyes hurt?" he asked.

Yuna sullenly pouted and pressed around her eyes as if to massage the strained muscles. *Oh, boy.* The ends of Soohyuk's lips pulled up toward his cheekbones. Yuna was now standing in front of him. She could sense that he was standing there in expectation of something.

"Were you out here for long?" she asked, already knowing the answer.

"I was. Let's go home." He reached out a hand toward her. Yuna hesitantly reached out hers as well. Soohyuk waited without saying anything. When her hand finally touched his, he simply held it firmly.

Yuna blushed. The feeling of her small hand wrapped in his large one tickled her heart.

A whisper escaped her smiling lips. "It's nice."

"Hmm? What's that?"

"I said, it's nice to hold hands with you," she said a bit louder.

"Sleeping with me would be even nicer," mumbled Soohyuk, cracking a smile.

Her face warmed, probably turning as red as a tomato. Thankfully, he started to walk without any further remarks. They walked side by side back home. Yuna's heart beat to the rhythm of their steps. *So, this is what dating feels like.* This must be how he was planning to train her heart. She suddenly wondered what kind of a person the woman he lived with before was. *Did he act this kindly toward her too?*

When they crossed the road and entered the alleyway where they could spot their building at the other end, Yuna raised the question. "Why did you let her move in with you?"

"Who?"

"The woman you said lived with you before."

Soohyuk rubbed his chin with one hand and mumbled, "Oh, her. She said that her apartment was undergoing renovations."

Yuna stopped walking and looked at him. She'd never dated anyone before. Soohyuk was an extremely honest man, but she still wanted to make sure. Who were his eyes on now?

"Did you tell her that you liked her too?" In spite of herself, her voice trembled like a leaf.

Soohyuk stopped walking as well and looked at her.

"I'm just wondering," said Yuna quickly. "I don't know much about you to begin with, and I'm a little worried you might still have some feelings left for her."

He tightened his grip to stop her hand from wriggling and slipping out of it. "I never had any feelings for her from the start. I just told her that I would try."

"What made you say that?" she asked.

"She kept following me. To the point that it made me think I should at least give it a try."

"But?"

"I failed. I didn't want to like her. I said that I'd try, but I really didn't. She then reciprocated by banging some stranger on my bed. All the while claiming that she loved me."

Yuna started to walk again. "She wasn't very nice."

Soohyuk continued moving alongside her, but he didn't reply. In his opinion, it was more that the woman couldn't control her lust than that she wasn't nice. He was now starting to get what she must have had to go through. It must have been a little like what he was feeling now. But he knew Yuna, shy as she was, would not understand him. Like he didn't understand that woman at the time.

"It's all in the past now," he said.

"I guess. Since I'm the one holding your hand now." Yuna sheepishly smiled and swung their clutched hands forward and back like a child. "Umm, I have another question."

"Shoot," he said.

She wanted to ask him what he thought of her smile, but she was overcome with embarrassment when she was about to. Her face grew hotter by the second as she felt more and more bashful.

"Are you just going to keep me hanging?" he asked.

"Never mind, it's nothing," she mumbled.

"What is it? All the more reason to ask if it's nothing."

Shoot, I shouldn't have said anything in the first place, she thought. Surrendering to his persistence, she asked with utmost awkwardness, "What do you think of my smile?"

It all happened in a flash. Soohyuk let go of her hand to wrap his arm around her shoulders instead and kissed the crown of her head.

"Mr. Cha…" She nervously pushed him away in response to his sudden action.

"It makes me want to do this," he answered as he pulled her even closer to him and kissed her on her forehead. She tensed, not knowing what to do.

"All right, all right," he said soothingly as they stepped into the building. When they arrived at the apartment, he closed the door and said, "I'm going to hug you and kiss you now."

Yuna didn't have enough time to escape his reach. All she could do was put her hands on his chest as he grabbed her waist with both of his hands and kissed her on the lips. *Ba-boom, ba-boom.* Her heart started pounding. His lips gently caressed hers as if to calm her down. She could taste the winter wind on his lips. She closed her eyes to relax a bit more. That allowed her to feel him even more intensely. She could feel Soohyuk Cha, the man who claimed her heart, even more closely now.

Soohyuk unbuttoned her coat and pushed his arms in between the fabrics to pull her closer to him. He'd wanted to kiss her like this from the moment she asked that question. He leaned farther down to feel more of her lips. He was dying to know what her tongue hidden behind the lips tasted like, but he held himself back as hard as he could.

"Mmm…" A moan escaped his lips. The supple feeling of her waist in his hands sent shivers through his body.

Yuna's back was now arching downward in an effort to back away from Soohyuk as he pushed his body closer and closer to hers. Still not wanting him to let go of her, she slightly opened her mouth. Then in a split second, his tongue pushed its way through her lips like it had been waiting for permission. His hand brushed up along her spine and cradled her neck, stopping her from backing away any farther.

Feeling her body betraying her, she tried her hardest to push back against the desire to flee and opened her mouth a little wider. When he responded by tightening his arm wrapped around her waist, she started to pant.

Soohyuk sensed her response and immediately loosened his arm. But he still lightly pecked her lips again to show her how he was feeling. Every time he kissed her, Yuna's eyes closed, then opened again like she was blinking in slow motion.

When the endless streams of short kisses finally ceased, she whispered, "I'm sorry."

"No, you're getting damn good. Too damn good, really. You're going to start playing me like a violin soon," he said.

Yuna broke into giggles. *Oh, what am I going to do when he speaks like that?*

But she gladly played along. "Well, I am glad I am just too damn good for you."

He pulled her close to his chest and laughed out loud.

CHAPTER 2

$\mathscr{A}$s Ms. Seo busily prepared breakfast, she called out, "Today's breakfast is a ham and egg sandwich, Hwihyun."

Hwihyun stepped into the kitchen wearing a crisply ironed button-down shirt. "Why, thank you."

"Well, well, well, what do we have here?" She looked him up and down and raised an eyebrow in amusement. "You never wear button-down shirts. Not even if I iron them for you."

"Dr. Cha always wears button-downs," said Hwihyun, sitting down at the table.

"That is true," she answered.

Hwihyun mumbled something she couldn't hear.

"Sorry, I didn't catch that. What did you say?" Ms. Seo asked as she laid down the finished sandwich and orange juice in front of him.

"I said, it looks nice. It sort of makes him seem dignified. I don't like him that much, you know, because of his foul mouth. But...he seems pretty all right as a doctor. I can, I don't know, sense his professional mindset," he said.

That was more or less along the lines of what had been on

Hwihyun's mind lately. His father—and Ms. Seo's ex-husband—Dr. Cho had told him that he was going to step down from his place as director and go back to being a doctor. Hwihyun had been surprised, of course. He'd never thought that Dr. Cho would resign from his position on his own.

"It's about time I went back to being a proper doctor again," Dr. Cho had told him the other day at lunch. "There aren't any other reasons for this than that, so don't think too hard about it."

Hwihyun hadn't been able to think of anything to say in return, because he sensed that it was the divorce that had brought his father to this decision.

"Do not forget that you came all the way up to where you are now on your own, without my help," Dr. Cho said, while Hwihyun just sat there and listened. "You earned your place. You are going to be a greater doctor than I or anyone ever was. So, I should at least try to set a good example for such a great son and show what a true doctor should look like instead of just treating VIPs."

What a doctor should look like. A true doctor. As Hwihyun listened, his thoughts had gone to Soohyuk Cha. *What makes a doctor?* The first thing that came to mind was Soohyuk's shirt. All kinds of things got on the clothes of someone who worked at an emergency room, and yet, Soohyuk always insisted on wearing his white button-down shirts. It had to be a heck of a lot of work to maintain that, but he did. It wasn't much, but it was enough to let Hwihyun catch a glimpse of his mindset.

Now, Ms. Seo let out a soft peal of laughter.

"You're making me feel embarrassed. Stop laughing, Mother," said Hwihyun, his cheeks warming. Ms. Seo turned around to hide her smiling face from him. Hwihyun smiled bitterly as he looked at her back. He hadn't told her about Dr. Cho. His father had promised he would tell her later himself.

"How would I be able to call myself a father if I asked you to do that too?" he'd said.

Hwihyun let out a long sigh and started to eat his breakfast.

Ms. Seo turned around when she heard him chewing on his food to look at him. She was prouder and prouder of him by the day. It had been a long, long time since she last saw Hwihyun all properly dressed up like that. Finding an admirable aspect in someone and trying to take after them was not an easy thing to do. Hwihyun was already a doctor with an impeccable attitude by any standard. She couldn't even think of anything he could improve on. But he seemed to have reconsidered the basics after seeing Soohyuk. She couldn't be prouder of her son for trying to become even better.

"This is really good," he said.

"Is it? I'm glad." She smiled again.

"Even Dr. Cha wouldn't be able to give his speech about not eating anything a stranger gives him and all that if he tried this," he said proudly.

Ms. Seo's eyes automatically went to the remaining bread sitting on the counter. Her mind wandered back to the abalone porridge she'd tried to give to him. He'd refused to eat it, much to her disappointment. Although, Soohyuk seemed ever so slightly different nowadays.

Her lips clamped shut with resolution.

A little while later, Ms. Seo arrived at the emergency room. She spotted Soohyuk sitting in front of the monitor as soon as she stepped inside. Ms. Seo took some deep breaths and walked straight over to him, and lightly cleared her throat.

Soohyuk answered without even looking up. "Can I help you?"

Ms. Seo showed him the paper bag in her hand. "I made a little extra food while making breakfast for my son this morning. I thought you might like to taste it."

"I'm fine." Soohyuk declined at once, as she'd expected. It hurt much more than she thought it would, but she was not going to back down so easily today.

"I'm not saying that you should taste it right now," she said. "Have it as a snack when you're hungry later. I'll leave it with Ms. Jeon. I know you never get to eat on time."

He didn't even bother to answer this time.

"If you're perhaps allergic to something—" she started.

Soohyuk coldly interrupted her. "I have someone already taking care of me, so leave me alone. Continuing to do this when I have already said no is harassment."

Someone taking care of him... He probably meant that woman. She recalled Soohyuk pulling her into his arms in front of all those people at the mall. In Ms. Seo's eyes, that woman seemed to be the only person he let his guard down to. It would be a lie to say that she wasn't hurt by the way he spoke to her, which bordered on being utterly rude. He wasn't wrong, but she was starting to wonder if he was cutting her off so sternly for another reason.

"Is it because you think I might ask something of you? Because I'm the director's wife?"

Soohyuk looked up at her with cool eyes and said, "Is that really that important? Being related to the most powerful man in this hospital? What a strange family. First Dr. Cho, and now you?"

Ms. Seo bit her lip, realizing her mistake. "I'm sorry, I didn't mean it that way."

"If you do this again, I will just throw it in the trash can. It almost feels like you want to see me do it."

His voice was so cold that she found herself trembling. *Was I wrong?* Everyone else said that there wasn't anything different about him, but Ms. Seo could definitely see that something had changed. Such was the feeling she got while watching him all week. He somehow seemed brighter, softer, and more energetic.

That was why she'd been able to get up the courage to try again. But…

"I'm sorry for the disturbance," she quietly apologized as she took back the bag she'd offered. As he said, giving him things again and again when he'd already declined her food was harassment. She certainly sensed that he took it that way. *But he didn't have to put it like that. It was just a kind gesture.* She couldn't help but feel hurt.

He glanced at her and said, "I'm sorry I couldn't say it in a kinder way. Please think of it as my not knowing how else to say it."

That short remark made all her sadness melt away. Yes, she was right. There was an almost imperceptible change about him. She could feel her lips smiling again.

When she nodded, he mumbled, "It makes me look bad when you smile like that."

"No, it does not. I know that you're a good person, Dr. Cha," she said.

Suddenly, an unfamiliar expression surfaced on his face, then disappeared. It was an expression of perplexity intense enough to make her beam. It was only visible for a split second, but it was adorable enough to make all her sadness disappear.

At the end of the day, Soohyuk returned home after working overtime as usual. Fatigue seemed to be crashing over him like waves and devouring him. He remembered with relief that tomorrow was Saturday, his day off.

The apartment was silent when he entered. Yuna wasn't there. *She must have gone to Minjoon's.* "I suppose she's not back yet," he mumbled to himself.

He took off his clothes and took a hot shower. He couldn't stop yawning as he shampooed his hair. After drying himself, he immediately proceeded to crawl into bed. His legs felt like they were made of lead. He would go pick up Yuna after taking a brief nap...

———

Soohyuk's shoes were at the entrance, but the apartment was plunged in darkness. Yuna quietly closed the door. *He might be sleeping,* she thought. But when she started to look around on her tiptoes, she couldn't find him anywhere. Not in the office, and not in the kitchen.

Yuna took off her coat and walked to his bedroom. They were dating, and she was receiving at least three hugs a day and countless kisses, but she'd never set foot in his bedroom without his invitation. But there were no invitations today, let alone any other sound. *He must be exhausted,* she thought.

The room was dark. All she could hear was his steady breathing. Yuna tiptoed to the bed. She wanted to see his face. The light coming through the cracked open door allowed her to make out his face. This was the first time she'd seen him asleep. Yuna suppressed a giggle. The way he slept with a large pillow tucked between his legs made him look like an innocent child. It even made her change her mind about leaving after just sneaking a peek.

Yuna carefully put both of her hands on the bed and leaned over to get a closer look. *So this is how he sleeps...* She smiled. He wasn't doing anything, but even so, a surge of happiness filled her. She gathered the courage to reach out and touch his tousled hair. It didn't feel like she thought it would. She thought that it would feel cool and slick like he seemed on the outside, but instead it was soft and pliable. That feeling wiped away more of her fear, allowing her to caress his hair over and over.

When he moved, she pulled back her hand instantly like a shameplant.

"What time is it…?" he asked drowsily.

She answered, "It's past six. You must have been exhausted."

"Yeah…" he mumbled, rubbing his eyes with both of his hands like a child. She suddenly felt bad for him. He never came home on time because he always worked overtime. Instead of running away, Yuna sat next to him.

"I'm going to lay my head on your thigh," he warned in a gravelly voice, so he wouldn't startle her. Then, he scooched closer to her, while at the same time reaching out to pull her leg toward him. He then proceeded to hug her leg like a giant pillow.

Ba-boom, ba-boom. Her heart started to pound. She could feel his face on her thigh and her leg was completely bound by his arms. She gulped. It didn't seem to do much for her drying throat. Still, she didn't wiggle out of his reach. She didn't push him away either.

The two sat there like that for a couple minutes.

"Can I ask you something?" he asked.

"Sure," she answered.

He opened his mouth with his head still resting on her thigh. "I've been wondering this for a while. When *the incident* happened, why didn't you get therapy? I don't think your brother would have ended up limping now if he had gotten proper treatment then too."

Yuna's body stiffened. Soohyuk moved a little again to wrap his arms around her waist, saying, "If you did, we would've slept together by now."

"No, we wouldn't have. I would have slow danced with you first," she said.

"Sure, you might have. But then you would have slept with me right away," he said.

God help this man. But that made Yuna think back on that time again. The time when she was aggrieved like she never was again in her life. The time when she learned that not having parents made everything worse for a child. Yuna then realized that she hadn't told Soohyuk about herself at all. She suddenly felt her self-esteem dropping again. He was a doctor. A talented, *renowned* doctor.

"Soohyuk," she said.

"Yes?" he answered.

"What do you like about me?"

He didn't hesitate before answering. "You're cute."

Yuna took a deep breath. She felt like she had to tell him. It seemed like she at least owed that much to a person she was now in a relationship with. After all, she had asked him about his past as well.

"We had very limited access to treatments," she started.

The perpetrator's parents had come and caused a scene as Yuna was forced to recount what had happened over and over to the police—how she had come to this part of town to stand up to her bully, and had instead been dragged inside a shed and found herself trapped in darkness with a man. His parents had screamed that she was trying to get in the way of their son's future, even though he was the one who had traumatized her. They even said that they would press charges against her brother, Yoonjae, for assault. They were frightening people. Yuna had never been more frightened by anyone.

In the end, Yuna and Yoonjae had agreed to let everything go under the condition that the parents wouldn't press charges. After having to visit the station multiple times because of the two, the director and the staff at the orphanage had turned their backs on Yuna and Yoonjae. As a result, Yoonjae was provided with the bare minimum of the treatments he needed, and Yuna barely got any at all. They didn't consider an invisible trauma of the mind a valid enough trauma.

Soohyuk said, "I'm waiting. Whenever you're ready."

Of course. He was a man who had to get his answer one way or another. *All right, I'll tell him,* decided Yuna.

Yuna took a deep breath, then said everything in one breath, as if she were rapping. "It was just us two, Yoonjae and me. There wasn't anyone else to take our side. We were only orphans, after all. So, Yoonjae ended up limping because he didn't get the proper treatments, and I just agreed to let everything go because I wasn't hearing anything nice."

Soohyuk pushed himself up onto his elbows. She could see his eyes flash even in the dark.

"Just you two?" he asked.

"Yup, just us two. Yoonjae and me," answered Yuna. She calmed her breath again. *This is not a flaw,* she reminded herself. *This kind of a childhood is nothing to be ashamed of. I was raised to be a decent human being under Yoonjae's protection.* "Our parents passed away in an accident, and Yoonjae and I were sent to live in an orphanage."

Suddenly feeling anxious when Soohyuk remained silent after hearing that confession, Yuna added, "If it makes you nervous that I grew up as an orphan…"

"No, no. Do you remember your parents at all?" he asked.

"No, not at all," she said.

"I'm going to touch you," he warned before raising his hand to cradle her face. His hand felt warm.

Feeling encouraged by that warmth, she asked, "Does my being an orphan make you nervous?"

Soohyuk shook his head. "No. You turned out well. Despite only having your brother around while growing up."

Yuna smiled faintly. He was talking as if he were far older than she was. "Yoonjae is the one who had a hard time as a child because of me."

"I'm going to kiss you," he warned.

The moment she closed her eyes, she felt his lips against hers. It was a gentle kiss that warmed her heart.

When their lips parted, he told her again, "You really are a good person. A much better one than I am." She could feel his sincerity because it was delivered in such a matter-of-fact manner.

She reacted without realizing and nodded. "Mhmm."

Soohyuk's face suddenly brightened up with a smile. He urgently whispered, "I'm going to kiss you for real this time."

The hand cradling her face sneaked into her hair and held her head firmly in place. His lips overlapped hers at the same time, and soon his tongue made its way into her mouth.

Yuna put her hand on his shoulder. She felt her body being lifted into the air and within seconds, she was on his lap. They'd never kissed in such an intimate position.

"Hmm." A bizarre sound escaped her lips. She truly was at a loss for what to do. Tears kept welling in her eyes. *Stop that, you idiot,* she tried telling herself.

Soohyuk's keen senses caught that, but he couldn't let go of her. When the tears rolled down her cheeks, he finally managed to bring himself to a halt.

"How are you going to slow dance with me like this?" he asked.

The heat in his breath made her feel guilty.

"I'm sorry. I should never have asked that. Will you forgive me?" he added.

Yuna cracked a smile at his overly serious apology while wiping the tears with both hands.

"Monkey's butt is red…" he teased her.

Even when she hit his chest with her hands, he quietly let her smack him and apologized again. "I'm sorry. Please forgive me."

He sounded so serious that she had no choice but to stop. Taking a deep breath, she asked, "Do you want me that much?"

"Yes," he answered as directly as he could. "I didn't want to stop."

Yuna took another deep breath. Yes, this was Soohyuk Cha. A man who was nothing but honest.

"All right, then. I should give you a reward since you stopped for me. I'll go on a date with you tomorrow. You're off, right?" she asked.

"I am."

"Then let's spend the day together tomorrow," she suggested.

Soohyuk answered, smiling, "It would be an honor."

Saturday morning came. Soohyuk looked around the empty apartment, then glanced at Yuna. She was lying on her stomach, reading a book. It was the perfect time to do something together, but there wasn't anything to do because he disliked leaving the apartment so much. Maybe they could watch a movie, but all he had for a screen was his computer. With her, he wanted to watch something on a big screen, a TV perhaps, on their comfortable living room couch. Of course, it would take a few days for a TV to get here and to have it installed even if he ordered one now, but he for sure was not going to make the same mistake the next time he was off. *An investment for the future,* he thought.

Slinking down next to Yuna, he asked, "Do you want to go outside?"

"To where?" she immediately responded as if she'd been waiting for him to ask that.

"That mall we went to last time. I have something I want to get," he answered.

She gave him a surprised look. "Really?"

"Really."

Yuna stared at him like she couldn't believe what he was saying, then said, "But you don't like crowded places. Especially after what happened last time."

"You'll be there. I'm not going to stay ten feet away from you this time. And I'm warning you now, I'm going to be holding your hand because I feel like I will not be able to come back home if I lose you," he said.

It almost sounded like he was buying whatever he was buying because of her. Like he was going outside for her.

Yuna nodded enthusiastically with a grin and answered, "Mhmm."

Soohyuk beamed at her. "Whenever you answer like that, you remind me of the, what's it called, the bobblehead dog. You're as cute as a bitch...ouch!" She'd pinched his chest.

"What did I say about that word?" she said.

"What should I say then? It means a female dog, which you really look like, and I find that cute," he said.

Getting up on her feet, Yuna said, "Then just say that I'm cute. Not, 'I'm as cute as a bitch.' "

Rubbing his aching chest, he answered, "You're really cute. I could just bite your cute little face off and crunch, crunch, crunch..."

She crossed her arms and gave him a hard look. "Soohyuk."

"Yes?"

"Keep it up like that, and things will not look up for you. That's a warning," she said.

Soohyuk shut his mouth at once and got up on his feet.

The mall in Jamsil on a Saturday was as crowded as they'd ever seen it. Yuna felt as if she were being pushed around by all the people rather than walking side by side with Soohyuk. Every time she was pushed to one side by someone, Soohyuk tightened his grip on her hand and pulled her close to him.

"Maybe we shouldn't have come," said Yuna, biting her lip.

"There were just as many people before too," he said, but he couldn't hide his frown. A large crowd. Indistinguishable murmurs. He was starting to feel nauseous again, just like before. He grabbed her hand more firmly.

Feeling his hand tighten around hers, Yuna glanced up at his face. It didn't look very good. She didn't need much explanation to understand what was going on because she knew how private of a person he was.

"Should we just go? Come on, let's go. We can come back on a weekday when we have time," said Yuna, pulling on his hand.

"No, it's all right. I can do this. And I want to sit on the couch with you watching a movie my next day off," he insisted, but he had no idea what was going on. He'd been fine when he came back here to find Yuna before. He didn't feel nauseous then like he did now. "Just don't let go of me and don't lose me," he said.

But as he took another step, Soohyuk froze in place like a statue.

"Soohyuk?" Yuna called, looking up at the suddenly frozen Soohyuk. He was gazing into the distance like he couldn't hear her. That look on his face… Yuna automatically took a step toward him to soothe him, and gently called his name, "Soohyuk."

The look on his face was vulnerable, easy to break. It was a look that gave her the courage to calm her fears and continue holding him in her arms. Soohyuk was still unmoving, his eyes looking out at something she couldn't see. Yuna felt a pain in her heart. Her brows narrowed and her eyes started to water.

There wasn't anything different about his expression. It was as impassive as usual and his eyes as cold and sharp as usual. But he seemed sad. She sensed a sorrow hidden under that impassive mask.

Pulling at his hand so his arm wrapped around her shoulders, she whispered, "Hold on to me. I'll never let go of you."

Soohyuk suddenly snapped back to his senses. It happened in a brief moment, but thousands of pieces of memories passed through his mind. His heart painfully wrenched. Evidence of that pain showed on his forehead. When he started to hyperventilate like he was having a panic attack, because he didn't know what to do with everything he was feeling, she said, "I've got you. I'm not going to let you get lost."

It happened in the blink of an eye. Soohyuk pulled her into his arms. It was almost like he'd been waiting his whole life to hear those words.

***

Soohyuk waited for Yuna while leaning against a thick pillar. Yuna had gone to get something to drink. He'd told her that there was no need, but Yuna had begged to differ.

"Please do as I say. You have low blood sugar right now. You need to consume something with sucrose," she'd insisted.

"I don't like sweet drinks," Soohyuk had complained.

"Too bad. Do you realize how pale you look right now? I'll be right back, so stay put over here. Don't go anywhere."

When Yuna insisted that strongly, Soohyuk couldn't argue with her. So, he'd just nodded. Now, he was leaning against the pillar and inattentively watching people come and go.

A large crowd... Indistinguishable murmurs... Memories sifted through his mind again. His height had been completely different back then. *Probably around this height,* he thought as he kneeled to lower his stance. Now, he was looking at people's waistline instead of looking down at them from a couple inches above their heads. The passersby looked like walking pillars. Hundreds of those pillars were crowding his view. Soohyuk stayed in that position for a moment and looked around.

"We're playing hide-and-seek," a kid's voice said. Soohyuk turned his head to look back. *"You're it."*

No one was there, but he felt like someone was nodding. He stood back up. Was this a memory of his? If so, who had he shared that conversation with in this memory?

His head started to ache, and he touched a hand to his temple. He had no idea why things were coming back to him, though in pieces, when they never had before. Was it because he was trying, for the first time in his life, to find his birthparents? Or was it because he was in Korea? His lips pulled to one side as he sniggered. *Yes, perhaps that's it. Perhaps these pieces are coming back to me because I've done something for a change.*

Back in the States, every day was a battle of survival. He was met with discrimination, kids his age who were just psychotic, and people who hated him for no reason wherever he went. There was only one way to go about his life while not losing his mind in the midst of all that, by not thinking of receiving or giving affection to anyone. It was a lesson he'd learned early on in his life.

The snigger on his lips disappeared. *Oh, now I see. It's Yuna...* He, who had heeded to that lesson all his life, was starting to feel affectionate toward someone. He, who had never reached out first to anyone before, had reached out to her. He could see it now. It was Yuna's influence.

Soohyuk let out a long sigh. *Yes, that must be it.* His affection toward Yuna must have brought a change somewhere deep inside his heart. And that brought back those memories or imaginings or whatever they were. Soohyuk thought things through once more. He was becoming more and more certain that he was correct. None of this had happened before he realized he liked Yuna. *In that case...*

He took out his cell phone to call the detective's office. There was no need to pressure the incompetent detective, who couldn't find anything anymore. He should be able to do it on his own with Yuna by his side. After a couple rings, the detective agency picked up.

Soohyuk said with utmost disinterest, "This is Soohyuk Cha."

"Yes, Mr. Cha."

"I would like to conclude the investigation on my case."

"Splendid. We will conclude it immediately."

It was a little annoying how quickly they complied, but they had advised him to stop weeks ago, because they weren't getting anywhere. After hanging up, Soohyuk continued to stand by the pillar and waited for Yuna.

"What's taking her so long?" he complained under his breath.

Still, he stayed put as she'd told him to. After all, it was he who didn't want to lose her in a nauseating place like this. After however many minutes passed, some staff members appeared and started to build a stage in the empty area in front of a large store. Some kind of an event was happening, because it was a Saturday.

As he was mindlessly watching them set up, Yuna finally appeared with something in both her hands.

"There was a really long line, sorry," said Yuna.

"What is this?" Soohyuk asked, taking the cup full of yellow liquid from her.

"Mango and banana. I've watched you for some time and you don't eat nearly enough fruit. So, you're going to have some like this. It should be pretty sweet too," Yuna answered with a cup full of pink liquid in her hand.

"And what's that?" he asked.

"Strawberry and banana," she said before putting the straw in her mouth and taking a sip of her smoothie. She eyed him as if to tell him to go on and drink his.

He absentmindedly looked at her eyes, then her lips. Her lips, which displayed a variety of different shapes on a daily basis, were enrapturing.

"Stop staring at my lips and drink," Yuna ordered.

With a wry smile, Soohyuk complied and took a sip of his smoothie. *Bleh!*

Watching him frown like he'd just sipped the most disgusting drink in the world, Yuna nonchalantly said, "Suck it up and drink. All of it."

It wasn't enunciated perfectly because she still had the straw in her mouth, but Soohyuk understood anyway. He didn't take his straw out of his mouth, though he kept his frown.

Now that she was actually looking, his lips were quite something. She couldn't take her eyes off of them. Her mind wandered to memories of the countless kisses from him. And that deep, deep kiss. She had to try so hard to not pull back whenever he kissed her like that and enjoy the moment instead. But it was almost like the fear had become a part of her over the many years since the incident. *What to do, what to do.* She wanted to be free from the restraints of the trauma. She wanted to feel free in her own body.

Suddenly, Soohyuk said, "I'm going to touch you."

Yuna focused on drinking on purpose to not wince. She didn't pull away when his hand caressed her hair, followed by her neck. But all the tiny hairs on her nape rose.

"It's all right," he said.

She blushed with embarrassment. *What if it really became a part of me? Do I have to live like this for the rest of my life? How can I reclaim my freedom?*

"No matter how much your body rejects me, I'm going to keep touching you," he said, then lowered his head to rub it against hers as if he were teasing her.

You have no idea how much that relieves me, do you? You have no idea how much I like you when you say that you won't give up on me even though you know me, do you? Pretending like her heart wasn't tickled by that at all, she said, "Drink. Stop trying to get out of it."

Her breath smelled of strawberries when she said that. *Would her lips taste like strawberries too? Or like banana?* he wondered. But

Soohyuk soon straightened his posture to shake away the temptation. He knew she wouldn't be pleased if he kissed her at a place like this.

"Are they doing something here?" asked Yuna.

"I don't know. This is too sweet. Do I have to keep drinking it?" complained Soohyuk.

"Yup. For the sugar," said Yuna sternly, not budging an inch as he expected.

Having no other choice, Soohyuk slowly drank the smoothie one sip at a time. As he did, someone climbed onto the stage.

"Hello!" they called.

"They're starting," said Yuna, consumed with curiosity about what they were going to do.

"I'm going to hold your waist," Soohyuk said, wrapping his arm around her waist and pulling her toward him as if to protect her. Even more people were gathering now. Whatever they were going to do on stage, they'd already succeeded in gathering a crowd. Yuna kept getting bumped by the people in the process. No one dared to bump into Soohyuk, but they bumped into Yuna freely, as if she didn't matter. He tried to get her a seat, but all the seats were taken in the blink of an eye. Soohyuk pulled her in front of him instead and guarded her with his own body.

Yuna couldn't breathe. He was standing right behind her. With all of her attention focused on what was behind her, she could almost hear his heartbeat. He'd hugged her several times before now, but never this close. *Ba-boom, ba-boom.* Her heart pounded like it was about to burst. She could barely breathe.

He chuckled. "Breathe."

His reminder made it easier.

"Remember, we need to slow dance as soon as possible," he said, continuing to chuckle.

In her memory, he always sounded impassive, cold, or snide. But hearing a new tone in his voice was quite delightful. Her lips drew a smile. "I'm sure we will someday. I think that day will be very special."

Soohyuk lowered his head with a smile and whispered in her ear, "I think so too." He then pulled her even closer to his body. She leaned into him a bit more comfortably than she had before now that she was more relaxed.

The event Yuna had been so curious about finally started. Actors came onto stage to put on a musical. She'd never seen a musical before, but she'd heard the song they were singing now. She stared at the stage. This was the first time she was seeing anything like this. The only "cultured" activities she'd done before now were watching animations with Minjoon and listening to the radio, because she couldn't go to a dark concert hall or a theater alone. But hearing them sing live right in front of her made her heart pound. It was a familiar song, but it sounded more special than usual.

"She's bad," Soohyuk commented from behind, but it didn't matter. To Yuna, this was what the angels' singing would sound like.

"Do you want to leave now? I'm done with my smoothie," asked Soohyuk.

"No, just a little longer," said Yuna.

Soohyuk scowled. He couldn't bear listening to that actress sing because she was such a terrible singer. She must have been the worst musical performer he'd ever seen. But Yuna didn't seem to mind. She appeared completely enchanted by the actress.

Yuna turned around to look at him and said, "I've never seen anything like this. It's so amazing."

Soohyuk's eyes focused on her twinkling eyes. They seemed watery, as if she were close to tears. *Oh boy... Why does every face this woman makes look so cute?*

Yuna turned her gaze back to the stage. His arms wrapped tighter around her waist, but it felt fine. Probably because she was too preoccupied with listening to the musical. She didn't even realize that she was leaning back into his chest more and more.

Two songs ended in a flash. This time, a very petite woman climbed on stage, wearing a tight-fitting black dress. She was much smaller than the woman who was just on stage. But her volume was no compare. The song began like the whisper of a breeze, then swept over Yuna like a storm.

Yuna asked Soohyuk in a trembling voice, "Do you know this song by any chance?"

"I do," he answered.

"What's the title?" she asked.

" '*Ich Gehör Nur Mir*,' " answered Soohyuk.

Yuna pinched the back of his hand on her waist. She couldn't understand what he'd said.

"It's from the musical *Elisabeth*..." After thinking for a moment, he continued, "It means something like, 'I Belong Only to Me.' "

"Does it? I love it. I think I might cry," choked Yuna.

This was a song he liked very much as well, "*Ich Gehör Nur Mir* (I Belong to Me)." Soohyuk noticed that Yuna's body was slightly trembling. Like the song was rippling through her. She patted her eyes with the back of her hand. They were already watery, so he supposed she was now really crying. *How she gets touched by the smallest things like this...* Soohyuk held her even closer to him.

This was only a short performance for entertainment, so the show ended after one more song. Walking amidst the scattering crowd, Yuna said, "I've never heard someone sing this close to me. I think that's why it felt so different."

She was clearly still lost in the magic of the song. He could tell by the way she was excitedly chattering while walking very close to him. She seemed to not even notice the fact that she was holding on tight to his hand and was almost leaning all her weight on him as she walked.

"You liked it that much?" asked Soohyuk.

"Yes. How do you know the song, by the way? Is it a song you like too?"

Soohyuk looked into her eyes as they looked up at him with visible evidence of her emotional response to the performance.

He answered, "It is a song I like too. What did you like so much about it?"

"Her yearning for her freedom," answered Yuna.

They might have been the exact words she needed right now. For she also yearned for her freedom. Freedom from the past. Yuna took a deep breath in. She needed to ask him something before the effects of this song wore off. Before she was drained of this courage.

"Do you want to have a drink with me tonight?"

"A drink?" he asked.

"How much can you drink?" she questioned.

"I'm not sure. I don't drink that often. Do you want to?" he said.

"Mhmm." Yuna nodded.

Watching her answer with a nod like that wiped all other thoughts away from Soohyuk's mind.

"All right then. Let's have a drink. I'm off, after all," said Soohyuk.

"Are you sure it'll be all right? What if they call you again?" asked Yuna.

"They won't this time. Dr. Park has given an order not to call me when I'm off," said Soohyuk.

It was true. Dr. Park, the head of the emergency room, had told the other staff to let Soohyuk rest when he was scheduled to and to call him instead if they needed someone.

"Oh, thank god." Yuna sighed.

"So what do you want to drink?" asked Soohyuk.

"So-Mac, duh," she said with a smile.

"What's So-Mac-Duh?" Soohyuk frowned. "That doesn't

sound very good."

At times like this, she couldn't help but feel that he really was from another country even though he looked like a Korean.

"It's So-Mac, not So-Mac-Duh. Soju and beer mixed together," she explained.

"Ah, I see." He nodded.

"Let's get some beer and soju on our way home, then," she said.

Soohyuk glanced at her clearly excited face. Would they be able to get a little closer if they drank? Would they be able to do all the things they couldn't before? *No. Will we be able to slow dance like she wants to, at least? I hope so.*

"Sure," he answered.

When he'd taken a couple steps with her like that, he suddenly heard the child's voice from before again.

"We're playing hide-and-seek."

"You're it!"

Soohyuk stopped and turned around. He even forgot Yuna for a second as she stopped as well, looking at him with curious eyes. There was no one there. The voice was coming from his head. Still, he could not step away.

Yuna quietly waited for him. She didn't ask any questions either. She simply took his expression in. *Who is he looking at with such a sad face?*

After a long operation that spanned over twelve hours, Hwihyun threw himself on a bed in the hospital staff room and fell asleep, unable to bring himself to go all the way back home. He was too tired to take even a single step more. At least the operation had been successful.

Sleeping as soundly as a baby, he suddenly mumbled, "Found ya, Hwiyin…"

CHAPTER 4

Following a successful shopping experience, Yuna showered first when they arrived home and excitedly connected the Bluetooth speaker to her phone while Soohyuk showered. The song from earlier at the mall had been stuck in her head ever since the show ended, and she couldn't wait to listen to it again. She opened a search engine and typed in the title. When the song was coming out of the speaker at last, her heart started to pound again. *I belong to me.* Yuna clenched her fists. The more she listened to the music, the braver she felt.

Soohyuk came out of the shower, drying his hair with his hand. "What are you doing?"

"Listening to that song," she answered.

Wearing loose sweats, he stopped on his way to the table and said, "Did you like that song that much?"

"I did. Come sit. I'm almost done."

"All right," he answered, but his feet wouldn't move. Her face was slightly elated in a shade of pink, as if that tiny sound coming out of the Bluetooth speaker was all she could ever wish for. *Hmm...* Soohyuk's brows narrowed, and he thought hard for a moment. He wanted to do something about that tiny sound.

Unaware of all of this, Yuna was busy finishing cooking.

"One moment," he said before going back into his bedroom. Yuna placed the sliced and sautéed cucumbers, zucchinis, carrots, and mushrooms one by one on their plates, then quickly sautéed the beef marinated in bulgogi sauce. Today's dinner was bibimbap.

"I can't believe he didn't know what So-Mac is," she said, shaking her head. *Then again, he doesn't eat out with his coworkers.* She wasn't even sure if he was a heavyweight or not. She'd never seen him drink at all. He didn't even smoke, but that was perhaps because he worked in a pediatric emergency room. If it was professionalism that stopped him from drinking and smoking, he really was a perfect doctor. She couldn't believe once again that the man who liked her so much was such an amazing man. Or maybe it was proof that she was a much better woman than she gave herself credit for. So, she was determined to be brave tonight.

"All right, I've decided," she said to herself.

"Decided on what?" he asked, coming out of his bedroom with something in his hand.

Startled, she quickly said, "Nothing, nothing. What's that in your hand?"

"A CD. Let me play something with proper acoustics for you. Hold on," he said as he went into the office and turned the computer on. He had a large collection of CDs, because he had a habit of watching and listening to something he liked over and over again. It was one of the things he'd taken great care in when he was packing for Korea.

The music started playing. But it wasn't in Korean.

"If this is still all right with you..." Soohyuk stopped mid-sentence. His eyes were fixed on Yuna. She was looking at him with true joy beaming out of her eyes, like she couldn't be any happier. This really wasn't much. And yet...

"This is so thoughtful of you," she said. "Thank you."

Butterflies filled her stomach whenever she found him looking at her like this. His eyes were so cold, and yet so deep at the same time that she felt like she would never be able to reach their full depth. Yuna grinned with slight awkwardness. She had a strong hunch that today was going to be a very special day in her life.

"Come sit," she said.

When Soohyuk came and sat on the chair with his eyes still fixed on her, she sat on the chair opposite to him and asked, "Are you really sure it'll be fine to drink So-Mac?"

"I don't drink that often because I choose not to, not because I'm unable to," said Soohyuk.

"Huh. So, you are a heavyweight?" asked Yuna.

"Probably." He shrugged. "I'm not sure because I've never drank until I blacked out, but I definitely have never gotten drunk."

"That's not what I expected. I can't really picture you drunk because I've never seen you drink. But first, let's eat. I made bibimbap. It's bad to drink on an empty stomach."

"Okay."

Yuna pushed the bowl of bibimbap, vibrantly embellished with various thinly sliced vegetables and beef, toward him.

"It looks beautiful," he exclaimed.

"You can just mix it without adding pepper paste. I seasoned the vegetables," said Yuna.

"Okay."

Soohyuk couldn't eat spicy food. Sometimes, he seemed like he was a pickier eater than her nephew, Minjoon. Yuna brought her bowl to the table as well and sat across from him.

He suddenly said, "I'm sorry for making you work."

"Don't worry about it. Watching you eat well makes me happy."

Hearing her say that, Soohyuk finally allowed himself to mix the bibimbap. Yuna had actually wanted to eat and get drinks out somewhere. But she'd ended up making dinner as well as snacks to eat with their drinks at home, because the thought of eating out in public made Soohyuk nervous. He'd felt bad the entire time she was cooking, but he finally could shake off that guilt. He scooped up a big spoonful of the bibimbap. Crisp vegetables and well-seasoned beef danced in his mouth in harmony.

"How is it?" she asked.

He gave her a thumbs-up. That was enough of an answer for her. She looked at him with a proud smile. Watching him eat what she made always greatly delighted her. Soohyuk couldn't eat anything spicy like an eight-year-old, but he could *eat.* She could always see that he enjoyed eating her food as well, which doubled her joy of cooking for him. Watching him eat often inspired her to cook even tastier things for him.

While he cleared the table after dinner and did the dishes, Yuna set the table for the next menu: pork katsu and Japanese-style fish cake soup.

Soohyuk opened the fridge and put down the beer and soju on the table.

"Let me make it," interrupted Yuna. She then mixed the beer and soju according to a special recipe she'd learned from Kyungjo, her brother's wife.

Soohyuk took the glass she offered and lightly clinked his glass with hers. He tried a sip. He'd never had soju since he came to Korea, but he'd had beer every once in a while. So-Mac tasted a little lighter and sweeter than just beer but still left a slight burn in his throat.

"What do you think? Is it all right?" asked Yuna.

"I think I'll be as drunk as a skunk," mumbled Soohyuk after taking another sip.

"I'd better run then. I don't want to be with a skunk."

Soohyuk cracked a smile and emptied his glass. There was something strangely addictive about So-Mac.

"Have some food," offered Yuna. Soohyuk dipped a piece of

katsu in the sauce, then pushed it into his mouth. A symphony of crunches filled his mouth.

"You're an amazing cook," mumbled Soohyuk through the katsu.

"Try some soup too. It's Japanese. I think you'll like it. It's not spicy at all."

Soohyuk tried a spoonful of the soup as she suggested. He couldn't help but smile at the warmth and sweetness spreading through his mouth.

"I knew you'd like it," said Yuna. She then noticed that his glass was completely empty. She mixed a second glass of So-Mac and pushed it toward him.

"Is there a recipe for this?" asked Soohyuk.

"Everyone has their own perfect ratio, if you will. Mine was taught by my sister-in-law. I think this tastes the best for me," answered Yuna.

And so, the two drank. So-Mac had never tasted sweeter. It probably tasted even sweeter because they hadn't drunk in a while and they were listening to music they both liked. The two finished four glasses together without even realizing.

As she was starting to feel the alcohol, Yuna slowly loosened her barrier.

"You really like pork katsu, don't you?" commented Yuna. She was feeling even more comfortable now. *Good thing I made a lot,* she thought. His fork didn't seem to stop moving.

"I tried it for the first time when I came here. When you gave me that sandwich," answered Soohyuk.

"Really? Don't people make it a lot at home?" asked Yuna.

Soohyuk shook his head. "Not even once."

"Huh. That's unusual."

"Is it? Why?"

"Pork katsu is very easy to make," she explained.

"It would probably have been hard for her. She has probably never even heard of it," said Soohyuk automatically. Kate was a good enough person, even if she didn't make him any pork katsu. She was in fact a very good person who'd even divorced her beloved husband for a boy who had no relations to her. The moment he'd started making money, Soohyuk had begun sending her a moderate amount of money every month to repay her love. He hoped that she could live a more comfortable life, even if it were by a small degree.

Yuna observed him with her glass pressed against her lips. She knew that he had some trouble finding the right words to say, but at times like this, it almost felt like he did it on purpose. Why else would he not even use the word "mom"? *Or maybe "she" isn't his mom. Yeah, that must be it. Why else would he avoid calling her "mom"?*

"You must come from a wealthy family to have a hired cook," said Yuna.

Soohyuk couldn't help but crack a smile at Yuna's preposterous speculation. *A wealthy family? Please.* He sneered in his head. Kate should've listened to Danny. She should've adopted more abandoned orphans and gotten that stipend.

"No, not at all. We always had a giant pile of unpaid bills on our table," said Soohyuk as he emptied his fifth glass.

Yuna was thrown off by his unexpected answer. She couldn't even hide her bafflement because she was drunk.

"Are you disappointed because I don't come from a rich family?" asked Soohyuk.

"No, I'm not that shallow, thank you. And I'm self-made myself, so I don't care about people's backgrounds."

"Self-made? How could you be self-made?"

"It means that I grew up to be a great human being without other people's help. Are you self-made too?" asked Yuna.

Soohyuk crossed his arms as he thought for a moment, then answered, "I think so. Though there was someone who protected me."

Kate. All the alcohol was making it easier for him to realize once again how much Kate had sacrificed for him. He'd never be able to repay her even if he tried his whole life. Soohyuk rubbed his face with both of his hands.

Yuna chuckled and said, "What a great lady she was for protecting you." She sounded sincerely grateful instead of just throwing polite rapport.

"Why does it sound like you want to thank her?" he asked suspiciously.

"Because I do want to thank her. If it weren't for her, I wouldn't have met you. And if it weren't for you, we might have wasted our little Minjoon's precious time. Also, you don't seem like the type of person who would admit to having owed just anyone," Yuna said with a giggle.

"Me?" said Soohyuk as he got up from his seat to get more beer. He tried mixing So-Mac himself this time. There was way more soju in both their glasses this round, but neither of them noticed. They were becoming more and more drunk.

"Maybe you don't realize, but you come off as really arrogant sometimes," said Yuna.

"That's harsh."

"Isn't that why you eat lunch by yourself every day?" she teased.

"Shush and drink," he said.

They clinked their glasses again. He chugged half the glass at once. *Wow...* It was good. His throat burned a little quicker than before.

"So, why do you then? Why do you prefer to be alone?" asked Yuna.

"It's not necessarily because I don't enjoy the company of someone else," he started.

"Then why?"

Yuna suddenly felt exceptionally drunk. And Soohyuk seemed more handsome than ever. Her eyes were now fixed on him. Because he was sitting across from her, her fears completely disappeared.

"I just hadn't met the right person yet," answered Soohyuk.

She got on her feet to lean over the table with an alluring smile. "And have you met one now?"

Soohyuk's face turned expressionless. She couldn't tell what was going through his mind at all. His face looked too cold without a smile.

She sat back down and said, "Smile. Please, smile. You're making me feel embarrassed."

Soohyuk then faintly smiled and tousled his short hair with one hand.

"See? You look so handsome when you smile. All right. Cheers to your handsomeness!"

When their glasses were emptied, Soohyuk got up again and mixed more So-Mac.

"Hold on, you're going too fast. I might get drunk if we keep going like this," said Yuna.

"What happens when you get drunk?" asked Soohyuk.

"When I get drunk?" Yuna giggled. "I keep laughing. And then I start crying at the tiniest thing that moves me."

Looking at her with an unreadable expression, he said, "You really turned out well, even though it must not have been that easy for you growing up."

"All thanks to Yoonjae. See, Yoonjae is..." She paused as she sprang up from her seat and posed as Superman. "A Superman."

"All right, all right. Yes, yes, I get it. Aren't you quite the drinker?" said Soohyuk with a grin.

Yuna ran a lap around the living room with her arms still in the Superman position. He chuckled. He could tell that Minjoon had influenced her. After all, he'd seen them dancing together so many times.

Following that line of thought, he asked, "That kid, your nephew. How is he?"

"He's being treated like a king every day. Enjoying Kyungjo's daily massages. He starts school next week," said Yuna.

"I see. How is his walking?" asked Soohyuk.

"He doesn't say that he gets tired or that it hurts anymore. Maybe because of those massages," said Yuna pensively.

"Really? He doesn't get tired?" asked Soohyuk with his head cocked to one side.

"Nope." Yuna scurried back to her seat across the table from him.

"You haven't told him yet?" asked Soohyuk.

"Not yet."

"I see," he said, then stared at her.

Minjoon's parents were doing their best for Minjoon. He could tell that first day when they came to the emergency room for him to examine their son. He could also see through Yuna how much they loved the child, who had been diagnosed with a condition that was not easy to treat.

He then asked, "And how are you?"

He'd been worried about Yuna from the beginning. He was worried about her even in this very moment. It was not an easy thing to give up something of their own, but Yuna had done that —given up her shop. And for her nephew, not even her son. Just like Kate.

"Not fabulous, of course. But that's all the more reason for me to try harder. Enjoy every single moment of this life, not miss anything," said Yuna as her voice slightly trembled.

Shoot...is she crying?

"Come here." Soohyuk held out his hand. Yuna got up from her seat and walked around the table to come to him. He pushed his chair back to make more space between him and the table, then pulled her onto his lap. The tears running from her cheeks soaked his shoulder.

"I'm sorry. I'm drunk." Yuna hiccupped.

"It's nothing. You're more than welcome to get drunk any time," he said, then felt her lips smile.

"Hmm, this is so nice." She hummed affectionately. And drunkenly.

Soohyuk suddenly gulped. He'd had a very hard time stopping himself from taking her by the waist when she'd leaned over the table before. And now...he couldn't help but focus on the sensation of her weight on his thigh. As well as her supple body and her sweet scent.

Suddenly, he saw her face coming close, then felt her lips press against his. This was the first time she'd kissed him first. His eyes slowly closed. Her lips were so warm and sweet that he wanted to taste them the best he could. His hand dug into her hair and her arms wrapped around his neck.

He opened his mouth to take her lips and gently sucked on them. She opened her lips as well instead of pulling back and took him in. A sudden, intense tingle from deep within his gut made his hair rise. He could feel every movement of hers as if all of his senses were focused on them. He leaned his head down to kiss her lips even harder. He pushed his tongue in between her lips to taste her as much as he wanted and pulled her even closer to his body. His heart was racing a mile a minute because of the sensation of her soft breasts pushed against his chest.

When their lips finally parted, her lips were slightly swollen from the rough kiss. He couldn't stop staring at those lips.

"You know what Kyungjo told me?" said Yuna. "She told me that if there's a man I liked, I had to make my move. *That's how you get 'em*, she said."

Oh, boy. She must be really drunk now too. She couldn't stop smiling even while saying things that normally would have embarrassed her. Soohyuk gazed into her eyes. Everything about her seemed to entice him. Even the slight flutter of her eyelashes seemed to be inviting him. His entire body tensed.

"So, are you going to make your move on me right now?" he asked.

Yuna returned his intense stare that almost made it seem like he was planning on swallowing her whole.

"Have you met the right person now?" she asked.

His black eyes were all she could see now.

"What if I have?" he asked.

"Then I'll make my move," said Yuna as she pressed her lips against his. She could feel him smile under her lips. The smile let her in on a lot of things. First, he liked her. In fact, he liked her very much. Second, he wanted her very much as well.

Soohyuk couldn't stop smiling. Who knew this little woman who was as jumpy as a bunny could be this forward? Their lips lined up against each other comfortably like she was smiling as well.

"Do you like me?" he asked. He'd never directly asked her this before. She hadn't reciprocated when he'd told her that he liked her before either.

But this time, she nodded with certainty, saying, "Mhmm."

"How much?"

Sensing the heat hidden in that question, she looked at his slightly blushed face.

"I really want to sleep with you right now, so come on. Tell me," said Soohyuk as he pulled her tight against him. So tight that she could feel... *him,* very clearly, over the loose sweatpants. An involuntary shiver went through her body. He caressed her back soothingly, whispering again, "Tell me."

The hand caressing her back felt so hot that she could feel its trail as it kept moving. She gulped. *Yes, time to claim my freedom. I'm not going to live in fear for the rest of my life.* She didn't want him to have to warn her beforehand every time he touched her. She wanted the man she liked to be able to touch her naturally like any other couple. But, boy, he was staring at her so intensely that she felt like she was about to die from embarrassment.

"Can you close your eyes?" asked Yuna.

"Why?" he asked.

"Just do it, will you?"

He pouted like he was about to complain, but he still closed his eyes. *Yes, he's a good man who knows to listen from time to time.* And shouldn't she pay him back for being so good? No, actually, it was she who wanted it more. *I want to confess my feelings to him.*

"I like you very much," she said. Soohyuk didn't react, like his ears were completely clogged, so she added, "Very, very much." As she continued to confess her feelings, his brows started to narrow. "The moment you first showed up in front of my shop. The moment you reached your hand out to take the heavy grocery bag. The moment you stopped in front of the entrance and didn't enter until I told you to come in. The moment you stayed with me until I was fine instead of leaving me when I collapsed."

Her voice was starting to sound watery. It seeped into his heart like a sweet shower of rain after a draught.

"The moment you noticed Minjoon. The moment you comforted me. And the moment you took my hand. I found myself liking you more and more each of those moments," she said, then caressed his face and kissed his frowning forehead. "You have no idea how much I wanted to get up and dance when you told me that you liked me." She burst into laughter. "Oh god, I'm so drunk. But it feels so good to say that out loud." She couldn't stop laughing. *Hooray! I finally found the courage to do it! Today must be the day I actually should let myself dance in joy. Who knew such a day would come for me?*

Soohyuk slowly opened his eyes at the sound of her joyful laughter. Yuna was beaming. She looked so cute that his heart started racing again. He grabbed her nape with one hand and slowly lowered his head to press his lips against hers.

Yuna accepted his kiss with a smile. Holding her, Soohyuk sprang from his seat. He couldn't hold it in any longer. He wanted Yuna. Her legs wrapped tightly around his waist.

"Wait," she said.

"What?" His voice was hoarse with excitement and almost sounded aggressive. "I really want you. I want to sleep with you right now." He kissed her neck without even being able to wait for her answer. He wanted to kiss her bare skin. He wanted to have all of her.

"We haven't slow danced yet." Her voice was now as hoarse as his.

Hearing that, he headed to the bedroom while still holding her. If romance was what she wanted, he would give her romance.

CHAPTER 5

"All right. Let's first choose a song," he said.

She was still hanging from his neck, but it didn't feel heavy at all. This was the first time he'd been this close to someone else, but it didn't feel uncomfortable either. *Must be because it's her.*

Soohyuk hurriedly sifted through the CDs. It was her wish to slow dance with a man. It probably meant more to her than making love with a man.

"Damn it, where the hell is that?" He cussed in English before he could stop himself, feeling irritable that he couldn't find the right CD.

"Shhh…" she whispered as if to calm him down. "I'll wait for you. I can take it slow."

Ha! Soohyuk scoffed. He soon found the one he was looking for at last. He headed straight to the office with her still hanging from his neck, then played the music he found with a great effort: "Only Hope" by Mandy Moore.

"Do you know how to slow dance?" he asked with his hands safely supporting her buttocks.

She answered mischievously, "Oh, of course not. This is my first time, after all. You?"

He turned the lights off in the room instead of giving an answer. Moonlight shone on her like it was perfectly planned. As he gazed into her twinkling eyes, they slowly started to move. It was awkward at first because he didn't know how to slow dance either. He never liked standing this close to another human being, let alone doing anything more. He'd drawn an invisible line and built an invisible wall between him and everyone around him, but now one of those walls was crumbling down.

Eventually, they found their rhythm. Slowly swaying side to side with her in his arms seemed like enough.

Soohyuk leaned in. Yuna raised her head in response. Their faces were now angled perfectly for a kiss. He gently took her lips. Shivering from her sweetness, he took hold of her breath.

They continued to dance in the moonlight.

Their movement softened a bit more. The already loosened barrier between them now seemed to have completely vanished as the gentle steps continued. Her fingers dug into his hair, then tightened to make him face her.

She then bravely proclaimed, "I'm going to make my move now."

"Please do." He smiled.

Soohyuk headed to the bedroom with her still in his arms. He carefully laid her down on the bed and took off his top and threw it on the ground. His fingers were now trembling uncontrollably. He'd never thought that he would be this consumed by the desire to sleep with a woman in his life. He had no idea how he was going to remember this day in the future, but he was sure of one thing: he was now in a new world where there was only him and Yuna. And he was looking at her for the first time in that world. *Yuna Lee and Soohyuk Cha.* He would never forget this moment when she changed him forever.

Suddenly, she sat up and took a deep breath in.

"Are you all right? Do you feel lightheaded?" he asked, reaching out to pull her toward him and caress her back. *This really isn't easy for her,* he thought. The depth of her trauma was not to be overlooked. It was enough to make her fear and dislike men for her whole life.

"No…umm…" she mumbled. At least her heartbeat was fine. It wasn't irregular. She smiled sheepishly in the dark, saying, "You're so hot right now. You seem really strong." She reached out to touch this chest. It was firm. And hot. This was the first time she was touching someone else's body.

She brushed her fingertips along his collarbones. She then touched his shoulders at the end of either collarbone. The strength of this man made her fingertips tingle. She put her palms against his chest. He could feel his hair rise as he felt her touch with heightened senses. Looking into his eyes, Yuna traced her hand down his torso. Smooth, firm sides. The bellybutton. The trail of black hair she could feel under the bellybutton that led down and down to where his pants started. She brushed the part that had been as hard as rock for a while now.

He gulped. But he failed to swallow back the rough exhales as well. She could feel his jagged breathing against her skin. The sensation from her hands told her that the man in front of her was strong. And yet, that same strong man was shivering under her touch.

Yuna leaned in to trace her hand down his thighs, then straightened her back again. "Now you make your move."

Soohyuk quietly reached out to touch her hair, which was inundated with fragments of the moonlight. He could feel her trembling, just like he was. He brushed her shoulders. How small they were! The bed rocked when he climbed on top of it. Kneeling, he took both of her hands into his. He explored the hands that chopped those vegetables every morning in a delightfully brisk rhythm. The back of her hands, her palms, her fingers, her nails.

He took a deep breath in at last, telling her, "Let me know if you can't take it."

"Would that change anything?" she asked.

With a mischievous smile, he answered, "Nope. But I thought I'd at least say it. Don't all gentlemen do that?"

Her nervous heart relaxed again at his unexpected joke.

Yuna answered, "You already are a gentleman. Why else would I be doing this? I loved the slow dance. I felt like a proper woman."

"You are a proper woman," he said.

"No," she said while adorably shaking her head. "I was an all right person, and now I'm about to transform into a proper woman. Thanks to you. I would never have dreamed of doing anything like this if it weren't for you."

Soohyuk gazed at her unbearably adorable face, then said, "Yun."

"Yes?"

"I really like you."

She blushed, smiling. "Then I'll trust you with my transformation."

"I see you're not objecting to my calling you 'Yun,' now. Why the change? Is it because you're drunk?" he asked as his hand sneaked inside her top. His hot hand touched her bare skin.

"You didn't pay attention to the movies, did you? All couples have nicknames for each other," she said.

"I think you're trying to fool me because you know I wouldn't know."

"Nope. I'm going to think of a nickname for you too. You're just going to have to suck it up." When she burst into laughter again, one side of his lips pulled into a sly smile.

He mumbled, "You're so unpredictable sometimes. But it

somehow makes you even cuter. So much so that I want to taste all of you."

Wait, does he actually mean... Before she could react to his direct words, he almost ripped her top off of her body and threw it on the floor. Her bra soon followed the same fate. She learned once again from his next move that she really did know this man. His lips arrived at her breast. "Ha!" she exclaimed without realizing. His large hand then proceeded to wrap around her upper body to lay her down on the bed.

Soohyuk opened his mouth a little wider to taste her nipple. He'd wanted to do that since earlier in the evening. He wanted to touch her. He grabbed her waist with both hands. The sensation of her bare skin against his was more than he could ever imagine. He touched her smooth skin with his thumbs and tasted her as much as he wanted to with his tongue. She quivered, not knowing what to do.

It hurt and she was scared, but at the same time, she was drawn to the intensity of his hands grabbing her like they were outside of his control. She didn't have the words to describe what she was feeling because this was the first time she'd felt it. She definitely did not want to stop him. He moved to the other breast when the first one started to ache. He then moved a hand that was grabbing her waist to grab the breast that was soaked from his attention.

"Your breasts are the best of all the soft things I know," he growled with his teeth sunk into her skin. Sharp pain from it pierced through her. That shiver reached deep inside her lower abdomen in a flash. It tingled so much that her hips bucked upward on their own. She was running out of breath now. His hand slid down her lower back this time. It lifted her hips until she was pressed against his part between his legs.

As hard as a rock, it pressed down on her lower abdomen. He rubbed himself against her. He then lowered the angle a little to rub himself in a more intentional way. He explicitly revealed how much he wanted her, not hiding anything.

Yuna threw herself into his storm-like throes of passion. To be frank, it was impossible for her to gather any more courage. It almost felt like she had used all the courage she had for the remainder of her life just to touch him. That was all she had left in her. So, she let him take the lead instead. She trusted Soohyuk with herself. And that trust was rooted in their slow dance in the moonlight. *This is a man who would specially pick out a song to slow dance with me,* she thought. So, she was certain that she would never regret it with a man like him.

Yuna moved both of her hands to reach her fingers into his hair while he continued to suck her breasts like he was obsessed with them. His hair felt soft against her fingers. Soohyuk's lips now slid up to her collarbones. He then reached up to kiss her chin. *Oh...* She yelped without realizing and shrunk into herself. Her skin had become so sensitive that even the slightest touch came across as pain. Soohyuk took her head in one hand and pulled down her pants with the hand that had lifted her hips.

"Open your eyes," he growled like he was consumed by an aggressive storm of passion. Yuna, who'd had her eyes closed for some time now, opened her eyes to find him staring into her at an alarmingly close distance. The way he stared at her made her blush every time. Yuna's eyes moved before she could stop herself to avoid his gaze.

"I'm not going to forget tonight," he said. Her eyes moved back to meet his. "I hope you don't either."

Yuna gulped and said, "No, I'm not going to either. Not that slow dance, at least."

He cracked a smile. It was such an innocent-looking smile that she couldn't help but smile as well.

"Let's dance again later. We're both bad, so don't expect too much, though," he said.

"Mhmm," she said.

He stared at her for a moment. "Do that again."

"What?"

"Mhmm," he said.

"Mhmm?"

"Yes."

"Mhmm," she said.

Every time she said "Mhmm," she slightly nodded.

"I guess I really do like cute women," he mumbled.

As she blushed at his sudden comment, he got on his knees to pull the one remaining piece of fabric off of her body and throw it on the floor. He then threw off his loose sweatpants and underwear at once. Yuna's head arched back the next second. His hand was now at her inner thigh. He slowly caressed it over and over to help her relax. He didn't even realize that he was as tense as she.

When his hand finally touched her most intimate place, she gasped. All the muscles in his body tensed at the same time. They could both barely breathe. They were overwhelmed with dizzyingly primal instincts. The back of his hand lightly rubbed her intimate spot. He then felt it with his fingers. He could feel her wetness. Pleased with her reaction to him, a flash of a smile appeared on his face.

He leaned down until his entire body covered hers and attacked her lips. His tongue slipped inside as her mouth opened. At the same time, his finger reached into her hot channel. She slightly frowned. An unfamiliar sensation was filling her up.

He paused for a moment like that. He wanted to give her at least a little bit of time to get used to the feeling. But when her heat squeezed in around his finger, he couldn't help but move. He twisted his finger inside to enjoy her warmth, savoring her increasing wetness.

Yuna was mesmerized by his kisses. She couldn't think straight as he continued to taste her and feel her to the point that she kept forgetting to breathe. His touch was so intense. It didn't leave any room for her to feel any fear.

Suddenly, he raised himself from her, saying, "I'm going in."

She could feel his hard head at her slick entrance. She breathed in and held it, freezing in her position. He tickled her face with his fingers like he couldn't bear how adorable she was. *Oh...* She frowned. Excruciating pain overwhelmed her, as if her body was splitting in half. His hand caressed her lower abdomen as if to soothe her.

He was frowning now, too. He felt like he was about to let go. The indescribable sensation of drowning himself in her drove him crazy.

He couldn't hold himself back any longer. He wanted to throw himself in her like this. He added a little more force to pierce her as she let the first man ever in her life inside. Her body was trembling where they were connected, and his heart was racing. More than anything, he could feel the most basic desire to claim her devour him.

He moved. He slid all the way out to the entrance, then slammed in at once. Yuna gasped. It was too deep too early. Her face turned sideways, then dug into the sheets. Soohyuk grabbed her pelvis. He was trying with all his might to go slow. Veins popped out on his arms and his temples. This was his first time as well, but he knew that he had to go slow. But it was hard. He continued to move in the same manner and dug into her deepest place. He couldn't help but speed up. His instincts were whispering to him that greater pleasure awaited him.

Yuna turned to face up again when his hands grabbed her breasts. He was squeezing them as hard as they could take it. He suddenly lifted her hips a little bit. "Ha!" A strange sound escaped both their lips at the same time. Soohyuk's mind went blank because of the way her warmth squeezed in around him, and Yuna's went blank because of the way he was going faster and deeper by the second.

In a primal state, they were now panting. The wet sound of their movements filled the room. His passion was making something as hot as fire bubble from deep within Yuna. He became more and more primal. He ceaselessly attacked her. She gasped and screamed. She didn't know enough to know what an orgasm felt like, but he was making her forget everything. In this moment, he was all that she could feel. He was *everything*.

Suddenly, he pulled himself out and took out a condom from the bedside drawer. Yuna could guess that he'd probably bought that the very next day he told her he wanted to sleep with her. He probably had been waiting all this time with that already prepared. *Well, that's the man I chose.*

Soohyuk filled her up again once the protection was on. He then thrusted aggressively into her as if he was trying to crush her. She couldn't catch her breath again. She was shaking like a ragdoll. When her throat was so dry that she couldn't even swallow anymore, he stopped his thrusts with a grunt.

He leaned his head down to rest his forehead against hers. As their rough pants slowly synched into one, an obsessive thought overcame his mind: he didn't want anyone ever to intrude on their precious, private world.

She belongs with me, and only me. I want her to be my everything. And I want to be her everything.

When Yuna brushed his sweaty hair back and kissed him, he kissed her back. It felt like a storm had just passed. Her whole body ached, but she'd never felt freer. Her entire body felt light, as if something that was stuck had finally dissolved. He kissed her forehead, her cheeks, her lips, her nose, then continued down to her neck and her breasts.

"Hold on," he called, then climbed down as the bed rocked again. She heard him go into the bathroom, followed by a sound of water running, then saw him emerge with a wet towel in his hand. He carefully wiped her body with the towel.

"We should change the sheets," he said as he picked her limp body up in his arms. Heading to the bathroom again, he called over his shoulder, "I'm going to wash those sheets, so don't you dare touch them."

"Why?" she asked.

He leaned down to kiss her. "Because I want to. And now, I'm going to give you a bath, because I want to as well."

Wearing one of his cotton shirts and only that, Yuna watched him change the sheets. He certainly was a man who was good at organizing. She could tell by the way he expertly smoothed out the wrinkles.

After finishing the task, he straightened his back and asked, "Aren't you hungry?"

"Are you?" she asked.

"Yeah. Let's eat something," he said.

She looked longingly at the bed. She just wanted to throw herself on that bed and fall asleep. But not even giving her enough time to attempt that, he pushed her out of the bedroom. After sitting her down on the chair, he opened the fridge.

"Hold on, I'll make you something," he said. Wearing his sweats again, he took out several eggs and a pan. Covering her mouth as she yawned, she looked at the clock. It was nine o' clock. It had felt like they were at it for hours, but it was only nine.

"I won't ask you how it was," he said nonchalantly, to the point it came across as arrogance. "Because I know it probably sucked."

Rubbing her lower abdomen that was aching like he was still inside her, she mumbled, "Not necessarily. It was my first time, is all. More than anything, it felt... freeing."

"Freeing?" he repeated.

"I thought I'd never be able to do it." She blushed so red that she looked like she was about to combust, then added, "I'm glad I got to do it with you. It feels like a weight is lifted off my shoulders now. Like I can finally breathe. I'm really glad I decided to like you."

Soohyuk came to her in a flash and leaned in to shower her with passionate kisses. Yuna kissed him back instead of backing away. After a quite literally breathtaking series of kisses, he went back to the stove.

Skillfully frying the eggs, he said, "I'll try not to be too aggressive next time. It was my first time too, so it was a little hard to control."

Yuna raised her brows like she couldn't believe him.

"Let's eat first, recharge, and then start again from the slow dance."

But the moment he laid down the plate of fried eggs on the table, Yuna gasped. "You're going to eat all of this?"

There were six eggs on the plate.

He said in a serious tone, "It's not enough, is it?"

"Soohyuk," she said like a warning.

Walking back to the fridge, he said, "First, eat. You're not getting any sleep tonight, so don't even think about that."

Soohyuk tossed a little in his sleep with the faint dawn light cozily filling the room, hours later. It was dim at first, but it slowly grew brighter. He frowned and moved his lips as if he were dreaming about something.

Suddenly, he jumped and snapped up, wide-awake. His heart was pounding so hard that he could almost hear it in his ears. He sat there for a moment, waiting for his breath to calm down again, and glared at the darkness. Then, he felt Yuna's warmth by his side. He reached out to caress her bare shoulder. Having used up all her energy, she didn't even realize he was touching her.

He lay back down next to her. Reaching out his arm, he rested the fast-asleep Yuna's head on it, and hugged her. Their bare skins touched affectionately.

He closed his eyes and drew her closer to him. He tried to calm himself down like that, but it wasn't easy.

He gave in at last and spat out what he'd realized in his sleep. "Dammit, I thought I was two years older."

CHAPTER 6

At last, the long-awaited day came for Minjoon to start school. Yoonjae, Kyungjo, and Yuna all stood side by side with their eyes fixed on the young boy, who was participating in the first-day-of-class ceremony. Yuna sneaked a glance at Yoonjae. Her brother wasn't one to express his feelings through words like his wife, Kyungjo. Instead, he showed them through his eyes and actions. Like now. He was looking at Minjoon with the warmest eyes ever, as if he were looking at his most precious treasure in the world. She glanced at Kyungjo next. Kyungjo wasn't even blinking, like she was trying to burn every second of this moment into her memory.

Yoonjae unexpectedly broke the silence. "What a handsome boy. He's the best-looking kid up there."

Yuna smiled, sensing the boundless depth of affection embedded in his comment. Kyungjo didn't reply. She just stared at Minjoon. Yoonjae took Kyungjo's hand into his. She glanced at Yoonjae, then faintly smiled. He looked at her with a gentle smile as well.

"It's a shame. He wanted his teacher to be a pretty lady like his mom," said Kyungjo. Minjoon's teacher was a man well in his 60s who seemed like he was close to retirement.

Yoonjae replied, "There are pros and cons to everything. He seems like an experienced teacher, so I'm sure he'll take good care of Minjoon."

"Oh, he'd better. Or else, I'm not going to hold back." No one dared to disagree with Kyungjo. No one knew how long Minjoon would be able to attend school. Whether it was only for a day or a month, they all wanted him to enjoy the new social experience as much as possible. Wasn't that what first grade was for anyway? For the children to have fun with their new friends?

The short ceremony soon ended, and the parents were guided to their children's homerooms along with the students. On their way, Yoonjae said, "The caravan should be finished by this week. I'm going to take it for a trial run when it's done."

"That's good to hear," said Yuna. "Where do you think Minjoon would want to go first?"

"I think probably Suncheon Wetlands. He was so disappointed when we couldn't go last year. Even though he kept saying he wasn't."

"Yeah, I bet he was. You have no idea how many stick figures about the trip he drew and put up on my shop's wall."

Yoonjae chuckled. "You're going to come with us on the first trip, right? The caravan was your gift. You should come try it out."

Without hesitating, Yuna answered, "Of course, of course I'm coming. I'm sorry to duck out, but I need to go back home and pack some lunches."

"Thank you so much for coming. I know how busy you are," whispered Kyungjo as she held Yuna's hand tightly.

The scheduled retirement ceremony for Dr. Cho was being held at S University Hospital at that time. Hwihyun stood in the back of the room, looking at the stage and his father with mixed feelings.

Dr. Cho was giving his speech. "Thank you all so much for trusting me with such an important role for so long. I now plan to return to my original place as a doctor..."

Hwihyun brushed back his hair, which was just long enough to cover his ears. The day had really come. He'd known that it was coming, but seeing it happen in person made his heart wrench. Rubbing his aching chest, he looked around. Ms. Seo was nowhere to be found. She'd learned about Dr. Cho's retirement only yesterday.

"Going back to being a doctor...that must not have been an easy decision for your father," she'd said.

"I think so too," Hwihyun had replied.

"Right, right. Your father never liked heavy titles like that. He only wanted to take it on in the hopes the position would help him find your brother, Hwiyin."

"Yes, I know," Hwihyun had answered as he watched Ms. Seo prepare dinner with a much more stoic expression than usual.

"It had to happen at some point. I'm sure your father will feel much more at ease now."

It would've been easier if there weren't any love left between them. Ms. Seo would've taken the sudden news of his retirement much more easily then.

As Hwihyun half-listened to his father's speech, his mind wandered back to the other thing Dr. Cho had told him recently.

"Your mother had this strange idea that Hwiyin disappeared on his own, not because he was kidnapped," he'd said.

"He... It must have been because of me," Hwihyun had said.

"No, no. Definitely not. But just in case your mother...like before..."

"I get what you mean. I'll keep an eye on her," Hwihyun had

assured him. He knew Dr. Cho was worried that she might become depressed again.

"If anything happens, be sure to contact me too," said Dr. Cho.

"I will. I'll take care of her, don't worry."

"It's not your fault."

"I don't know. But if I hadn't said that then… Anyway, I get your point," Hwihyun said.

When his brother Hwiyin disappeared at the amusement park all those years ago, and Ms. Seo was half out of her mind because she couldn't find him anywhere, Hwihyun had innocently told her, "We're playing hide-and-seek. I'm it."

"Hwihyun, did you see someone take your brother? Did you?" she'd asked frantically.

"No, he's hiding, I told you. I need to find him now," Hwihyun had said.

"Hwihyun, stop! Please, if you saw something, tell me. Which way did he go?" she'd shouted.

No one had paid any attention to what he was saying back then. He was smarter than his peers, yes, but he was still only a five-year-old child. A scared child watching his mother slowly lose her mind after losing her son. They all thought that he was telling a lie to comfort his mother. But he could still remember, as if it had happened yesterday, Hwiyin saying, "You're it." He'd even dreamed of finding Hwiyin a couple nights ago.

Hwihyun pressed his stomach with one hand. He wasn't feeling great. *Maybe I shouldn't have eaten breakfast.* He'd been fine for a while, but he guessed his chronic condition was acting up again. He'd often had indigestion since he was a child, as did Hwiyin, mostly because of the stress from dealing with their grandmother, Ms. Jung, who always expressed such animosity toward Ms. Seo. Actually, Hwiyin had usually had it much worse than him. He would often find Hwiyin throwing up by himself whenever Ms. Jung screamed at their mother.

Hwihyun mumbled to himself bitterly, "He always pretended

like he could take it all, but it was all just show. He was actually really sensitive." It was true. Hwiyin had always screamed back at Ms. Jung whenever she spewed hateful words at Ms. Seo. Adults yelled at him quite a bit for that, but they more often said that he wasn't like a child at all.

But knowing that his brother threw up behind their backs, Hwihyun knew that Hwiyin had indeed still been a child, no matter what they said. But he didn't realize that at the time. Back then, he didn't even think for one second what Hwiyin must have been going through while throwing up till his eyes turned red. He only looked up to Hwiyin because he thought that Hwiyin must be incredibly strong to be able to go against Ms. Jung like that when he didn't dare say anything back.

Well, you did it, Hwiyin. You freed Mom, he said to Hwiyin in his imagination. Divorce had never seemed possible, given how much Dr. Cho loved Ms. Seo and how he was never going to let her go. But it had happened.

And you freed Father, he added. Once when Dr. Cho was severely drunk, he'd said something like, "You need a certain amount of power to receive help, you see. There isn't a funeral home in this country that I haven't been to using my title. Yes, I was afraid every time the phone rang that it might be for a child who had no relatives they could identify. Still, I went. If that was all it took to find Hwiyin…if all it takes for Hwiyin to find us is my climbing to a higher position of power than I am in now, then I'm going to do it."

Dr. Cho wasn't someone who gave any value to titles and power. But because of such reasons, he had become the director of this hospital. And as a result, his time remained frozen.

"You really are a wunderkind. Look at me, I've achieved nothing," Hwihyun mumbled.

He snapped back to reality at a sudden roar of applause. Dr. Cho had finished his speech. Now, he was back to being a professor and a doctor instead of the director. Hwihyun watched him wave to the crowd as they showered his father with thunderous applause for a moment, and then he turned around. Out of the corner of his eye, he saw someone familiar.

"What's he doing here?" he mumbled to himself. It was Soohyuk. The range of places one could expect to find Soohyuk in were extremely limited: the pediatric emergency room, the waiting room outside the operation room, and the staff room. Those were the three and only three places. And yet, there he was, standing against the wall with his arms crossed, looking as cold and expressionless as ever.

"I thought he wasn't interested," Hwihyun mumbled again. A sudden annoyance at Soohyuk bubbled up from deep within him. Dr. Cho had tried so hard to scout him, and he had ignored it all.

Hwihyun strode over to Soohyuk and teased, "Fancy seeing you here, Dr. Cha."

Soohyuk glanced at Hwihyun. "What do you want?"

It was a discouragingly cold question. Hwihyun snapped back, "Sheesh, nothing. It's just that I know how precious your time is to pay a visit to the director's retirement ceremony."

Soohyuk stared at Hwihyun. It was more of a glare than a stare, as usual.

"Why couldn't you make some time for Dr. Cho at least once? A single cup of coffee couldn't possibly hurt," added Hwihyun.

"My refusal upsets you that much?" asked Soohyuk.

"It does, in fact, yes," Hwihyun answered, emphasizing each word. It was strange how he felt more and more comfortable around Soohyuk every time they had an interaction. He felt like he could say whatever he wanted to say without any repercussions. He was someone who always smiled. He very rarely got angry. But whenever he was with Soohyuk, his heart burned with passion and his tongue turned sharper and sharper. "Are you going to eat lunch alone again today? You really should try to have some company from time to time. You might end up going a little cuckoo if you don't."

He was getting angrier and angrier that Soohyuk had ignored Dr. Cho. He was now almost attacking when he said, "I get that this place might still be a little unfamiliar for you, but you need to make more of an effort to fit in. A hospital is an organization and a society of its own."

"Are you done now?" asked Soohyuk, maintaining his coldness without budging an inch.

"No, I have a whole list to get through," snapped Hwihyun.

"Fine. Let's meet outside of work later and continue then."

The two stood side by side with their arms crossed, as if they were having a fight.

"What do you mean by that?" asked Hwihyun.

"I'm asking you to have a drink with me," said Soohyuk.

Hwihyun blinked at him in disbelief. "Really?"

They looked at each other. Their eyes were at around the same height, both of them standing just over six feet tall. Soohyuk turned his gaze back to the stage. Dr. Cho seemed to be about 5'9", and Ms. Seo seemed to be about 5'5".

A sudden understanding was stirring inside him. Something he might've known for a long time, but part of him hadn't wanted to accept it.

"What's your number?" asked Soohyuk as he took out his phone.

"This feels a little weird. Haven't you also never attended team dinners?" asked Hwihyun, his brow furrowing.

"Rumors are truly running rampant here, aren't they? How juvenile," Soohyuk sneered. But it somehow didn't upset Hwihyun. He must have gotten used to the way Soohyuk spoke without even realizing.

"My number is zero, one, zero..." Hwihyun said as Soohyuk entered his number on his phone. "What's your number?"

"I'll call you when I'm free," said Soohyuk.

Hwihyun cracked a smile. *What a ridiculous man.* "You really do march to the beat of your own drum."

"It's very unlikely that I know for sure when I'll be free beforehand, as someone who works at the emergency room. Don't tell me you weren't aware of that," said Soohyuk.

Hwihyun shrugged. "All right, then. Please do call me. I can't wait to have a drink with you."

"I will," answered Soohyuk.

Hwihyun scanned him again with great scrutiny. It wasn't anything new, but his snow-white shirt and crisply ironed gown were just as astonishing as ever.

"What are you looking at?" asked Soohyuk.

"Do you know a good laundry cleaner? It seems like you do," said Hwihyun. He was living with his mother, but he didn't ask her to do his laundry because he'd lived on his own for a long time. Moreover, she wasn't living with him to do his chores for him. She was living with him to shower him with the affection he'd been longing for. So, Hwihyun got his laundry done at a cleaners like he'd always done. "Come on, sharing is caring. Don't hoard all the good resources."

"I don't go to a cleaners," said Soohyuk.

"Then where? Don't tell me you clean and iron your clothes yourself."

"I do."

"You're joking," said Hwihyun, shaking his head. He didn't believe him one bit.

The two continued to banter in the same manner for a little longer. No part of it was productive, of course. All useless chatter. But neither of them wanted to stop.

After a while, Soohyuk changed the subject. "So, what happens to you now that the director has resigned?"

"Do you realize how insulting that question is?" said Hwihyun.

Soohyuk stared at him almost like he was trying to challenge him. It strangely reminded Hwihyun of that day during his childhood when his brother Hwiyin said, "You're it." Hwihyun felt a sudden sharp pain at his chest. He pressed down on the spot that stung with one hand, swaying. His forehead was covered in sweat in seconds. *Damn it, not now!*

"How are you going to *climb the ladder* now?" asked Soohyuk, noticing Hwihyun's suddenly changed expression and his hand pressed to his chest.

"I wasn't planning on climbing any ladders to begin with," said Hwihyun quietly with sweat trickling down his face. "Excuse me." He stumbled as he turned around. His stomach felt tight. The world started spinning.

When he dangerously swayed in his step, Soohyuk grabbed his arm, saying, "You have indigestion." He touched Hwihyun's now ice-cold hand.

Hwihyun looked at Soohyuk with unsure eyes. Something about this felt familiar. Hwiyin used to do this when they were younger. He'd come and massage his hand for him. Indigestion was a chronic problem of theirs, and Hwiyin had it a little worse than Hwihyun. But they tried to take care of it on their own instead of going to their mother. *Being sick really does a number on you*, thought Hwihyun. *Look how emotional I'm getting, thinking of Hwiyin.*

Right then, Soohyuk interrupted his nostalgic, emotional moment. "You look like a three-day-old corpse that was brought back to life and then was drowned again. I'm taking you to the emergency room."

Oh, for god's sake...why is he like this? thought Hwihyun.

Hwihyun slowly blinked. He must have fallen asleep. He jumped and sat up straight, like he was startled.

"Shh, you can sleep a little longer if you want. I haven't seen you that sick in a while, kid," said Dr. Cho. Or Professor Cho, now that he'd resigned—though of course, he was still a doctor, even if he wasn't the hospital director anymore. "People told me that you were in the emergency room. I must have stressed you out a little too much."

"I'm fine now. I had too much breakfast when I wasn't feeling that well, like an idiot," grunted Hwihyun.

Professor Cho looked at Hwihyun with mixed feelings. He was the reason his sons had indigestion so often.

He said quietly, "I'm sorry. I'm sorry for letting things go this far. For making you sick now too."

"I'm an adult now, so it's my own fault. Stop apologizing. I don't want to hear it," said Hwihyun rather coldly. Then he tried to smooth out his crumpled shirt at least a little. It would be better if it were immaculately crisp like Soohyuk's, but... *What a cheapskate. What's so bad about sharing who cleans his laundry? It's not like they're going to stop taking his clothes because they have one more customer. Seriously, what a cheapskate.*

"So, why were you looking for me?" asked Hwihyun.

"I wanted to have lunch with you," answered Professor Cho.

"Sorry to disappoint you, but I don't think I'll be able to have lunch."

"Do you want some soup then? I can bring some to the staff room if..."

Hwihyun reached out to grab his hand. "I'm all right, Father. You don't have to be this worried. I'm an adult."

That stung Professor Cho's heart. It sounded to him like his child was asking why he hadn't been there for him when he was young and in need of help. He didn't have a single thing to say in his defense. He was a horrible father who shouldn't even call himself one.

"Go, eat. I can take care of myself," added Hwihyun.

Suddenly, footsteps approached and the curtain around his bed was yanked to the side. Surprised, Hwihyun and Professor Cho both turned around to see who it was. It was Soohyuk.

Soohyuk gave a slight nod to Professor Cho, then pushed a

bag he was holding into Hwihyun's face. "Eat porridge," he said casually, in a way that sounded almost like an insult. Then he added, "You'd better eat the whole thing. This is hard to get." With that, he turned around and left.

After examining the package, Hwihyun started to chortle. *Did he really just buy me porridge?* The *Soohyuk Cha?* It was from Soohyuk's favorite shop, A Tasty Meal. He hadn't realized they made porridge too. There wasn't anything about a porridge on their blog. *Soohyuk really must be a VIP customer.*

"I guess he'll be skipping lunch," commented Hwihyun. This was probably Soohyuk's lunch. How else would he have gotten hot porridge from A Tasty Meal this quickly? *I guess he knows a thing or two about indigestion,* thought Hwihyun as he cackled. *He looked like he was about to pass out that day at the mall, but he insisted he was fine when Mom and I offered to help.*

"Hwihyun?" Professor Cho carefully called him, like he was worried about his son cackling like a madman.

"I'm fine, Father. I just can't stop laughing when I think about Dr. Cha. He only eats food from this place. I'd better buy when we go for that drink," said Hwihyun.

"You're having a drink with Dr. Cha?" Professor Cho couldn't believe his ears. *But I thought he didn't spend time with anyone outside of work.*

"He asked me to have a drink with him sometime. I'm really going to see the end of that man when we do."

Professor Cho smiled at Hwihyun's boastful proclamation.

"You know, he might end up staying here," added Hwihyun.

"What makes you think that?"

"He has a woman he likes."

Professor Cho's eyes widened.

"I saw them when Mother and I went to the mall the other day. He's dating a very cute woman. According to Mother, he said that she's someone who feeds him."

"Well, that is good news. If he stays, the two of you will be the yin and yang of this—" began Professor Cho.

His son interrupted him. "Father."

"All right, all right," said Professor Cho.

"Anyway, I'll be sure to avenge you, Father," said Hwihyun resolutely.

When was the last time they'd talked this comfortably? Usually, it was hard to even find something to talk about. But Soohyuk, being their common interest, was making their conversation continue to flow without any awkwardness.

"You should first focus on getting your health back, son," said Professor Cho.

Smiling wearily, Hwihyun answered, "I will. Don't worry."

CHAPTER 7

Soohyuk stood in front of the mirror in the bathroom. He stared at his reflection.

"Many years have passed," he murmured to himself in English.

He thought of Dr. Cho and Hwihyun. Anyone could see at one glance that they were father and son. Hwihyun even had Ms. Seo's gentle eyes. *But what about me?* He kept gazing at himself in the mirror like he was seeing it for the first time. He soon raised his hand to touch his eyes. Unlike Hwihyun, his eyes seemed cold and aggressive.

"You've really had it hard, Matt. Look at your eyes. They're more like Danny's than Kate's," he said to his reflection.

He'd spent years of his life carefully watching his stepfather, and walking on eggshells around him every minute of every day so he wouldn't ruffle his feathers. Soohyuk looked down to avoid his eyes, which reminded him of Danny's. People tend to grow to look like the people they live with. Like a way of protecting oneself, if you will. Like they can only survive if they can prove that they belong in the pack by taking after the leader in one form or another. That must have been what happened with Soohyuk. The simple reason of wanting to be beaten at least a little less and be accepted as part of the family by Danny must have brought this change.

Soohyuk looked into the eyes of his reflection again. He'd become extremely emotional when he spent the night with Yuna. His whole being had burst with his desire for her as he made love to her over and over. That must have woken the memories that were locked away deep within him. He'd had a dream. And a lot of them had come flooding back to him.

"They're still not all there," he mumbled.

He recalled the day he was taken to the orphanage. The voices of people he couldn't remember flitted through his mind, people who interrogated him in a violent way and talked about him like he wasn't there:

"Whoa, what's up with him? Why is he so big? Hey, kid, how old are you?"

"Ew, why are you throwing up? You're so disgusting."

"What are you, mute? Why aren't you saying anything? What's your name?"

"What an idiot. Where did they find him? He wasn't kidnapped, was he?"

"Since when did we care about all that? Anyway, we need some documents on him to get the stipend. He looks like he's around eight. Just write on the form that's he's eight years old and hand it in."

"No one's even going to take him. He's too big and stupid."

"Who cares? We just want the stipend."

Soohyuk's face grew pale. He started to feel nauseous. Yuna had prepared porridge for lunch for a reason. He'd been fine for a couple days, then this morning, he'd suddenly fallen ill. The hazy pieces of memories that weren't even complete were tormenting him, making him sick. Were they bad memories? How bad could they be to make him this sick?

He turned the water on to wash his hands as he looked at his face in the mirror again. No matter how hard he looked, he couldn't find any part that looked like his birth parents. He'd become a total stranger. Suddenly, the grudge he was holding against them melted away. Of course they couldn't recognize him when they'd stayed the same while he'd changed this much. It had been such a long time. Would they even still remember him?

"It would be nice if I could remember my age, at least. To think that I thought I was two years older than I actually am for all those years..." He frowned. His head was starting to ache.

When he entered the pediatric emergency room after not eating anything at all for lunch, he was already on edge. The first person who came into his view was Ms. Seo.

"How was lunch?" she asked with a warm smile. Soohyuk glared at her instead of answering. Ms. Seo winced and cocked her head to the side. "Did something happen?" she asked.

Soohyuk walked past her without answering. When he saw Ms. Seo, knowing now who she was, something that was sleeping deep inside his heart awoke. Anger. He remained consumed with that anger for the rest of the day. Consequently, the emergency room staff suffered much more than usual.

While she waited for Soohyuk to come home, Yuna checked on the granola bar she'd made for Minjoon. "Okay, it's hard now. I'll just take one bite..." She cut off a piece and took a bite. The granola, nuts, and dried fruit all came together very well. It was a lot less sweet and unhealthy than the granola bars they sold at the store because she used honey instead of sugar.

"Mmm, delicious." She smiled. It was an instinctive response to eating something so yummy. "I'm sure it'll be good enough for Minjoon too."

She was paying great attention to Minjoon's snacks. She wanted to make sure she was providing him with the most balanced, nutritious food she could make. Kyungjo was busy nowadays for a similar reason. She was learning how to cook from Yuna and also taking massage classes. No one thought that the time Minjoon was given was too short anymore. The family had sworn to each other that they would help maintain Minjoon's health to the best of their abilities for the medicine that would come out sometime in the future.

And in order to do that, they had to continue living and working hard. One difference was that Kyungjo was now trying to find something she could do while staying with Minjoon, so she could run to him whenever he needed her help.

The things Yuna could do in their busy lives were things like this: making snacks. Yuna divided the batch of granola bars into two containers, one for Minjoon and one for Soohyuk. Soohyuk was actually a pretty picky eater, though he didn't look like one on the outside, so he tended not to heed to a balanced diet unless she forced him to. He very rarely ate vegetables, fruits, nuts, and the like. It was truly a wonder that he kept his slim figure while sticking to a diet that consisted mainly of meat.

"If he doesn't want to eat them on his own, I'll make him," she said resolutely.

After organizing the granola bars, Yuna started her usual end-of-cooking cleanup. As someone who cooked, maintaining a clean work environment was one of the most essential and basic rules she followed. Sweat was all over her forehead by the time she finished. She started to take her clothes off. Now, it was time to get ready to leave. She was going to Minjoon's to have dinner with the family.

While she was in the shower, washing herself under the stream of water, the front door opened and Soohyuk entered, looking wearier than ever. He was feeling a little less nauseous now, but he was starving because he hadn't had lunch and was also slightly dizzy because he'd been looking at blood all afternoon in that state. Today really hadn't been a great day for him.

"I'm home," he said, exhaustion thick in his voice. The sound of water streaming out of the shower greeted him. Instead of going right inside after taking off his shoes, Soohyuk leaned against the wall for a moment and listened to the trickle of the water. It was the sound of someone other than himself being home. For the first time today, his shoulders relaxed.

Rubbing his face with one hand, he mumbled, "You're all I have, Yun."

Ms. Seo, Professor Cho, and Hwihyun all did not recognize him. He'd understood them for a brief moment because it was he who had changed so much, but that all changed again. Soohyuk had anticipated that the moment when he found his parents wouldn't be a warm, emotional one. It had been twenty-seven years, after all. They were separated when he was six years old, and were reunited when he was thirty-three. He didn't feel any affection for them. Instead, he was angry at them because all the pain he'd had to go through for those twenty-seven years had come rushing back to him. And when it did, how he became adopted no longer mattered. Only all that he'd had to go through mattered. Only the fact that they were the cause mattered.

Soohyuk closed his eyes. He hated them. He hated them. He hated them with all his heart. *It would've been better if I never remembered them.*

"No, I can just ignore them. I don't need anyone. I just need you, Yun," he mumbled to himself as he quietly knocked on the bathroom door. "I'm home, Yuna."

The door soon opened and her head poked out. "Welcome home. You're later than usual."

"There was a patient who got in an accident," answered Soohyuk as he took his coat off and unbuttoned his shirt. He threw the sweaty shirt in the laundry basket and was taking off his pants when she came out of the shower wearing a bathrobe.

"You're done already? I was just about to join you," he said as he hugged her waist and kissed her neck. Yuna blushed. They'd spent the whole weekend together, but she was still shy. Soohyuk held her tight in his arms. His anger was fading away with her in his arms.

When he finally let go after kissing her again and again, she mischievously protested, "Phew, I thought my ribs were going to break." Cracking a smile, Soohyuk brushed her wet hair. "Go take a shower," she said.

"Okay," he answered.

By the time Soohyuk came out of the shower, she was already all dried and dressed. She told him, "I'm going to Minjoon's. I'm having dinner there tonight. Your dinner's in the fridge, so you just have to warm it up later."

Soohyuk pouted. He knew that she always went to Minjoon's at this time of day. He didn't have any grievance with that because he knew how much Minjoon's family meant to her. But it was different today. He was getting angry again. It felt like the safe little world of their own he was relying on was starting to falter.

"Do you have to stay for dinner?" he asked sullenly.

Yuna paused on her way to the door. "Today's a special day. Minjoon started school today," she said.

That didn't help make Soohyuk feel better. *Minjoon, Minjoon, Minjoon.* He was getting all the attention in the family. But he'd barely gotten any attention until he met Yuna. He had gotten Kate's, but that wasn't enough. A part of his chest ached. *I must be jealous. Of an eight-year-old, too. What a sucker. Seriously. You're a real sucker, Soohyuk.* He didn't say anything more.

Yuna returned to the kitchen. Something seemed off about him. He didn't seem like his usual self.

"Hyuk," she called his new nickname. But he didn't answer; his back was still turned toward her. Yuna quietly looked at him. Yes, something seemed off about him. He seemed...on edge.

Like he was all worked up. "Did something happen at work today?"

"What do you mean?" Despite the stinging tone of his voice, he didn't even turn around to face her.

"Working in an emergency room, I'm sure things don't always go well and results don't always come out great. How does a doctor like you, who works so passionately to the point that it looks like you're willing to give your own life to the patients, handle all that stress?" she asked.

"There's no particular stress from that. That's just the way things are," said Soohyuk with utmost nonchalance.

She looked at him with wide eyes. She couldn't believe what he was saying. How could someone who worked as hard as Soohyuk not be stressed out? He suddenly felt like a stranger to her. He didn't seem like the Soohyuk she knew. Yuna fell silent as well.

Soohyuk clasped his hands tightly. *I'm such an idiot, really.* What was he doing, taking his anger out on Yuna? He didn't expect himself to be this irritated by the fact that she was going to leave without him. Soohyuk slowly turned around to face Yuna, who was looking at him with concern.

He mumbled, "I'm sorry. It's been a long day."

Yuna approached him with her arms open, and he hugged her tightly. He buried his face in her shoulder. He didn't want to be without her for even a second. He held her even more tightly. He didn't want her to leave him by himself. But he didn't show that. He didn't want to add any pressure to Yuna by telling her what was on his mind. Yet at the same time, he could not bring himself to let go of her. He just kept tightening his arms around her.

Yuna patted his back with her small hand at last, saying, "I need to go now. I'll come back as soon as possible."

"Okay," he said, then finally managed to let her go after she hugged him back even tighter. He followed her to the door.

While watching her put her shoes on, he said, "Call me when you're done. I'll come pick you up."

"No," she responded without any hesitation.

Soohyuk scowled. "Sometimes, I wonder if you realize that you're an adult." He didn't mean to chide her; it just slipped out.

"Soohyuk," she warned.

"You're not some girl who needs to get her daddy's permission to live with her boyfriend."

"Soohyuk Cha, we agreed to talk about that later," Yuna snapped.

Soohyuk's lips sullenly clamped shut again. They were now sharing a bed, but it was a private affair of their own. And the two had different opinions about this. Soohyuk didn't care if the whole world knew, but not Yuna. She was careful about everything.

He let out a long sigh at last. "I'm sorry. Guess I'm just really tired today. Go have dinner with your family."

"Are you sure you'll be all right?" she asked.

"I'll be fine after I take a nap. Have a great evening," he said.

Soon, Yuna disappeared out the door. Soohyuk stood there for a long time after she left. The apartment was completely silent. Like the quiet before a storm. He felt like he was a ticking bomb that could go off at any moment. Rage kept bubbling up inside him.

He leaned his head back and covered his eyes with both hands, mumbling, "Dammit. They're driving me nuts. And they're living happily ever after by themselves!" They were smiling even though that crazy old cow, his grandmother, was still alive and well. He'd had to go through so much pain to the point that even his face had changed, and they were smiling.

"Dammit!" He was starting to feel sick again.

CHAPTER 8

When Yuna returned, the apartment was quiet. She found Soohyuk asleep in the bedroom, lying on his side. Tiptoeing out of the room, she took her clothes off, showered, changed into comfortable clothes, and then returned to the bedroom. As she kneeled on the bed, he turned around like he sensed that she was there and reached out a hand, mumbling, "You're back…"

"I am," said Yuna, taking his hand. She brushed his hair when he moved to lay his head on her thigh. He must have been really tired. He did not take naps that often. "Did you eat anything?"

"No, I wasn't feeling well." He wrapped his arms around her waist and buried his face in her stomach. His breath slowly warmed her skin.

"Let me make you some porridge then." She began to get up.

He tightened his arms around her, stopping her from leaving. "Later. I want to stay like this for a little bit."

"All right," she answered.

Soohyuk just breathed while holding her like that. He really was feeling a lot calmer than before the nap. But he could still feel the rage quietly bubbling beneath the surface. It would return as soon as he faced them again at work tomorrow. But his head was clear enough now to focus only on Yuna.

"How's the kid's teacher? Is he all right?" he asked. Yuna hesitated for a moment. "Tell me. Whatever it is," Soohyuk reassured her.

"Kyungjo had a meeting with him today. Because you have to let the teacher know about a severe condition like Minjoon's. So, she did, but apparently he didn't respond as expected."

"Ah, a typical old grandpa who only looks after himself," said Soohyuk.

"Kyungjo didn't go that far, but I think he really might be, so I'm worried." Yuna sighed.

"Tell her to keep a close eye on him. You'd think that kids are the ones who cause most problems, but it's really the adults."

"Yes, that's what I told her."

"It's not going to be an easy ride for her," he mumbled.

"I know, that's why I'm so worried. I was hoping the teacher would help Minjoon," she said.

"If he says anything to the kid, bitch-slap him."

Yuna cracked a smile. She recalled a recent news segment on the violence in classrooms caused by overprotective parents and so on and so forth. *But he wants me to bitch-slap the teacher.*

"He at least told her that he will pay special attention to Minjoon." With that, Yuna paused. *What's best for Minjoon? Wouldn't it be better to tell him about his condition? What if he hears about it from someone else before we tell him?* But it wasn't that she couldn't understand Yoonjae and Kyungjo's position. How could she not? She also wanted to see even a single day more of Minjoon being the bright kid he'd always been.

"It's hard to tell if it would be better to tell him about the condition or not, isn't it?" asked Soohyuk, almost like he'd read her mind. "It's a dilemma I often witness, but I suppose it feels different to the people who have to make the decision. Anyway, it's something the parents themselves have to decide and take responsibility for. It's not something an outsider should try to meddle in."

For a moment, Yuna felt a coldness enter her heart. It wasn't because of the realistic nature of his advice. It was because of the cold way he'd said it. This was about Minjoon, not any other patient of his.

"Well, how levelheaded you are," she muttered.

"I know." His nonchalance stung her more painfully than any insult he could say.

"He's my nephew. How could you say it like that? What, is that your professional advice?" she said.

Soohyuk fumbled to raise himself to sitting. "You want my professional advice?"

Yuna's heart sank when he asked that. *What is he going to say? What if he talks about Minjoon like that too?*

"All right, here's my professional advice, then." Soohyuk flashed his cold black eyes. They frightened her. He was being too cold right now. She'd never seen him like this.

When he was about to open his mouth, she quickly interrupted, "No, don't. Don't say anything. I don't want your professional advice."

Soohyuk leaned his head to one side with a cold smile and said, "I thought you did."

She shook her head. "Not right now. You're being too cold, too pragmatic. I think I'll cry if you say anything at all about Minjoon like this. Even if it's the truth. Even if it needs to be said."

"Yun."

"Let's just not say anything anymore today," she said.

"You want me to shut up?" he asked.

Yes, Soohyuk was acting strange today.

"Yes, shut up. I'm going to go make porridge." Her voice trembled, but she sternly turned around.

He could sense her anger. Soohyuk lowered his head and

buried it in his hands. This wasn't good. Not good at all. He felt like he was going crazy.

Yuna turned back around for a moment when she reached the bedroom door. "If you have anything you want to say to me, say it after you've calmed down. Then I'll listen."

Soohyuk sat there like that for a long time after she left.

Yuna stood in front of the sink, trying to take deep breaths. Her heart was racing. She was both frightened and sympathetic of the new side of him she saw today. He looked cold and unstable. She mumbled to herself, "There has to be a reason. He wasn't like that even in the morning. Or yesterday. Yes, there has to be a reason."

It was true. He'd been kind to her all weekend, and this morning too. Something must have happened.

With a sigh, she opened the fridge at last. She was going to make his favorite beef porridge. She had to pay extra attention while preparing the vegetables because her hands kept trembling, like his unstableness had passed on to her. Forcing her eyes wide open, she started to precariously slice the washed vegetables into thin strips. The knife seemed to continue to try to escape her hand. This didn't happen often, but when it did, she always ended up hurting herself.

Ouch!

"Of course." She groaned. The knife had really cut through her skin and drawn blood. She heard quick footsteps approach her from behind, and before she could turn around, Soohyuk snatched her hand.

"It's nothing. It didn't go in that deep," she said, thanking her instincts for retracting the finger so quickly.

Soohyuk still didn't let go of her finger. He pressed on the wound until it stopped bleeding, then checked how deep it was once it stopped. Thankfully, it wasn't that deep, as she'd said. One bandage would suffice.

"Was it because of me?" he asked.

She didn't answer. She didn't look at him either. She only showed her back. Soohyuk quietly stood behind her, watching her shoulders tremble, then slowly said, "There's something I haven't told you yet."

Yuna turned around to face him.

Looking into her eyes, he said, "I was adopted."

Soohyuk observed her reaction. He wasn't going to miss the slightest hint. But she just kept staring at him without saying anything. His eyes nervously looked for signs. He felt like he couldn't breathe. Would she change her mind and start to dislike him now, because he'd kept such a big thing from her? Just as his chest began to tighten, she quietly took his hand.

A long sigh escaped Soohyuk's mouth. She was holding his hand, and yet, he was still nervous. He'd never told anyone that he was adopted himself. Even when he was filling out the application form to come to S University, he hadn't listed all his family history like most Koreans did. He'd come all the way here relying only on himself and his own history, as Soohyuk Cha and no one else. But did she see him as Soohyuk Cha as well? He desperately hoped she did. Soohyuk's head dropped until his forehead was leaning against her shoulder. He wanted to lean on her again.

Yuna brushed his back with a gentle hand. *Adopted.* It was enough to surprise her, but her heart was beating tranquilly. Maybe a part of her had expected something like this. His shaky breath seemed to painfully knock on her heart. She continued to silently brush his back, trying to console him.

The things he'd said and the expressions he'd made slowly came back to her mind one by one. The way he'd frowned and acted irritated when they talked about his parents, how he'd called his mother "birthmother," the time he'd said that he learned Korean from a neighbor and that there was someone who took care of him, but he hadn't called that caretaker his mother... All of those must have been hints. Who would be comfortable talking about themselves? Even she, who was sure that she'd been raised to be a decent human being by Yoonjae, had hesitated before telling him that she was an orphan. Moreover, he was adopted. She took that as his childhood being more miserable than her own. She'd been protected by Yoonjae. She'd seen kids who were adopted at the orphanage. Most of them didn't end up in a very happy place.

"Say something," he murmured.

After taking a deep breath in, she said as sincerely as she could, "I admire you for becoming such an amazing adult. Look at you, you're such a great doctor."

Soohyuk couldn't help but laugh. He'd never thought of himself like that.

"Really, you should be proud of yourself. Like I am. You're much more awesome than I am." She pulled him into her arms and said, "It must have been hard."

"No," he automatically lied. He didn't want to tell Yuna. He didn't want her to change the way she thought of him. She might end up pitying him if she learned how he was raised. Even if she denied it herself, he might misunderstand her gestures as pity. He was too proud to be pitied by anyone. A lot of people misunderstood him already, saying that he was cold, rude, and distant because he was adopted. So, he couldn't ever let Yuna know.

That thought drove him down a spiral of confusion. *What does it mean to be* me? He wrapped his arms around her waist like he was clinging to her and pulled her closer.

Yuna didn't ask more questions after hearing his short response. She understood that he didn't want to talk more about it right now and that telling her that he'd been adopted was enough to hurt him or throw him into an emotional spiral. Or at least, that's how she would've felt if she were in his shoes.

When Soohyuk straightened his back at last, he held her

finger that wasn't bleeding anymore and said, "Let me fix it for you. Please forgive my behavior."

Yuna answered with a silent laugh, "I've already forgiven you. So, don't think too much about it."

Soohyuk didn't say anything, but there was a certain coldness in his eyes. But Yuna could see through that now. He was being overly silent because he was feeling extremely defensive. She had a feeling he'd lied when he said that he didn't get stressed out from his job. No, he instead seemed like the type to pile all the stress inside himself.

He took out the first-aid kit and treated her small wound with great care. He disinfected it, put some ointment on it, and then put a waterproof bandage on it.

"I don't need anything for dinner," he said while putting everything back in the box.

She shook her head. "No, you need to eat something. You look awful right now. I feel bad because there's so much I want to do for you, but there isn't much I can actually do. So, I'm at least going to make you dinner..."

Yuna couldn't finish. Soohyuk suddenly pulled her into his embrace, burying her face in his chest.

CHAPTER 9

The weather warmed up more and more by the day. Soohyuk started to wear less clothing, and thinner shirts as well. Yuna walked him out to the door. He'd had night shifts all last week, but this week, he'd been assigned morning shifts.

"I'll come by during your lunchtime," said Yuna.

"No, don't. Just send it with the other ones," he said.

She frowned. "Hyuk."

"No, really. You need to get some rest too. I wouldn't be able to come out to see you even if you came anyway." When he leaned down to kiss her, she comfortably accepted his kiss. "See you at dinner," he said before leaving.

Yuna could finally let go of the breath she'd been holding once she was alone. *I really wanted to give it to him in person today.* When she'd returned from the grocery store earlier this morning, she'd found him coming out of the office looking like he'd been up all night. It wasn't that much of a surprise to see him like that, since she knew that he studied whenever he had time, but he seemed a little different today. He was extremely pale like he'd seen a ghost. Still, he kept his mouth shut.

She was certain multiple bad things were happening in his life in a row. Her sensitive intuition had caught that, but he still would not open up. She didn't know what it was, but there certainly was something bothering him. He was clearly becoming thinner and more on edge by the day. He didn't even eat as much as before.

"Wait, did he find his birthparents?" she thought out loud. *What if that was the reason he came back to Korea?* It wasn't a rare thing. She'd seen several kids who were adopted overseas return after they'd grown up to reconnect with their roots. Maybe Soohyuk wanted to do that too.

Yuna buried her face in her hands, feeling perplexed. The worst-case scenario kept playing in her head. Finding his birthparents wasn't that bad on its own. But what if he'd seen them going on about their lives so happily without him? That was truly the worst thing that could happen.

"I hope not. He's actually a rather sensitive man," she mumbled. It was true. She could tell by the way he treated her, like how he never missed a single thing. The way he was as a doctor was probably rooted in his innate sensitivity. *I mean, think of that slow dance. Who else in the whole wide world would ever have slow danced with me in that situation?* She'd become even more certain since they'd started sharing the same bed. He was a man who was both cold and sensitive.

Yuna's heart ached with sorrow for him. That must've been what happened: he'd learned something about his birthparents that wasn't encouraging.

"I really hope not. He shouldn't be hurt any more than he already was," she said.

But this wasn't something she could just bring up to Soohyuk. He wasn't keen on exposing his vulnerability in front of her. Still, having to watch from the sidelines like this was also frustrating. Yuna let out a long sigh when she recalled his ice-cold eyes.

Ms. Seo entered the pediatric emergency room, greeting people with a warm smile, as always. Her eyes first searched for Soohyuk. She hadn't had a chance to see him all last week because he was working night shifts. She couldn't wait for him to come back to work in the mornings again.

The moment she spotted him, her eyes lit up. He was checking the chart of the patients from the previous shift before putting on his coat. Tightening her grip on the container she was holding, Ms. Seo took a deep breath. He'd warned her last time that he would throw it in the trash if she offered something to him again, so she'd changed her plans to work on the people around him rather than going for him straight away.

"I wonder how he's feeling this week," she muttered. When he'd started talking politely to everyone, thanking people, and not even showering the guardians with profanity for some time, people had begun to say that he'd turned soft. But for some reason, he'd reverted back to his original attitude a couple days ago. He didn't even speak in Korean unless he was talking to the patients. The nurses also said that he became enraged at the smallest mistakes. More than anything, he'd turned so utterly cold. And every time he saw Ms. Seo, he glared at her like he wanted to strangle her.

She had no idea what had happened. She'd been thinking that his girlfriend was having a good effect on him, but that had changed all of a sudden. That thought naturally led to her wondering if they had broken up. And that thought then led to her bringing this container in this morning.

Ms. Seo walked over to the desk and brightly greeted the staff. "Good morning, everyone."

"Good morning, Ms. Seo," they all warmly greeted her back. Except one person. Soohyuk didn't even look up from the charts. He looked completely absorbed in his work.

Pushing the container full of kimbap and sandwiches she'd made early in the morning toward the head nurse, she said, "I made a little something for you all. Just a little snack."

"Oh, Ms. Seo, you shouldn't have," said a nurse.

"It was no trouble. I just made a little more while making Hwihyun's. Don't get mad at me if it tastes bad." Ms. Seo smiled.

Suddenly, Soohyuk chimed in. "Why would anyone bring anything so bad that people would get upset?" She couldn't understand him right away because he was speaking in English, but she could tell that it wasn't anything nice by his cold tone.

Tense silence ensued until the head nurse, a dire supporter of Soohyuk's, broke it with a cheerful smile. "Thank you so much. I'll make sure everyone gets a bite." She then leaned in toward Ms. Seo and whispered, "He hasn't been doing that great recently. So, don't take it personally."

A sharp *bang* pierced the room as Soohyuk slammed the desk with his hand. Silence ensued again.

Glaring at one of the residents, he snapped, "How could you get the spelling wrong?" He sounded colder than ever. The resident, who was rejoicing in his long-awaited break time, turned stiff at once.

"Dr. Cha—" he started in Korean.

"Explain it to me so I can understand. You're not having trouble understanding me, are you? This is basic English," Soohyuk continued in English. Blushing at the continued berating, the resident fell silent. "All right, I'll change the question then. Do you realize that your mistake has changed the diagnosis of this patient?"

"I'm sorry," the resident barely squeaked in English, pale with fear. It had been smooth sailing for a while, but it seemed like Dr. Cha's bitchiness was back in full. But he didn't really have much to say in his defense, because it clearly was his fault.

"Fix it, and precisely record why you had to fix it on the chart. Notify the patient of this as well," ordered Soohyuk.

"Yes, sir."

"Do it right when I ask you nicely," Soohyuk warned while looking over the next chart. "I've told you multiple times already that this is a record of life and death."

After checking the last charts, he put on his gown and disappeared to check on the patients. When the gathered residents who were working this shift scattered as well, the head nurse said to Ms. Seo, "Like I said, he hasn't been doing that great lately."

"He's not sick, is he?" she asked, her worried eyes fixed on Soohyuk as he approached a patient. He'd grown a lot thinner in the week she hadn't seen him. And much colder and tenser. *What if something really has happened?* She couldn't help but worry about him.

"Dr. Cha isn't someone who would open up about himself in any situation. But another doctor did say that he threw up in the bathroom this morning," said the head nurse.

"Oh, really?" Ms. Seo's brows narrowed with concern. But he still seemed kind when he was addressing his patients. He was still the best doctor any patient could ask for. *So then, why did he change his attitude toward the staff all of a sudden?*

Ms. Seo spent all morning watching Soohyuk, to the point that he said to her, "Are you stalking me? Why are you staring at me like that?"

She failed to say anything in return, even though she perfectly understood his English, because he was acting so aggressive.

"You have a knack for making someone feel very uncomfortable," he growled.

Ms. Seo's face fell. He was mad at her, she could tell. And that somehow made her heart wrench.

"I'm sorry," she managed to answer in English, only for Soohyuk to scoff and turn his back on her.

The busy emergency room suddenly settled down as the clock struck noon. Thanks to the endless stream of patients finally ceasing, Soohyuk had a moment to catch his breath. He leaned against the chair and fidgeted with his phone in his hand. He was afflicted. He kept entering Kate's number and erasing it. His brows narrowed as he struggled to come to a decision.

He'd remembered something about Kate earlier this morning. He didn't know why it had to happen today, but the memory was bad enough to crush his previous conclusion that at least Kate was good. It had kept him up since early in the morning and forced him to struggle on his own without Yuna by his side. He'd started feeling nauseous again and ended up throwing up in the staff bathroom.

"I have to know," he muttered.

He had to hear her side of the story. He still very clearly remembered all that she had done for him, so he at least had to give her a chance to redeem herself. But… Soohyuk lowered his head and rubbed his forehead with one hand. It felt like he was slowly falling apart.

Someone softly cleared their throat. He looked up. Ms. Seo was standing there.

Soohyuk frowned. Hers was the one face he did not want to see in this moment. He clamped his mouth shut and glared at her.

"Sorry for the intrusion, Dr. Cha," she said. She had a feeling he was going to be relentless with her, judging by the way his eyes were shooting daggers at her, but she was determined. She gathered the courage to hold out the medicine she'd gotten for him at the pharmacy and said, "I heard you were feeling a bit queasy, so I thought this might help. It's for indigestion."

Soohyuk quietly reached out his hand to take the medicine she was offering. When Ms. Seo started to smile, she heard a small *tap*. Soohyuk had thrown the medicine into the trash can.

"Dr. Cha?" she said, but he didn't even answer. He'd already said no. He'd already warned her that he would toss anything she gave him in the trash.

Letting out a long sigh, she said, "I'm sorry. I knew you would do this, since you said that you would last time. But I had to do something when I heard that you threw up this morning."

Soohyuk gazed at her with cold eyes. *How could anyone be that cold?* she wondered. But Ms. Seo continued softly without evading his eyes, "I know I shouldn't say this, but I can't help wanting to take care of you." She gave him a warm smile.

Looking at that smile, he coolly spat out, "It must be nice to be able to smile whenever you want."

"I'm sorry?" She blinked.

Soohyuk turned his back to her.

Perfectly understanding that she was very much not welcome here, Ms. Seo said, "I'm sorry, Dr. Cha," and turned to leave.

"I'm so sick of hearing that," muttered Soohyuk.

She winced, but she continued walking. *How could he change this much all of a sudden? How could he be so cold?* A certain sorrow filled her aching heart.

Soohyuk got up from his seat and went into the staff room. He finally dialed Kate in the empty room. After a series of rings, Kate picked up.

"Soohyuk! My, my, how nice it is to hear from you. I was about to call you anyway. Happy birthday!"

Soohyuk slightly gasped. Birthday…the birthday the orphanage had arbitrarily assigned him. The new fragments he'd recalled that morning slowly turned into a certain truth. He now had no choice but to bring it up.

"Kate, I wanted to ask you something," he said.

"Yes, of course, anything."

"You gave them money, didn't you? What did they say when they asked for it?" he asked straightaway.

"What are you talking about, Soohyuk?"

Soohyuk clenched his jaw in an effort to hold himself back from erupting like a volcano.

"Soohyuk? Matt?"

"I remember now. What those people at the orphanage said when they were cackling about you sending them money. They said that I was a blessing," he said through gritted teeth.

"Matt…"

He tried to control his emotions by grabbing a handful of his hair as he continued, "When you first brought me home, your family was very affluent. But it all crumbled down in one fell swoop when Danny lost his job. I couldn't remember why that happened, but now I do."

"Matt, listen to me first. Matt…"

"No, you listen to me," interrupted Soohyuk. "It was because of you. Because you got that loan without letting Danny know. The loan you got so you could buy me. I bet you didn't think that Danny would lose his job."

"Matt, please…"

After taking in a deep breath, he continued, "If everything in the world went according to the law, or common sense, none of this would have happened. I would never have been sent to that orphanage, and you would never have been able to buy a child without all the hoops you'd have had to jump through in the US government."

"I knew from the first moment that you would be my…"

Soohyuk grimaced. "So, this was the truth you wanted me to find. You just wanted me to acknowledge how much you had to pay to get me."

"Hold on, Matt, listen to me for a second. Yes, you're right. I paid the orphanage. Because they said that that was the only way they were going to let me take you. I knew from the first moment

I saw you that you would be my son. Like it was our destiny. I didn't want you to be sent to some other family."

Soohyuk let out a shaky breath while roughly rubbing his forehead with one hand. Danny was right in the end. He had been sold for money indeed. Danny's rage against him was going to happen in one way or another since the moment he was adopted. He was, after all, the child who ruined the family and got in between the two of them.

"Matt, did you hear what I said?"

He suddenly realized why all of this had come back today. Because today was his stupid fake birthday.

Soohyuk said through gritted teeth, "I never thought I'd say this, but Kate, Danny was right in the end. I was sold for money. Though, the person who sold me wasn't my birthmother. But Kate, you know what? You were the one who made Danny hate me in the first place. Because of you, I had to live in hell for all those years." He could hear Kate's shaky breath from the other side of the phone. But Soohyuk continued without relenting, "I'll never contact you again. Please don't ever call me either. I will, however, keep sending you money. Goodbye."

"Matt, wait! Matt! Matt!"

Ignoring Kate's desperate cries, Soohyuk ended the call. He then proceeded to block her number. But that wasn't enough. He threw the phone on the ground as hard as he could.

Soohyuk was not at his high for the rest of the day. He was scowling the whole time he was working and became furious whenever someone made a mistake. Everyone had to walk on eggshells so as to not set him off. They had no other choice because he was by far the best pediatric emergency medicine specialist. His quick and precise eyes and impeccable techniques from real life experience and arduous studying were truly incomparable.

"I think something really did happen to Dr. Cha," whispered one of the nurses to the head nurse. "He won't say a single thing. He at least showed that he was listening even if he didn't always respond before, but not anymore."

Instead of answering, the head nurse watched Soohyuk very carefully sew a wound on a patient's face, making sure that it wouldn't leave a scar. He was as careful and skilled as any respected plastic surgeon. The child's mother could watch the procedure at ease from the side thanks to him.

"Did we do something wrong?" asked the nurse.

"Enough now. Everyone has their ups and downs. There's no need to overanalyze everything. Don't tell me you haven't had days when you were down. See? You have too. I know how irritable you get on those days."

"Why do you always take his side? You should be on our team."

"Oh, don't you worry, I am on your team," said the head nurse.

"Really?" she asked in disbelief.

"Yes," the head nurse answered halfheartedly, with her eyes still fixed on Soohyuk. She carefully scanned his clamped lips, serious eyes, and stiff neck. He hadn't even eaten lunch today. She'd brought him the kimbap and the sandwich Ms. Seo made, but he declined without even a moment of hesitation. It would all make perfect sense if she blamed it on his well-known antisocial tendencies, but she didn't want to.

As someone who'd worked with countless doctors, she believed that their personalities did not matter in the emergency room. What mattered were their skills of precision, speed, and a sense of responsibility. And Soohyuk had all three of them. Of course, it would be even better if he were sweet and kind as well, but she'd never seen someone that perfect in her life. The reality was that it was hard to even find a doctor with a balanced set of the three virtues.

But something had started to change within Soohyuk. He'd started becoming soft, like he was slowly opening up. Every so often, he'd say things that didn't sound like mockery. It was truly astounding. He was so widely known for driving people up the wall whenever he opened his mouth until then. And even when he did, there was always an understandable reason behind it. He was someone who hated tricks, after all.

But he'd shut back up a couple of days ago. Now, he refused to communicate with anyone, like he had built high walls to separate himself from the world. And he was slowly suffocating the people around him with his eyes, which became colder and colder every day. The effect was slowly rippling through the emergency room. He had so much influence in the pediatric emergency room that not even Professor Park ordered him to do anything anymore. Some people even called him a tyrant without a title.

There had to be a reason for all of this. He wouldn't do this without cause. *Is it because of stress?* she wondered.

"What to do… He does seem like the type to hold it all in," she mumbled. He had to get stressed out from time to time, since he was human too. Taking care of ill people must take up a lot of energy as well. *How does he cope with all that?* Other people shook most of it off by chatting during lunch hours or team dinners, but Soohyuk didn't do that. In fact, he didn't interact with anyone here at the hospital.

Soohyuk started walking toward her while taking his gloves off. The head nurse quickly smiled. She wanted to always greet this young doctor with a smile.

"My phone is…" he started to speak in English.

"I'm sorry, Dr. Cha, but my English isn't that great," she interrupted.

Soohyuk answered in Korean. "My phone is not working. You will not be able to reach me through my number." To be precise, he'd broken his phone. At the moment, it didn't matter much, because Yuna never called him while he was on the clock. And she was the only person, other than Kate, he ever talked to on the phone.

He leaned against the desk and crossed his arms. He hadn't told Yuna about much as of now. But she had noticed as well that he had changed. He didn't know how much more he was going to change. The only thing he knew for sure was that his behavior was hurting her. His insisting on being alone until now was to make sure he didn't hurt anyone. But ironically, he was holding on to her, the most precious person in his life. He did not want to let her go, even though he knew that he was hurting her.

"There should be a lot of cell phone carrier stores on the way to your apartment from here," said the head nurse. Soohyuk didn't answer. The way he stood there with his arms crossed, he seemed like he was lost in thought. But he somehow seemed a little unhinged at the same time. She was sensing a certain vulnerability about him that made him seem like a hurt child.

"Dr. Cha," she gently called. Soohyuk snapped back to reality and looked at her. "We need you, Dr. Cha. I'm really sorry, but you're the first person who comes to mind in the most serious situations. So, please, get a cell phone. I think I'll be too anxious to fall asleep at night if you don't."

Soohyuk just quietly stared at her. Looking into his cool eyes, she said once again, emphasizing each word, "We need you."

Soohyuk closed his eyes. Then he quietly mumbled, "Fine."

"Thank you so much, Dr. Cha." She smiled.

Ms. Seo watched the head nurse and Soohyuk from a distance, then turned her attention back to the child in her arms.

"Yes, I know, I know. Hold on just a little longer. Mom will come soon," she soothed the child. She was watching the girl while her mother left for a brief moment to retrieve some things from home, as they'd been told they would be admitted overnight. The five-year-old girl had been diagnosed with pneumonia and now was waiting before being admitted. She lay limp in Ms. Seo's arms. She was as light as a feather after all the coughing, so it wasn't hard to continue holding her like that. Her little hands grasped Ms. Seo's top.

"Mom…" Her voice trailed off, then turned into a cough. Ms. Seo patted her back to help her spit out the phlegm. Her cough continued on without ceasing.

Suddenly, Soohyuk called out from behind, "Put on your mask." Ms. Seo automatically smiled. He was speaking in Korean again. That little gesture made all the embarrassment she'd felt from before melt away.

"It's a little hard because both my hands are occupied. Can you help me?" she said.

Soohyuk looked down at her with his cold eyes. Her eyes shone gently with warmth, and her lips formed a comfortable smile that clearly showed she was happy to see him. And she smelled of something sweet... *Birthmother...* Soohyuk took out a mask from his pocket and put it on Ms. Seo himself.

"Thank you, Dr. Cha," she said.

He simply nodded and continued going his way. He would be going home in a little bit. And Yuna would be home. Waiting for him. His lips made a faint smile. It was the first time today he'd smiled. He missed her. Very much.

<hr>

"I'm home," he called.

"You're early today," Yuna answered from somewhere in the apartment.

"Thank god," he mumbled.

Soohyuk headed straight to the kitchen when he heard her bustling in there. Yuna was in the middle of the last step of today's work, uploading pictures of the day's menu. But she paused and opened her arms wide toward him.

More crushing her ribs than hugging her, he mumbled, "I missed you."

"Me too," she answered, caressing his arms tightly wrapped around her body. The hug continued for a long time. Brushing his hair, she whispered, "How was your day?" He didn't answer. And that was enough of an answer for her. He hadn't had a great day. "How are you feeling? I was worried because you looked so sick this morning," she said.

"I'm all right now," he answered.

Oddly enough, all the nausea that had been pestering him all day disappeared the second he arrived home. He hadn't felt any hunger all day, but now he did. It was probably because Yuna was there. Everything felt much better when she was with him. He was definitely unstable. He was a full-grown adult, and yet he couldn't control himself and was letting his mood swing like a rollercoaster. It was embarrassing. But he couldn't help it. He couldn't let go of her either.

"Go take a shower. I'll make you some snacks," she said.

"No, I'm not hungry," he answered. He actually was hungry, but he didn't want to ask her to make something for him. He didn't want to do anything that might burden her. That was the least he could do.

"Go work. I'll find something to eat if I get hungry," he said.

Yuna unwrapped his arm from around her and looked into his face. Bags were visible under his piercing eyes, showing his exhaustion. His forehead seemed to be bearing all the weight of the world on that little spot between his eyebrows. He, who usually said everything and anything that came to mind, even if it was rude or destructive, was choosing to stay quiet.

"Soohyuk," she called.

Straightening his back, he immediately cut her off. "Don't ask anything."

Yuna still went on. "Then complain to me."

After all the time she'd known him, liked him, lived with him, she was getting used to him, and maybe she was also becoming more like him. Regardless of his coldness, she said what she wanted to say. "Why don't you ever complain when you look like you're about to die from stress or something? Whatever it is, spill it. You have to just rant sometimes and let things out."

Soohyuk's hand paused mid-air as he was trying to unbutton his shirt. He hadn't expected this response from her.

"If you don't even want to do that, then have some fun with me and loosen up," she continued.

Soohyuk looked so cold when his face became expressionless. He seemed like he was an emotionless machine. But when he was smiling, he looked like a completely different person. He seemed like someone who could control himself well whatever came, but here he was, without his smile. She missed his smile so much.

Soohyuk threw his head back and took a deep breath in. He filled his lungs with Yuna as if she existed all around the apartment. He took another deep breath then another, then finally looked at Yuna. "Do you want take a shower together?" he asked.

Yuna pushed back her chair to get up from her seat, saying, "You know I normally don't do this sober, right?" She walked over to him and threw herself into his embrace, wrapping her own arms around his waist. Soohyuk leaned his head down to give her a brief but intense kiss.

"I know," he whispered in a husky voice as he pressed his lips against hers again. His tongue naturally found its way into her mouth as her lips parted. He wrapped his arms around her waist as well and leaned farther down toward her. Her tongue gently slithered across his. It was such a sensual feeling that the hairs on the back of his neck rose. Soohyuk moved one hand to cradle her neck and started kissing her even deeper. He sucked her lips, interlaced his tongue with hers, swallowed her saliva, and breathed in her breath.

A warmth spread through one side of his heart. Only she warmed him up like this. He didn't know what he would do without her. Every day, he hastened to get back home to see her even a little quicker.

Her hands started to unbutton his shirt. His kiss always made her feel braver than usual. His lips pecked her face, then her ear. A short moan escaped her lips.

"I like it when you moan for me like that," he whispered, stamping his lips on her neck so hard that he could leave a mark.

"Mhmm," she hummed.

Soohyuk grinned. She was so adorable whenever she said "Mhmm" that he didn't know what to do with her. Caressing her back with both of his hands, he brushed her shoulder and collarbone with his tongue. Her body smelled delicious.

Every time he tasted her collarbones with his tongue, she struggled to straighten her quivering body. Her legs wanted to give in, so it was not an easy fight. Her fingers trembled as well, making it harder to unbutton his shirt. When she finally unbuttoned it all the way, she pulled the hem out of his pants and felt his bare flesh with her lips. She kissed his chest and left a mark like he had. As she did so, she put her hands on his belt buckle. The bold move made her heart jump. She had always been shy in the beginning steps of making love, because she couldn't completely shake away her shyness and fears.

But his kiss kindled her inner fire.

His fingers sneaked into her hair and forced her to look up. His lips aggressively took hers. Making its way in through her parted lips, his tongue unabashedly revealed its desire to claim her. She gasped. It was so intense that her whole body wanted to go limp.

He suddenly turned her around and pushed his hand into her loose lounge pants. His hand covered her most sensitive spot in seconds.

Another moan escaped her lips. He was touching the soaked place as if it were his. He firmly rubbed it with his palm. She leaned her head against him. Leaning down to kiss her exposed neck, he stroked the place dripping in anticipation of him. Her body was opening up to its limit and trembling. His body trembled with excitement as well.

Soohyuk forced himself to stop before he became even more excited. He quickly undressed her and threw his clothes on the ground as well. Letting his part that was hard with anticipation show, he grabbed her hand and led her to the bathroom. Warm streams of water rained down on them. It soaked the two naked lovers as they touched and kissed each other. Soohyuk was kissing her intensely, like he was going to devour her with both his hands holding her face in place. Pushed back by his fervor, she was now leaning against the cold wall. But she didn't even notice its coldness; her body was running so hot that she could completely ignore it. His hand fumbled to grab the soap. With her lips trapped between his, he started to lather her body with it.

He lusted after her body. He firmly grabbed her round breasts and rubbed her flat stomach, his hands covered with slippery bubbles. He snatched her full buttocks, only forcing himself to let go so he could lather her slick, long legs as well. His hands were now slithering up her thighs. He gently rubbed her as if he were kissing her, then started lathering soap on himself.

Yuna joined in. Like he had done, she got soap on her hands and started touching him. Her hands slid down past his firm chest and slim waist to the part that was wanting her so badly.

"You've become so brave. I feel like you might end up taking control, if you go like..." He abruptly stopped mid-sentence when her hand slowly stroked his part, making him quiver.

"You feel so soft," she said in the most alluring way he could imagine. That was all it took. He pulled her hand, which was driving him crazy, out of the way and quickly finished washing himself. He then rinsed off all the soap left on their bodies. He hastily took out a condom from the cabinet and put it on.

He lifted her body up into the air. Her legs searched for a place to hold on to, then wrapped around his waist. He filled her up at once. *Oh...* It felt like electricity was coursing through her body. Every time he roughly thrusted and rubbed himself and her innermost flesh, that sensation got stronger.

It felt so good Yuna thought she might die. She clung to his neck. It felt like he was pushing himself all the way up to her stomach every time he thrusted. Making love with him was always like this. No hesitance. No hiding how much he wanted her. But he wasn't expressing that out loud anymore. Panting like an animal while letting her back grind against the wall every time he pushed himself in, Yuna grabbed his hair and leaned forward to press her lips against his. With a loud groan, he moved even more aggressively.

She threw her head back as an ecstatic sensation swept over her till her sight went black. But he wasn't there yet. Soohyuk pushed her higher and higher. Heat spread throughout her body, drying her throat. Still, he continued, making her thrash again and again.

At last, he quivered with a short grunt. The violent wave of pleasure from the release swept through his body. Yuna wearily leaned her head against his shoulder and panted. Soohyuk didn't pull himself out. The faltering pleasure was scaring him. His part, which had shrunk after the release, seemed to intensify his fear.

"Soohyuk?" she called, but he didn't budge. He just held her in his arms.

He was afraid to let her go. He was afraid that she might leave him alone if he did. *How ironic,* he thought. *I lived my whole life alone... But being alone, without Yuna, is scary. Being in a space where Yuna is no more is scary.* He pulled her even closer to his chest.

Soohyuk shifted in bed when he heard a voice from the distance. *Hmm...* A warm hand patted his back. He squirmed toward the source of the warmth. Once he rested his head on her thigh and buried his face in her belly, he felt at ease again. *She must be on the phone with someone,* his sleepy mind thought. He could feel the vibration every time she spoke.

"When? You want to leave this Friday and come back on Sunday?" she said.

Soohyuk suddenly felt his mind snap out of the slumber. *What?*

"So what if it's all green? We can see what Suncheon is like in the spring, then in the fall," she continued. His body stiffened.

"That sounds good. I'll leave as soon as I finish the deliveries on Friday."

Now, he was wide awake. Soohyuk opened his eyes and looked up at her chin.

"Nope, I'm not going to bring anything. Everyone knows how good the food is in Suncheon. We can also stop by Gwangyang on the way for some bulgogi and cockles." Yuna laughed. Soohyuk lifted himself to sitting from her lap. With a smile still lingering on her face, she put down her phone, saying, "It's Yoon-jae. He wants to go to Suncheon on the caravan this weekend."

"And?" he asked.

"It's the first trip on the caravan, so I'm going with them. I don't work on weekends anyway," she said.

Suddenly, a sharp jealousy he didn't even realize he'd been hiding inside shot out. "Yes, yes, to be with your *family*, surprise, surprise. You do realize that can all shatter to pieces just like that, right?"

"What do you mean by that?" His sharp words were starting to get on her nerves. But she still calmly waited for his explanation.

"I don't understand why that matters so much to you. No matter how hard you try, you'll just be a stranger to them in the end," he spat out.

Yuna clenched her jaw. He was being overly aggressive. But it was understandable. He was adopted, after all. And judging by the way he was talking, the family who'd adopted him must not have been a happy one. *Yes, he must have been raised in a worse environment than I thought.*

Something changed inside of her, all of a sudden. She wasn't angry. If someone had said something like this to her in the past, she wouldn't have understood why right away and would have become furious. But now, her heart ached for him. She could feel all the terrible things that he must have experienced, as if they'd happened to her. And they hurt. A lot.

Yuna frowned like she was about to burst into tears, but calmly asked, "Did you grow up in that bad an environment to make you think of families like that?"

Instead of answering the question, he curtly said, "Don't go." With that, he rose from the bed in his naked form, the exact way he fell asleep after making love with Yuna. This was like a slap in the face after a sweet nap. His hands even began to tremble as he opened the drawer to take out a change of clothes.

Yuna watched him put on his clothes, then said, "I'll try to be as clear as possible. I'm not a stranger to them. Yoonjae's family is my family, and I cherish my family. I will do all that I can do to protect them and will try my hardest to make them happy." Soohyuk clamped his mouth shut. "You said that you don't understand why they matter so much to me. Then, Soohyuk, tell me. What are we going to be?"

"How am I supposed to know?" He spat out the first thing that came to mind. He was feeling more hurt than ever. It annoyed him. And everything about this made him angry. *Why do I have to be alone?*

"You don't know? So, you haven't given any thought to *us*?" she said.

"What am I supposed to have given any thought to? And why should I?" he asked.

Yuna started to turn pale. He sounded so negative that her heart started to tremble. She blinked for a long time in an effort to force her blank mind to start working again. Yes, perhaps they didn't have to think about *them* like he said. Liking someone didn't always lead to loving someone, and loving someone of course didn't always lead to marrying that someone. Strangers became lovers, then became strangers again and again. But it was still a shock. *It's us.*

She continued blinking while trying to figure out if she'd misunderstood something. *No, I heard him correctly.* The direct manner in which Soohyuk spoke had one big upside: it left no room for any misunderstandings.

We *don't exist in his planned future.*

Swallowing, she opened her mouth. "All right, then. I need some time to think about this."

"Think about what?"

She was lost in thought again. Soohyuk had just shown her that liking someone didn't mean that she could accept everything about that person. This was proof that she had a limit. *So, what are we supposed to do now...?*

Suddenly, he warned, "Don't say anything you might regret."

Cracking a smile, Yuna raised her head to look straight into his eyes and answered, "You're the one who's already said something you might regret."

CHAPTER 11

Soohyuk was sitting on the bench with his mouth clamped shut. A plastic bag sitting next to him containing a sandwich and a cup of coffee he'd bought at a nearby café kept rustling in the wind. But he continued to draw a blank, looking ahead, replaying that Friday morning in his mind like he couldn't hear anything.

"Have a good trip," he'd said reluctantly, belatedly accepting that he couldn't change her mind about going on this trip with her family.

Yuna had stared at him with her black eyes for a moment and answered, "Mhmm," but in a frighteningly plain way, not the adorable way he liked.

"So, are you just going to go? You don't have anything to say?" he asked.

"Not yet. I said I needed some time to think about it. So, wait."

"Yun," he called.

"Stop. I don't want to listen to you right now."

"Yuna," he called again.

She'd been smiling the whole time, but something about it felt different. He couldn't quite put his finger on it, but his keen intuition told him that something was wrong.

"And take care of your own meals while I'm gone. It's not like you didn't know how to get food until you found me, right?" she said.

"Tell me why you're mad at me," he insisted.

"I'm not mad at you."

"Then what is it?"

Yuna didn't answer. Instead, she just smiled. As he looked at her smile, he felt his heart slowly shatter to pieces.

When he'd returned home after work in the afternoon, she was already gone. He'd called her right away, but her phone was off.

Soohyuk pressed on his aching temples with his thumbs. *No Yuna. No Yuna even at home.* He took out his cell phone from his pocket and dialed her number again. *Is her phone still turned off?* Right when he thought that, it started ringing. He instantly brightened up. *I'll be able to hear her voice soon.*

"Hello?"

Soohyuk frowned. A child had picked up the phone.

"Who is this?"

It was obvious it was Minjoon. Soohyuk hesitated. She was keeping their living together a secret from her family. And if he spoke now...

Minjoon interrupted his thought. "I'm in the middle of playing a game, so I'm hanging up. You can try again later."

With that, the call ended. Dumbfounded, Soohyuk just stared at the screen. "Ha, haha, hahaha." A hollow laughter escaped his mouth. When it stopped, his hands started to tremble. His heart hurt like it was being torn to pieces. He'd never felt this kind of pain before. He pressed his aching chest with his hand. *Yuna...* He frowned. A certain longing swept over him in waves. His lips started to tremble as well. How was he to get through another day without her? Or, rather, would he be able to?

Soohyuk gritted his teeth. It was time to get back now. His lunchtime was coming to an end.

He took a deep breath in. Air rushed in and clawed at his throat. Every part of his body ached. He rubbed his pale face with his hands. His eyes felt sandy. But he had to focus now. He lightly slapped his face with his palms.

He soon got up from his seat, tossing the unopened sandwich and the untouched coffee right in the bin.

"Try some of the spicy crab, Kyungjo. It's so good," said Yuna while placing some crab covered in red spices on Kyungjo's plate. She then placed a fat cockle on Minjoon's.

"What about me, Yuna?" asked Yoonjae.

With a teasing smile, Yuna answered, "You have Kyungjo. You should be asking your wife, not me."

"Stop discriminating," he answered, pretending to pout.

Seeing that, Minjoon tried very hard to scoop the cockle in his plate with his spoon and said, "Hey, you have me, Dad. Let me just..."

Click clack. Kyungjo, Yoonjae, and Yuna all looked at Minjoon's hand. The spoon kept crashing into the plate like he couldn't use all of his fingers correctly. Minjoon stuck out his tongue and tried even harder to scoop the cockle. After a few more tries, he suddenly frowned like he was holding back tears, then switched to a smile. He said, "It's a little hard with adult spoons. Can you do it for me, Mom?"

No one could react at first. They only stared at Minjoon's stiff hand. They were all drawing a blank until Minjoon hid his hand under the table, saying, "I really like the cockles, Aunt Yuna. Hurry, peel some more for me. I'm going to eat them all."

They all snapped back to their senses and started peeling the cockle with exaggeratedly bright smiles, making cockle bibimbap, exclaiming in delight over every bite of the side dishes and such. Then Minjoon said, "Mom, can I play baby today?"

Kyungjo's eyes started to turn red. "Do you want to?"

"I do. Feed me lots of cockles when I go, *ah*." He opened his mouth like a baby bird.

"All right, my sweet baby," she answered.

Minjoon laughed like the mischievous boy he was. He danced in his seat as if he couldn't be more excited and he thought this was the most delicious food ever.

When they finished their meal at last, they got back in the car and soon entered Suncheon Wetlands.

The wetlands were far bigger and far more beautiful than they'd expected. The land before them looked like an ocean of green. Green waves danced this way and that, following the wind. Salty wind warmly caressed their faces as it passed.

"Worth the trip. It's really nice," said Yuna.

"It is, isn't it?" said Kyungjo.

Kyungjo and Yuna watched Yoonjae and Minjoon fish for crabs in the mudflat with strands of reeds. When they touched a crab's claw with the reed, the angry crab clenched on the reed. All they had to do next was pull it up.

"Dad, Dad, hurry, hurry," exclaimed the excited Minjoon. He was completely preoccupied with watching his father pull up crabs. "I want to try! I want to try too." After Yoonjae repeatedly showed him how it was done, Minjoon took hold of the reed this time.

"Yuna," Kyungjo quietly called while keeping her eyes fixed on the two.

"Yes?" Yuna answered.

"You sensed something weird with Minjoon too, right?"

A long sigh escaped Yuna's lips. She'd been holding it in since they were eating at the restaurant. The quick shifts of expression on Minjoon's face had been lingering on her mind.

"I've been sensing that something's off with him for a while now. He's become too bright," Kyungjo continued mumbling as if she were talking to herself, while Yuna listened. "So, I asked his teacher if he saw anything, and he said that he couldn't even tell that Minjoon was sick because he's so bright all the time. And Minjoon says that it's so nice to go to school, and that he's so happy."

Yuna looked at Minjoon. He was busy reed-fishing with a very curious expression. And he looked so happy. But it was not at all like the happy face he was making at the restaurant. There definitely was a difference.

Yuna asked, "When are you going to tell him, Kyungjo? Shouldn't we tell him now?"

"We should. I just haven't determined how yet. I mean, how much are we supposed to tell him? That he won't be able to walk? Or use his hands? Or that his spine will cave? And that it will get hard even to breathe?" Kyungjo started to sound exasperated.

"Kyungjo," said Yuna, trying to calm her down.

"I don't know, Yuna. I want to be a wise mom. Not a mom who wastes time crying. But there's just so much I don't know all of a sudden," said Kyungjo. Yuna reached out to hold Kyungjo's cold hand. She continued, "We still need to tell him, I know. But you know, Yuna, I find myself wanting to believe what his teacher said, ironically enough. I want to believe that he's so bright right now because he's happy. And then I keep stopping myself from telling him because I want him to be happy for just a little longer, just one day more."

Yuna brushed her stiff back. She could feel the pain Kyungjo was experiencing.

Minjoon turned around toward them and waved at them. Grinning almost out of reflex, the two started waving back at him. They then looked into each other's faces.

Shoot, I know who Minjoon's taken after. He'd taken after all of them. Even his trying to hide his sadness was like them. Yuna's mind then automatically went to Soohyuk, the man who hid his emotions under a cold mask.

When they finished dinner after leaving the wetlands near sundown, Minjoon fidgeted with Yuna's phone and asked, "What are we doing now?"

"We're going to look at the stars back in the caravan," answered Yuna.

"Can I play games on your phone?" asked Minjoon.

Yuna chuckled. "It ran out of battery because you were playing games on it earlier. It needs to charge."

Twinkling his eyes, Minjoon asked, "So, we'll go look at the stars *and* play games?"

"Wouldn't you not be able to see the stars if you were playing games?" said Yuna.

They hadn't been able to see any stars through the clear roof of the caravan the night before because the sky was so cloudy. Yuna and Minjoon were of course very disappointed. But tonight, the sky was clear.

"Of course, I'll be able to. It's settled, then, stars *and* games." Minjoon grinned.

"Oh my god." Yuna jokingly rolled her eyes.

"Aunt Yuna," Minjoon called, making his cute face. Yuna couldn't help but nod.

The night sky looked like a carpet embellished with stars. This was the reason her brother Yoonjae had made sure that the roof was made of a clear material. So he could show Minjoon the stars at night, rain if it rained, the blue sky when it was clear, and the gray sky when it was cloudy, even when he was lying down.

"It's so pretty, Aunt Yuna," mumbled Minjoon.

"I know," replied Yuna.

Minjoon turned around to face her and grinned.

"Why are you smiling like that?" she asked.

"Is your phone charged yet?" he said.

Minjoon was having a hard time not thinking of the joys of playing games once he got a taste of it.

"Have you had enough of the stars?" Yuna smiled.

"Yup," said Minjoon.

"Are you sure?"

Minjoon looked up at the sky again and said much more maturely than she'd expected, "We're going to sleep under that sky riddled with stars tonight. How much more could I see the stars? Plus, tonight's not the only night."

"Oh, wow, Minjoon. When did you grow up to be such a charming young man? Where did you learn to say things like that?" Yuna exclaimed. She was genuinely surprised. She'd known that Minjoon was very expressive with his words, but this was more than she'd ever imagined.

Minjoon answered boastfully, "I thought of it on my own."

"You're so amazing, really," she said.

"So, can I play some games now?"

"All right, all right, you can," she relented.

With a wide grin on his face, Minjoon took her phone and turned it on. With his eyes fixed on the starting screen, he mumbled, "Aunt Yuna."

"Yes?" she answered.

"Thank you for gifting me such a great caravan. I'll never forget this," he said.

Yuna frowned. *Why did you grow up so fast? You didn't have to.*

"Aunt Yuna," Minjoon called again.

"Yes?" she answered again.

"I love you." He smiled.

Yuna leaned down to kiss the crown of his head and said, "I love you too, Minjoon Lee."

Minjoon was soon lost in the game. Yuna lay down on her

back next to him and looked up at the night sky riddled with stars. She'd never seen so many.

"Lots of stars out tonight, Minjoon," she muttered. But her nephew was too focused on playing the game with his tongue sticking out to answer. Yuna turned her head to look at him for a moment, then let out a long sigh and looked back up at the sky.

So many thoughts had crossed her mind today. She could understand what Kyungjo was going through, and she could sympathize with Yoonjae, who had to use extra energy to walk while carrying the exhausted Minjoon on his back. She could understand their hesitance and their desire to believe what Minjoon's teacher said. Her thoughts then led to Soohyuk. *What am I going to do?*

Suddenly, Minjoon said, "Ugh, he's calling again." He sounded irritated.

"Who is?" answered Yuna, looking at the screen as well. As soon as she did, she reached out and snatched the phone out of his hands.

"Just hang up and give it to me, Aunt Yuna. I was in the middle of a very crucial moment," whined Minjoon.

"This is mine, you know," she said.

"Oh, come on!" The boy sighed.

The sound of shaking breath hit her ear as she lifted the phone. Soohyuk was just quietly there on the other side of the phone, not saying a single word.

Minjoon reached out, complaining. "Give it to me. He's not saying anything again, right? He didn't before either."

As soon as Minjoon started speaking, the call ended before she could say anything. With the phone clutched in her hand, she asked Minjoon, "Before? Did he call before too?"

"Yeah. When I was just about to have some fun."

"Really?"

"Yes! I asked who it was, but he didn't say anything. I swear," said Minjoon.

"Okay, okay," she answered. A sudden memory flashed in her head.

"What are we going to be?"

"So you haven't given any thought to us?*"*

It was probably Soohyuk who'd called before. He probably couldn't say anything because it wasn't her who picked up. She fell silent. *What am I doing right now?*

She frowned. She should have asked herself too. No, she should have asked herself first. She was the one hiding her relationship with Soohyuk from her family, what *they* were going to be. Perhaps it was she who first thought that they'd break up. Perhaps that was why she was hiding Soohyuk from her family. And perhaps by doing so, she'd made Soohyuk not have faith in her.

Minjoon brought her back to reality by sneakily taking the phone out of her hand while she was lost in thought. He then proceeded to go back to his game.

"Oh my god, Minjoon Lee. What do you think you're doing?"

"Oh my god, playing a game, obviously." Minjoon grinned.

Tousling his hair, Yuna answered, "You little rascal. But I shall allow thee to play thine game since you said such a poetic thing earlier."

"Thanks, Aunt Yuna," said Minjoon.

"I'm going downstairs," said Yuna.

"All right," he answered.

Yuna kissed the crown of his head once more and got up to go down to the first floor of the caravan.

"Yoonjae, Kyungjo. Are you sleeping?" she called softly.

"No, not yet," answered Yoonjae.

Making up her mind, Yuna said, "Can I talk to you for a second? I need to tell you something."

Yoonjae and Kyungjo stared as Yuna's face displayed a wide array of expressions. She became red, then pale, then serious. Then she smiled, then her cheeks turned red again, then blue…

"Have you turned into a chameleon?" Yoonjae commented at last. "You always have a surprise announcement for us whenever your face turns all those different colors."

Kyungjo chimed in while cutting fruits next to them, "That's right. Whenever she says that she needs to tell us something, a big change happens. She first said that she wanted to move out, then that she wanted to start her own business." She broke into joyful laughter.

"Why are you laughing?" asked Yoonjae.

Dividing the beautifully cut fruit onto to plates, Kyungjo answered, "Because there's only one thing left that Yuna could surprise us with."

"What's that?" he asked, still not catching on.

"One second. Let me go give this to Minjoon," she said as she got up with one of the plates in her hand. She walked up to Minjoon, still busy playing his game on the second floor bed, and said, "Minjoon Lee, have some fruits."

"All right, Mom." Minjoon blew kisses to her with both his hands and exclaimed, "I love you, Mom!"

Kyungjo grinned. "I love you too, son!" She then returned to Yoonjae and Yuna after blowing kisses to him with both hands as well. "Isn't that right, Yuna?" she asked.

Yuna leaned against the wall and looked at Kyungjo. She should've known her sister-in-law would beat her to it. She was good. Yuna took a deep breath in. Thanks to Kyungjo starting on the subject, it was much easier to make her announcement.

When her face finally returned to its normal shade, her lips opened as well. "I like someone."

Yoonjae's eyes widened.

"And this man made me want to try to overcome my trauma for the first time," she continued.

Both Yoonjae and Kyungjo knew how easily frightened Yuna was. All she'd managed to create after years of trying was a mask: back straightened, head held high, and saying what she had to say without crying. That alone took practice, and she had forced herself to keep at it because it was necessary to live her own life. But she hadn't tried to go any further than that. Overcoming trauma wasn't something that could be done with sheer willpower. It couldn't be done with pills either. It needed an emotional shift strong enough to heal an old wound. But Yuna hadn't wanted to become close with anyone. Until now.

Smiling, Yuna added, "And I want to try harder. For the both of us."

Yoonjae quietly observed Yuna's eyes, which now looked at ease. They seemed to be telling him that she was done thinking this through and had gotten over her fear. *Is my Yuna really in love? My little Yuna?*

"Do we have any beer in the fridge, Kyungjo?" asked Yoonjae. His mouth suddenly felt dry after hearing his sister's announcement.

"One second," said Kyungjo as she got up from her seat and returned with three cans of beer from the fridge. Yoonjae opened two of them and handed them to Kyungjo and Yuna before opening one for himself and taking a sip.

He then asked, "Does he like you back?" Yoonjae couldn't bring himself to use the word *love.* That was too cheesy.

"He does. He was the first to say that he liked me," answered Yuna.

Yoonjae took another sip. "So, how much are you going to try?"

"All the way through," answered Yuna.

The two stared at each other. Kyungjo didn't step in on purpose. Yoonjae was looking at Yuna right now from the perspective of a parent. They were two siblings who'd been sent to an orphanage together, who'd only had each other to rely on but cherished, understood, and loved each other more than anyone else in the world. At first, Kyungjo had had a hard time understanding why Yoonjae treated Yuna like she was a child when he often leaned on her, and she was the same age as Yuna. But after she'd learned what had happened to Yuna, she understood.

Back then, Yoonjae told her, "I could've gone astray, taken the wrong road, you know. But every time I was at a crossroads, I looked at Yuna relying only on me, and I just couldn't. It felt like I'd be bringing Yuna down with me if I made the wrong decision."

Kyungjo smiled. Earlier, she'd felt like she was in hell when she was thinking about Minjoon, but watching these two siblings reminded her once again that life was full of hope and happiness. *This is what life is*, thought Kyungjo. *It would be swell if all was well all the time, but that doesn't happen. All that you get from filling your world with ugly things and crying about it and resenting it is regret for wasting all that good time with resentment. Yes, I'm an adult. And a parent. I'll cry when I have to cry, but I'll cry less than Minjoon and smile a lot more.* Her smile widened.

Yoonjae suddenly asked, "What kind of a man is he?"

"He was adopted, and I don't think he was too happy growing up. He's very cold, but it all just feels like a defense mechanism," said Yuna, not hiding anything. Neither she nor Soohyuk knew how their relationship was going to end. But that wasn't what mattered. She'd been thinking of the final destination, but not how she was going to get there. And what, in this world, had a beginning and an end but no middle?

Yoonjae blatantly scowled. "Yuna, I'm sure you've seen a lot of adopted kids yourself as well, but they're a little different from us."

"I know," she answered. There was a huge difference in having someone to lean on and not having anyone to lean on. Yuna quietly continued, "I was raised to be a decent person thanks to you. He seems very successful on the outside, has a great job and everything. But he's cold. And he doesn't socialize with people that much."

Suddenly, Soohyuk's voice echoed in Yuna's head. *"Don't go."*

Had she really understood him? Soohyuk was completely on his own until now. And now, he had her. Had she truly understood what she meant to him?

"Don't go."

No, she had not. She had not, even though she held enough significance to him for him to beg her not to go. How could she have not known that? A smile slowly appeared on Yuna's face. Now, she knew. She'd told him that she needed some time to think about this. And now, she had a sense of which direction she needed to head toward from now on.

"Yuna, I don't know about this," Yoonjae continued when Yuna was looking at him again. "I'm very glad you've found someone who makes you want to try to overcome your trauma, but why did it have to be someone like that? Can't you try to stop at just liking him a little bit?"

Kyungjo nudged his side with her elbow, but he couldn't hide his concern. *Adopted.* He'd seen a fair number of bad-case scenarios that started from adoption. He'd seen a lot of homes that couldn't provide an already lonely and vulnerable child with a stable enough environment to grow into an adult. And he'd seen many a person who grew up to hold a pessimistic view of the world with an invisible tag following them around every-where. *Why did she have to fall in love with someone who was adopted?* She deserved better. Like someone who'd shower her with love.

"No, I can't, Yoonjae," Yuna said without an ounce of hesi-tance. "It's someone you both know, too. His name is Soohyuk Cha, and he's a pediatric emergency medicine specialist. I'll introduce you to him soon enough. He didn't like that I was hiding the fact that I was living with him from you anyway."

Yoonjae couldn't believe his ears. "What? What did you just say?"

"The friend I'm staying with right now is him. I'm sorry I

didn't tell you. The thing is, though, I had to take a big step out of my comfort zone to go to him. And I could do that only because I liked him so much and I wanted to see him even a tiny bit more often," said Yuna.

"Yuna…" At a loss for words, Yoonjae's voice trailed off.

"I was happy with just being with him because I didn't have enough courage to turn it into something more," said Yuna, "but Soohyuk came to me first, saying that he liked me and that he wanted to be more than friends with me. So, I made sure I didn't miss that opportunity."

Yoonjae gazed into her eyes, twinkling with confidence in herself. *She means it. She really likes him. She's so sure of her feelings that she's willing to open up about everything.*

Yuna took a sip of beer to quench her throat and said, "You know what, I wasn't being honest. I don't just like him. I love him."

Kyungjo glanced at Yoonjae. She was getting slightly worried that this man, who saw his sister as someone he'd have to protect always and forever, might not be able to handle all of this.

"So, whatever path we are on, whatever end this leads to, I'm going to follow it all the way through, making the most of the journey I can," declared Yuna.

"Slow down, Yuna," said Yoonjae. "Think this through just once more."

"No, there's nothing to think through. Yoonjae, you've raised me to be a good person. Have faith in that and let me do this. I want to become a good woman now, for him," said Yuna with determination, holding her head high.

Yoonjae fell into deep silence. Her sudden announcement was probably a lot to take in. So, Yuna waited until Yoonjae broke his silence himself.

After a long time, her brother finally opened his mouth. "Kyungjo, you were right yet again. Remember when you said that there was something about the way that doctor looked at Yuna?"

"Maybe I should become a psychic." His wife laughed. Yoonjae chuckled as well.

When they quieted down again, Yuna reached out to take her brother's hand and said, "Yoonjae."

"Yes?"

"Thank you for looking after me for so long," she said.

A sudden lump in his throat prevented him from answering. He wanted to say something encouraging to her, but he was too choked up to get any words out.

So, Kyungjo spoke for him. "Good luck, Yuna. We'll always be on your side."

"Thank you, Kyungjo." Yuna smiled.

CHAPTER 12

Soohyuk took off his gown and sat down on his chair in the emergency room. Letting out a long sigh, he started to look over the charts before leaving. He'd worked overtime again today. Blood and vomit from the patients stained his white shirt. He'd already changed into a clean shirt twice, and this was the last spare he'd brought. The emergency room felt like a battlefield even more than usual today. His shift had ended hours ago, but he couldn't just up and leave.

"Thank you so much for your work today, Dr. Cha." The head nurse smiled at him.

Soohyuk nodded. He'd saved three children today from the brink of death. He'd clung onto their lives, blocking the streams of blood gushing from their bodies with his own body. The energy he'd poured on the patients today was probably incalculable.

The nurse added, "You're going straight home, right? Get lots of rest. Lots and lots of it."

Soohyuk still didn't say anything in return, but she didn't mind. She wouldn't have minded even if he had thrown a sudden fit after the day they'd had. Nothing could outweigh the weight of life. Her eyes caught Soohyuk's hand holding the computer mouse slightly tremble. Her heart ached, seeing that.

Suddenly, she saw something in Dr. Cha's face and couldn't believe her eyes. Was he...smiling? His lips were definitely drawing a slight curve. She had no idea what it was that was making him smile, but...she never wanted him to stop. The first smile she'd ever seen on his face was so utterly pleasing.

Soohyuk briskly walked along, in a good mood for the first time in days. Yuna was coming back today. He felt like he should do something in honor of that, something that would make her happy. His weary body suddenly felt like it was full of energy again. And happiness. Even the splitting headache was gone.

"Maybe I should make dinner," he mumbled to himself, speeding up. He should be able to make some pasta, at least, with one of those tomato sauces they sold at the grocery store. He'd get some garlic bread from a bakery on the way home as well. "Yes, I'll make dinner."

Yuna smiled as soon as she walked inside their apartment. The place was clean and spotless. Not a single patch of dust could be found, even though she'd been gone for three long days. She knew that Soohyuk usually liked to keep things clean, but she'd never seen him pour this much attention into it. She checked the kitchen, the living room, the office, the bathroom, and finally, the bedroom. A new set of sheets was on the bed.

"He really tried," she mumbled. It was obvious he'd set aside a large chunk of his free time to clean in order to impress her. She took a set of neatly organized clothes out of the same drawer he used after taking a shower, then went into the kitchen to make dinner.

"I hope he found some things to eat," she said to herself. She didn't want to find out he'd have starved the whole time. That would make her too sad.

A series of *beeps* came from the front door. Soohyuk was home. Yuna leaned against the sink and waited for him to find her.

Soohyuk's heart skipped a beat when he entered the kitchen. He froze like a statue for a moment and couldn't move an inch. He stood like that until Yuna finally smiled and shrugged.

He dropped the bag he was holding on the ground. He walked straight toward her, held her face in his hands, and kissed her. A shiver ran down his spine. The moment her breath seeped in through his lips, his heart, which had been silent like it was hibernating, woke up and started to beat again. *Ba-boom, ba-boom.*

He finally managed to stop kissing her when he was forced to gasp for breath. While he recovered, he pulled her into his arms. His hands ran up and down along her spine again and again. How he missed her small body that fit perfectly into his, and how he missed her warmth... He didn't want to let go. When he leaned into that feeling, all the things he had been holding inside gushed out.

"I was afraid you might not come back. But I wanted you to not come back at the same time," he said as he pulled her even closer to him. He was afraid she might push him away. But she didn't. Instead, she dug deeper into his embrace. That encouraged Soohyuk to open his heart to someone for the first time. *Yes, now is the time. Tell her everything now, since you have the courage.*

His mind racing, Soohyuk continued, "You were raised very well. But not me. I was abused as a child. I don't even know if the me I am now is the real me or the made-up me. I had a horrible childhood. To the point that I couldn't even remember how I ended up at the orphanage, or my age, or even my name."

Yuna caressed his back as she quietly listened to his confession.

"And then suddenly, I started remembering things. Little bits and pieces, out of nowhere. And soon, I could see them," he continued in a hoarse voice. He swallowed, then said, "Not even the detectives could find them, but it turned out that they were much closer to me than I thought. I was enraged beyond reason. It felt like my very existence was being denied."

Yuna wrapped her arms around his even tighter.

"I know I shouldn't be taking this out on you, but I can't control it," he said. "I'm anxious and scared that I might be abandoned again. And at the same time, I was worried I might be breaking you too every time I hurt you. I already drove my adoptive parents to divorce. You really mean a lot to me, but I don't know how I'm supposed to protect you. I don't know how I'm supposed to take care of myself either. I really don't know what to do." And with that, he stopped talking. He just quietly held her in his arms with bated breath, as if he were waiting for her final verdict.

After taking a few moments to organize her thoughts, she slowly started speaking. "Yes, so, I've been thinking about a way we could do this." Yuna leaned back a little to look into his eyes. "Let's start again with just the two of us."

"Just the two of us?" he asked.

"Yes, we'll start working on building the two of us. I'm sure the next step will naturally reveal itself, as will the path we should take. And I'm sure you'll find along the way that you're not someone who could break anyone. You're too warmhearted to do anything like that. I can tell by the way you take care of your patients and me. You have a very warm heart. So, I really don't think you had anything to do with your adoptive parents' divorce. That was just a choice they made as independent adults. You shouldn't blame yourself for that."

"Yun," he said.

"Any adult who abuses a child is a bastard. No buts, no what-ifs. No excuses. They're a bastard, and that's all there is to it," she said firmly. He faintly smiled. "Forget about them. Let's start with us. Let's start loving each other the way we deserve."

We... That word rippled through Soohyuk's heart.

Yuna continued, "And I owe you an apology. I'm sorry for hiding you from my brother and my sister-in-law. That was not very mature of me. It was my own choice to be with you, after all. So, I told them yesterday that I'm living with you. That you're the man I love. I should have told them a long time ago. I'm sorry it took so long. And I'm sorry I left you so unsure of us."

Soohyuk's eyes started to turn red. His world that had seemed so unstable before now had a new anchor to secure it. His anxious mind began to calm down. *Just the two of us...*

Taking in a deep breath, Soohyuk said, "I don't like you. I love you."

Yuna felt her eyes start to become hot.

"I love you, a lot," he said again.

Hot tears trickled down her cheeks. In a shaky voice, she reciprocated, "I love you too. Very much."

"Say it again," he said.

"I love you," she whispered.

"Again," he said.

Yuna repeated, obliging to his request, "I love you. I love you very, very much." Looking into his red eyes, she continued to whisper, "I love you, Soohyuk Cha. I love you." She would keep telling him a thousand times, or ten thousand times if that meant this man who must have craved this for so long could feel her love, and if it made him smile again.

Yuna confessed again with her whole heart, "I love you." He pulled her into his arms and hugged her as tight as he could.

Early the next morning, Soohyuk snapped out of his slumber. It wasn't because of a displeasing memory this time. It was different. A certain rhythm was stuck in his head. He could hear it so clearly that it brought him back to reality. "Ha." He quietly laughed. *It must be because of what she said.* This melody must be ringing through his head because Yuna had suggested that they start over with just the two of them.

He looked over to check on Yuna. As soon as he was sure that she was fast asleep, he started humming the melody before he could stop himself. *"Hmm, mm hmmm..."*

It was the chorus of "Just the Two of Us" by Will Smith.

Professor Cho woke up early in the morning as usual and quietly walked into the bathroom. Looking at his reflection in the mirror, he lathered shaving cream on his chin and shaved the stubble that had grown overnight. He did this every morning. Shaving mechanically, he glanced at his bedroom reflected in the mirror. It looked grim and depressingly empty.

"You should give up now, you know," he said bitterly to himself. Ms. Seo, the mistress of his heart, was not ever going to come back. Let alone forgive him. And yet, for so long, he'd been holding on to that inkling of hope that once he found Hwiyin, he would be forgiven by Ms. Seo and Hwihyun. His most dire wish was that he would be able to live again with his family and only his family, even if it was just for a passing moment.

He looked at his reflection in the mirror. There stood a man withering away with age. This was not what he had envisioned for himself. When he let go of his hope, he felt the sudden weight of time. He looked at his hair, turning grayer and grayer by the day. The thought that he might not be able to realize his wish left a dent in his heart for the first time.

He quietly cleared his throat to hide his vulnerable heart. "No, I can't give up until I've tried everything," he said to himself. He was still looking for Hwiyin. But he wasn't getting much response nowadays. "It doesn't mean that I've looked everywhere already, no, it does not," he mumbled again. He was determined to protect Ms. Seo's hope until his last day, even if he had to let go of his own. He was going to return Hwiyin to her, no matter what it took.

He started moving his hand again. A large, hollow, empty space greeted him when he stepped out of his room after changing. He paused and looked around the massive house. His heart felt just as empty and cold. Fixing his eyes ahead, he started walking. When he reached the staircase, he could hear his mother bustling on the first floor, no doubt making breakfast. He'd already told her multiple times that he was going to skip breakfast because he was having digestive issues, but it was no use.

He walked down the stairs with his hand brushing the bannister. The memory of Hwiyin and Hwihyun's high-pitched laughter echoed in his ears. A faint smile appeared on his face. He could almost hear his sons shouting, "Dad!" He paused for a moment and closed his eyes, picturing the two mischievous boys clinging to his legs. "Are you coming home early today, Dad?" they used to say. "Can you come early and play with us?"

Professor Cho's eyes grew hot. He wanted to answer and say that yes, he would of course come home early today, but his sons were no longer there to hear it. His smile disappeared. He moved his feet forward numbly. When he reached the first floor at last, his mother, Ms. Jung, appeared with an apron around her waist.

"Time for breakfast, Professor," she said.

He paused once more and said to her, "Mother, I don't want to eat breakfast. Please don't do this again."

"None of that, now, Professor. A man must eat to have enough energy for work. Come here and take one bite, at least," she said.

His expressionless eyes stared at her. He then said in a bitter tone, "You really do think of me as your property, don't you, Mother? You always do everything as you please."

"What are you talking about, Professor? What wrong have I done you? There is no one in the world who loves you more than I do," screeched Ms. Jung, suddenly becoming serious.

Professor Cho impassively answered, "I live like a dead man thanks to you, Mother."

Ms. Jung's lips trembled. "That again. Would you be finally happy if I took that fool of a girl back in as my daughter-in-law? Would you be able to discern what you should and should not say to your mother, then?"

Hearing that she was once again blaming everything on Ms. Seo, he told her as clearly as he could, "The day you go find my family will be the last day I call you my mother."

"Professor Cho! Are you really trying to kill me?" she cried.

A smile appeared on his face. But his voice was colder than ever. "You never know who will die first, Mother. You could end up killing me instead of the other way around."

"How dare you say such a thing to your mother…and all for a woman who drove her own babe to death." She shook her head, trembling with fury.

"If you spend even a single day in an emergency room, you'll know that I'm speaking the truth," he said. Ms. Jung's lips quivered again. Not even batting an eye at her response, he continued, "I've told you countless times now that Hwiyin's disappearance was not her fault, but mine and yours. Her leaving me was also my fault and yours. Not being able to see Hwihyun is also my fault and yours. All of this misery is our fault."

Taking one step toward him at a time, she pleadingly reached out both her hands and said, "Don't do this. My days are already numbered, so what use does all this fighting have? It certainly doesn't make me happy. Who, if not you, Professor Cho, would understand me? Do you think I lived through all those hard times for myself?"

He always hated hearing her call him Dr. Cho, or Professor Cho. Those titles weren't rooted in respect when they came from her mouth; they were more of a way to brainwash him. A constant reminder, of sorts, that she was the one who'd made him who he was today, and he should never forget that.

"Why don't you remarry, then?" she asked. "Who will take care of you when I'm gone? Let me look around. I'm sure there's someone good, someone right for you out there."

"Please, just stop talking," he mumbled.

"Professor Cho!" Her brows narrowed again with fury. "If you want to get rid of me so much, just cast me out in the streets. You know I will never resent you. And how would anyone dare to say anything when it is my most beloved who cast me away?"

He'd once suspected she might have Alzheimer's disease, because it was so hard to get through to her. He'd actually run the tests on her without her knowing. But they'd come back negative. This was all coming purely from her true nature and her love-hate relationship with her son. She'd never admit to it, but she loved her son the most in the world and hated him the most in the world at the same time. This chain was never going to break until the day he finally ceased to exist. *What does it really mean to be a parent?* he wondered.

He turned his gaze to look around the barren house. It felt too large. It was empty, but it was so filled to the brim with Ms. Jung's obsession that he could barely breathe. He had to do something. Ms. Jung might go looking for his ex-wife if they stayed here. And Ms. Seo might leave for good if that happened, to somewhere he would never find her again. That was the last thing he wanted.

A sudden urge made him open his mouth and ask, "Don't you think this house is too big, Mother?"

Ms. Jung looked at her son with sharp eyes. He was a foolish son who was still bewitched by that mindless girl, but he was her only child. He was all that she had and she would carry him in her heart till the day she died.

"I think I should go away to the quiet countryside," he said. "Leave the hospital for good. This place isn't right for me."

"Professor Cho!" she screamed.

"Have a nice day, Mother." He bowed his head and headed to the front door. Ignoring the painful slap on his back delivered by Ms. Jung as he passed by, he put on his shoes and stepped outside.

He sighed. He felt like he could finally breathe again.

Upon arriving at the hospital, Professor Cho had his morning coffee at the café in the lobby with the other specialists. This was the time when his mind woke up to its usual clarity. He started his day by talking about the small things of life as well as treatments, as usual.

Suddenly, Dr. Jin, the newly appointed hospital director who'd come down for coffee as well, grabbed his hand. "Professor Cho, I have something I'd like to discuss with you. Do you have a minute?"

The two had been colleagues since medical school and were still close friends. They called each other by their first names when they were alone, but addressed each other more formally in front of the younger doctors. Professor Cho excused himself to the others and sat at a separate table with Dr. Jin.

"What is it?" Professor Cho asked.

The enthusiastic Dr. Jin got right to the point. "You know that pediatric emergency medicine specialist?"

"Dr. Cha? What about him?"

"He's become really famous. There was this huge event at the pediatric emergency room a couple days ago. Well, I mean, that place is always like a zoo, but it was especially bad that day. To the point *the* Professor Park cried, 'Enough!' "

"Really? What happened?" Professor Cho sipped his coffee, his eyes twinkling with curiosity.

"Three kids fell on top of metal posts with some kind of molds on them while playing at a construction site. All three of them were diagnosed with gastrointestinal perforation," Dr. Jin quickly explained.

Professor Cho frowned. He always became nervous whenever he heard stories of children getting hurt, because he couldn't help but think of Hwiyin getting hurt like them.

"Everyone else was starting to give up because they were losing too much blood, but that Dr. Cha alone didn't give up," Dr. Jin continued. "He apparently used his own fingers to cover the perforations and stop the bleeding. The police came to investigate the accident, and the reporters came, and Dr. Cha saving the children was caught on camera."

Chills ran down Professor Cho's spine. His mind was automatically picturing how Soohyuk must have saved them.

Spitting on his face out of excitement, Dr. Jin kept talking. "And that made the news. Our hospital! Our pediatric emergency room so appropriately was put under the spotlight when all the other emergency rooms were being bashed by the media. They even said that there was a doctor here who was like a reincarnation of Jun Heo himself."

Professor Cho rubbed the goose bumps on his arms.

"You're getting goose bumps, aren't you? I did too! I found those clips and watched them and my, oh my, did I get goose bumps. I've never seen a guy who's as awesome as him." He leaned in and said in a softer voice, "I've always completely supported your pediatric emergency room project, you know. Which was why I was so disheartened that it wasn't receiving the attention it deserved. You have no idea how happy I am your blueprint for the future is finally

getting some light. The only problem is, actually, that Dr. Cha—"
Dr. Jin quickly looked around and continued in an even lower voice, "Everything is proceeding as planned, but he wouldn't take the deal. So, I invited him to dinner, and you know what he said?"

"That he doesn't eat anything a stranger gives him," said Professor Cho with a chuckle.

"Yes, exactly! A full grown man, talking like a child! So, I asked if I could talk to him for just a little bit then, and he declined, saying that he didn't have time. Was this the same way he kept turning you down?" he asked.

Cracking a smile, Professor Cho answered, "Yes, that was exactly the way he turned me down. I asked him again and again, but it was no use. Listen here, though, because I heard from a very reliable source that he now has a girlfriend."

Dr. Jin's eyes widened. "Really? Have they set a date yet?" It was a question befitting such an enthusiastic man.

"Ha, come on, now. You're getting ahead of yourself. But it does mean that there is some hope now, doesn't it? In addition to that, I heard Dr. Cho made plans to go drinking with Dr. Cha," said Professor Cho, referring to his son Hwihyun.

"Is that so? Dr. Cho's done us a huge favor," exclaimed Dr. Jin.

"Indeed he has. They're about the same age, so it should be easier for him to get through to Dr. Cha," said Professor Cho.

Unable to control his excitement, Dr. Jin clasped his hands tight. "What can I do? Should I give him my credit card and tell him to put everything on it? If he becomes the head of the pediatric emergency room... Wow, imagining it alone is making my heart race."

His excitement was truly contagious, as Professor Cho was starting to feel its effect on him. Dr. Jin chewed cubes of ice in an effort to calm himself back down. When he finally succeeded in doing so, he said, "Building a world-class pediatric emergency room was your dream for so long."

"It was, it was indeed," Professor Cho answered.

"That dream is going to come true now. I am going to build on the blueprint you created and make sure it comes to life, no matter how hard it's going to be," he said resolutely.

Professor Cho chuckled. They were on the complete opposite spectrum of personality as people, but were a better fit for each other because of that.

"Professor Park's already thrown in the towel when it comes to Dr. Cha," said Dr. Jin.

"Really? That proud man?" asked Professor Cho.

"He's more of a braggart than a proud guy. Anyway, he was talking about Dr. Cha as if he's completely sick of him, and he said that he's a prick, but he really is good so I should keep him here no matter what," answered Dr. Jin.

"Well, I'll be darned, the real deals are always recognized wherever they are. I was the only avid fan of his at first, but now, it seems like his fandom is expanding by the day," exclaimed Professor Cho.

"That's right. It's Jun Heo, *the* Jun Heo. He doesn't even practice traditional medicine and they're calling him the reincarnation of the greatest doctor in the history of Chosun," chuckled Dr. Jin.

Professor Cho grinned as well. Jun Heo was a doctor who had treated all his patients with all his heart regardless of their background. Perhaps that was the reason he was so widely appraised. Hearing that people were comparing Dr. Cha to such a renowned figure made him gleeful, like he was the one everyone was talking about.

Dr. Jin's face turned serious all of a sudden. "Shoot, I hadn't thought of that."

"Thought of what?" asked Professor Cho.

"He's all over the media now, so he's going to get countless job offers from other hospitals. No pediatric emergency room has ever gotten any spotlight like this, so everyone's going to try to poach him under the surface," grunted Dr. Jin.

Professor Cho frowned. "Right, I hadn't thought of that either. I'll tell Hwihyun to have that drink as soon as possible."

"I'd be grateful if he could do that. So, when are they meeting? Should we pretend like we stumbled upon them by accident and join them?" Dr. Jin said with a grin.

"They haven't even set a date yet. Don't get ahead of yourself," warned Professor Cho.

"All right, all right. Can I have a date and a place by the end of the day, then?" asked Dr. Jin.

"Dr. Jin," warned Professor Cho again.

"Hem, hem, fine. I should still give Dr. Cho my credit card now, though, right?" asked Dr. Jin eagerly.

Professor Cho shook his head and chuckled. Dr. Jin wasn't someone to get this excited this easily, but right now, he looked like the happiest kid in the world who had just gotten the most thrilling news. *It's good that he still finds moments like this*, he thought to himself. *Who says old people have to be calm and composed all the time?* Thanks to his jolly friend, his day was brightening up as well.

"By the way, why do you think Dr. Cha doesn't eat anything a stranger gives him? It's a little silly, isn't it? Like he'd had a bad experience after eating something a stranger gave him," said Dr. Jin.

"Who knows, maybe that did happen," answered Professor Cho. There had to be a reason why a very self-assured thirty-five-year-old adult would say that. Like people avoiding food that gave them horrible food poisoning.

"Have your morning coffees with me from now on, Professor Cho," said Dr. Jin.

"Now, now, dear friend, I enjoy the company of younger blood better," teased Professor Cho.

"At least until I strap Dr. Cha down. I'll of course buy the coffee. Who would I trust and rely on, if not you?" pleaded Dr. Jin.

Professor Cho chuckled again. He was actually planning on having a meeting with Dr. Jin in the afternoon about quitting his job at the hospital. It was a sudden impulse that had made him say that to his mother in the morning, but on his way to work, he'd started to think that he really should leave the city. If he left Seoul, Ms. Seo and Hwihyun would be able to find a peace of mind at least.

But talking to Dr. Jin changed his plans a tiny bit. His friend's enthusiasm was rubbing off on him. He would only leave for the countryside once he saw how their plans with Soohyuk went down. Building a world-class pediatric emergency room was the big goal Professor Cho had had in mind from the beginning. If they could keep Soohyuk here, his dream would basically have come true. *What an interesting fella he is. He's already a young doctor, which you don't see that often, and on top of that, he's a very promising one. How nice it would be to have him here to represent S University Hospital along with Hwihyun.*

"Why aren't you saying anything?" Dr. Jin pestered.

Professor Cho jokingly said, "I'll think about it if you buy sandwiches as well."

Dr. Jin answered with utmost sincerity, "Then I shall."

Yes, I'll stay here just a little longer. And I'll work on clearing my mind in the meantime. Discovering an obsessive side to him, much like Ms. Jung, he thought to himself, *I really am her son, aren't I?* A flash of bitterness appeared on his face, then disappeared.

"Hurry, call Dr. Cho. Ask him when he's going to see Dr. Cha," badgered Dr. Jin.

"Come on, now." Professor Cho laughed.

"Should I do it, then? I have to give him my credit card anyway," continued Dr. Jin with haste.

"Haha. Take it easy, my friend," said Professor Cho, but he soon gave in to Dr. Jin's persistent nagging and called Hwihyun.

For some reason, his heart started pounding painfully as the phone rang. He was afraid his son might ignore him and decide not to pick up. His heart beat harder the longer the ringing continued. Finally, it stopped.

"Yes, Father?"

His face brightened. "Hello, Hwihyun."

CHAPTER 14

*H*wihyun settled on the terrace with Ms. Seo during their lunchtime and opened the boxed lunches they'd ordered.

"So, this is the boxed lunch from A Tasty Meal, huh?" asked Ms. Seo.

"That's right. The one Dr. Cha eats every day," answered Hwihyun.

"Oh, dear…it's probably covered in MSG," mumbled Ms. Seo.

Handing a set of chopsticks and spoon to her, Hwihyun said, "I know you wouldn't like me saying this, but their food is good. It's easy on the stomach too. Honestly, they sometimes have things that are tastier than my own mother's cooking." When Ms. Seo looked up from the food, he grinned.

She said with a gentle smile, "That mother of yours had better try a little harder."

"I could not agree more. Please, enjoy. My treat." He grinned again mischievously when she exaggeratedly looked askance at him. They then started eating. As Hwihyun said, the food was very good. The omelet was perfectly seasoned, and the charcoal grilled pork was truly incredible.

"It's good. Especially this grilled pork," commented Ms. Seo.

"Their main menu is always meat. They always include it in the menu in some shape or form," replied Hwihyun.

"People must love it," said Ms. Seo.

"It's really popular. A lot of people at the hospital are ordering it now too. I wonder if that's why they put up a notice saying that they're only going to sell a hundred boxed lunches a day from now on. I think they said it was because of some personal reason or something. Anyway, the point is, you have to order fast if you want to get one," said Hwihyun. He thought to himself, *Unless you're* the *person who doesn't apply to that one hundred limit and can have specially made menus that perfectly suit your appetite.*

"Really? A limited number of orders. Huh. The competition must be intense. Was this place always famous?" she asked.

"I'm not sure about that. But people started thinking they could trust it since it's what Dr. Cha eats every day. You know how persnickety he is. That's why I ordered it the first time too," said Hwihyun. Ms. Seo grinned and put some of her grilled pork on Hwihyun's plate. His had already disappeared into his stomach because of his habit of eating his favorite dish on the table first.

"Oh, Mother, you really don't have to...but you already have, so thank you." Hwihyun giggled.

Ms. Seo affectionately watched her son devour the pork. It almost felt like they were on a picnic with the breeze tickling their skins. *How lucky I am to be able to eat lunch with my son on such a beautiful day... Today really is a special day,* she thought. Revealing that happiness in her voice, she said, "Thank you for growing up to be such a wonderful man, Hwihyun. I love you so much, son." Hwihyun's bright smile filled her heart with love.

When they finally finished their lunch and were having coffee from the vending machine as dessert, Hwihyun asked, "Dr. Cha's busy, right?"

"Of course, he's busy. He works overtime every day,"

answered Ms. Seo. Soohyuk Cha was one of the few doctors she'd encountered who still had enough burning passion to voluntarily work overtime. A smile emerged on her face as she thought of the conversation she'd had with the head nurse about how he was starting to soften up again after a streak of hostility.

"You know, Dr. Cha apologized for creating an unpleasant work environment during the morning meeting," the head nurse had told her in a whisper.

"Did he?" asked Ms. Seo.

"I didn't expect him to apologize. But his apology was…very him."

"What did he say?"

"He said he was sorry for being such an ass." The head nurse had giggled, and Ms. Seo had smiled even wider.

She hoped he wouldn't suffer. She hoped things would work out between him and his lady as well, so he wouldn't have to be alone. Nothing made a person more adverse than loneliness.

Hwihyun continued, "Oh, maybe that's why he hasn't called me yet. We were supposed to meet up for a drink soon, but he never called me after that."

Ms. Seo's eyebrows rose in surprise. "A drink? With Dr. Cha?"

"Yup. I wonder if he even drinks that well." Hwihyun laughed.

"Really? That's unexpected."

"I know. I wasn't expecting it either. And I definitely wasn't expecting him to ask me first." Scratching his head, he mumbled to himself, "Oh boy, Father's going to be disappointed."

"Why would your father be disappointed?" asked Ms. Seo.

"Do you by any chance know that the pediatric emergency room's been on the news?" asked Hwihyun.

"Of course I know. You have no idea how many ambulances we got after that. We were swamped," remarked Ms. Seo.

"Dr. Jin's officially on the move to keep Dr. Cha here. Father's agreed to help because he's already an avid fan of Dr. Cha's. But the problem is that Dr. Cha still won't let them in. He never makes time to negotiate the terms, he's busy when he's working, and when he's done, he goes straight home. And while all that's happening, I made plans with Dr. Cha to go for a drink," explained Hwihyun.

"Wow, you have a lot on your shoulders," said Ms. Seo.

"I really do. But I first have to see him in order to drink or talk or whatever else, except, it seems like he's too busy." Hwihyun sighed.

"I think I heard that he's off tomorrow…" started Ms. Seo, but she was interrupted by a sudden ring of Hwihyun's phone.

"Hwihyun Cho speaking," said Hwihyun as he answered the phone.

"This is Soohyuk Cha."

Hwihyun tightened his hand around his phone involuntarily.

"Are you free this evening?"

Hwihyun answered right away. "Where should we meet?"

"I don't know what's around the area at all. I'll go wherever you suggest."

"Sounds good. I'll text the time and address to this number soon," said Hwihyun.

"All right."

"See you in a couple hours, then," said Hwihyun again.

"All right."

After he hung up, Hwihyun punched his fist in the air and shouted, "Yes!"

<hr>

Soohyuk looked at the beaming Yuna after hanging up. "Are you happy now?" he asked.

"Yup, I'm happy now," she answered, smiling.

"I might end up drinking a lot. It's not like we'll have a lot to talk about, you know," he said.

Trying to cheer him up, Yuna said, "That might happen, since you know him but he doesn't know you. But I think just listening to him, or even just sitting with him would be beneficial enough. Maybe it'll help all those lost memories of yours come back."

Soohyuk scratched his forehead with a grimace on his face.

Yuna reached out to cradle his face, saying, "They might be memories you don't like. They might be memories you erased because they hurt so much. And you might hurt a lot from poking around to find them again." Soohyuk gazed into her warm eyes. "But I'll be with you. I'll be right here with you, so you don't have to hurt alone. And the most important thing to remember is that whatever those memories may be, they're all already in the past. So, let's not allow the past to hold you back anymore," she gently coaxed.

"Are you sure you'll be all right?" he asked. This might be their Pandora's box. And he might not be able to handle what was inside and end up hurting her again. He'd told her about himself over the past couple of days: about how he was sold from the orphanage for money, about Kate and Danny, about Danny abusing him both physically and mentally, and about how he'd hid the fact that he was being abused because he wanted them to continue being happy. And all the while, the pain from those memories manifested itself in forms of hurtful, curt words and behaviors in front of Yuna. He even had nightmares, forcing Yuna to be as sleep-deprived and tired as he was in the mornings.

And yet, Yuna continued to stay by his side and attentively listen to him. And when Soohyuk finally brought himself to tell her why he wanted to become a doctor, she broke into tears. Watching her cry, he oddly felt like something was finally being freed inside him after years and years of captivity, even though she was the one crying, not him. He then found himself telling her about his family being at S University Hospital.

The moment she'd heard that, she'd started to persuade him. She'd quietly cajoled him, asking him if it wasn't true that he asked Hwihyun to have a drink with him because he wanted to talk to him in person. And after days of persuasion, he'd finally set the date today.

Yuna said cheerfully, "We should get you ready now."

"What do you mean?" he asked.

"You can't go out and drink on an empty stomach. You're going to feel horrible tomorrow. It's a little early, but I'll fix you dinner." Heading to the kitchen, she added, "You've never tried dried pollack soup, have you? It's the best hangover cure in the world."

Soohyuk watched her make an early dinner while swaying her hips to a song only she could hear. He had a hunch that he would not be able to say no to her when she looked at him with those trusting eyes, like the hunch he'd had that the food made by someone who enjoyed cooking as much as she did would definitely be good. Soohyuk cracked a smile. *So what if I can't say no to her? All that matters is that she's with me.*

When the time came for him to leave the apartment, Soohyuk hesitated. He stared, no, glared at Yuna as he did whenever he was looking at her, trying to figure out how to describe what he was feeling right now. Any stranger would have taken his glare wrong, but not Yuna. Sheepishly smiling, she gave him a tight hug.

"You're afraid," she whispered. He hadn't wanted to acknowledge it before, but it was true.

"A little. And a little annoyed. He's always smiling," grumbled Soohyuk.

"People smile when they're sad too. Like me and Kyungjo," said Yuna.

Soohyuk cradled her face with both his hands. His ice-cold eyes looked intensely into her warm eyes as he said, "Don't hide your sadness when I'm with you. I'm aware how coldly I reacted when you were telling me about Minjoon before. It's a lifelong habit, so it's a little hard to fix."

"I understand," she answered.

But Soohyuk shook his head and said, "No, don't understand things like this. Don't let me continue living as an ass like that. If you have anything you want to talk about, I'm here. If Minjoon's parents have any questions, give them my number. I'll be happy to talk to them."

Hot tears welled in Yuna's eyes. Surprised, he asked, "Why are you crying? Did I say something wrong again?"

"No," she said as she wiped the tears with the back of her hand. "You said Minjoon's name for the first time. And I'm so grateful you did."

Soohyuk watched her smile and wipe her tears for a moment, then said, "I've really done you wrong." He bent forward to lean his forehead on hers. "Forgive me. I'm sorry. So, don't feel like you have to hide things from me."

"All right," she murmured. He lightly kissed her lips and pulled her into his arms. The heat radiating from her body warmed up his cold heart. It was thanks to Yuna that he'd learned cold hearts could break easily, like ice. He'd just never noticed that before because he had been keeping his distance from others until now, so his heart wouldn't have to suffer from damaging impacts.

Releasing her from his embrace at last, he said, "See you in a little bit."

"Have fun," she answered.

He kissed her again while putting his shoes on. "I'll keep in mind what you said about people smiling when they're sad too."

Yuna answered with a wide grin, "And I'll keep in mind to lean on you whenever I need to."

Reaching out to pat her head, he said, "See you soon."

"Mhmm," she answered with a cheerful nod.

———

Hwihyun entered the bar while rubbing his face, which was stiff with tension. It was a quiet rooftop bar at a hotel with a wide range of drinks and snacks available that he had carefully picked out for Soohyuk, assuming that he wouldn't like loud places since he liked to eat alone.

Heading to the reserved table, he mumbled to himself, "I hope I'm not digging my own grave here."

When he'd told Dr. Jin that he was going to see Soohyuk tonight, he'd found Dr. Jin to be much more excited about the news than he was. He'd even insisted on giving Hwihyun his personal credit card, which Hwihyun had a very hard time refusing.

"Dr. Jin, I make enough money to buy him a drink," Hwihyun told him in an effort to stop him.

"You think I don't know that? Think of this as just a little gift from your father's old friend. No need to think of it as anything else," said Dr. Jin with a wave of his hand.

"Oh, I think it's a little hard not to think of it as something else," said Hwihyun.

"No, please, don't. I'm not expecting anything out of this. You know I know what Dr. Cha is like. I know this is only the first step."

"Really? You're really not expecting anything out of this?" asked Hwihyun in disbelief.

"Of course not! Seriously, no pressure whatsoever," answered Dr. Jin, but his eyes looked so determined that Hwihyun couldn't help but feel the pressure. "He's the man who's going to make your father's decades-long dream come true. We need to get him on our side," Dr. Jin added.

"My father's dream?" asked Hwihyun.

"It's the dream he's been holding on to since Hwiyin left." Seeing Hwihyun's surprised expression, he continued, "You didn't know. I can see why he didn't tell you, because I know what his mother is like very well. But...Hwihyun, I do want you to know this at least. That's how we all grew up. With our parents' sacrifices engraved in our very bones. I wouldn't have had another choice but to do the same as your father if I were in his shoes. Anyway…" He paused for a moment, then continued, "After Hwiyin went missing, your father wanted to build a world-class pediatric emergency room. Can you guess why?"

This was the first time Hwihyun had heard about this, but he could immediately see why. "Yes. Because of Hwiyin. Because he might have gotten hurt but not had access to the right treatment."

"Not so different from your mother staying at the pediatric emergency room. So, be sure to get Dr. Cha on our side. I give you permission to film anything we might be able to use against him when he gets drunk," said the resolute Dr. Jin.

"Dr. Jin, I'm pretty sure that's an express ticket to jail," said Hwihyun jokingly.

"Hahaha. You're right! I didn't think I'd ever hear you threaten me, kiddo. Anyway, this is the beginning of something great, so make sure you don't step off on the wrong foot. I'm trusting you, Dr. Cho." He chuckled before leaving.

Now, Hwihyun sat in his seat at the bar and looked over the nightscape of Seoul. *A world-class pediatric emergency room.* He'd felt pressured since the moment he heard that story. "I didn't know you were planning something like that," he mumbled to himself. He'd also realized that there was no point in trying to determine who was suffering and hurting the most in his family. He, Ms. Seo, and Professor Cho were all suffering and hurting an equal amount.

"I have to do this right," he said again to himself. He wanted to help his father even if it was for this one single thing. Professor Cho was a stoic man, but still a generous father who let all his sons' mischievous pranks slide. He'd never told them that he loved them out loud, but there was always love in the way he looked at them.

He hadn't gone to see his father outside of the hospital since the divorce, even though he knew that he was Professor Cho's favorite friend to drink with. To his father, Hwihyun was not just a son, but a friend he felt comfortable enough with to do silly things in front of and the only person with whom he could express his love for Ms. Seo to his heart's content.

At first, he only wanted to free himself from the implicit responsibilities he had because he was his father's "son." Then he suddenly found himself feeling sympathetic toward Professor Cho. He came to a resigned conclusion that there were some things in the world that were just out of one's control. As time passed, he could see more and more of what kind of a life Professor Cho had been forced to lead. Ms. Seo and Professor Cho. He kept feeling like he was losing balance between them. So, he was not going to see Professor Cho until he regained that balance.

"I still hope he takes care of himself," he mumbled again. He'd learned through watching Ms. Jung that dedication could sometimes become toxic. It would be swell if everyone could get along and be happy, but who would ever be able to debilitate her obsession? *No one*, he thought. It was a very unfortunate thing that there were some things in the world no one could change.

Hwihyun muttered to himself again, "I should check on how Father's doing when I get to work tomorrow." He'd noticed that Professor Cho was suddenly looking much older lately.

"You came early," a cold voice said, startling him out of his thoughts.

CHAPTER 15

Soohyuk strode into the bar and plopped down on the seat across from him.

"I like being on time." Hwihyun smiled. "So, what's your poison?"

"So-Mac," Soohyuk answered.

Hwihyun broke into laughter before he could stop himself. He'd thought Soohyuk didn't give a rat's ass about Korean culture. *But wow, So-Mac. Okay.*

"Why are you laughing? You're being very rude," Soohyuk said as his eyes flashed with displeasure. He'd said So-Mac because he liked drinking So-Mac with Yuna. How dare this man laugh in his face?

"My apologies. I'd made an assumption that you wouldn't know that much about our culture since you don't come to team dinners and such," said Hwihyun.

"So, your culture is to laugh in people's faces like that. Got it. Thank you for teaching me such a great custom," spat Soohyuk.

Hwihyun grinned. "Oh, come on. It was a mistake. We came all the way here after such a long wait. Let's have a drink and have a good time."

Soohyuk shut his mouth. He knew his nervousness was making him lash out. He took a deep breath in and put down his jacket by his side, saying, "All right."

"So-Mac it is, then. Do you want anything to eat?" asked Hwihyun.

Thinking that everything at the bar would taste bad, since none of it would be made by Yuna, he said, "Any kind of dry snack will do."

"Sounds good." Hwihyun ordered the drinks and snacks right away. But even after the booze and the food arrived and they'd had a couple rounds of So-Mac, neither of them said a word. They just glanced at each other from time to time and remained resigned in their silence.

After a couple more minutes of that, Hwihyun lightly sighed and said, "I wasn't expecting anything less, but you really aren't the talkative type, are you? You haven't said a single word."

"You were the one who said that you had a lot to talk about with me," Soohyuk shot back.

"Oh, so you were waiting for me all along?"

"I was," Soohyuk answered curtly.

Scratching his head, Hwihyun said, "Well, I'd like to hear about your experience first, actually. How do you like working at S University Hospital? If you have any concerns, please tell me. I have some connections, so, you know, I can talk to the upper management."

Soohyuk mumbled in between sips of the So-Mac, "I don't care much for S University Hospital, I've seen people with far powerful connections than you, and I'm just an ordinary doctor who's got nothing but his skills."

Hwihyun sneered at that. "Gosh, you can't help being blunt, can you? I really do feel a little weird when I'm with you. Like maybe I should start being blunt with you too."

"I have no idea what you're talking about," answered Soohyuk.

Emptying his glass of So-Mac at once, Hwihyun explained,

"In short, you make me feel comfortable, but in a weird way. By the way, your Korean is so good that sometimes it makes you look like you're pretending not to understand on purpose."

"The guy who worked at the cleaners wasn't that eloquent a man," remarked Soohyuk.

"The guy at the cleaners?"

"He's the one who taught me Korean in the States." He was indeed the man who'd helped Soohyuk relearn the Korean he'd forgotten. But most of the things he taught were profanity and other vulgar expressions. Like most people's experience when learning a new language, the bad words stuck in his brain much faster and easier.

When he'd told Yuna about that, she'd said, "That makes sense. I was wondering how you learned all those expressions just from R-rated movies. But there was another factor, huh?"

"I did learn some of them from the movies," Soohyuk had insisted.

"You're going to have to work on that a little bit. Korean expressions aren't as straightforward as you think. No one says exactly what they mean. And you should learn to stop cussing."

"You want me to practice talking more."

"Exactly. You really are smart. You already perfectly under-stood what I meant! It's only going to get better from here. We'll keep practicing," Yuna had said happily.

Hwihyun ripped a piece of jerky to put it in his mouth. "Oh, I see. I suppose your parents don't speak any Korean."

Glaring at Hwihyun with his ice-cold stare, Soohyuk answered, "They don't."

Hwihyun glanced at him, cracked a smile, then said, "Don't you have anything you want to ask me?" He paused, then said, "Now that I've said that out loud, it sounds like something someone would say during a first date."

"I want to make this clear once and for all: I'm not queer. Also, are you talking like that on purpose?" asked Soohyuk.

"Like what?"

"You seem tense. You don't look comfortable at all."

"Me? Tense? I'm very comfortable right now." Hwihyun laughed.

Suddenly recalling what Yuna had said, Soohyuk cocked his head. *People smile when they're sad too.* Now that he was looking at Hwihyun's smile from up close, it seemed very tense.

"Really?" he said. "Well, I'm glad you're comfortable. I guess that's just your smile, then."

"What's wrong with my smile?" asked Hwihyun.

"The ends of your lips kind of shake when you smile. You know how the muscles get tired if you force a smile, and they start screaming? It looks exactly like that."

Hwihyun shook his head with his arms crossed and gazed at Soohyuk for a moment. *A forced smile...* He'd always done that. He'd always tried his very best to smile. "You're very honest. People usually at least try not to be so blunt with me," he said.

"Hmph, that's why it's so ridiculous. How do they not find someone prancing all over town, bragging about his mediocre parents not ridiculous?" Soohyuk sniggered.

Hwihyun frowned, slightly offended. "Are you describing me?"

"If you weren't one of the actually good doctors, I wouldn't have even talked to you. How pathetic is it that a man has nothing but his parents to brag about? What a piece of shit," laughed Soohyuk.

Hwihyun's jaw dropped. He hadn't noticed at first that Soohyuk had cussed because he was talking in such a cold tone. But when he replayed what he'd said in his head because he sensed something weird, he realized that Soohyuk had cussed like it was no big deal.

"So you should stop bragging about your dad too," continued Soohyuk. "And don't say things like, 'I have connections.' You have enough to brag about yourself."

"Do I?" asked Hwihyun. He was a little dumbfounded because he'd never heard anyone talk like this to him. Then it occurred to him that Soohyuk had complimented him. "Thank you. For saying that," he quickly added.

"Glad you at least know," said Soohyuk as he pulled the bottles of soju and beer toward him to mix So-Mac himself.

Watching Dr. Cha suddenly made Hwihyun feel a little depressed. He hadn't thought that he'd be drinking So-Mac up here at this fancy hotel rooftop bar. Though he had had an inkling that he was going to be hit with some strong words tonight.

"Drink." Soohyuk offered him a glass. Hwihyun drank without a word. He'd fallen silent, since Soohyuk had told him not to say things like "I have connections." So, the two men just quietly sat there and drank. Hwihyun was a notorious heavyweight, but Soohyuk seemed to be no worse than him.

"What do you say we go somewhere else if we're just going to drink So-Mac?" asked Hwihyun. "I need some hot soup."

"Let's go." Soohyuk got up from his seat without protest and took the bill. "I'll take care of this round."

While Soohyuk paid the bill at the cashier, Hwihyun disappeared into the bathroom. Soohyuk mumbled to himself as he waited for him to return, "I don't know what I'll tell Yuna. He doesn't want to talk, and frankly, neither do I."

A significant amount of time passed, but Hwihyun was still nowhere in sight. Soohyuk followed him into the bathroom at last. He was leaning on the sink with his hands on his head, facing down.

"Are you all right?" asked Soohyuk.

"I haven't had this much alcohol with barely anything to eat in a long time," said Hwihyun, feeling a little flustered. He was much drunker than he thought he would be. He blamed it on their drinking So-Mac without even talking on and on, which very rarely happened. Something else was different from usual too, but he couldn't put his finger on it. *It's weird. I never get this drunk.*

"You're a heavyweight, aren't you, Dr. Cha?" Hwihyun mumbled.

Soohyuk just watched Hwihyun mutter to the sink, unable to even hold his head up.

"I remember when I passed the GED and drank soju straight from the bottle." Hwihyun broke into a laugh. "I was kind of smart, so I quit school after a while and took the GED right away. I got into S University's med school first place, and kept on going. Being a specialist for four years already at the age of thirty-two is pretty impressive, isn't it? And I served my time in the army, too." Hwihyun added, "I don't normally go bragging about myself like this."

"Now you say that." Soohyuk sniggered.

Hwihyun broke into joyful laughter, then said, "All right, enough of the Hwihyun Show. Let's go to the next place. It's one of my go-to's."

Having sobered up a bit, Hwihyun led the way again. This time they went to a crowded pub. Spicy-smelling steam was billowing from everywhere.

"Their fish roe soup is amazing," said Hwihyun as they settled down at a much smaller table than before. Thanks to that, they were sitting much closer to each other now.

"So-Mac?" asked Hwihyun.

When Soohyuk nodded, Hwihyun called the server and ordered. While they shared another couple rounds of drinks, the soup came. But that was all for him. He asked Soohyuk if he'd like to order anything, but Soohyuk shook his head. He didn't want to have to suffer again after eating the wrong thing.

Soohyuk watched Hwihyun just quietly drink for a while, then asked, "So, when are you going to get to the things you wanted to talk to me about?"

"Hahahaha. I'm sorry, but I can't remember. I'll tell you when I remember later," laughed Hwihyun.

Soohyuk crossed his arms and gazed at Hwihyun for a while. "When did you get your high school diploma?"

"My high school diploma? Oh, you mean the GED," said Hwihyun.

"Same thing," mumbled Soohyuk.

Hwihyun shrugged. "When I was sixteen. And then I left home when I was seventeen for college."

"Is that early?" asked Soohyuk.

"It is in Korea. Seventeen-year-olds are thought of as just boys here because they don't know how to do anything. Like, my apartment was a pigsty, and all I ate were prepackaged meals. But it was still nice to live by myself," answered Hwihyun.

"I'm sure Ms. Seo helped a lot," said Soohyuk.

Hwihyun cracked a smile and replied before he could stop himself, "Not at all. Mother was, umm…umm…going through a rough time in her life."

Soohyuk's eyes narrowed. Hwihyun's smile was changing a little to something looser and freer. He was starting to laugh at himself instead of laughing to appear happy. *He's getting drunk,* thought Soohyuk. Hwihyun was now pouring pure soju down his throat. Soohyuk didn't bother to stop him.

After emptying two shots of soju in a row, Hwihyun grinned and said, "I'm sorry. I don't know why soju tastes so sweet all of a sudden. Don't worry, I'm not one of those people who do stupid things when they get drunk. I'm the heaviest weight of all the heavyweights at S University Hospital."

"Yes, I had a feeling you might be when you said that you drank soju straight from the bottle at seventeen, Hwihyun," said Soohyuk.

"Hey! You just called me by my first name! I'm going to start calling you by your first name too."

He's drunk. Oh, he is so drunk, thought Soohyuk gleefully. He, on the other hand, felt like he was becoming more and more sober.

"My mother likes you." Hwihyun pointed at Soohyuk and added, "She doesn't normally compliment people, but she compliments you. And that makes me feel jealous. I had to work so hard over the years for her to notice me, but she noticed you right away."

That was true. He was jealous of Soohyuk. Every time Ms. Seo complimented him, expressed concern about him, or wanted to do something for him, he felt jealous. But the truth had only burst out of him because his barrier was lowered thanks to the alcohol. *Oh, shoot.* Hwihyun rubbed his face with one hand.

"Now we're getting somewhere. Say whatever's on your mind, Hwihyun. It's all right," said Soohyuk. He was starting to gather things he could tell Yuna, like his birthmother having a rough period in her life and Hwihyun foolishly being jealous of him. They weren't fragments he could easily piece together, but he was still going to be sure to remember them.

Hwihyun grinned again. There was something familiar about his grin now. It was just like the way he'd smiled when he was a child. The last time Soohyuk had seen Hwihyun before he came back to Korea, he was grinning and waving at him as if to tell him to hurry up and go hide.

Soohyuk frowned. A sharp pain shot through his chest.

"But I just don't get why she likes you," Hwihyun continued. "I've never seen someone as unkind as you. And no one ever talks to her like that at the hospital. Because, you know, she was the director's wife."

"How astounding. A director, no, not a director anymore but a professor now, and a respected wife of the former director, and a doctor. What an utterly amazing family," commented Soohyuk.

Pouring soju in his glass and So-Mac in Soohyuk's, Hwihyun said, "My family was broken into pieces a long time ago, so that's all we have left to brag about. I'll apologize if I sounded like a prick, so let's move on."

"What do you mean it was broken into pieces?" asked Soohyuk.

Hwihyun emptied his glass at once, then mumbled, "We're an unhappy family."

Soohyuk's heart started to ache even more.

"Devoid of any laughter," added Hwihyun as he poured more soju and drank that too. "I'm sure yours was a happy one?"

"Not at all," answered Soohyuk.

"Ah, well that makes me feel much better," laughed Hwihyun.

"I was beaten all the time." Hwihyun's expression changed at that. But Soohyuk continued like it was nothing, "Why do you look so shocked? Child abuse happens everywhere, doesn't it?"

When Hwihyun still didn't brighten up, Soohyuk cracked a smile and refilled his empty glass for him. "It's all in the past. No need to look so sad," he said, but he was feeling sad, too, because of the face Hwihyun was making.

Then all of a sudden, Hwihyun changed his expression again and asked, "What do you think of staying at the pediatric emergency room for good, then? I'm actually here on a secret mission assigned by Dr. Jin. S University Hospital is very interested in keeping you here." Soohyuk didn't answer. "Can you at least think about it and tell me later, Soohyuk?"

"Do you think calling me by my first name's really going to get you the deal?" asked Soohyuk jokingly.

"Oh, please. You were the one who first called me by my first name," Hwihyun said with a scoff.

"Aren't I a few years older than you?" retorted Soohyuk.

Hwihyun grinned and replied, "Fine, I'll call you Dr. Cha. There's only one person in the world I call 'Hyung.'" He suddenly looked up as if he'd heard something. He then started to groove to the rhythm of the background music drowned in the chatter of the people. "Did you know that Will Smith began as a rapper?

You know that song, 'Just the Two of Us?' The owner here likes old songs, so I hear it from time to time when I'm here. It makes me feel something new every time I listen to it."

How coincidental, thought Soohyuk. It was only a couple nights ago that he hadn't been able to fall asleep because that song's melody was stuck in his head.

Hwihyun's eyes suddenly turned red. He quietly said, "It was my brother's favorite song. He had such a good ear that people said he was a genius since he was very young. He was especially gifted in the linguistic areas."

As soon as he said that, Soohyuk felt as if fireworks were going off in his mind. Past memories started flooding in. The amusement park in July, playing hide-and-seek with his brother, a stranger giving him food. Getting lost as a six-year-old. *Ba-boom, ba-boom.* His heart started to race. The sudden rush of memories shook him, but a deep corner of his mind sighed in relief.

Hwihyun sprang to his feet and walked to the cashier. He walked so straight that Soohyuk forgot he was drunk for a second. But when he heard the same song starting over from the beginning as Hwihyun walked back to their table, Soohyuk frowned. *He must be drunker than he looks.*

Hwihyun spread out one of his hands, saying, "I asked him to play it exactly five more times. And he said yes, because I'm a regular here." He laughed.

Soohyuk quietly drank his So-Mac while listening to the music. He could hear it as clear as day now, even through all the noise. His toes started wriggling to the rhythm, and they both sang along to some of the lyrics.

Hwihyun ordered more drinks as he said, "Let's drink like there's no tomorrow. We can just sleep in tomorrow."

"I think you've had enough," said Soohyuk, shaking his head.

"Nope! I'm not drunk at all. Look. Completely fine, right?" Hwihyun spread his hand open in front of Soohyuk's face. It wasn't shaking at all. His voice was clear too. He really seemed completely fine, on the outside. But after a couple more shots of soju, Hwihyun violently mumbled, "It keeps bugging me."

"What?" asked Soohyuk.

"Thinking that you had a childhood like that is making my blood boil. Is that why you became a pediatric emergency medicine specialist?" asked Hwihyun.

"Yes," answered Soohyuk, not particularly trying to hide it.

Hwihyun brushed his hair back with both hands and clamped his mouth shut.

"Why are you getting upset? I was the one who was getting beaten," said Soohyuk. Hwihyun didn't answer, but his jaw tensed even more. Was he thinking of Ms. Jung? Or was he thinking of the abuse they'd had to endure in their childhood?

Soohyuk's keen eyes examined Hwihyun's face. And he found what he was looking for. Hwihyun still looked a lot like he had when he was young. He'd said himself that he grew up in a broken family, but it didn't show at all. Soohyuk found himself feeling a little jealous, then grateful, then envious again. *And here I am, looking so different that no one can recognize me...but maybe I still should be grateful, since I at least know now that I wasn't abandoned.* Not knowing what to do with his mixed feelings, Soohyuk stopped talking as well.

As time passed, Hwihyun became drunker and drunker until he finally started blacking out. Soohyuk could tell by the way he kept repeating his words. He seemed to get more forceful each time.

"Stop ignoring my father. Have a cup of coffee with him," pleaded Hwihyun.

"You like Professor Cho, don't you?" replied Soohyuk.

"What kind of a son doesn't like his father? Even if his father didn't give him everything he needed. Shoot. I keep taking Father's side. Mother's going to be heartbroken if she finds out..." Hwihyun's voice trailed off for a moment, then he grinned. "Still, have a cup of coffee with Father. He likes you too, you know. Think of it as a favor to your new friend and have a cup of coffee with him in the morning."

"I don't really want to," muttered Soohyuk.

"Oh, come on, stop being such a wuss. I know how nice you can be, like when you're with your girlfriend," protested Hwihyun.

"Hey, that's private. You'd better not tell anyone," snapped Soohyuk.

Hwihyun broke into a guffaw, saying, "Wow, I can't believe it. You sounded just like my brother just now."

Soohyuk beamed. *Is he finally recognizing me?* But that wasn't it.

"I guess all narcissists are the same. Threatening laymen like me. *You'd* better not tell anyone what I said tonight," Hwihyun added.

Soohyuk's face fell with a rush of disappointment. So, he quietly asked instead, "Do you even remember what you've said?"

Hwihyun thought for a moment, then said with a grin, "Nope. I don't remember anything. Let's see… Oh, I did have one thing to say. Stop ignoring my father. Please, just have a cup of coffee with him. He likes you too, you know. Can't you just think of me as one of your friends even though we're from different countries, since we're working at the same hospital?"

Soohyuk leaned back in his chair and gazed at Hwihyun. A lot must have changed within the family since he'd disappeared. *A broken family devoid of any laughter.* And Hwihyun must have had to grow up by himself again. Without even a brother to lean on this time.

"You've come a long way," said Soohyuk.

"What? What did you say? Oh, hold on," said Hwihyun as he got up from his seat again.

"What is it?"

"I want to listen to that song again. Hold on a sec. Did I tell you I'm a regular here? I'm a regular here," shouted Hwihyun as he walked over to the cashier again.

A faint smiled appeared on Soohyuk's face. *I'm glad you made it this far so well, Hwihyun.*

When he finally returned to his seat, Hwihyun said, "I didn't tell you, did I? This song by Will Smith was my brother's favorite…"

CHAPTER 16

*Y*una kept stroking Soohyuk's back as they lay there on the bed, facing each other in silence. When he'd returned home around midnight, he looked completely sober, though he did smell heavily of alcohol. And now, he was holding her in his arms in bed, lost in thought.

"Are you all right?" she asked at last. She was worried urging him to go see his brother might have led to an unpleasant result.

"I remembered a lot of things." He finally started talking as he pulled Yuna closer to him. It was getting hard to breathe, but she didn't push him away. Instead, she wrapped her arms around him as well. "We all went to an amusement park when I was young, and the woman just sat there, staring at nothing and bored to death. She didn't do anything with the two of us. It wasn't much fun, and I got bored. So, we played hide-and-seek. I made my brother seek, and I hid."

Hearing him say "the woman," Yuna realized that he hadn't accepted Ms. Seo as his mother yet. But that was all right. At least he'd gone to see his brother today. That was much better than just hating them and not doing anything, in her opinion.

"And?" she asked.

"Hold on," said Soohyuk, trying to focus on his memories. Something didn't feel right about this part. Had he really played hide-and-seek because he was bored? It felt like something was missing. The beginning was a little foggy too. He was a genius. And so was Hwihyun. So, why had they played hide-and-seek at the amusement park? They must have been cautioned not to go out of sight of the adults when they were in a crowded space. Soohyuk shook his head. He figured it would still be beneficial to try to connect everything into one piece, since he did recall a lot of things.

"I couldn't find my way back. And my brother couldn't find me..." He paused again. The more he tried to piece things together as he explained them to Yuna, the more questions he had. Did he not go back to try to find his family, or could he not go back? His thoughts automatically led to the time he'd run into Ms. Jung, his grandmother, in front of the emergency room. His brows narrowed into a hostile frown. She was still the same crazy old bat she was back then.

"I can't tell if I got lost or if I didn't go back on purpose. I can't remember," mumbled Soohyuk. Yuna kissed his forehead as if to encourage him. She then kissed his lips. His eyes closed as he felt her warm kiss. It was light and brief, but enough to make his heart pound.

His lips caught hers before she could pull away. His kiss was neither as soft nor light as hers was, but it was charged with heat to the point that she could feel it in her very soul. When they finally managed to break apart, he was left wanting more but much more relaxed at the same time. He hadn't realized how tense he was until now.

"I somehow got lost and someone offered help. There was this man who tried to calm me down by giving me yogurt. I think the yogurt was drugged, because I fell asleep immediately after eating it. I didn't normally like yogurt, but I was too hungry to say no. So, I ate it." Soohyuk paused again. He could vaguely remember the man saying something...something very important that he couldn't remember.

He frowned deeper. Something about this didn't feel right. More importantly, why hadn't he told anyone his name and his home phone number? The woman would have come for him then. Or had she not? Had she been glad when he disappeared?

He suddenly felt like a storm was sweeping through his mind, blowing all the memories up into the air. It was almost like someone was interfering, saying that none of this mattered anyway.

Yuna watched him as his eyes turned cold. It seemed like the parts he couldn't easily remember were making him mad. His lips were tightly shut as well. Was he regretting it by any chance? Was he thinking that he shouldn't have gone to see his brother tonight? Embracing the silent, cold Soohyuk, Yuna waited for him to start talking again.

And at last, he did. "Kate couldn't bear children. So, she was looking to adopt when she found me, a boy who couldn't remember his name or age. But I don't understand why I couldn't remember any of that. I was smart."

"Even if you were smart, you were still a six-year-old child. Children are children, no matter how smart they are. I'm sure you were in a state of panic. It only makes sense that you couldn't remember anything," Yuna said in a soothing voice.

Whether he'd been in a state of panic or not, he hadn't made it back home. He'd eaten drugged yogurt and ended up at an orphanage where the board only cared about collecting children to receive a government stipend. It was Kate who'd come to save the now stupid boy who had nowhere else to go. He didn't know what she'd liked about him, but Kate had paid every last penny they asked for and brought him all the way to the States.

"Maybe. Anyway, I went to the States with Kate, where a lot of things happened, like I told you before, and here I am now," he concluded.

Yuna hugged him tightly instead of answering. Soohyuk hugged her back and buried his face in her neck. He took a deep breath in. His body finally relaxed. He was quite relieved after connecting all the fragments into one piece. There still were some missing parts, but he had a feeling that it was up to him to find them again. To work through the storm that was blowing away all the memories. Perhaps it was he who'd created that storm. A voice inside him was confirming that suspicion. He was the one interrupting the process.

"What was your brother like, by the way?" asked Yuna. "How much did he drink? I heard he's a heavyweight."

"He's definitely not a heavyweight. He kept repeating the same thing over and over like a parrot toward the end. It was hard to even get him in a cab home because he got too drunk," answered Soohyuk.

Yuna chuckled. He still sounded as impassive as before, but it didn't sound like he was mocking Hwihyun at all.

Soohyuk softly added, "He did come a long way, though."

Yuna's smile widened. She hadn't expected him to say something like that. *Today's meeting was a success,* she concluded.

She looked up at him. "Can I ask you something?"

"Sure."

"Umm…what kind of a mom was Kate? It's just that I don't have any recollections of my mom. I've only heard stories through Yoonjae," she said.

Soohyuk looked into her deep eyes. *Right.* He hadn't even considered that Yuna must not have any memories of her parents. After thinking for a moment, he started, "When I first saw Kate…"

He calmly told her about his relationship with Kate. Thinking of her now, since the moment he'd remembered she bought him with money, made him feel nothing but anger and resentment. But as he recounted the first time he saw Kate to Yuna, moments of love and affection started to come back to him one after another, like the time she'd held him in her arms and sang him a lullaby when he was having a nightmare, or how she'd held his hand when walking outside, or how she'd always smile when she looked at him. She used to give him sweet candy when he was hiding and crying, to cheer him up. Then, finally, he thought of how she cried and hugged him, saying that she was sorry for hurting him.

A shiver ran down his spine. Kate. What would have happened to him if it hadn't been for her? The hairs rose on the back of his neck. He'd said some awful things to her for buying him with money, but what kind of an adult would he have become at such an orphanage if she hadn't taken him home? His heart suddenly felt like it was being torn into pieces. He'd broken Kate's heart. He'd done the most ungrateful thing a person could do, even though he would definitely not have ended up in a better place if Kate hadn't taken him.

"Soohyuk?" Yuna gently called, caressing his trembling body. His sudden shaking seemed so painful, and she wanted to help make that pain go away.

"One second, Yuna," said Soohyuk as he pulled her to his chest so she couldn't see his face. Tears rolled down his cheeks. Hot tears of regret that burned his skin and heart. His body was shaking uncontrollably. Yuna quietly waited for him. She could feel his tears at the crown of her head.

At last, he starting speaking in a shaky voice. "I've said something I shouldn't have to Kate. I blamed all my pain on her. Even though I can't even imagine where I would have ended up if it weren't for her and her protection." He was ashamed and embarrassed of himself.

"You love her. That's why you were mad at her," said Yuna.

Soohyuk nodded. "She raised me like her son..."

"You *were* her son. You were her only son."

A sudden tightness filled his chest, to the point where he couldn't breathe. Yuna was right. *Her son.* Kate had always called him that. Soohyuk raised his hand to wipe the tears from his face. He took deep breaths as he rose to sitting.

Seeing that he was looking for his phone, Yuna realized what he was going to do. When she got out of bed to give him some privacy, he pulled her hand. She sat back down next to him.

He dialed Kate's number. It didn't take long for her to pick up, like she'd been sitting by the phone waiting for him to call.

"Matt," she said.

Soohyuk took a deep breath in and said in one breath, "I'm sorry. For acting so mean."

She was silent for a few seconds. Then, she burst into sobs.

"I would not have reached where I am now if it weren't for you. I'm sorry for blaming everything on you, Kate," said Matt.

"No, Matt, it was my fault. I made you like that. You stopped smiling and became lonely because of me. I am the one who ruined such a sensitive boy full of love like you. It was fair of you to blame me."

Soohyuk listened to her guilt-ridden confession, then answered, "Mother."

He could hear her gasp in astonishment.

"Mother, thank you for raising and loving such an ungrateful son like me," he continued. Unable to form any words, Kate just sobbed. So, he said, "I love you, Mother."

Kate continued to cry for a long time after that. Yuna firmly held his hand. She couldn't understand all of what he said, but she did understand "Mother." And she could hear Kate crying through the phone. Like two streams coming together as one river, their hearts were connected once more. Tears welled up in her eyes. Soohyuk had called Kate "Mother." Yuna didn't have to think long about how much that must have meant to Kate, as she could already see it in his gentle expression.

He ended the call and turned to face Yuna, saying, "You inspire me to be a better human being."

Yuna gave him a sheepish smile. His lover sitting under the

moonlight looked so precious and sweet that he couldn't even dare to reach out his hand to touch her.

So, he confessed again instead, "I love you. Truly, I love you. So much."

Yuna anchored her feet on the bed and cradled his face with both hands. She pressed her lips against his lips, which kept whispering, "I love you." She pushed her tongue through the crack between his lips to tantalize him. *Boy, have you come a long way, Yuna Lee,* she thought to herself. *You used to tremble when even his fingertips touched you.* His lips, holding the words of his love, tasted so sweet.

He pulled her into his arms as he stood up. He carefully placed her feet on top of his so she could come to standing as well, then walked forward like that to the CD player. A serene music started to play on the lowest setting. With her standing on his feet, Soohyuk started to dance. Yuna wrapped her arms around his neck and leaned her head against his pounding chest. Feeling her relaxing, he tightened his arms around her and pulled her closer to his body.

A smile appeared on Yuna's face. The man she was sharing this joyful moment with was so beautiful that she felt like she might burst into tears.

"I love you," she said. "I can't help smiling whenever I look at you. Like I've been infected with happiness or something."

Gently chuckling, Soohyuk pulled her even closer. He wouldn't have been having this kind of a moment had it not been for Yuna. He would never have experienced this comfortable happiness he was feeling right now if not for Yuna. It seemed like it was thanks to this new feeling that the resentment he'd been holding against his family had subsided. He tightened his arms around Yuna. He couldn't imagine a life without her anymore. There was no point in living without Yuna.

Soohyuk leaned down to kiss her passionately and said as sincerely as he could, "I want to marry you."

Yuna broke into joyful laughter. "Are you proposing to me right now?"

"Who else would I be proposing to? You're all I have. What do you say we get married tomorrow?"

"No. I want to get married in December," she said.

"No. That's too far away."

"December is my least favorite month, because that's when I was sent to the orphanage," said Yuna. Soohyuk stopped dancing and quietly gazed at her. Still bearing a bright smile, she continued, "So, if I get married in December, it will turn into my favorite month. Because you will make my Decembers the happiest months."

Thinking about how trusting she was with him made Soohyuk's eyes get a little watery.

Yuna whispered to him, "Can you wait for me?"

Hugging her tightly, Soohyuk assured her, "Of course, I can."

He then started dancing again with Yuna standing on his feet.

CHAPTER 17

*P*rofessor Cho was sitting at a table drinking coffee with Dr. Jin early in the morning. Dr. Jin was too curious to know how Soohyuk and Hwihyun's meeting had gone the other night, so he'd come down to see him. But Professor Cho didn't have much to tell him. Hwihyun had blacked out and could barely remember anything.

"Dr. Cho must be under a lot of stress right now. It's not easy to get a heavyweight to blackout," said Dr. Jin, as if he hadn't played any role in adding to Hwihyun's stress.

"Yes, he must be, since someone kept pressuring him with his credit card," said Professor Cho pointedly.

Dr. Jin chuckled and changed the subject. "The coffee is very nice today."

Professor Cho gave a faint smile instead of an answer.

"We're going to send out a recruitment notice today," said Dr. Jin.

"It's finally starting?"

"It is," answered Dr. Jin. "First things first, we need to get us a good team. But Dr. Cha needs to accept the offer first. He was even offered a professorship at the university, but he turned it down right away. He prefers being out in the field."

"I thought so," said Professor Cho.

"He really is something, that Dr. Cha. Now, how on earth to get him is the question…" Dr. Jin's voice trailed off when he heard quick, deliberate footsteps approaching them.

Someone pulled out the empty chair next to him and plopped down. It was Soohyuk. Stunned, the two stared at him. Soohyuk put down his cup of coffee on the table and looked back at Professor Cho. Completely flabbergasted, the professor and Dr. Jin now glanced at each other. They hadn't been saying anything bad, but they had still been talking about him behind his back, strictly speaking.

Dr. Jin forced himself to swallow the shock and said, "Nice to see you, Dr. Cha."

Soohyuk nodded in answer and took a sip of coffee. His eyes were fixed on Professor Cho. His stare was so cold and intense that Professor Cho had to retrace what he had said in his mind to check if he'd said anything wrong. Or had Hwihyun done something? No, he hadn't said anything wrong, and Hwihyun wasn't someone to do harm to another person. He widened his shoulders a little.

"I came for coffee," said Soohyuk impassively.

The two men brightened up when they heard that. Who'd have thought that *the* Dr. Cha, whom they'd failed multiple times to set up a meeting with, would come to them on his own?

Dr. Jin quickly said, "Why don't you just sign a contract with our hospital? We'll do our best to meet your conditions, so why not a lifetime contract, while we're at it?"

Dr. Jin was way ahead of himself as usual. Soohyuk didn't answer. He only glared at Professor Cho as if he was about to start a fight.

Not evading his intense glare, Professor Cho looked at him

with gentle eyes and asked, "Aren't you tired? I heard there are too many patients in the pediatric emergency room nowadays."

"I am tired," answered Soohyuk.

Dr. Jin butted in again. "Speaking of which, we're going to recruit more specialists. We will make sure our pediatric emergency room has the best staff in the whole world."

"That sounds like a great idea," said Soohyuk.

"We're planning on purchasing additional helicopters and expanding the facilities once we have the staff. But it will take a long time for all of this to happen," said Dr. Jin.

"It will. I'll be looking forward to it," answered Soohyuk. Both Dr. Jin and Professor Cho beamed.

"So, why don't you sign the contract now?" asked Dr. Jin hopefully.

"I'm drinking coffee right now," said Soohyuk so coldly that it made Dr. Jin's excited eyes lose their twinkle. But he was not going to give up.

"I hope you know that it was you, Dr. Soohyuk Cha, who made us move in this direction," said Dr. Jin. Soohyuk looked at him for the first time this morning.

Looking into his cold, almost inhuman eyes, Dr. Jin continued, "Professor Cho here was the one who planned all this, but it is you who made everyone burn with the determination to make it come true. We were all infected by your passion. So, you'd better look out. Because I don't give up that easily."

"Professor Cho was the one who planned this? Did you always have an interest in the pediatric emergency room?" asked Soohyuk.

"What parent in the world wouldn't want children to be treated properly, before it's too late?" answered Professor Cho.

"That's strange," said Soohyuk. "As far as I know, this country doesn't acknowledge children's rights at all. Do people here even treat children as equal human beings?"

Professor Cho blushed. It sounded like Soohyuk's retort was

aimed at him. His throat tightened and his heart ached. *Children's rights. Rights to be loved, to be allowed to dream.*

Sensing what was happening, Dr. Jin quickly cut in, "You're a very passionate man, Dr. Cha. I like that. Yes, doctors like you should be the ones protecting our children."

"Do you not agree?" Soohyuk said with his eyes fixed on Professor Cho, as if he couldn't even hear Dr. Jin. "Have you always been interested in children's rights, Professor Cho?"

"Now, now, no need to be so aggressive. Why would he have dreamt about this if he had no interest in it? And this dream of his isn't something others can easily think of or make come true," said Dr. Jin, trying to diffuse the tension.

"I'm waiting for Professor Cho to answer," said Soohyuk.

Professor Cho gulped and finally brought himself to say, "I haven't always been interested in it. But I…"

Grabbing his cup, Soohyuk muttered, "All the patients who come to the pediatric emergency room are children. Children who cannot express themselves fully and do not even have the right to make decisions for themselves. I believe a world-class pediatric emergency room should start from a wish to create a space where the children's rights come first. How else would the staff be qualified to call themselves world-class pediatricians?"

Both Dr. Jin and Professor Cho were at a loss of words. They'd never thought of it like that. Children's rights. It was like their belief that doctors only needed to be good at their jobs had been shattered.

After a couple moments of silence, other than the sound of someone sipping coffee, Professor Cho said, "I learned something new today. Thank you, Dr. Cha." When Soohyuk shrugged, he added, "This is why we want to keep you here. I think we'd have a lot to learn from you. I'm not going to let go of you, at least, either."

Soohyuk made an odd face. He knew Professor Cho hadn't said that because he recognized who he was, but it still made him feel good. He still hated him and loved him at the same time. He remembered the strong back that carried him when he was sick. He used to think while on his father's back that his father had a very wide back, which in truth had nothing to do with the actual size of his back but his heart. From what he could see when he was young, his father had a very big heart. So big that it even reached out to the horrible Ms. Jung. That was why he hated him and loved him at the same time, both then and now.

Soohyuk took another sip of coffee with his eyes still fixed ahead. Dr. Jin and Professor Cho were now quietly drinking their coffee too, not knowing what else to say.

Soohyuk finished his coffee first and said to Professor Cho, "I just had coffee with you."

"Yes, you did just have coffee with me," replied Professor Cho.

"I sat down with you and had coffee," said Soohyuk again.

Professor Cho frowned. "Yes, that is true as well. Why are you saying this?"

"Tell Dr. Cho that when you see him later. That we sat down together and had coffee."

Chuckling, Professor Cho asked again, "Why?"

Soohyuk got up from his seat. "Ask Dr. Cho. Excuse me, then."

He sounded so cold that Professor Cho and Dr. Jin didn't even dare to stop him. But the two were already very satisfied with their conversation with him. Hwihyun had done them a great service by making the immovable Soohyuk come all the way out to the café in the lobby. So, they didn't stop Soohyuk as he nodded to them and turned around.

Dr. Jin waited until he was far enough away and then said, "He got us."

"Oh, he got us good," said Professor Cho.

"He's better than I thought. Talking about children's rights when we're all busy as hell just keeping them alive. I would have thought that he was just full of it if someone else said that, but for some reason, it doesn't feel like that coming from him."

"It does make us think again about what we do," said Professor Cho.

"He's a little too cocky, but I like him," said Dr. Jin.

Cracking a smile, Professor Cho said, "You must really like him to say that you like a cocky doctor."

Dr. Jin waved him off. "Oh, that's because they like to talk about big things when they're actually totally incapable of them. People like him aren't cocky because they're conceited. It's just a way of staying true to themselves."

"Well, I've got to say, I'm grateful you say that."

"Why would you be grateful?" asked Dr. Jin.

Chuckling, Professor Cho answered, "Because you let me know that I'm not the only fan of his."

"Silly man." Dr. Jin chuckled as well.

Professor Cho raised his eyes to look at the disappearing Soohyuk in the distance. Suddenly, his heart started pounding. There was something familiar about the way he looked from the back. He'd never realized until now because he'd never looked at Soohyuk from this far back, but he kind of looked like Hwihyun. It could have been due to the fact that the two were about the same height and build, but there was something else too. If he hadn't known it was Soohyuk, he would've thought it was his son.

Professor Cho mumbled to himself, "They look so similar…"

***

Soohyuk strode across the lobby. He'd done this purely for Hwihyun. Hwihyun had asked him over and over the other night why he wouldn't even have a single cup of coffee with Professor Cho. So, Soohyuk had granted his wish. He could do at least that much for Hwihyun, as a reward for growing up so well on his own.

His lips started to draw a warm smile. *A world-class pediatric emergency room.* That wasn't the first time he'd heard about it, thanks to the head nurse adamantly updating him on the process. She'd told him that Professor Cho had been trying everything in his power to bring the pediatric emergency room to the next level, but it kept getting pushed back by the other departments and never ended up happening. But this time was different. Professor Cho had been pushing for it harder than ever, with him as the central piece to the plan. Having a proper pediatric emergency room here would be a good thing, both objectively and subjectively, since more children would be able to access treatment in time.

He didn't hate the idea of being a part of it. *I was going to settle here once Yuna and I got married anyway,* he thought.

As he was walking across the lobby, his phone rang.

"Soohyuk Cha speaking," he said.

"This is Yoonjae Lee."

Soohyuk stopped walking.

"Yuna's brother, Yoonjae Lee."

"Hello, Mr. Lee. Nice to speak to you," said Soohyuk.

"Nice to speak to you too. I heard from Yuna about the wedding."

"Yes, we are planning on getting married in December," said Soohyuk.

"Please don't take this the wrong way."

"I will not," said Soohyuk.

"Please make her happy. To the best of your ability."

Soohyuk couldn't say anything for a moment. A lump in his throat was stopping all words from coming out.

"Yuna means the world to me. So please, make her happy."

"I will make her happy. Don't worry about that," said Soohyuk finally.

"All right, then. Thank you."

"Wait. How is Minjoon doing now? Has the way he gets up in the morning or the way he walks changed at all?" asked Soohyuk.

"Not yet."

"And does he still laugh a lot?" said Soohyuk.

"He started laughing even more ever since he started playing that video game he likes."

"Yoonjae," said Soohyuk. Yoonjae fell silent for a moment, like he wasn't expecting that. Soohyuk continued, "You haven't told him yet, have you?"

"No…but we're planning on telling him soon."

"I know it's a difficult decision to make. Please let me know if you need my help," said Soohyuk.

"Oh, thank you. That's very kind of you. Why don't we have dinner together sometime soon?"

"Yuna knows my schedule, so you can talk to her," said Soohyuk.

"Sure."

"Also, Yoonjae," said Soohyuk.

"It feels a little weird to hear you call me that." Yoonjae laughed lightly.

"Thank you for calling me," said Soohyuk.

"And thank you, too. For helping me learn that you're a much better man than I expected."

After the call ended, Soohyuk put his phone away. Right then, the alarm in the emergency room started blaring loudly. Soohyuk reacted without a moment's pause.

As he was putting on his gown he'd placed on a chair, the head nurse came straight over to him and said in a rush, "Patients from a car accident are on their way. All four of the family have been badly injured. The parents, at least, are conscious, but the two children are not."

"When will they be arriving?" asked Soohyuk.

"In ten minutes. Here is the report from the paramedic," she said as she handed him the report.

He quickly scanned it and ordered, "Empty two intensive care units. They may be suffering from cerebral hemorrhage, so contact the other departments for support."

"Yes, sir."

Soohyuk looked at the residents, who were watching him with nervous expressions, and said, "Dr. Jung and Dr. Park, follow me. Dr. Ji, Dr. Kim, you go with Professor Park."

While they were busily running around to get ready for the incoming patients, a siren rang from afar. "Get ready!" Soohyuk shouted.

"Yes, sir," the others answered.

The ambulance came to a halt at last, and the parents and the children were sent to separate emergency rooms. The staff quickly surrounded the children. They weren't looking good. They were wearing seatbelts at the time of the accident, but they ended up getting sandwiched between the trunk and the front seats when a car crashed into them at great speed from behind. The perpetrator was drunk at the time. He'd shattered the lives of a family that was happily going on their trip as a result. The medics said he'd tried to run after crashing their car and was only caught when some nearby citizens chased him down.

Soohyuk and the other doctors all cursed the drunk driver who got away with minor injuries as they clung to the flickering lives of the children. They were losing too much blood. Soohyuk tried everything he could to stop the bleeding. He reached inside the ripped skin to find the source of the gushing blood with his fingers. The child was only going to get a chance at getting to the next step if he could stop the bleeding.

After a couple tries, he managed to find the source. But while he was waiting for the child's vital signs to come back to normal after taking care of that, a long *beeeeeeeep* came from the machine. The child's heart stopped.

Immediately reaching for the defibrillators, he said, "Someone go check on his parents and bring whoever can move."

"Yes, sir."

The child's life was slipping away. Everyone assumed Dr. Cha meant they should let the parents be with the child in his last moments.

Soohyuk tried with all his might to get the child's heart pumping again. He was so focused on it that his shirt was getting drenched in sweat.

The nurse who had stepped outside came back. "The dad is here," he said.

"Get him in gear and bring him in," said Soohyuk.

"Yes, sir."

The father collapsed onto the ground as soon as he laid eyes on the dreadful state of his son.

"Now's not the time, Dad. Come here and hold his hand," said Soohyuk. The father crawled next to the child. "Come on, Dad, you can do this. You need to help me save your boy."

The father held his son's hand as tight as he could, with tears streaming down his face. "Can you feel that? Dad's here, holding on tight to you. Daddy's never going to let go," he sobbed.

Beeeeeeeeeep…

Soohyuk did not give up. The father, watching him, started to calm down and focus on the task at hand as well. "It's Dad, Chanho. Dad's right here. Open your eyes and look at me."

"That's good. Keep going," said Soohyuk.

"I love you, my son. I love you so much. So, come on, open your eyes!"

"Come on, kid. Come back to us. Your dad is here!" Soohyuk continued to encourage the father as he clung on to the boy.

And the child responded at last.

Beep, beep, beep, beep.

He and his sibling were led straight to the operation rooms, owing to the doctors from the other department quickly taking over. Hwihyun was in charge of the child with cerebral hemorrhage.

When his shift finally ended, Soohyuk went up to the waiting room outside the operation rooms to check on the progress of the surgeons. The children's father was sitting with their mother, who'd undergone temporary treatments for her broken arm and broken ribs. She would have to have surgery as well because of the way her bones had broken, but she insisted on waiting until the children's operations were finished.

"Thank you so much, Doctor," said the father. Both his eyes and his wife's were bloodshot from crying. "Thank you for giving them the opportunity to go into operation."

Soohyuk nodded.

They all sat together, waiting for the results. Not long after, a middle-aged woman appeared.

"Excuse me, are you the ones who got into that accident at Chungmuro?" asked the woman. When the parents looked at her with suspicious expressions, she said, "Oh, please, please forgive him just this once. My husband's really not that kind of a man. He just made a mistake. Please, forgive him just this once."

Soohyuk raised his head and stared at the woman.

"This is not the place for this. We'll see you later at the police station," hissed the father.

"Please, please," she begged. "My husband is a good man. We have a child together too. We're all going to starve if he goes to jail. Please, just this once. I heard you are both lawyers. We're living off a truck driver's salary. We don't even have the money to go through a lawsuit. And he's seriously regretting what he's done right now at the station. It was a mistake. Just a mistake."

"We'll talk about this later!" said the father again. But still, the woman would not budge. She even kneeled down on the floor as if she were protesting.

She looked at Soohyuk and asked, "You're a doctor, right? They'll live, won't they? Won't they?"

Soohyuk quietly said, "You should be ashamed of yourself. Living isn't just barely breathing on a hospital bed. How would you like to live with all your bones broken, your body paralyzed from cerebral hemorrhage, and a heart that could stop at any minute? Would you be able to say that's living even if you're the one who has to live like that?"

All of their gazes shot toward Soohyuk when they heard his cold voice.

He continued, "This is a hospital, you shameless woman. A place where life and death are only minutes apart. How could you think to bitch and moan about your puny little problems at a place like this? You seriously should get yourself checked out. Also, a mistake? Didn't he try to run after the collision? He completely changed the lives of two children and shattered a family's happy future, and you're saying it was only a mistake? I'm scared to think what'll happen next time he makes another *mistake.*"

The security guards approached and pulled the woman up by force as she thrashed and struggled to stay in her place.

"What, so you never make any mistakes? You think being a doctor makes you a god or something? How dare you talk to me like that!" she screamed.

"I'd never make a mistake like that. And try thinking from their perspectives for once, you crazy cow. The kid in that room right now could've been yours. You're telling me, if it were your child, you would be jumping up and down in glee if someone came up to you and said it was all just a mistake?" said Soohyuk.

The woman didn't dare say another word to that and quietly followed the security out.

"Thank you, Dr. Cha," said the father.

"How dare she say it was only a mistake when that kid tried so hard just to stay alive?" spat Soohyuk, shaking his head in anger. "There's got to be a special place in hell for idiots like that."

Looking determined, the father said, "I will make sure that driver pays for this even if I have to fight for the rest of my life. I swear it on my name."

"Glad to hear that," said Soohyuk.

They continued to sit there and wait. At long last, the lights turned off in the other room, and the nurses and doctors coming out one by one all gave them hopeful news. The parents started to cry tears of joy. Finally, Hwihyun came outside and walked straight over to them to notify them of the results.

"The surgery was successful and they are both in stable conditions," he said, then went on to give a more detailed account in a composed manner. After listening till the end, Soohyuk got up from his seat.

When he was walking down the stairs, he heard someone running toward him from behind.

"Dr. Cha!" called Hwihyun.

Soohyuk stopped and looked up at him. "Do you have something to say to me?" he asked.

"I just wanted to say thank you," said Hwihyun with a smile, as Soohyuk looked at him without any expression. "Thank you for drinking coffee with my father. And for not telling anyone about the things I said."

"Do you remember everything?"

"Not all of it, just bits and pieces. Anyway, thank you. See you around, then," said Hwihyun before running back up the stairs.

Soohyuk mumbled, "You really did come a long way, kid."

CHAPTER 18

The next day, Hwihyun was sitting out on the terrace with the lunch he'd asked Ms. Seo to make all set and ready, just waiting for Professor Cho to join him. The first thing that came to mind when he'd finally sobered up after his night out with Soohyuk was his father's health. He'd checked as soon as he arrived at work the next day, and thankfully, nothing out of the ordinary was found during his check-up. But he couldn't stop thinking about his father. He felt like he'd been too disinterested and cold toward him.

Suddenly, footsteps approached him and Professor Cho appeared.

"I'm sorry I kept you waiting. There were so many patients," said his father.

"No worries. I just got here too," said Hwihyun.

Professor Cho halted for a moment as he squatted down to sit on the chair. He'd found the laid-out lunch.

"What is all this?" he asked.

"Mother made it. Have some, Father," offered Hwihyun, but Professor Cho couldn't bring himself to grab his chopsticks. "What is it?" asked Hwihyun.

"Did your mom know who you were going to eat it with?" asked Professor Cho.

"Can't you tell? There's fried pollack right here," answered Hwihyun.

Professor Cho gently smiled. That was his favorite. The two began eating their lunch.

"Still as good as ever," remarked Professor Cho.

"You should be thankful. It's gotten so much better than the first time around." Hwihyun sighed.

"What do you mean?"

"Mother hadn't cooked in a while, so it was too salty or too bland at first, you know. But she got the hang of it again pretty quickly. And then it just kept getting better and better. It got even better when I encouraged her a little." He giggled.

"All right, all right. Yes, thank you for offering to share such a delicious meal." Professor Cho chuckled.

Hwihyun watched him take a moment to savor every bite as if he were trying to taste everything down to the atom. His eyes paused on his father's graying hair. The lines on his forehead seemed deeper, and most of all, he looked lonely.

"Dye your hair when you get the time, Father. You look like a grandpa," said Hwihyun.

"Do I?" replied Professor Cho.

Hwihyun nodded. "And wear a brighter colored shirt. You look sick."

Professor Cho touched his hair with a faint smile and said, "No one tells me things like that."

"Of course no one does. I'm telling you only because I'm your son."

Professor Cho laughed. "Who would I pretty myself up for at this age? It's fine, I'll live."

"You do have one person you would want to look good for, for the rest of your life," said Hwihyun pointedly.

Professor put down his chopsticks for a moment and looked at his son. "Hwihyun."

"Yes?" Hwihyun raised his head from the food to look at him as well.

"I'm thinking of quitting soon," he said. Hwihyun's smile faded. "I'm going to quit as soon as I know what's going to happen with Dr. Cha," he continued.

"Why?"

"Because of my obsession," he said with a smile, but that word felt like a dagger to Hwihyun. "Even though I already ruined both of your lives and your mother's because of my love, I just can't let it go. I can't stop thinking that I'd do anything to live with you, and Hwiyin, and Yoonkyung just once more."

He had tried to stop. He'd tried with all his might to stop thinking of them the way he did. But it didn't work. He just could not give up.

"That'll happen eventually. You don't need to quit your job," said Hwihyun.

"No, my obsession will make life harder for you and Yoonkyung again. So, I need to put an end to it," said Professor Cho.

Hearing him talk as if he'd already made up his mind frustrated Hwihyun. He'd thought his family had been shattered to pieces long ago. He'd thought that all there was left to his family was the façade they put on. But if Professor Cho left Seoul… If he left too after Hwiyin left…

"No, Father. I don't think you should," said Hwihyun.

"Hwihyun."

"No, listen to me. I don't think you should. Please reconsider," he said adamantly.

"Hwihyun…" Professor Cho's voice trailed off.

"Let's eat. It's getting cold," interrupted Hwihyun.

The two ate in silence. When they were almost done, Professor Cho asked, "By the way, did you bring that too?"

Hwihyun's eyes moved in the direction he was pointing, toward a bag of lunch that had been sitting all by itself since he first came outside.

"No, that's Dr. Cha's. I guess he's eating outside because the weather's so nice," said Hwihyun.

"But lunchtime is already almost over…"

"Dr. Cha rarely eats on time. But he still seems to enjoy his food," said Hwihyun.

"That place must be really good, then," said Professor Cho.

"It's ridiculously hard to order from there. I failed a couple times."

"Really? It's that popular?"

"Yup. Are you done? Should I get us some coffee?" asked Hwihyun.

"Sure. We'll have ourselves a full-course meal," said Professor Cho.

Hwihyun brought back two cups of coffee. While he was drinking it with Professor Cho, he heard quick footsteps. Soohyuk appeared and paused when he saw the two of them sitting there, but soon nodded to them and sat in front of his bag of lunch.

"The weather's nice today, Dr. Cha," said Professor Cho.

"It is." Soohyuk gave a short answer and opened the lid. The lunch Yuna made for him revealed its glorious self. A smile creeped on his face. Today's main menu was a handmade hamburger. A salad made with shite kimchi she'd specially made for him, French fries, and a scone were neatly laid in the container as well. A tomato was sitting in the corner as dessert.

The other day, Yuna had decreased the limit of orders per day from two hundred down to a hundred. It was for Soohyuk and Minjoon.

Yuna had said while posting the notice on her blog, "I'm thinking of drawing back the scale a little."

"Drawing back the scale? What do you mean?" Soohyuk had asked.

"You know how I was trying to sell two hundred boxed lunches a day? Well, that's getting a little hard. And a little too time-consuming. I want to spend more time with you and Minjoon."

It was true. As orders had multiplied by the day, she'd had to get more and more ingredients during her morning grocery runs to the point that she could barely carry them home. For a person who could not ride in taxis, it was not an easy task. Soohyuk drove her whenever he had time, but she felt too guilty for making him do that. Moreover, she would get so tired by the end of the day from preparing so many meals that she couldn't spend much time with her family. So, Yuna had made the bold decision to cut back. That had ironically made her brand even more popular. Her blog was blowing up every day.

But she always made space for her one special customer, Soohyuk.

"You really must be a VIP there, Dr. Cha. You've gotten something off the menu again," said Hwihyun.

Soohyuk shrugged and took a big bite out of the hamburger with the thick, luscious patty in the middle. The juice from the meat, molten cheese, sweet sauce, jalapeño, and crunchy lettuce danced in harmony in his mouth. Her food was the best. He realized it all over again every time he ate it.

When he was halfway through the burger, Professor Cho said, "Don't eat alone over there. Come join us. We'll stay until you finish."

Soohyuk hesitated for a moment. He recalled Hwihyun's drunken, disorganized, concerned rant about his father.

"Mother's going to be heartbroken if she finds out, but I'm worried about Father. I keep thinking of bad things happening to him now that he's alone, like him falling ill or even passing. Maybe this is why everyone says there's no use raising a son. They all run to their dads

when they grow up. I tried my best to be loving like a daughter, but I guess I was just another annoying son."

A father he loved and hated.

Soohyuk got up from his seat. He took big steps toward their table, with his lunch in his hand, and sat down in an empty seat.

Hwihyun looked at him with an expression of utter shock. It was almost like he'd just seen a miracle.

"No getting up before I finish eating," said Soohyuk.

"Of course not," said Professor Cho. "By the way, I didn't know you were that much of a heavyweight. You're better than our Hwihyun, I heard."

"His habit is repeating what he said, it seemed," answered Soohyuk.

"Really? So, that's what happens when he gets drunk," exclaimed Professor Cho.

Hwihyun quickly jumped in. "No, that doesn't count. That was purely because Dr. Cha here kept drinking without putting any solids in his stomach. I mean, what kind of a man doesn't even slow down to match other people's paces? That only happened because I drank on an empty stomach. I swear that will never happen again."

"Is that so? Let's go out another night and see what happens," Soohyuk answered straightaway.

Hwihyun couldn't believe his ears. Was Soohyuk trying to be social right now? "You're not joking, are you?"

"Why would I joke about something like that?" answered Soohyuk.

"All right, then. Let's set a date right now," said Hwihyun excitedly. He'd had an oddly freeing experience when he drank with Soohyuk. That was probably why he'd drunk to the point of blacking out. Why else would he have done that? He had no clue where he'd gotten the idea where that whatever he talked about with Soohyuk would stay between them, but he'd been having so much fun just drowning himself in alcohol that he hadn't even wanted to go home. In any case, this Soohyuk Cha had a peculiar power over him.

"I'm free on…"

Professor Cho watched the two sit side by side with their eyes on their phones to set a date. Hwihyun always had a smile on his face and was liked by everyone because he was so social, but as his father, Professor Cho could see through that. His son always seemed precarious, as if he were standing at the edge of a cliff. But right now, he seemed at ease.

Suddenly, an offer escaped his lips. "What if I joined you too? I'll buy."

Hwihyun and Soohyuk looked up at the same time. The professor's heart started pounding hard like it had that morning, when he was looking at the back of Soohyuk. He couldn't quite put his finger on it, but there was something very similar about the two of them. Their eyes and their overall feelings were quite different when he took a closer look at them, but there still was something about them.

"Hold on a second," said Soohyuk. He took out a flashlight from his pocket and got up on his feet to lean his body toward Professor Cho. "Let me take a look at your eyes."

It was an order. Slightly surprised, Professor Cho took off his glasses and showed his eyes to Soohyuk.

"When was your last check-up?" asked Soohyuk.

"About two months ago, no irregularities found," answered Hwihyun instead.

Soohyuk took a look at both of his eyes and said, "I'd recommend you do two more blood tests. It could be Gilbert's syndrome, considering that there were no irregularities found during your check-up two months ago. We'll know for sure once we have the results. Come with me to the emergency room after I finish eating."

He was so used to talking in an authoritative manner that it came out as a mixture of orders and recommendations. He'd at least started using a lot fewer obscene expressions, all thanks to Yuna's constant reminders.

"Are you saying that you're seeing signs of jaundice in my eyes?" asked Professor Cho.

"Yes. Unless the whites of your eyes are naturally yellow?" asked Soohyuk.

"Well, no."

"Then we'll go do some bloodwork," said Soohyuk firmly.

"All right," said Professor Cho at last, sensing from his sternness that he was not going to change his mind no matter what he said.

"We'll do one today and another one in a week. Then we'll set the date for drinks once we have all the results," said Soohyuk.

"So, you're letting me tag along?" Professor Cho grinned. *Why am I getting so excited? Is it because I'll be drinking with Hwihyun after such a long time? Or because I'll be with both Soohyuk and Hwihyun?*

"Sure, if Dr. Cho agrees," said Soohyuk.

"What do you think, then, Hwihyun?" asked Professor Cho.

Hwihyun jumped and looked up, asking, "About what?" He was still thinking about what Soohyuk had said just now about Professor Cho. He hadn't spotted it. He hadn't even thought about it. All he, his own son, had done was bring lunch and tell him to dye his hair because the results from his check-up seemed fine.

Soohyuk interrupted his thoughts. "No need to feel so guilty, Dr. Cho. It's just that I'm much more used to being around children than adults. They all say they have a stomachache when you ask them which part of their body hurts. So, I'm used to finding signs on my own."

Hwihyun calm down a little when he heard Soohyuk's explanation, which made sense to him as well.

Professor Cho spoke up again. "I asked, what do you think about my coming drinking with you two?"

"If the results look fine, sure," said Hwihyun. "No reason to say no when Dr. Cha says he's fine with it and it's your wallet we'll be raiding. I'm going to reserve the most expensive place there is. Although, I'm sure we'll end up drinking So-Mac again."

"So-Mac? You like So-Mac?" Professor Cho asked Soohyuk, a little surprised.

"I do," he answered.

"So do I," said Professor Cho, beaming again. The glum that was hovering over him was suddenly and completely gone. He had no idea why he was getting this excited, but he was. He was so happy, like one of his oldest wishes had come true, that he didn't know what to do.

Soohyuk and Hwihyun took in this memorable sight of their father.

***

Ms. Seo noticed Professor Cho, Hwihyun, and Soohyuk all coming into the emergency room, and frowned. Soohyuk brought Professor Cho straight into one of the exam rooms and prepared to draw blood. Her feet started stepping toward them on their own.

"What is it, Hwihyun? Is there something wrong with your father?" Her voice started trembling. Was there something wrong with Professor Cho? Why else would they be drawing blood right now?

Looking affectionately at his mother, Hwihyun calmly explained, "Dr. Cha found signs of jaundice in Father's eyes. But there weren't any irregularities found during his recent check-up, so he's suspecting it might be Gilbert's syndrome. We'll know for sure once we have results from both blood tests."

"Oh, I see. But isn't Gilbert's syndrome serious too?" asked Ms. Seo, anxiously grasping Hwihyun's gown.

Squeezing her hand on his gown, Hwihyun said soothingly, "No, it only comes up temporarily when the patient is tired and stressed out. All he needs to do to get better is rest. I'll let you know when the results come back."

"Yes, all right," she answered, but her shaking hands couldn't seem to calm down.

Ms. Seo held her son's hand tightly and watched Soohyuk draw blood from Professor Cho's arm. They soon walked out together after Soohyuk finished and put the order in.

"Honey, are you all right?" asked Ms. Seo.

Professor Cho looked over at her, saw her anxious eyes, and faintly smiled. *Honey...* She hadn't called him that in a long time. He reached out and warmly caressed her back. She didn't pull away either. *Today must be the day all my dreams come true,* thought Professor Cho. *Look how happy I already am.*

CHAPTER 19

After finishing the day's work, Yuna started to make something to give Minjoon for a snack. He'd become even bubblier after their first trip on the caravan. She couldn't help but wish that he would stay that bubbly and happy, even if it was exaggerated. So, she was just watching Minjoon. It was a nerve-wracking thing to do, but no one had a definite right answer. They couldn't hastily make judgment on what would be the best for him.

Yuna minced the vegetables into small bits and put them in the bowl. She then started to rip the boiled chicken breast pieces into thin strips. She was making a sandwich. Suddenly, the phone in her apron started ringing. She wiped her hands and pulled it out of the pocket.

"Oh, it's Minjoon," she mumbled.

Minjoon called her at times to ask what the day's snack was going to be, or to tell her what he wanted to eat.

"Minjoon!" she exclaimed.

"Aunt Yuna! What's today's snack?"

He really did love to eat.

"A chicken breast and vegetable sandwich," answered Yuna.

"That sounds good."

"What do you want for dinner?" asked Yuna.

"Aunt Yuna."

"Yes?" she answered, a sudden knot forming in the pit of her stomach. Something was off.

"Can you come get me, Aunt Yuna?"

Yuna started rushing. She ripped off the apron, left the disorganized table she hadn't had the chance to clear yet, and leapt to her feet.

"Of course, I'll come right away. Where are you?" she asked.

"First, promise me you won't tell Mom and Dad."

Tears welled up in her eyes within seconds.

"Of course, I promise. I'll never tell them until you say that I can," she quickly answered.

"I'm at school. In Classroom Five."

Yuna cursorily brushed her hair with her fingers while running to the bedroom to grab her wallet, then left the apartment.

"Aunt Yuna." Minjoon sounded like he was trying to hold back tears.

"Yes? I just left home. I'll be there in about half an hour. Can you wait that long?" said Yuna.

"My legs feel weird. I can't walk." He started wailing out loud.

Yuna broke into a run as soon as she got off the elevator and got into a cab. She'd even forgotten that she felt suffocated in cabs. The only thought in her head was that she needed to get there as fast as possible. She called Soohyuk as soon as she got in the car.

Soohyuk's phone rang as he finished looking over the hospital charts. It was Yuna. "Hi, what's up?"

"Soohyuk, can you come help me? Our Minjoon…"

Soohyuk calmly listened as she explained everything with a trembling voice, then said, "I'll be there as soon as I can. Wait for me, okay?"

"Mhmm." He could tell she was panicking.

His shift had ended long ago, so he moved right away. He took off his gown and gestured for the head nurse.

"Yes, Dr. Cha?" she answered.

"How do you call a private ambulance?" asked Soohyuk.

"I'll call one for you," she promptly answered.

"Thank you. Right now, please," said Soohyuk. He then talked to Yuna on the phone again while almost running to the changing room. "You heard that, right? I'll be there with an ambulance, so stay there."

"Mhmm." Her voice was shaking uncontrollably.

"Where are you right now?" asked Soohyuk.

"In a cab. But I'm fine. I'm fine."

Soohyuk frowned. She was still claustrophobic. She couldn't breathe in small, enclosed spaces. It was probably purely her love for her nephew that had made her take that cab.

Moving even more quickly, Soohyuk said in a quiet voice, hoping it would soothe her, "Yuna, open the windows on both sides. And follow me. Take a deep breath in, and breathe out. Right now." Her uncontrollably shaking breath made him anxious, but he continued, "He's going to be fine. I'll be there soon. So, keep doing as I say. Deep inhale, then slow exhale."

Soohyuk rolled up his gown and tossed it in the corner, took his things, and left the changing room at once. Every second counted now. Yuna needed him.

"Trust me, Yuna. Minjoon is going to be fine. Don't make me have to worry about you more," said Soohyuk.

"Mhmm."

Soohyuk broke into a sprint.

———

Yuna waited for Soohyuk on a chair in Classroom Five with her arms wrapped tightly around Minjoon. Minjoon had been so relieved to see her that he'd wrapped his arms around her neck on her lap and fallen into deep slumber. She was relieved by this as well, for it allowed her to hide her racing heart and sneak a call to Yoonjae.

She gently kissed the crown of her nephew's head. A pleasant smell wafted from him. *How ironic,* she thought. *He was panicking because he couldn't walk, but he smells of warm, cozy sunshine. Like a doll I could hold tight in my arms.*

"Why did you want to grow up so fast?" she mumbled through her exhales, which were still shaky because of her pounding heart. How Minjoon had found out about himself didn't matter. Neither did it matter how accurately he knew what was happening to him, nor how much he knew. The most pressing issue right now was that Minjoon didn't want to be in pain for the adults. That was why he'd felt like he should hide the oddities, smile even more brightly, and make the adults tear up by saying something an old man would say.

Yuna whispered, "You just live forever as Peter Pan. You just travel the world like the Little Prince and fool around like Minjoon."

She'd told Yoonjae to wait in the lobby at S University Hospital with Kyungjo. She'd made a promise to Minjoon, so she had to keep it. If she didn't, Minjoon would lose the last person to call the next time he needed someone. And that was what she'd emphasized to Yoonjae, too, when she told him to sit tight and wait even if he felt like he was going to go crazy.

Brisk footsteps echoed in the hallway outside. They didn't sound like one person, but two people. Soon, the door slid open and the school's security guard appeared, followed by the panting Soohyuk. Yuna burst into tears before she could stop herself the instant she saw him. She was so relieved; it felt like all the energy was draining out of her body. Soohyuk rushed over to Yuna and reached his arms out to hold both her and Minjoon at the same time.

"Well done, Yuna. You've done so well," said Soohyuk, even though he could sense deep in his heart what kind of a state she was in right now. Her entire body was drenched in sweat, and her heart was still racing. He patted her back, thinking that she really was insanely brave even though she was easily scared. Yuna was a good woman and a good aunt, who would be a good wife and a good mother. This was the woman he loved.

When he sensed that she was calming down again, he turned his gaze on Minjoon and said, "Shall we go now? I'll take the kid."

"Mhmm," she answered.

The moment he took Minjoon from her lap, his keen eyes caught Yuna's palms. They were bloody from her nails digging into her skin so deep. Realizing what he was looking at, Yuna showed him her palms instead of hiding them. Both of them were bloody, showing how scared she'd been all along.

"I'll take care of those when we get to the hospital, so hang on a little longer," said Soohyuk.

"Mhmm," she said again.

Soohyuk leaned down with Minjoon in his arms to kiss the top of Yuna's head. He was once again falling hard for her bravery.

Holding Minjoon in his arms, Soohyuk started to walk. He hadn't brought the stretcher on purpose because he knew that Minjoon would freak out. Children often thought that they were gravely ill when they were on a stretcher, even if it was for a minor injury. When he'd taken a couple steps like that, he turned to check on Yuna. She was still standing back in the doorway of the classroom.

"Are you okay? Can you walk?" asked Soohyuk.

"I can," she answered with determination.

She tensed her shaking legs. She was so out of energy that her legs wanted to go limp like they were an octopus's. But now wasn't the time for that kind of nonsense. Not wanting to seem weak, she clenched her teeth. That little gesture somehow fueled her with new energy. But she was now walking awkwardly like a robot because her legs were too tense.

"Just go first. Don't wait for me," said Yuna through gritted teeth.

"No, that's all right," said Soohyuk. "We can wait. Nothing's going to happen to Minjoon right now. And if we leave you here, you're going to end up walking all the way to the hospital. You can't ride anything right now, whether it's a cab or a bus."

He was right. She was already panting, out of breath. So, Yuna clenched her teeth even harder and tried her best to walk a little faster. Soohyuk was walking slowly ahead of her, so he wouldn't wake Minjoon, and so he could walk side by side with her. Seeing that helped her relax a little. He was waiting for her. Her eyes betrayed her again and started to water.

"Take your time, Yuna," said Soohyuk.

"Mhmm," said Yuna, wiping the tears with the back of her hands.

She tried even harder to walk. She followed Soohyuk like a stiff robot.

When they got on the ambulance at last, Soohyuk quickly checked on Minjoon. He checked his heartbeat, his breath, then the reactions of his legs. While he did that, Yuna texted Yoonjae because she knew he'd be waiting anxiously.

We're leaving the school right now. Don't forget, you absolutely have to wait. I'll call you as soon as he asks for you and Kyungjo.

The reply came quick, as if her brother had been staring at his phone this whole time.

All right. We're at the lobby right now.

"Let's go," said Soohyuk to the driver, and the ambulance started to move. Soohyuk reached out to pull the crouching Yuna toward him.

She whispered in a barely audible voice, "I'm so scared."

"Of course you are," said Soohyuk.

He hadn't ever tried to empathize with the guardians of his patients before. But not anymore. He brushed her shoulders and kissed her temples in an effort to share her pain. He wanted to do whatever was in his power to lessen her pain.

"The fact that he's been hiding it until now hurts more than anything," said Yuna, rubbing a hand down her arm. "It means that we weren't trustworthy enough."

"No, you, Yoonjae, and Kyungjo are really handling this well. I've seen bad cases, you know. Minjoon's every day is a holiday compared to those kids," said Soohyuk.

"Still…"

Tightening his arm around her, he said, "Don't blame yourself. You couldn't have done more than you already have. Nobody could. You've done so well."

Yuna quietly leaned her head on his shoulder. His warm consolation and support seemed to envelop her like a soothing blanket. His warm lips touched her temple. Yuna felt braver when she felt that warmth. And as she did, a new worry started to creep in.

"I don't know what I'm supposed to do when he wakes up," she mumbled.

Soohyuk looked at the soundly sleeping Minjoon. Eight years old. Still just a child, no matter how hard he pretended to be mature. He wondered why he'd called his aunt instead of his parents. And then it hit him.

"What a bold kid he is." He chuckled.

"Hmm?" asked Yuna.

"I think you can just be your usual self with him," he said.

"Hmm?" she asked again.

"It seems like Minjoon thinks you're some kind of super-woman who can take on whatever the world throws at you. Just cry if you feel like crying."

Yuna looked up at him. "What do you mean?"

"Children have a tendency of hiding it from their parents when they get sick. Partly because they're afraid of going to the hospital, but also because they're afraid they'll become a burden to their parents in some cases," explained Soohyuk. "It's the same with kids who are bullied. They hide their pain for their parents."

"But Minjoon's too young for that kind of stuff," said Yuna.

"Because he is young, his mind works in a simpler and a purer way. He's basically burying his head in the sand, but he doesn't realize that. It would be a problem if he kept that to himself, but thankfully, he has you. You're honestly not that tough either, but he doesn't know that. So, what can you do? You just have to be his superwoman."

"That's good, then," said Yuna, smiling a little. "Really good. I'm sure he'll slowly realize how Kyungjo and Yoonjae really feel as he keeps talking to me about whatever he's going through. He'll then realize how many people there are to support him."

Soohyuk gazed at her with an odd expression. It was an extremely optimistic thing to hear when he knew how tiring it must've been to take a cab despite her fears, follow him even when her legs wanted to give in, and listen to the complaints of a sick person.

"You're such an amazing woman," whispered Soohyuk.

"Really?" said Yuna.

"Really. I've never seen a woman as amazing as you are."

She bit her lip. "I wanted to become a really amazing woman for you… I'm glad you think I am one."

Soohyuk leaned his head sideways to rest it on her head. Yuna began to relax as his breaths tickled her hair. Moreover, Soohyuk had told her that she could cry if she wanted to cry when Minjoon woke up, so she didn't have to worry about that anymore. What Soohyuk said was exactly the thing she'd needed to hear.

"I'm really glad I have you," whispered Yuna.

"Me too," replied Soohyuk.

"Thank you, for being with us," she said.

Being with us... Soohyuk's jaw clenched. His heart was suddenly aching. Something he couldn't control was trying to rip out of his heart. But something else blocked it from coming out. Maybe the hatred that was still inside him. Yuna started caressing his shoulder, and he realized his body had tensed up. Her hand felt warm and affectionate, like she'd completely calmed down. Now, the person needing consoling was Soohyuk, not Yuna.

"I should be the one thanking you, for being with me," Soohyuk choked out.

When the ambulance arrived at the emergency room at last, he carefully brought Minjoon up into his arms. Minjoon opened his eyes.

"Aunt Yuna…" he mumbled.

"Yes, she's right here," answered Soohyuk.

Minjoon stared at the man holding him and asked, "Lego Man?"

Soohyuk asked Yuna, "What will he call me when we get married?"

"Uncle Soohyuk," answered Yuna.

Soohyuk then said sternly to Minjoon, "Then you can start calling me that right now."

The doors to the emergency room burst open.

oonjae kept fidgeting with his phone as he waited and waited for Yuna's call. He was anxious, but he'd made a promise, so he had no choice but to wait.

Someone suddenly asked, "Would you like me to go take a look for you?"

Yoonjae's eyes found Ms. Seo, who was sitting next to Kyungjo. It was a true boon that they'd run into her when she was on her way back home after her volunteer hours ended because she'd recognized them at once. It had taken Yoonjae a minute to remember she was the one who saved them the day Minjoon was diagnosed and they were in a state of panic. Thanks to her taking Minjoon on a tour around the hospital, Kyungjo had been able to recover from the shock. Seeing Ms. Seo again brought Yoonjae a rush of relief and cheer. It was like he'd found a shed of light after being in complete darkness for a long time.

When she'd heard that they were waiting for Soohyuk to bring Minjoon, Ms. Seo had decided to stay a little longer. She'd held Kyungjo's cold hands, consoled them, and brought them water.

Now, getting up from her seat, she said, "Wait here. I'll go take a look."

"We would really appreciate that," answered Yoonjae.

She nodded and started walking. Kyungjo got up from her seat as well, like a magnet.

Yoonjae pulled her back down, saying, "Not you. They told us to wait."

Kyungjo sat back down in her seat, looking pale. None of this felt real to her. Her eyes wandered aimlessly. No amount of mental preparation could've been enough for the impending reality. Minjoon's attempts to be considerate of them made her feel like she was going to lose her mind.

Yoonjae said to Kyungjo, "Hang in there. I think they should be arriving soon."

Suddenly, Kyungjo came back to life. She forced her limp back to straighten, then slapped her face hard with both hands.

"What are you doing?" said Yoonjae.

"I need to come back to my senses," she said through gritted teeth. Her brows narrowed as if she were going to cry. She slapped her face once more and said, "I'm not going to cry. Even if I do cry, I'm not going to bawl like a baby."

Yoonjae caught her hands before she could slap herself again. Leaning his forehead against hers, he whispered, "Yes, I know you won't. You're a strong mother. So, let's get through this as a team."

Kyungjo nodded. *Mom. Yes, I am Minjoon Lee's mom.* She took a deep breath in, then gazed at the entrance to the pediatric emergency room.

Yuna was standing next to Minjoon in the exam room. They had just filled out all the forms to be admitted in order to run a more thorough test and were waiting for another room to open up.

Soohyuk asked Minjoon, "When did it become hard?"

"To do what?" asked the now calm Minjoon, as if he had forgotten all about what happened earlier.

"When did it become hard to walk, I mean," said Soohyuk.

"It's not," replied Minjoon cheerfully.

Yuna leaned down toward him and said, "Minjoon, you have to tell the truth to doctors."

"It really doesn't hurt. I only did that because I wanted to see you," pouted Minjoon.

Soohyuk gazed at him with narrowed eyes.

Minjoon didn't meet his eyes. Yet, he said with exaggeration, "Seriously. I'm fine now, Aunt Yuna. Take me home."

Yuna looked at Soohyuk as if she were asking for help. Minjoon could walk again now, not at all like when he couldn't move an inch from his seat back at the school. As soon as he felt better, Minjoon had started hiding his pain again.

Soohyuk quietly said, "Can you give us a second, Yuna?"

"Soohyuk," said Yuna.

"Just give us a second," said Soohyuk again.

Minjoon widened his eyes and held on to Yuna's hand. "Where are you going, Aunt Yuna?"

"I'll be right outside," answered Yuna.

"No, don't go. I don't want to be alone with this man." Minjoon desperately clung on to her.

"I'm not 'this man.' I'm your uncle. Go, Yun," said Soohyuk.

"You're not even married yet!" cried Minjoon.

"Why does that matter when we're already living together?" exclaimed Soohyuk as well.

Yuna jumped when she heard that, but he'd already told Minjoon.

"Aunt Yuna?" asked Minjoon.

"He's right. He's going to be your uncle soon, so no need to worry," said Yuna before reluctantly leaving the exam room.

Ms. Seo found Yuna walking out of the room right away. She scurried toward her and waved at her.

"Hello, I'm a volunteer here," said Ms. Seo.

"I remember you from before," said Yuna. "You do such great work here."

Ms. Seo grinned. She could see how adorable Yuna was even at one glance. "You're Mr. Yoonjae Lee's sister, right?"

"Yes, that's correct," said Yuna.

"He's waiting in the lobby right now. He wants to know how things are going."

Yuna answered with a fragile smile, "I'd hate to disappoint him, but he's going to have to wait a little longer. Soohyuk's inside talking with Minjoon right now."

"Oh, all right. I'll tell him that, then. I can't even imagine how hard this must be, but they're holding up so well out there right now. It seems like you are too." Ms. Seo smiled.

"Thank you so much for looking out for us," said Yuna as she held Ms. Seo's hand.

Ms. Seo felt a sense of gratitude toward Yuna. She seemed like such a kind person. That was probably why she was having a good influence on Soohyuk.

"It's my job. I'll go and tell them, then," said Ms. Seo before nodding to Yuna and leaving the emergency room.

Yuna kept waiting in front of the exam room after she left. After a while, she started to notice something odd. The staff were all glancing at her. *Why would they... Did Soohyuk say something about me?* she wondered. Then she thought of their wedding in December. Butterflies found their way through the cracks of her worry-filled mind. *What a strange thing life is,* thought Yuna. *It always finds a way to make you want to live the happiest you can.*

Feeling embarrassed for some reason, Yuna glanced inside the exam room to avert her eyes. Soohyuk and Minjoon were glaring at each other as if they were having a fight.

"I wonder what they're talking about," Yuna mumbled to herself.

***

Soohyuk gazed at Minjoon stubbornly keeping his mouth clamped shut, then reached out to slowly press on his thigh.

"That hurts," protested Minjoon.

"Don't lie to me. I know you can't feel it that well yet. You may have fooled Yuna, but you can't fool my eyes," said Soohyuk.

"Well, you're wrong," proclaimed Minjoon.

"When did you realize you're sick?"

Surprised to hear such a direct question, Minjoon looked at him with wide eyes.

"Why do you look so surprised? Don't you know that doctors can see through everything? Are you still going to try to fool me?" said Soohyuk, crossing his arms.

"You're not a doctor when you can't even fix it," snapped Minjoon. "You're a fake doctor."

Soohyuk grinned and pressed different parts of Minjoon's body with both hands. His reaction was noticeably slower this time.

"You knew. Someone must have babbled it all to you," said Soohyuk.

Minjoon bit down on his lip. "Is it...is it true? I heard my teacher talking to another teacher about, I think, muscles? Am I really sick?"

"You are. You have muscular dystrophy," answered Soohyuk truthfully.

"Am I going to die then?"

"Is that what that meathead said?" said Soohyuk.

"Meathead?"

"Yes, meathead. Someone who doesn't even know what to say and what not to say is a meathead, what else?" answered Soohyuk.

Minjoon cracked a smile and muttered, "He said that I'm a real bother. That he's so sick and tired of my mom calling him every day."

"What a nasty meathead." Soohyuk shook his head. "How dare a teacher say something like that about his student. He shouldn't have become a teacher if he thinks kids are bothersome."

"What's going to happen to me?" asked Minjoon.

"You will die, eventually, of old age. Me, Yuna, your mom, your dad, all of us are going to die of old age," said Soohyuk.

Minjoon slouched. His eyes started to water, and within seconds, thick drops of tears were rolling down his cheeks. Soohyuk crossed his arms and observed Minjoon. He'd thought so before too, but this kid was much quicker at picking up subtle cues and was also more considerate than most other kids his age. He could only guess how much Minjoon must have struggled until now on his own.

"Minjoon," said Soohyuk.

"Yes?" hiccupped Minjoon.

"Do you want me to give you a more detailed explanation of your sickness?"

Minjoon nodded as he wiped the tears with the back of his hands.

Soohyuk leaned forward to look at the boy eye to eye, then carefully began, "The sickness you have is a type of muscular dystrophy, where your muscles literally do not listen to you. Like today. You wanted to walk, but your legs wouldn't listen to you. You wanted to stand up straight, but your back wouldn't listen to you."

Seeing Minjoon's eyes twinkle with curiosity reminded Soohyuk of Yuna. It made him smile.

"But there are ways to help you even when your muscles don't listen to you. There are wheelchairs that will allow you to sit, and the new wheelchairs that are coming out now can take you anywhere you want to go. There are braces that will help you to straighten your back if you want to, and physical therapy that will help your muscles stay awake and not fall asleep. More than anything, there's a medicine in development that's going to come out soon."

"Really? There's a medicine coming out?" asked Minjoon.

Soohyuk nodded. "There's one that's already been approved, but I think it would be inappropriate for you because they haven't concluded the clinical trials."

"Really? I'm going to be healthy then?" said Minjoon.

"It will not perfectly cure your condition. But it will definitely make moving much easier for you."

"Umm, that medicine," mumbled Minjoon.

"Yes?" said Soohyuk.

"Isn't it expensive?"

"It is."

"Then I don't want it," said Minjoon.

Soohyuk reached out to wipe away his tears, asking, "Why not?"

Minjoon quietly sobbed, unable to speak.

"You can cry out loud. This is an emergency room. Everyone who comes here cries," said Soohyuk.

Minjoon shook his head with tears still streaming down his face. "No. Mom and Dad are going to be sad if they see me crying."

Soohyuk didn't say anything more, but took out his handkerchief and gave it to Minjoon. Then, he stood there and watched Minjoon sob, trying not to make any loud sounds. A strange sensation filled him again, like something was trying to rip out of his chest but something else was blocking it. Soohyuk rubbed his chest.

After a few more moments, Minjoon said through his sobs,

"Then Dad's going to have to work even more than he does now, and Mom's going to have to go through a lot too. Because they'll need to make a lot of money for me."

"Why should you worry about that? You're only eight," said Soohyuk.

"Because I like Mom and Dad so much. Because I love Mom. Because I don't want them to have to suffer because of me. It's not like I'm going to get healthy anyway," sobbed Minjoon.

At those words, Soohyuk felt the final pieces of his lost memories come flying back. His heart pounded like it was about to burst. His brows narrowed. *Oh god... Oh god...* He suddenly felt like he was in a dream state. Ms. Jung's screams echoed in his mind.

"Your mother wouldn't have had to go through all this if it weren't for you! Do you think I like doing this? You're a bastard conceived out of wedlock, nothing more! You ruined my son's life! You ruined your mother's life too! Everyone would have gone about their lives happily if it weren't for you!"

Soohyuk's eyes watered. He covered his mouth with one hand.

He'd loved his mom, Ms. Seo, so much. He'd wanted to do everything in his power to save her from the abuse she put up with. So, he'd fought with his grandmother. But that only made things worse for his mom. *Because of me... If I weren't there, Mom wouldn't have married Dad.* His grandmother was wrong. It wasn't his mom who'd ruined his dad's life. It was his dad who'd ruined his mom's life.

He'd had a certain hunch. He'd been worried since a certain point that his mom might just let go of herself. Especially when she would look at him with that blank stare. She didn't even have enough energy to protect her two sons from the verbal abuse. She was wilting away. So, he thought, *She'll go looking for me if I disappear. She won't think of ending her life, then.* Six years old... He'd loved his mother too much.

All the lost memories were back. He was the one who'd forced himself to erase all his memories, so he could keep playing hide-and-seek. No one else.

Suddenly, the door to the exam room opened and Yuna stepped inside. She had a very determined look on her face. Before Soohyuk could readjust to the present, Yuna lightly smacked Minjoon.

"What was that for?!" shouted Minjoon. He started to cry out loud, like Yuna's appearance had worked as a sort of reassurance.

Soohyuk didn't dare say anything. He'd never seen her so angry. In his eyes, she seemed furious.

"You're still just a tiny kid! You can't even wipe your own butt yet!" shouted Yuna back.

"I hate you!" bawled Minjoon.

"Yeah, yeah," said Yuna.

"That was a secret. You can't say that out loud in front of Uncle Soohyuk!" cried Minjoon.

"Ha, that's nothing compared to what I'm about to say."

"There's nothing more!"

"Of course there is. How about the time you made a horn with your hair in the middle of a bath and fell face-first on the ground while dancing?" said Yuna.

"No, Aunt Yuna," wailed Minjoon as he clung to her sleeve.

Soohyuk frowned a little at Yuna. She seemed like she was being mean on purpose. He couldn't understand what was going on. *Isn't she upset? Then why does she look so mischievous?*

Yuna blatantly teased Minjoon, "I'm going to tell him that you got twenty percent on your spelling quiz once too."

Funnily enough, Minjoon fought to refute everything she said through his tears. "You said that you once got ten percent. I got ten percent more than you did."

Soohyuk started to smile. *I get it now. I get why she's doing this.*

"That was because I was only eight years old at the time. Only eight years old, silly. And I didn't pretend like I was all grown-up already. Also, what kind of a grown-up cries like that?" she continued.

Minjoon shouted back like he couldn't be more aggrieved, "I'm a kid too. I'm only eight years old too. And you said that you cried a lot even when you were old. You kept crying and made Dad come rescue you so many times even when you were all grown-up."

Yuna kneeled in front of her and looked into his eyes. "Did that make your dad not like me anymore?" she asked affectionately.

Minjoon looked into her eyes as well.

"Have you ever seen your dad say anything bad about me?" continued Yuna.

"My dad would never do something like that!" shouted Minjoon.

"Right? He loves and cares about me so much even though I'm just like a kid, right?"

"Of course!" said Minjoon with a determined expression, as if he were being challenged to defend his father's honor. *He really is just a kid, just an eight-year-old.* Yuna was very keenly reminding Soohyuk of that.

"How old are you?" asked Yuna warmly.

"Eight," answered Minjoon as he pressed his eyes with the back of his hands.

Yuna opened her arms to pull him into her embrace. "Yes, you're only eight years old. So, you just do what you want to do and leave all the worrying to the adults. We love you very much, so leave that all to us."

"But…" started Minjoon.

"You know, I took a taxi today. You know what happens if I get in a taxi, right?" said Yuna.

"You did?" Minjoon asked with wide eyes. He wasn't unaware of Yuna's claustrophobia. He'd seen her gasp for breath because she was having a panic attack, too. He'd been so scared that she might die then that he'd cried his heart out.

"I did. And I made it. Uncle Soohyuk helped, of course, but I could make it because of how much I love you," whispered Yuna.

"Really?" asked Minjoon.

"Really."

"But, Aunt Yuna…" started Minjoon again, but she interrupted him.

"Think about that tomorrow," she said sternly. She then patted his back and continued, "Leave all the worries to tomorrow. And when tomorrow comes, leave it again to tomorrow, and again, and again. You'll eventually start to see things you don't understand right now. You can think about all these when that time comes. You can do that."

"But I feel so bad. I feel like I've done something wrong to Mom and Dad. And to you," said Minjoon.

Pulling him closer, she whispered, "No, we're the ones who should be feeling like we've done something wrong. I'm so sorry we didn't realize what you were going through. We had no idea you were this worried. And you had no idea we make a lot more money than you think!"

"You make a lot of money?" asked Minjoon.

"Yup," answered Yuna.

Soohyuk sneakily chimed in, "I make a lot of money too. There's nothing for you to worry about."

Minjoon finally started to brighten up. But he soon frowned again. Yuna realized at once why that was.

"You miss Mom," she said.

Minjoon nodded. Of course he missed his mom. He probably wanted her to hold him in her arms and reassure him.

Taking out her phone, Yuna said, "So, I took a cab today, right? Isn't that amazing?"

"It is," answered Minjoon.

"What do you think Mom and Dad will take, then?"

"The car?"

"Nope, they're going to fly here," said Yuna.

Minjoon smiled. "Oh, come on, Aunt Yuna. I'm not that stupid."

"You don't believe me? Let's make a bet, then. How long do you think it'll take for them to get here?" asked Yuna.

"Umm…half an hour, since they're taking the car?" said Minjoon.

"What would you do if they came in five minutes?"

He looked disbelieving. "No way."

"Seriously. Okay, let's do this. If they really come in five minutes, promise me you'll tell us everything you're feeling, no matter how silly it seems, like you usually do. What do you say?" suggested Yuna.

Minjoon twisted his mouth, considering. "What if I win?"

"Then I'll make you kalbi patties every day."

His watery eyes started to twinkle without any signs of sorrow or distress. Yuna firmly dialed Yoonjae's number.

Soohyuk stood behind them in silence. He'd been playing hide-and-seek for too long. It took him nearly twenty-seven years to find his way back home. But Ms. Seo was still alive and well, so he'd succeeded. A bitter smile appeared on his face. The resentment and hatred he'd been holding inside him was now directed at himself. He was the cause of all this. It was he who'd made himself forget all those memories and not open up to anyone because he was afraid of hurting them. It was all him.

Hurried footsteps could be heard from outside. A moment later, the door burst open to reveal Kyungjo and Yoonjae.

"Mom!"

Kyungjo ran inside and pulled the surprised Minjoon firmly into her arms with a big smile. Minjoon dug into her embrace like a baby. Yoonjae hugged the two with his wide arms at once.

"Mom, Dad," murmured Minjoon.

Kyungjo kissed the crown of his head and tightened her arms

around him like he was her most precious treasure in the world. "My most beloved Minjoon Lee," she whispered.

"I was so scared…" said Minjoon.

"Yes, I know how scared you must have been."

"I didn't want to worry you, Mom."

"I know that's why you did that," said Kyungjo soothingly.

"It was my bad. I'm sorry for being sick," said Minjoon.

Tightening his arms around his wife and son, Yoonjae said, "No, you've done nothing you need to apologize for, Minjoon. Neither have we. None of us have done anything wrong."

"He's right, Minjoon. It's just that we've been introduced to a different, amazing world than the others. And we're going to be so happy in that world. Even more than now," said Kyungjo.

"Really?" asked Minjoon.

"Have I ever lied to you?"

Minjoon shook his head.

"We all love you so, so much. We'll do anything for you. So, all you have to do is enjoy this amazing world with Mom and Dad," continued Kyungjo.

"Really?" asked Minjoon again.

Yoonjae firmly answered, "Really. I promise."

"…Okay, then," answered Minjoon.

"So, you'll tell us everything next time instead of hiding it?" asked Yoonjae.

Minjoon glanced at Yuna. "Yes. I promised Aunt Yuna, too, so I will."

"Good. I'm so proud of you, kiddo." Yoonjae patted his head.

Soohyuk watched their heartwarming reunion for a little longer, then got up. Yuna followed him out of the room.

"Why don't you stay with them a little longer?" said Soohyuk. "I'm going to go see if there are any rooms open now."

"No, they'll be fine now. We're a pretty strong family," said Yuna.

Reaching out to affectionately brush her hair, he said, "It's going to be a long and hard fight from now on. But you'll make it, right?"

"Mhmm." Yuna nodded.

Soohyuk smiled. *Darn, she's cute.*

"We're going to have to pace ourselves, but we'll figure it out. We're going to make it," reaffirmed Yuna.

"I'll be with you, too. We'll make it till the end, all of us together," said Soohyuk.

"Yes!"

A smile of pure happiness appeared on his face. He then said, "Should we go take a look at your hands now?"

Yuna belatedly remembered what had happened to her palms. She had completely forgotten about them. "Once I see them get settled in. Let's have dinner with them after the tests, when Minjoon's allowed to leave."

"Sure," said Soohyuk.

The head nurse approached them and said, "Dr. Cha."

"Yes?"

"The room is ready."

"Thank you," said Soohyuk.

With her leading the way, Kyungjo and Yoonjae came out to the hall with Minjoon on his back. When Yuna started to follow them, Yoonjae stopped her.

"No, Yuna. You go on home and get some rest. You've done a lot today already. I bet you're going to have a fever," he said.

"It won't be that bad," said Yuna.

Yoonjae turned to Soohyuk this time and said, "She's definitely going to have a fever."

Nodding, Soohyuk wrapped his arm around her shoulders and pulled her toward her. "I'll come by tomorrow and check in," he said.

"Thank you for looking out for us," said Yoonjae.

"No problem," said Soohyuk.

The staff glanced at them as they walked past. They eyed each other as if to say that these people really were a tight family. And who knew Dr. Cha could be so kind? No, who knew he could even smile? They were all taken aback. When Dr. Cha smiled, he looked like a completely different person. His usual cold, hard demeanor melted away to reveal a much softer expression with smiling eyes.

Ms. Seo couldn't take her eyes off his face. Her heart was racing now. Something about his smile reminded her of Professor Cho. It had never occurred to her because she'd never seen him smile. But…

Ms. Seo scanned him from head to toe in search of places that were similar to Professor Cho and Hwihyun. Her gaze returned to his face. They locked eyes after a moment, because Soohyuk sensed her staring at him. Still, she didn't look away.

Soohyuk gazed at Ms. Seo. His lips drew a smile again, but only one side was pulled up like a mischievous child. She'd made it this long without giving up. Now she was standing in front of him, looking at him with such clear eyes and such a warm smile. Soohyuk's smile widened.

Hello, Mother.

CHAPTER 21

Soohyuk and Yuna headed home after he treated her palms. But when they'd only taken a couple steps, Yuna suddenly collapsed onto the ground like her legs had given out.

"Wait. My legs won't move," said Yuna. It was a crazy, heart-wrenching, but happy day.

Soohyuk crouched down with his back toward her, saying, "Hop on."

"No. That's embarrassing," said Yuna.

Soohyuk turned around and scooped her up in his arms without saying anything further.

"Hyuk," said Yuna.

"You said you didn't want a piggyback ride," said Soohyuk.

"I'd rather be on your back. I changed my mind. Come on."

Soohyuk let her down without saying another word and lowered down again with his back to her. His back seemed so wide today. *I wonder if he knows how grateful I am for him today,* she thought as she climbed onto his back. He started to walk slowly, almost like they were going for a leisurely stroll.

"Aren't I heavy?" asked Yuna.

"Not really," said Soohyuk.

"What do you want to eat when we get home? Do you want me to make you a sandwich?"

"I'm not hungry," said Soohyuk.

"Stop lying," teased Yuna.

"Okay, fine, I am hungry." He chuckled.

"What do you want to me to make if you don't want a sandwich?"

"I'd actually love some So-Mac. All my memories came back today," said Soohyuk.

Yuna slightly jumped. Her relaxed body tensed a little as well.

"Really? They did?" asked Yuna again.

Walking with her on his back, he calmly said, "So, I want to talk to you. Are you sure you'll be fine if I drink?"

She sensed he was worried about how tired she was. Grinning, she whispered, "I'll be fine with whatever you do."

"Then can we start with love?" asked Soohyuk.

"Yes," answered Yuna without hesitation.

Soohyuk sped up.

As soon as the door closed to separate them from the world, Soohyuk held Yuna tightly in his arms. He then lifted her chin to press his lips hard against hers. He'd been wanting to kiss her and feel her for hours. When she dug her fingers into his hair in response, he lifted her and took her shoes off. The shoes fell on the floor with a slight *clunk*. Her legs wrapped around his waist, and his hands found their way to her bottom to support her. Their lips joined once again.

His affection for her grew every time they kissed. It kept growing and growing.

Before she could do anything, she found herself lying on her back on the bed. Yuna struggled as he hurriedly ripped her clothes off. She'd sweated too much today. She grasped handfuls of her clothes in an effort to let him have her at her best. But he wouldn't let her. Her pants were soon tossed on the ground along with her underwear.

"Wait, Soohyuk. I want to take a shower first."

He stacked himself on top of her like he couldn't hear her, then aggressively took her lips as she tried to say something more. She had no choice but to follow his lead. She already knew very well that she couldn't stop him once he'd made up his mind. His tongue dug in frighteningly deep when her lips parted. He snatched her tongue at once and sucked on it as if it belonged to him.

His hand slid to the place that was revealed after he planted himself on top of her. He didn't hide his desire for her. He barely managed to stop vigorously kissing her till her lips swelled for a long enough time to whisper passionately, "I feel like I'm going nuts because I want you so much."

Enveloped in his fervid heat, she gazed at him and asked, "You want me that much?"

"To the point I only want to make love with you for the rest of our lives," said Soohyuk.

Yuna's heart reacted to his sincere confession. *Ba-boom, ba-boom.* Every time her heart beat, blood filled with her love for him coursed through her veins.

Soohyuk grabbed her hands. He pulled them above her head and pinned them down with one of his hands, while the other unbuckled his pants and pulled them down along with his underwear.

He started to carefully fill her up. Yuna held her breath. It was the same every time: the beginning was the hardest part. It was hard for her to let him in all the way. Knowing that, he took his time to fill her depths.

With an extremely satisfied moan, Soohyuk at last buried himself completely inside of her. He could feel her. He could feel her connected to him not only physically but emotionally as well. *So, this is what it means to make love...* He really did love her.

Yuna threw her head back. It was too deep from the start, as usual. He pulled out all the way to the entrance, then thrusted in till he hit her cervix. Yuna panted and moaned at his utterly vulgar movement of his hips.

Her moans drove him even crazier. He threw off his shirt he hadn't had enough time to take off and ripped off everything that was left on her body as well. Leaning down, he licked her erect nipples. One of his hands explored her hips and thighs, and the other caressed her breasts, which gently and alluringly shook every time he buried himself deep inside her. He took her bandaged hand and kissed her palm.

The sight of her was so titillating. Her skin was softer than silk. He roughly entered her, making her thrash as well. They grew more and more heated. The pants escaping their lips intensified. Her hand slid up his chest and pulled him closer when it was freed from his grasp. Their lips folded over each other again. He sucked on her tongue and swallowed her saliva. He couldn't take it anymore. He wanted to taste her everywhere. He did not ever want to leave her deep insides, but he had to in order to taste her. He boldly pulled out of her, then pinned her down with both hands so she couldn't run away.

When he lay down next to her and started to lick and taste her bare body, she squirmed to get out of his reach. She was worried she smelled from sweating so much. *Not this...* She protested, but it was no use. He was unable to contain his pleasure. She felt him bare his teeth from the excitement while kissing her. *Mmm... Ah...* It slightly stung, but that stinging came across as pleasure.

His kisses were never-ending. She thrashed again and again as he bit and kissed her entire body. The sensation was so intense that it felt like she could see flashing lights blinding her. When the multiple rounds of intense pleasure rendered her enervated, he came back to his place between her legs. She grunted as he thrusted inside her even stronger than before. Primal sounds filled the bedroom: rough panting, whispers of love they repeated to each other, kisses, and the wet sound they made as they rushed toward their climax.

All those sounds drove Soohyuk and Yuna further and further up.

Yuna could barely lift a finger. Their intense lovemaking had left her body sore.

Soohyuk looked at her with a grin, then leaned forward, whispering, "Come here."

Yuna let him take her into the bathroom in his arms. He skillfully bathed her, being careful with her injured hands like he'd done this a lot. Yuna leaned her head on his shoulder as he rubbed the soap over her body. Her mind was starting to become clear again. Like it was preparing itself to listen to his story. She hadn't heard him talk about his day yet, because he'd been too busy whispering words of love to her.

Soohyuk started to clean himself once he was done washing her.

"I'll meet you outside," said Yuna, feeling more energetic now.

"Okay," said Soohyuk.

She stepped outside after drying herself. She grabbed the clothes tossed on the ground and threw them in the laundry basket according to their color, then changed the sheets smelling strongly of them into clean ones.

After putting Soohyuk's change of clothes on the clean sheets, she took a moment to look at herself in the mirror. It was strange. Her body always felt as light as a feather after making love with him. Her skin glowed as well. And her face somehow seemed radiant.

"You're getting prettier, Yuna Lee," she mumbled to herself. Feeling embarrassed all of a sudden, she hid her face in her hands and scurried to the kitchen.

By the time Soohyuk came out of the shower, a delicious smell was permeating through the apartment. It smelled like the yaki udon she'd made him before. His stomach started grumbling.

When he almost ran into the kitchen, she greeted him with a grin. "Well, hello there."

She put the yaki udon on a plate and placed it on the table. Returning to the stove, she started stirring something that was boiling in the pot.

"What is that? You're making something else too?" said Soohyuk as he sat down and picked up his fork. He twirled a thick noodle around it.

"Yes. I wanted some soup, so I'm making a sausage stew called budae jjigae," answered Yuna.

"Can I have some too?" asked Soohyuk.

"Are you sure? It's spicy."

"You're making it, so it's all right. I'll just have a little diarrhea is all."

She frowned at him. "Hyuk."

Pretending like he couldn't hear her, Soohyuk stuffed his mouth with the yaki udon. Whatever she made, he was going to eat. Even if it were something spicy with tons of sliced chungyang pepper. He trusted her that much. *Just the two of us...* That's what she'd said. That they should start over with just the two of them. He was so happy about today because she was leaning on him as much as he trusted and leaned on her. *Stable.* Their feelings for each other and the ground they were standing on were both stable. When it just the two of them, at least. But... Soohyuk shook his head in an effort to shake off the foreboding feeling.

Yuna came and set down the budae jjigae, boasting its spicy

scent. Soohyuk jumped to his feet and brought over a bottle of soju, a bottle of beer, and two glasses.

"You want some?" he asked.

"Yes, please," said Yuna.

"Are you sure?"

Yuna sheepishly grinned and said, "I don't want to make you drink alone. I'll pace myself."

That warmed his heart. "All right. I'll take care of you even if you get drunk, so don't worry."

Yuna replied with an adorable smile, "Thank you. You're the best."

Soohyuk mixed two glasses of So-Mac and gave one to Yuna. After taking a sip of the cool drink, he picked up his spoon and tried the soup.

"What do you think?" asked Yuna.

"It's hot," he said.

"Of course it's hot. You need to blow on it."

Soohyuk did as she said. He scooped a slice of ham he liked and blew on it before putting it in his mouth.

"Is that better?" asked Yuna.

"It is better. It's really good."

"I'm glad."

The two focused on drinking and eating for a little bit.

After a couple glasses of So-Mac, Soohyuk finally began, "You know, people tend to lose themselves without even knowing it when they are repeatedly exposed to mental abuse, because they get used to it. They start to think that they deserve to be treated that way and end up becoming suicidal. That's what happened to her, too."

Yuna didn't know who he was referring to, but she attentively listened.

"Once you lose your sense of self, your love for your children starts faltering too. You want to do everything and anything for your children, but it stops at just being a thought. Your body won't follow through, and your will fades away too. The diminished sense of identity starts to destroy you, in a sense. Today…" Soohyuk paused for a moment to breathe. He continued, "Not every mother in the world is as strong as Minjoon's mother. And Minjoon's mother is able to be that strong because she has her husband and you supporting her."

He took a sip of So-Mac to swallow down the rush of emotions.

"That's really important," he continued. "That there's someone there to constantly remind you that you're not alone. But she didn't have anyone like that."

Who is he talking about? Could he perhaps be talking about his mother? Yuna wondered. Soohyuk had said that his lost family was at the hospital, but he had never specifically talked about them.

"She ended up getting married even though it was a marriage without a blessing, because she had me. And all hell broke loose. I remember that old witch spewing out hate at her relentlessly. She had a husband, but that wasn't enough to protect her. He was too kind to cut ties with that witch. He knew how much his mother had to go through, as well, to raise him. So, he tried to persuade her, praying that she'd change her mind. But he failed, and Mother was slowly dying."

Mother… The word, "Mother," in Korean had a great weight to it.

"We were abused a lot too. I was furious because of that, but worried at the same time not for me, but for my mother. I couldn't even sleep at night because I was so worried she might die. Father was busy working, so he didn't have a clue about any of this. The witch loved him so much that she didn't dare be that aggressive in front of him. Anyway, to me, it seemed like mother was dying. So, I thought of a way to save her." He grimaced and said, "And my solution was a game of hide-and-seek."

He let out a long sigh before continuing, "The reason I

couldn't remember was…not from the shock of being kidnapped, but from my own wish for Mother to stay alive until she had enough energy to find me. And I erased my memories because I knew I'd go back home when I got tired of hiding. I erased my own home, name, and age." He frowned as if he were about to burst into tears and said to Yuna, "It was all my choice in the end. I shut out my memories on my own, for Mother."

It was thanks to Minjoon that he'd found the last piece of a clue he thought he'd never find. What Minjoon said earlier had brought back his memory in its entirety. *For my family. For my beloved mom and dad.*

Yuna got up from her seat across from him and walked over to him to quietly give him a hug.

After taking a moment to breathe in her arms, he muttered like he was sneering at himself, "How ridiculous everything seems now. You have no idea how much I… How much I hated and cursed them until I came to Seoul—no, until not long ago, completely unaware of it all. You have no idea how much I hated them."

Still in her arms, he buried his head in his hands and continued, "I cursed them every time Danny beat me with his belt, and I cursed them when Danny pushed me off the staircase and broke my leg. I cursed them when I had to walk to the emergency room on my own, and I cursed them when I was bullied at school. I cursed them again when Kate chose me and was forced to divorce Danny. I always thought, if only they hadn't abandoned me, if only they hadn't sold me."

Yuna gently caressed his back as she kept listening.

"Horrible, isn't it? It was my decision, but I directed all the blame and resentment at them. And I hated my mother most, even though she was the one I wanted to save the most."

His voice trembled, heavy from bearing too much emotion. Still, Yuna didn't let go of him. Instead, she pulled him even closer to her. She wanted to let him know that she could understand him, even if she didn't express it with words. This man was very much like Minjoon in the sense that they both loved their families so much, to the point that they were willing to sacrifice themselves. But Soohyuk had had to come around a much longer and rougher road because he didn't have anyone to stop him.

"What's your real name?" asked Yuna.

Looking up at her, he answered, "Hwiyin Cho. I'm thirty-three years old."

As her eyes watered, Yuna teased, "Oh, no, and here you were, thinking you were two years older than you actually are."

"I know," said Soohyuk.

"So, who are your family members at the hospital? Can you tell me?" asked Yuna.

"My father's Sanghyung Cho. My brother's Hwihyun Cho. And...my mother's Yoonkyung Seo. My father and brother are doctors. And my mother is a volunteer at the pediatric emergency room," answered Soohyuk.

"Wait, Ms. Seo? The one we met at the emergency room today?" said Yuna, her eyes widening.

"Yes, she is my mother."

Yuna couldn't find anything to say for a moment. None of them recognized him, even though they were all so close by. *That must have been so hard for him,* she thought.

As if he realized what she was thinking, Soohyuk mumbled, "I've changed a lot. I was trying so hard to just survive that I... took after Danny. My eyes became cold and I never smiled, just like Danny. I was in a completely different world until now. No parent in the world would be able to recognize their son after he's grown to be such a different man."

Yuna gently caressed his face.

"They apparently weren't happy either. Hwihyun told me that his family became devoid of laughter. What have I done? I drove not only myself, but them into unhappiness too..." His voice trailed off.

"That wasn't your fault," said Yuna sternly. "That was the adults' fault. It was your parents' and the witch's fault for making you think that. All you did was love your family too much. Your only fault, if any, was that you loved your family the most when you should have loved yourself the most."

"Yuna, I can't reveal myself to them," said Soohyuk.

Yuna gasped. "Soohyuk…"

He shook his head. "I'm sorry, but I'm not brave enough to do that. I can't."

Yuna quietly gazed into his eyes. He looked into hers as well instead of looking away. The two stared at each other like that. It was Soohyuk who broke it off first. The hurt and guilt riddled in his eyes painfully dug into her heart.

Swallowing, Yuna carefully chose her words. "All right. Do as you wish. I understand what you're going through better than anyone. I happen to have a nephew who's too sensitive and full of love, just like you." Something hot tried to escape her throat all of a sudden. Barely swallowing it back down, she said, "But." She felt a lump in her throat this time. *Why is this man so sweet? Why is he so caring?* Struggling to keep down her sobs, she whispered, "Can you promise me that you won't run away if they come to you like you are magnets being attracted each other?"

Soohyuk's eyes started to water.

"I wish you would at least let them come if they want to talk to you about whatever it may be, or if they want to spend time with you, instead of pushing them away," she said.

Soohyuk felt a slight tinge of guilt. He was already planning on cancelling his plans with Hwihyun and Professor Cho. He was thinking of keeping a safe distance and trying not to run into them as much as possible.

It was Soohyuk who was gulping this time. He hadn't expected her to say something like this, and he knew he couldn't say no to her. This seemed hard to do. He didn't think he would be able to do this.

Yuna cradled his face in her hands and added while looking into his eyes, "I want you to do that. I think you'd be more comfortable if you did. I really do. I think it will help us become happier and stronger too."

Soohyuk just looked at her with his watery eyes without saying anything. Tears were welling up in her eyes as well.

"I'm always going to be here with you. So, even if you're afraid, try to fight it with me," she said.

She had a feeling that saying she thought his family would be still waiting for him, looking for him, and loving him wouldn't be of any consolation to Soohyuk. *Just the two of us.* That was what Soohyuk could comfortably take in. *The two of us.*

"For us. Promise me you won't run away for the sake of our happiness," whispered Yuna.

Soohyuk closed his eyes, then opened them. He nodded. There was no way he could have said no. Not to Yuna.

Then, Yuna awarded him with the most passionate kiss in the history of time.

———

That night, Professor Cho got a call from an unexpected person. Ms. Seo. Seeing her name pop up on his phone this late at night made his heart jump.

"Hello. Is something wrong? Are you ill?" he asked in a hurry.

"No, it's nothing like that. I just had no one else to call but you."

Professor Cho closed the book he was reading. "What is it? I'm here to listen."

Ms. Seo's voice was shaking.

"I think...I think I saw Hwiyin."

"What?" he asked, thinking of Soohyuk for some reason. "Where? Who was it?"

"Dr. Cha. I think he's our boy."

CHAPTER 22

Professor Cho and Ms. Seo sat across from each other early the next morning at a café. Both of their eyes were red from not getting enough sleep. Professor Cho looked at Ms. Seo. She was beaming, to the point that he could barely look at her. Sitting across from her right now felt so unreal because he hadn't seen her this bright in a long time.

"I couldn't sleep a wink," said Ms. Seo finally, after finishing half her cup of coffee.

"Neither could I," said Professor Cho.

"There's nothing definite yet, but the way he smiles looked just like you back when you gave me butterflies," she said sincerely. Her voice had a mixture of excitement and happiness to it that made his heart pound as well.

"I…I thought he looked a lot like Hwihyun when I saw him from the back," said Professor Cho. Ms. Seo's eyes twinkled when she heard that. "Everyone has a certain aura to them, and Dr. Cha's was so similar to Hwihyun that if I hadn't known it was him, I would have thought that it was Hwihyun. But…" He paused to pick up his mug and take a sip of coffee. "We have met many children, teenagers, and adults who didn't have a family. And there were those who looked surprisingly like Hwiyin…"

"I see what you mean," interrupted Ms. Seo. "You're saying that Dr. Cha could just be another man who looks like Hwiyin."

Looking at her with warm eyes, he said, "Our intuitions have never aligned like this, but I think we should still look into it a bit more."

"How would we do that?"

Professor Cho crossed his arms and got lost in his thoughts. He had considered a lot of options since early in the morning. He could do a DNA test, call H Hospital to ask about Dr. Cha's family…

Suddenly, Ms. Seo said, "I'm sorry, but I think I should tell you what I'm thinking first. Let's not go behind his back to do a background check. If he really turns out to be our boy and finds out that we figured it out by some test we ran or a background check we did behind his back, I think he'll be disappointed."

Professor Cho paused his thinking and looked at Ms. Seo.

"It's been twenty-seven long years," she continued. "I don't think any scientific revelation will make all those years between us go away. I know…what kind of a man Dr. Cha is. He is cold, levelheaded, and he never lets his guard down to anyone. Except one person. To a son like that, scientific proof is only a process of verification. I don't think that proof will warm our son up to us. So, just try to feel first. Try to feel our son as parents before running any tests. I think you'll be able to come up with a good way to overcome those twenty-seven years when you are certain about this like I am."

"So, you are certain about this?" asked Professor Cho.

She answered with the brightest smile, "Yes, I am certain. And I've been thinking about a way to overcome those twenty-seven years. I'm so happy I can think of the next step like this."

Professor Cho started to smile as well. "All right, we'll do that then. I made plans to drink with Hwihyun and Dr. Cha once the results of my second tests are out. I'll try then."

"Yes, that sounds like the perfect time. Please let me know what you think," she said.

"I will," he answered.

Looking out at the street covered in green outside the window, she said, "It's a beautiful world, isn't it?"

Professor Cho grinned.

When Soohyuk appeared on the ninth floor of the hospital, where the pediatric ward was located, the nurses and residents started buzzing about. They organized their stations and fixed their attire. It was their way of preparing for Soohyuk's visit.

It made sense, since their work was closely related to Soohyuk's. The pediatric ward was where the patients were sent to after he saved them. The first time he'd come to visit, they hadn't recognized who he was because he was in plainclothes, and they'd been faced with God's wrath. He'd started criticizing them on the businesslike manner they addressed the children, then gone on to yell at them for telling the children to stop crying. He'd even laughed in their faces when they told the children that only fools cried.

But they hadn't been able to say a word to him, because he wasn't saying anything that was incorrect. All they could do was complain behind his back that he was rude and arrogant. As time passed, though, people's assessment of him started to change. Something about the way he checked in on the progress of serious operations and the way he came all the way up to the ninth floor to see how the patients were doing touched their hearts.

The number of people complaining about Soohyuk had started to decrease at a certain point. When he stopped by to see a patient, they would follow him to see how he conducted himself with the children. Watching him awoke the passion that was sleeping within them. Naturally, they started to change as well. They thought things through once more before talking to the patients. They tried not to dismiss them for being young. Some residents even went to visit the emergency room during their spare time to learn how to better locate the children's veins. Soohyuk didn't once yell at the residents who were trying to learn. He never laughed at them either. He taught them again and again until they got it.

This morning, Soohyuk quickly headed through the pediatric ward to the room Minjoon was in. When he entered, Yoonjae and Kyungjo greeted him with delight.

"Are you finding everything okay?" he asked in a businesslike manner.

Kyungjo answered with a smile, "Absolutely. The staff here couldn't be kinder. This is all thanks to you, Soohyuk."

"I'm glad you think so." He then asked Minjoon while checking on him, "What about you? Any inconveniences, anyone bothering you without any explanations?"

"Not at all. They're all scared of you. You must be a really scary doctor," said Minjoon.

Yoonjae and Kyungjo awkwardly smiled at his honesty. It was true. Whatever his reputation was around here, everyone was being extremely careful and kind to them.

Soohyuk said, "They'd have no reason to be scared of me if they did their jobs correctly. You're leaving this afternoon once the tests are all done, right?"

"Yup. The hospital smells," said Minjoon, wrinkling his nose.

"It does. It smells bad," said Soohyuk. After thoroughly checking everything, he turned to face Yoonjae and Kyungjo and said, "Call me the day the results come back. I'll go with you."

"Thank you," said Yoonjae.

"Thank you so much," added Kyungjo.

Suddenly, her phone rang. Her kind smile vanished. "Excuse me for one second."

When she left with an angry expression, Yoonjae whispered, "It must be Minjoon's homeroom teacher."

"Nasty meathead," said Minjoon from behind as he burst into laughter.

"Would you like to have dinner with us later?" Yoonjae asked Soohyuk. "Yuna said you should be free."

"Sure. I'll come with Yuna in the evening," answered Soohyuk.

"Thank you so much for being here for us," said Yoonjae, reaching out to squeeze Soohyuk's hand.

Soohyuk held Yoonjae's hand tightly as well. When he stepped out of the room after saying goodbye, he found Kyungjo on the phone at the other end of the hallway. Her expression was so full of fury that he couldn't help but walk toward her.

"So, Mr. Han, are you saying that you've done nothing wrong? Have you no consideration of the pain and fear my Minjoon would have had to suffer?" she said.

"No, I'm not saying that," the teacher answered. "It was my mistake, yes, but it wasn't intentional. What kind of a teacher would be so irresponsible like that? But, Ms. Park, think about it. Weren't you the one who was getting anxious first? Why did you send him to school if it was going to worry you that much?"

"Are you seriously asking me that right now, Mr. Han? Is this how you treat all your students? Do you not have children of your own?" asked Kyungjo furiously.

"Of course I do. All I'm saying is that I wouldn't send a kid with that kind of sickness to school. You need to consider that it might be a hindrance to the other students as well. I'm trying to reason with you, here, Ms. Park."

"Fine, I'll try to reason with you too," Kyungjo spat through gritted teeth. "I will make sure no other children will have to spend their first ever year of school in a nightmare because of a teacher like you, although you don't even deserve to be called a teacher. I'm going to report you to the principal, the department of education, and the human rights commission."

"As you wish. I've done nothing to be scared of."

"Yes, I will do as I wish." She paused when she locked eyes with Soohyuk. She said in a more furious tone than she'd intended, "I just can't talk any sense into him. He keeps saying that it's my fault for sending Minjoon to school."

When Soohyuk held out his hand, Kyungjo handed him her phone.

"Hello, Mr. Han?" said Soohyuk.

"Is this Mr. Lee? I don't understand why you keep wanting to make this a bigger deal than it has to be. I've been teaching for thirty years, and I've never had to deal with something like this. No good for Minjoon's going to come out of this either."

"There is one good thing for Minjoon that's going to come out of this. He will learn that we have his back," said Soohyuk.

"Well…"

"How old are you, Mr. Han?" asked Soohyuk.

"What does that have to do with anything?"

"Are you over sixty?"

"I'm fifty-three!"

"Your metabolic rate is going to drop notably in the coming years," said Soohyuk. "Your skin will hang loose like a turkey's, age spots will cover your face and hands, you will experience urinary problems, and climbing the stairs will become harder by the day."

"Excuse me?" The teacher's voice rose.

"Your hair will lose its shine," Soohyuk continued, "and you will fear your heart might stop when it starts pounding unlike ever before when you walk just a little quicker than usual. Your face will be covered in wrinkles, your cognitive abilities will deteriorate, and your reflexes will become so slow that you will not be able to react to unexpected situations in time. Your thoughts will become more closed-minded, and you will turn into a pervert who rejoices in others' unhappiness."

"Excuse me, Mr. Lee! What is this all about?"

"I'm telling you the truth of how you will die. Do you know why your generation is so looked down upon? Because you want to be respected as an authority when you treat others like they're less than you. Meaning, you are thick, inconsiderate, and thoughtless. Also." He paused.

Kyungjo stared at him with her jaw dropped.

"This is Minjoon's uncle, not his father. And I just told you about the standard process of aging as a doctor. That is how you are going to age, and how you will die. If you don't believe me, come find me. I'll tell you more about it in detail. I am Soohyuk Cha, a specialist at S University Hospital's pediatric emergency room."

"Never have I been insulted like this in my life!"

"If a universal truth is an insult to you, what on earth was it that you told Minjoon? Mockery?"

"I, uh, well…"

"Here's Ms. Park again," he said.

Kyungjo took the phone with the shocked expression still on her face.

"If the meathead says he wants to see me, tell him to come to the pediatric emergency room," said Soohyuk.

Kyungjo smiled wide. "All right, Soohyuk."

"Excuse me, then." He nodded before walking toward the elevator.

Kyungjo watched him for a moment, then took a deep breath and said, "Kyungjo Park speaking."

"Ms. Park, I think I owe you an apology. When can I come see you? I admit, I hadn't thought things through."

"Yes, you do owe me an apology. And you will still pay for what you did. I'm not going to just forgive you," said Kyungjo.

"Let me first come talk to you in person."

"Fine. When will you be coming? We're leaving in the afternoon," said Kyungjo.

"I'll be there by two o' clock."

"All right. We're at S University Hospital, ninth floor on the west wing, room 904," she said.

"Great. Umm, Ms. Park, about the gentleman who just spoke on the phone…"

"He is Minjoon's uncle, and if you have anything you wish to say to him, I'll let you meet him," she said.

"No, no. That's not what I meant. I'll see you at two."

"Fine," she said. Hanging up, she ran to the elevator to find Soohyuk, but he was already gone.

Yoonjae watched with quizzical eyes as Kyungjo came into the room with a big smile. He'd never seen her smile like that after getting a call from Minjoon's teacher.

Kyungjo said to Yoonjae, "Yuna has a good eye, just like you."

"What do you mean?" asked Yoonjae.

"Mr. Han is going to come at two o' clock later to apologize," said Kyungjo.

His eyebrows rose in surprise. "Really? He was so stuck in his ways."

"Soohyuk got him good," said Kyungjo.

"Kyungjo," said Yoonjae as if in warning.

Kyungjo chuckled. "I couldn't be happier. Or more grateful. He really got him good."

Yoonjae ended up cracking a smile as well.

CHAPTER 23

As Yoonjae's family got settled into their seats at the Korean restaurant they'd made reservations for, Soohyuk and Yuna appeared.

"We're not late, are we?" asked Yuna as she sat down.

"Not at all. We just got here," answered Kyungjo.

When they all settled down, the waitstaff started bringing their appetizers. Yuna couldn't help but smile when she saw that Minjoon wasn't embarrassed he was having trouble using the chopsticks. It seemed like he'd grown during that one night he'd spent at the hospital. It was hard even for adults to accept their current selves, yet Minjoon was doing it. *What an amazing kid*, she thought.

As they ate, they shared about their day with each other. The test procedures, Minjoon's teacher coming all the way to the hospital and begging for them to forgive him, and how they were still filing a complaint.

"What a productive day you've had," said Yuna.

"Aunt Yuna, you have no idea how mad Dad got at Mr. Han. I've never seen Dad that mad," said Minjoon.

"Really?" Yuna smiled. "It must have been awesome to have someone so supportive on your side."

Minjoon sheepishly smiled with his spoon in his mouth. That smile was so adorable that everyone at the table smiled too. They were relived. Minjoon's smile seemed like a promise of a hopeful future.

When desserts came out after the main course, the subject of discussion naturally switched to Soohyuk and Yuna.

"So, what are your plans for the wedding?" asked Yoonjae.

They'd told them that they were getting married in December.

Soohyuk said, "We're planning on having it small. We're going to have the ceremony and the reception with only family, and we'll be making all the reservations. Yuna and I are the ones getting married, after all."

"I heard you're here as a part of an exchange program. Are you going to return to the States once it's done?" asked Yoonjae.

Grabbing Yuna's hand, he answered, "No, I'm planning on settling down here. I got a job offer at the hospital as well."

Kyungjo clasped her hands together, beaming. Of course, it didn't matter to her where Yuna lived as long as she was happy, but she couldn't help feeling relieved that she would stay by their sides. Yoonjae felt the same, although he didn't outwardly show his delight.

Hiding her wide grin with her hands, Kyungjo said to Soohyuk, "I'm sorry, I'm just happy." She then asked as quick as a cat, "So, what do you like so much about our Yuna?"

Yoonjae cleared his throat in an effort to stop her, but it was no use.

"What? I know you want to know, too. So, what do you like about Yuna?" asked Kyungjo again.

Yoonjae was now looking at Soohyuk too. Yes, he was indeed curious what drew this man to his dear Yuna.

"Everything," answered Soohyuk.

"Oh, come on, now," teased Kyungjo.

"Kyungjo," said Yuna and Yoonjae at the same time, frowning at her.

Soohyuk cracked a smile and answered, "I think Yoonjae's going to get mad if I get into the details."

"Oh, I see. Wow, are you cheeky," teased Kyungjo.

Yoonjae and Yuna looked at each other. There was something similar about Kyungjo and Soohyuk, though they hadn't noticed it before.

After a moment of silence, Soohyuk looked up at Yoonjae and said, "I don't know if you already know, but I was adopted. I assume that doesn't make me the most ideal match for your sister, in your eyes."

Yoonjae neither confirmed nor denied it.

"I grew up in an environment that was not so great, and I went through a lot of hardships, but I became a doctor thanks to my mother," continued Soohyuk. "My mother is working at a small rehabilitation hospital in the States. I'm going to invite her to Korea before the wedding, so I will introduce you to her then. I led a solitary lifestyle until recently because I don't particularly enjoy socializing, and I have strong opinions and passion for my work to the point that my previous coworkers in the States called me a tyrant."

He raised his hand to caress Yuna's shoulder. Yoonjae's gaze followed his hand. Yuna, who was always so easily frightened and would tremble if a man so much as came near her, was letting him caress her. In fact, she actually seemed to relax at his touch. He'd never thought this day would actually come for his Yuna, his baby sister.

"But I just can't say no to this woman. I always end up listening to her. I can't imagine a life without her anymore. I want to live with my first and last woman for the rest of my life," said Soohyuk as a smile as warm as the sunset widened on his face.

Yoonjae stared at his smile. He kept staring until Kyungjo nudged him in the side to say something nice to them. *Ahem, hem.* Yoonjae cleared his throat.

"I trust that you and Yuna will…" he started, but he soon choked up. He had a sudden flashback of the times he'd held Yuna's tiny hand as they were sent from one relative to another. He recalled that December day they were sent to the orphanage. And the nights when they relied on each other's warmth to fall asleep, frightened by all the strangers around them.

"Yoonjae," called Yuna.

Yoonjae's watery eyes looked at her.

"I'll be happy. Like you and Kyungjo," she said.

Even more tears welled up in his eyes. Yuna was no different.

"Yes, I know you will. But don't forget that I'm always here for you," said Yoonjae.

"Mhmm," answered Yuna.

"If he ever hurts you, you let me know," he said, with a serious look of warning.

"Mhmm," answered Yuna again.

Kyungjo grinned and said to Soohyuk, "You'd better get used to their love. There's no use being jealous."

A faint smile appeared on Soohyuk's face.

Professor Cho had been waiting for this day all week. The day he was getting the second test. As soon as he got a call from Soohyuk, he sprang to his feet. When he went down to the pediatric emergency room, he found Hwihyun waiting for him.

"I asked Dr. Cha to tell me when it was time," said Hwihyun.

"Yes, thank you for being here with you," said Professor Cho.

"I'm so excited to raid your wallet, Father." Hwihyun grinned.

"All right, now." He chuckled.

The two went into the emergency room side by side.

Soohyuk, who had been waiting for them, found himself looking away when they appeared. He tried not to, but he couldn't help it. But it didn't matter anyway, since they came walking straight toward him.

"Let's get this over with," said Professor Cho.

Hearing his gentle baritone voice made shivers run down Soohyuk's spine. Snippets of past memories came back to him.

"I don't want someone like you!" the young Soohyuk shouted.

"Someone like me?" said his father.

"I don't want someone who makes us cry everyday like you!" he screamed.

The Professor Cho of the present interrupted his remembrance and said, "Have you had lunch yet?"

Standing next to Professor Cho while he tried to strike up a conversation with Soohyuk, Hwihyun looked around the emergency room in search of Ms. Seo. He was worried because she'd had a light fever this morning. He soon found her. She smiled warmly when she saw him as well and made an "OK" sign with her fingers. Seeing that she already seemed like she was doing much better, Hwihyun relaxed.

"This way," Soohyuk said as he led the way.

Following him, Professor Cho mumbled, "Have you made your decision yet?"

"On what?" said Soohyuk.

"On the contract with our hospital," answered Professor Cho.

"You're too rash," said Soohyuk more coldly than ever.

Just listening to him made chills run down Professor Cho's spine. He now realized that Ms. Seo was right. Twenty-seven years. Even if it turned out that Soohyuk was indeed Hwiyin, the most pressing matter would be finding a way to bridge the gap of all those years.

"If you have any questions at all, bring them to me," said Professor Cho. "I'll make time for you any time of the day."

Soohyuk prepared to draw blood without giving an answer.

"Do you remember how delighted I was when you first came?" asked Professor Cho.

Soohyuk stared at him.

He continued with a grin, "I'm even more delighted now than I was then. The longer you stay here, the more it delights me that we're in the same space."

Soohyuk finished drawing his blood and said, "I'll let you know through Ms. Jeon as soon as the results are out."

Pulling down his sleeve and putting his gown back on, Professor Cho said, "I'm sure that it'll be nothing. Remember we said we'd all go for a drink? How's tonight?"

Pausing, Soohyuk thought for a moment. It would be uncomfortable. He wouldn't know how or what to say if he saw them privately when he was already feeling this uncomfortable around them. He didn't want to.

He impassively said, "If the reason you want to meet with me is the contract, I'll give you the answer right now. I will be staying here. So, no need to set private meetings with me anymore. Isn't that what you were trying to achieve tonight anyway?"

"No, no. That's completely separate from our plans for drinks. Hwihyun will give you a call. You have no idea how much I've been looking forward to this," answered Professor Cho.

Soohyuk narrowed his eyes. He couldn't pinpoint what it was, but he could sense that something had changed about the way he was talking to him. It felt somehow lighter and more casual. He could feel it as clear as day even though he couldn't quite put his finger on it.

From behind, a knocking was heard and Hwihyun peeped in. "Are you done?"

"Yes, Hwihyun. You'd better hurry up with that reservation. This guy seems to be getting cold feet," answered Professor Cho.

Hwihyun frowned. "We can't have that, now. We made a

promise. Didn't we, Dr. Cha? Of course, this is all if your results come out fine, Father."

Soohyuk stared at them. *If the results don't come out well...*

He quietly replied, "I'll be waiting for your call."

———

Professor Cho kept tapping his desk with his fingers, feeling anxious. The results should have come back by now, but they hadn't given him a call yet.

"Why is it taking so long?" he mumbled.

He recalled the way Soohyuk had stared at him. Cold eyes. Lips clamped shut. *Our boy...*

A knocking at the door pulled him out of his thoughts.

"Come in," he said.

The door slid open and a nurse peeped in. "Pediatric emergency room is on line one."

"Thank you," he answered.

He picked up the phone as soon as she left.

"Hello, Professor Cho. This is Sangoak Jeon."

"Hello, Ms. Jeon," he said.

"The results came back. You have no other irregularities, but you do have Gilbert's syndrome. I trust you already know, but you should..."

Professor Cho stayed on the line for a little longer without paying much attention to what she was saying before hanging up. It was Gilbert's syndrome, as Soohyuk had suspected.

"Not half bad," he said to himself, feeling especially proud of Soohyuk's keen eyes that had caught such a subtle sign.

He'd said that it might just be that Soohyuk and Hwiyin looked alike when he was with Ms. Seo before, trying to keep a cool head, but he found himself becoming excited every time he saw Soohyuk. *That cold, aloof young man being our son...* If it was true, what had made him change so much? Question after question arose in his mind.

His phone rang. It was Hwihyun.

"Did you get the call with the results yet?"

Professor Cho's eyes watered a little. Hwihyun was such a good son, and he'd only ever made him worried. He'd never made him happy.

"It's Gilbert," he said. "Make the reservation and let Dr. Cha know."

"Father…"

"I'll go wherever you want. I'll drink and talk about whatever you want, too," he assured him.

"All right. I'll give you another call after looking up some places."

Professor Cho hung up and waited for Hwihyun to call back, feeling anxious again. But he didn't have to wait that long.

"Hello?" he said as he picked up the phone.

"6:30 tonight, at Uh Young Boo Young."

"What? Where is that?"

"Uh Young Boo Young. It's a bar with really good jjigae. I'll text you the address."

"All right," he answered.

"Don't be late. And don't forget to bring your wallet. Their menu can get pretty expensive."

"Yes, all right," he answered again.

"Oh, by the way, Dr. Cha's a real heavyweight. Also, he's not very talkative, so you don't need to worry about him telling anyone whatever we talk about tonight. But you should refrain from these topics."

"Which topics?" he asked.

"Do not at all costs ask him about his family history. I know you're not someone who would, but I'm just mentioning it because I know how interested you are in him. Don't ask him private questions like that."

Professor Cho frowned. He was planning on asking various questions about Dr. Cha's family when they'd shared a sufficient amount of alcohol.

"Is there a reason I shouldn't?" asked Professor Cho.

Hwihyun was silent for a moment.

"…Father, can you keep a secret?"

"Of course I can," he said.

"He was apparently abused in his childhood. He only said it when we were getting drunk last time, but I think he was telling the truth. He made it sound like it was nothing, but it was upsetting to me. I don't know. It felt too close to home for some reason. So, make sure you don't ask him about his past, Father."

Professor Cho's face fell. *Abused. Our son was abused...* His heart started to race.

"Father?"

He was too shocked to say anything.

"Father, are you listening?"

He finally forced himself to speak. "All right, I'll be sure not to do that. Whatever you two talk about, I'll just listen. I won't get in the way."

"Thank you, Father."

"No, I should be thanking you," he said, feeling a sudden lump in his throat. Barely managing to swallow that back down, he continued, "For inviting someone like me."

"Oh, enough with that, Father. You're already bringing the mood down. I'm just excited to drink all the things you're going to buy us." The grin came through in Hwihyun's voice.

Professor Cho finally managed to say with a little more vigor, "Yes, drink your fill tonight. I'll be there to take care of you until the end of the night."

"Great, I'll see you soon, then."

"See you soon," he answered.

After hanging up, he got to his feet with a determined look on his face. He was going to take some preliminary measures. Time to put something in his stomach and drink a little something for the liver. He had two sons waiting to drink with him tonight.

After finishing the phone call he did not really want to make in the first place, Soohyuk went into the apartment building, lightly grumbling. He'd let five calls go to voicemail, but Hwihyun was persistent. He'd had no choice but to pick up on the sixth.

"Jeez, why are they in such a hurry?" muttered Soohyuk.

Now I don't even have time to mentally prepare myself, he thought with a frown. As soon as he'd picked up, and before he could even say anything, Hwihyun had told him they were meeting at the place they went to last time, Uh Young Boo Young, and that he would text him the address. "So, don't be late," he'd said. Soohyuk was about to tell him that he was busy tonight when he remembered what Yuna had said. So, he'd ended up telling him that he would be there.

"This is all because of you," he mumbled as he leaned against the cold elevator wall. Thinking of seeing Yuna soon made him feel better, at least.

The moment he opened the front door of their apartment, he heard Yuna's laughter and the sound of music. Yuna was on a video call with Minjoon.

"Oh, you're right. It does look different," she said.

"Now you try!" said her nephew. "I bet you can't do it as well as me."

"Whoa, whoa, is this a challenge to the great master? You should know by now how good my impressions are."

"Gorilla! Go!"

The next moment, Soohyuk had to cover his mouth with his hand to stop the laughter from escaping his lips. Yuna let her arms hang down low till they touched the ground and started jumping, grunting, "Ooh, ooh," like a gorilla.

"Giraffe!"

This time, she elongated her neck as much as possible and rose onto her tiptoes. Soohyuk was now shaking, trying not to laugh out loud. *Oh, man, this is good.*

"Python!"

Yuna went flat against the wall and started squiggling sideways in an S curve.

"What is that?"

"You can't see it if I do it on the ground," said Yuna as she kept squiggling.

"Wow, you're a genius. A genius!"

"Right?" she said, coming to a stop.

"Oh, yes! The best of the best!"

Lightly pounding her lower back, and feeling tired from all the squiggling, she looked at Minjoon on the screen.

"Does your back hurt?" he asked.

"Of course it does!" said Yuna.

"Oh, no, you're getting old! Mom never gets tired however much she dances."

"Oh, you just wait until you come back to Seoul," said Yuna as she teasingly threatened him.

"Are you mad, Aunt Yuna?"

"Yes, I'm mad." She made an exaggerated scowl.

"You won't be sad while you wait for us, then, right? You're not going to be lonely without us, are you? We'll be back really soon. In just one week."

Yuna burst into laughter. *Look at this little rascal.* "Were you just trying to make me feel better?" She hadn't yet noticed Soohyuk was in the apartment, witnessing her video call.

"Yup."

"Oh, Minjoon, I'm sorry to disappoint you, but I'm so happy I don't need to make your snacks for a full week. I could sing!" said Yuna.

Minjoon's laughter burst through the phone's speaker. "Mom says that you should just go to Uncle Soohyuk when you feel sad."

Yuna cracked a smile. Minjoon's family had left this morning to go on a week-long camping trip. They'd decided that Minjoon would stop going to school now. His condition was still getting worse every day, so they had a lot to talk about amongst themselves. This trip was going to bring a lot of change for them. A lot of good changes. Yuna suddenly felt a lump in her throat. Her breath started to shake.

"Don't cry, Aunt Yuna. I'll draw you pictures every day and send them to you."

"I don't want stick figures." Yuna sniffled.

"Oh, come on, now. Don't say no to my stick figures. I'll draw Uncle Soohyuk with you too this time."

"All right, send them to me. I will cherish them all. Also, Minjoon." Yuna paused.

"Yes, Aunt Yuna?"

"Have lots of fun. I promise I won't be crying the whole time," she said.

"Okay. See you in a week. Make kalbi patties for me when I get back!"

"I promise I will."

"I love you, Aunt Yuna. I love Mom, Dad, and you all equally."

"I love you all equally too." Yuna smiled.

Suddenly, an indistinguishable sound was heard, and Minjoon turned away from a moment. He came back onto the screen looking serious.

"Mom says you're lying. She's saying that you love Uncle Soohyuk the most. Is that true? What about me?"

"Ask Mom if she doesn't need help with dinner from now on."

"Mom says she's sorry."

"That's more like it." Yuna smiled again. "Have lots of fun, and I'll see you when you're back."

"Okay."

Soohyuk had been standing silently in the back of the room and watching them the whole time, amused by their conversation. When Yuna ended the call and turned around, she jumped at the sight of him.

She hadn't heard him come inside. Her mind automatically went to the impressions of a gorilla, giraffe, and python she'd just done.

She asked in a barely audible voice, "When did you get here?"

"A while ago," he answered with a smile, still leaning against the wall.

"You didn't...see everything, did you?" she asked, starting to blush.

"What? The gorilla? The giraffe? Or the python?" He caught Yuna before she could successfully run away and pulled her into his arms, saying, "You're so adorable. So adorable that I just want to bite your face off."

Soohyuk's lips pressed against hers, and in spite of her embarrassment, she kissed him back, welcoming his affection.

CHAPTER 24

It was on their crumpled bed, a little while later, that Soohyuk told her his evening plans.

"Really?" she asked.

Reaching his hand to brush her bare back, he mumbled, "I was going to say no, but then I remembered the promise I made to you."

Lying on her stomach, Yuna looked into his eyes and said, "Soohyuk."

"Yes?"

"How do you feel?"

He sighed. "I don't want to go. I don't want to see them, either. But I made a promise, so I'm going to keep it. I'm not going to run away."

Yuna grinned and kissed his forehead.

He closed his eyes to savor the moment, then added, "Also, he was being way too persistent. He wouldn't stop calling until I picked up."

"Who?" asked Yuna.

"Umm...my brother, Hwihyun," answered Soohyuk hesitantly.

With a bright smile, she whispered, "It's so nice to hear you call him that, Hyuk."

Soohyuk played with her hair, smiling.

After savoring that gentle tingle from his fingers, Yuna said, "This just occurred to me, but your brother…"

"What about my brother?" said Soohyuk.

"What if he's still playing hide-and-seek? He never found you. What do you think?" asked Yuna.

Soohyuk felt as if something hit him in the head. He'd never thought of it that way.

"You said it was a game of hide-and-seek. But he never found where you were hiding," continued Yuna.

Soohyuk lifted his naked body to sit up. A conversation he'd shared with Hwihyun before came to his mind.

"I'll call you Dr. Cha. There's only one person in the world I call 'Hyung.' "

"It was my brother's favorite song. He had such a good ear that people said he was a genius since he was very young. He was especially gifted in the linguistic areas."

'Just the Two of Us.' That was a song he'd taught Hwihyun. It was a song about what a father wanted to tell his son. Though Professor Cho never said it out loud, he wanted to believe that their father felt the same way about them as the father in the lyrics to his son. Later, Soohyuk had changed the lyrics to make the depressed Hwihyun laugh. But Professor Cho never caught on to the meaning of that or why his sons kept singing that song. He just kept listening without doing anything, even when they changed the lyrics into something much meaner out of spite.

After watching him think for a moment, Yuna whispered, "Good thing you're seeing them tonight, right?"

"Yes, I suppose so," answered Soohyuk.

"Can you help me up? I'll fix you something for dinner," said Yuna.

Soohyuk grabbed her hand to pull her up, then pulled her into his arms instead.

He whispered in her ear, "I love you."

———

Loud, indistinguishable chatter greeted Soohyuk as soon as the door to the bar opened. As his automatic frown started to turn into a nasty scowl, someone's hand shot into the air at the back of the bar. Soohyuk's eyes found Hwihyun at once. Both he and Professor Cho were already sitting in their seats when he arrived at the table.

"Hello," said Soohyuk.

"Yes, welcome," said Professor Cho. "It's a little crowded because it's Friday night. Is that all right with you? If you don't like the noise, we can go somewhere else."

"It doesn't matter," said Soohyuk.

"No? Great," Professor Cho answered, then started opening a bottle that was on the table. He offered it to Soohyuk and said, "First, drink this."

It was a drink that was supposed to help with hangovers. There was more than one bottle on the table.

"The sooner you start taking care of yourself, the better," he said.

Soohyuk coldly stared at Professor Cho, who opened the lid and pushed it toward him without even giving him a chance to decline.

"Am I still a stranger to you?" said Professor Cho.

Soohyuk replied, "It's more that I already had dinner at home. I don't need any."

"At home? Is there someone taking care of you at home? I thought you lived alone," said Professor Cho as he took a sip of the drink.

Soohyuk nonchalantly answered, "I live with my fiancée."

It was Hwihyun who showed a visible response to that. Turning toward Soohyuk in surprise, he asked, "Is it her? The lady you were with in Jamsil?"

"Yes," replied Soohyuk.

"Congratulations!" Hwihyun exclaimed. "I've been wondering, did she come with you from the States?"

"No, I met her in Korea," said Soohyuk.

Hwihyun's eyes widened. "Really? You met her here?"

"That's correct," said Soohyuk.

"Wow, I can't believe it. How did you two meet?"

"We just kept running into each other, and then I asked her to move in with me."

This time, Professor Cho's eyes widened as well.

"Is there something wrong with living with someone you love?" asked Soohyuk.

"No, no, that's not what I meant. I'm just surprised. Kudos to her, seriously," said Hwihyun jokingly.

Soohyuk shrugged and said, "Aren't we going to order something?"

Hwihyun looked a little confused. "But you don't like eating out."

"Yuna made me jjigae a couple times. It wasn't bad."

"Yuna?" asked Professor Cho.

"Yes, my fiancée's name is Yuna Lee," said Soohyuk.

"What a beautiful name. So, what kind of jjigae should we order?" asked Professor Cho.

"Budae jjigae. Without ramen noodles," said Soohyuk.

"What do you say, Hwihyun?"

"Sounds good to me. We're drinking So-Mac, right?" asked Hwihyun.

Both Professor Cho and Soohyuk nodded at the same time.

After ordering everything, Hwihyun undid a button on his shirt and said, "I'll show you what I'm really capable of tonight."

He glanced at Soohyuk, then muttered to himself, "Darn it. I still don't have anyone when even someone like him does."

"If you want to meet someone, you need to make time for that," advised Professor Cho.

"It's not that I don't have time. I just haven't given it much thought because I haven't seen any good examples," said Hwihyun.

Professor Cho's face fell when he heard that. No wonder Hwihyun had a pessimistic view of love when he hadn't set a good example of a happy family as his father.

"You're unable to find anyone because you're limiting yourself," said Soohyuk. "Try widening your view. Then you'll see that there are more than just unhappy people in the world."

Hwihyun couldn't help but be impressed with Soohyuk. He'd had an unhappy childhood as well, but he'd found love. *This man is really out of the ordinary in every way,* thought Hwihyun.

"Don't think that others' unhappy endings mean that you will end up unhappy too. Our lives are separate from our parents'," added Soohyuk.

His words felt like a dagger in his heart to Professor Cho. Especially because he was assuming to a certain degree that Soohyuk was Hwiyin.

A server brought over the budae jjigae and the drinks they'd ordered.

"Allow me," said Hwihyun as he took the bottles of soju and beer. Mixing the two, he said to Soohyuk, "I'm warning you now, the best of the heavyweights at S University Hospital is actually my father, not me. So, you'd better pace yourself. You might just end up wasted."

Placing three glasses of So-Mac in front of each of them, Hwihyun said with a flourish of his hand, "I present to you, my finest works."

"Thank you," said Professor Cho.

The three clinked their glasses and drank. The first glass of

So-Mac had a delightful bite to it. Professor Cho scooped the bubbling budae jjigae into bowls and gave the first one to Soohyuk and the second one to Hwihyun.

"You must be in a really good mood tonight, Father. I didn't expect you to serve the jjiage yourself," said Hwihyun.

"It smells good. Let's eat," said Professor Cho.

After eating a spoonful of the soup, Soohyuk mumbled, "It's not bad."

"The jjigae here is the best in the country, Dr. Cha. It's honestly better than Mother's jjigae." Hwihyun giggled.

Looking at him, Soohyuk said, "You must not have had good jjigae. This tastes all right, but I wouldn't say it's the best in the country. Yuna's is."

"Better than the jjigae from your beloved A Tasty Meal?" teased Hwihyun.

Soohyuk coldly replied, "That's Yuna's."

Hwihyun's eyes widened. *A Tasty Meal? It's Soohyuk's fiancée who makes that delicious food?* "I can't believe it," he mumbled.

"You should," said Soohyuk.

"I guess I'll just have to. Will you let me have a taste of your best jjiage next time, then, Dr. Cha?" asked Hwihyun.

"Why would I?" said Soohyuk.

"You said that it's the best. I'd really love to try it," said Hwihyun.

"Later," said Soohyuk.

"Promise?"

"Fine."

Soohyuk mixed the next round of So-Mac this time.

Looking at the glass Soohyuk placed in front of him, Professor Cho asked, "Is the reason you want to stay in Korea your fiancée, then?"

Cocking his head at Professor Cho's change of tone, which sounded a little friendlier than before, Soohyuk answered, "Yes."

"My gratitude to her." Professor Cho smiled.

Scooting closer to Soohyuk, Hwihyun asked, "You're seriously staying here because of a girl? Did your family in the States say they're fine with that?"

"Why should that matter when it's my life?" said Soohyuk. "More importantly, what more would I need when I found a good woman I am in love with? I'm the one who has to live with my decisions, after all."

Hwihyun was impressed, even though it sounded a little painful to him. "It still must not have been an easy decision to make. All of your things, friends, and whatnot are in the States."

"I'll bring the things I need. My mother will take care of the rest," answered Soohyuk.

Professor Cho slightly frowned when he heard Soohyuk say, "My mother." *Oh dear...what if Yoonkyung was wrong about him?*

"Drink," said Soohyuk.

After clinking his glass with Soohyuk's, Hwihyun finished his glass in one gulp, then said, "Aren't you going to finish yours, Father? It's getting cold."

Cracking a smile at his son talking as if soju and beer were the most precious things in the world, Professor Cho replied, "All right, all right. I will."

With that, the three drank endlessly. Empty bottles filled the table, then were cleared, then filled the table again, and on and on it went. Soohyuk suddenly thought that he was quite like Professor Cho if traits like these were genetic as well. Professor Cho could hold his alcohol. Impeccably. Hwihyun, on the other hand, was starting to become noticeably drunk.

"Dammit, it's me again," grumbled Hwihyun. "I don't get why, but I get drunk way quicker than usual when I drink with Dr. Cha. And it's not like we didn't have anything to eat this time either."

"You must feel very comfortable around him," said Professor Cho.

"I guess so, yeah. It's not like I have to be worried of what I'm saying, whether that's because I think he's going to tell other people or because he'll judge me. His mouth isn't all that clean either, you know," giggled Hwihyun.

Since they were on the subject, Professor Cho asked in a light tone of voice, "So, do you have any siblings, Dr. Cha?"

"Father," warned Hwihyun.

Professor Cho continued regardless, "Where do your parents live?"

"Father!"

He stopped at that.

Quickly catching on that they had already talked about him, Soohyuk said coldly, "I don't have any siblings. I don't have a father either. I only have a mother."

His unyielding tone made Professor Cho grow pale. He could almost hear Ms. Seo's conviction crumbling down. *What to do now... I don't want to see her disappointed.* Professor Cho cleared his throat, trying to reorganize his thoughts. He wasn't going to give up just yet.

"I see," he said.

Hwihyun suddenly stumbled up from his seat, saying, "I need to use the restroom."

"I'll go with you," said Soohyuk, leaving Professor Cho alone at the table.

Hwihyun looked a little unstable in the way he walked. Once he got inside the bathroom, he turned the cold water on like last time and stood in front of the sink with his head lowered down. He let out a sigh, then looked up at Soohyuk in the mirror.

"I'm sorry," he said. "I told Father about you. He likes you, so I had a feeling he'd try to ask a lot of things once we started drinking and all that. I only told him in order to stop him from asking all those questions. Anyway, I'm sorry."

"You have nothing to be sorry about. Water under the bridge," Soohyuk replied.

Cracking a smile, Hwihyun said, "No, I should be sorry. I told him partly because I didn't want to hear your story again."

"You mean you don't want to get to know me anymore?" said Soohyuk.

"No, that's not what I meant. I..." Hwihyun paused to turn around toward Soohyuk. "Hearing you talk about that, about how much you were beaten growing up, made me so mad. I couldn't remember most of the night because I blacked out, but I could still remember that part as clear as day. Did I tell you that my mother likes you too? Mother comes home from the hospital sometimes and tells me about her day, and it usually goes like, 'Guess what amazing thing Dr. Cha did today!' And one day, she told me that the times you have the strongest reactions at work are when you see a victim of child abuse come in. I used to not give that too much thought, you know, because it's none of my business." He paused and frowned. "But when I heard it from you, it didn't feel like it was none of my business. It felt like it was actually my business. I got so mad and angry, and I just wanted to go punch that bastard."

Soohyuk stared at Hwihyun for a moment, then quietly said, "You've had a lot to drink."

Hwihyun grinned. "Who cares? I'll just use that as an excuse to ask Father to take me home. Who knows if I'll become a cupid for Father, who is forever in love with Mother? Get what I'm saying?"

"Wait, aren't you all living together?" asked Soohyuk.

Hwihyun seemed to be feeling the alcohol more now. At least, that's what Soohyuk thought, judging by the way he was talking now.

"Did I tell you that my family's broken?" asked Hwihyun.

"Yes, you did," said Soohyuk.

"Wow, I did really tell you a lot that night. Anyway, my

parents got a divorce after years of living in separate homes. This is a secret, by the way. No one knows at the hospital," whispered Hwihyun.

"They got a divorce?" Soohyuk asked, wearing a serious expression now.

"They finally, at long, long last, realized what's truly best for each other." Hwihyun crossed his arms and continued as his voice slightly shook from the alcohol, "They were very unhappy. No, they were terribly unhappy. We all were, honestly. It feels like we've finally come out into the light after living in the darkness for years. It's all thanks to you, in a way."

"Me?" asked Soohyuk, surprised.

"They both like you, you see. Now they have something they have in common," answered Hwihyun.

"Where do you live, then?" asked Soohyuk.

"Me?" Hwihyun grinned. "I'm living with Mother now. We used to all live separately, you see. I'm sorry this is so late, but thank you. Mother started to change ever since you came to the hospital. She became brighter, full of energy, and she even started treating me with more certainty. Really, it's all thanks to you. So, thank you."

Soohyuk's expression slightly shifted again. He couldn't tell what he was feeling. *I had that kind of effect on my parents? ...Is that good? It is, right?*

"But Father will soon be leaving the hospital," added Hwihyun.

"He is? Why?" asked Soohyuk.

"He said that he was going to send in his two weeks' notice once you make your decision on the offer. He has a witch living with him, you see. Father..." Feeling a sudden surge of emotions, Hwihyun rubbed his forehead and murmured, "Shoot, I'm just babbling on again. He said that he was going to leave because he doesn't want to become a burden to Mother and me. I feel bad for him. It's not like he chose the witch as his mother. But he still can't just leave her, you know. Anyway, my thought on this whole matter is that he shouldn't leave. He needs to stay healthy, at least until my brother comes back. It's all for him that he's been planning to build a world-class pediatric emergency room."

My brother... Hwiyin Cho...

Soohyuk clenched his fists. His heart started to pound. He was suddenly very glad he'd listened to Yuna. Not everything was as it seemed on the outside.

"I just want him to come back now," mumbled Hwihyun.

"Where is he?" asked Soohyuk.

Unable to keep down the bubbling emotions, he spat out, "That damn bastard made me play hide-and-seek with him and still hasn't come out of his hiding place. That crazy asshole left me here all by myself and just disappeared."

With that, he turned back around to face away from Soohyuk. He splashed cold water on his face. His fingertips were still trembling. It was an anger he didn't even know was inside him. He'd locked everything away in his heart until now. Ms. Seo was unhappy, Professor Cho was unhappy, and Hwiyin was nowhere to be found, so he thought at least he should always be smiling. And in order to do that, he'd had to lock everything away. That was the only way he could smile.

"So, have you been *it* this whole time?" asked Soohyuk.

Hwihyun raised his wet face to look at Soohyuk through the mirror and mumbled as if he were under a spell, "What?"

"I said, have you been *it* this whole time?" said Soohyuk.

Hwihyun's lips moved on their own to say, "Yup. I'm still it."

Suddenly, Soohyuk reached out a hand to brush Hwihyun's hair. "I'm sorry."

Hwihyun blankly stared at Soohyuk, who turned around and left the bathroom. Something unreal had just happened. *That touch... The way he brushed my hair with his fingertips...* His lips formed a smile as his eyes started to water.

Hwihyun took a deep breath in. Those two words made all his anger melt away.

"You really are drunk, Hwihyun Cho. Look at you smiling like an idiot at that tiny apology. Oh, who cares. It's not like he's going to tell anyone about this," he said to himself.

He really did think that. He had a strong intuition that Soohyuk would never do something like that. So, he felt fine with whatever he wanted to talk about or did not want to talk about when he was with him. That was probably why he liked Soohyuk so much in the first place. It had made him keep insisting that he was fine and that he did not need to be sent home even if he ended up blacking out, the last time they drank together. He was going to hold out until the very end tonight as well.

"It at least feels good to get it out," said Hwihyun.

He'd never said anything bad about his brother until now. Just thinking of Hwiyin made his heart wrench. He'd never even dreamed that he was angry at him. And yet, all that anger was hiding inside him.

"I'm sorry."

A faint smile appeared on his lips.

***

"Where's Hwihyun?" asked Professor Cho when Soohyuk came back to the table.

"He's splashing some cold water on his face," said Soohyuk.

Offering him a glass, Professor Cho said, "I'm sorry for asking something like that."

"It's all right," said Soohyuk.

They clinked their glasses. The So-Mac tasted incredibly good. Professor Cho filled the empty glass again.

"You're going too fast. Take your time. You might become hammered if you go at that pace," warned Soohyuk.

Professor Cho chuckled at Soohyuk's concern for him. "I'll be fine. I'm feeling very good tonight. I'm not going to get drunk no matter how much I drink."

The two shared a couple rounds of drinks while they waited for Hwihyun to return.

"You are good," said Professor Cho. "I've never seen someone who can hold his liquor like you. You're not even getting drunk, like me."

"You're starting to slur your speech," said Soohyuk.

"Me? That doesn't sound right," denied Professor Cho.

But it was true. His pronunciation was increasingly becoming hard to understand. He'd even undone one of his shirt buttons, like he was getting hot. Something about that felt familiar to Soohyuk. It was the first thing Professor Cho used to do when he returned home from work: undo one button and hug his sons one after the other.

It had been nice to feel his father's warm embrace. He'd wanted to live happily with his father. And he had wanted to hear something from him.

Hwihyun returned to his seat, loudly announcing, "I'm in the mood for some pork katsu. Can I get the biggest pork katsu you have here, please?"

"Your mother makes the best pork katsus," said Professor Cho pensively.

"She does. Hwiyin liked it a lot too," said Hwihyun. He started pouring soju this time. "I actually didn't think we'd have much fun tonight. But this isn't half bad."

"No? I'm not getting in the way, am I?" asked Professor Cho.

"What do you think, Dr. Cha? Are you having fun?" asked Hwihyun.

"I am," answered Soohyuk. Though it surprised him a little, it was true.

Pouring soju into Soohyuk's glass as well, Hwihyun said, "Drink up."

The three clinked glasses again. The soju burned their throats and their stomachs on its way down. Soohyuk scowled. *Shoot.* He was suddenly feeling the alcohol.

They shared a couple more rounds until the pork katsu came. Stories that were forgotten as soon as they were spoken spewed out of their mouths. That continued even when the pork katsu came. The stories kept pouring out, and alcohol kept being poured down their throats like water.

When they were all as excited as they could be, Hwihyun suddenly said, "Hold on, hold on. Listen. Can you hear the music? I love the manager here. He's the man. I'm a regular here, you know."

It was "Just the Two of Us."

"He knows that I like this song," said Hwihyun.

"I like it too," chimed in Professor Cho.

Chuckling, Hwihyun said, "Wait, you do? Even after you heard me and Hwiyin sing it our way?" He then started singing along, "Just the two of us, we don't like Daddy, we don't like Daddy."

Professor Cho grinned. That was just the way he remembered the two singing the song. He'd just let them be because he knew that they never sang something like that in front of Ms. Jung or Ms. Seo. They only did that when they were alone with him. Like at the sauna. That was what they sang as they rubbed his back with a shower towel.

Hwihyun was having fun now. After doing all the rap with the appropriate hip-hop gestures, he started singing the chorus again, "Just the two of us, Daddy should be sorry, Daddy needs to change…"

Suddenly, Professor Cho's eyes widened. Soohyuk was mouthing the changed lyrics to a tee. No sound was coming out, but he could tell that he was singing the same words as Hwihyun. Tears welled up in his eyes within seconds. Before he could do anything, they started rolling down his cheeks. But he quickly blotted them dry so he wouldn't draw attention to himself when they were having so much fun.

While he was watching them, he started to really hear what the lyrics were saying. It was a promise a father was making to his son. His heart started to pound. He'd never realized that was what this song was about. Thinking again, that made sense, because he'd only heard Hwihyun and Hwiyin sing it and had never thought to listen to the original by Will Smith. Naturally, he'd never thought that it was a song with this kind of a theme. When a certain part started playing, his heart started beating even harder. He'd thought that they'd know even if he didn't say it out loud…but perhaps he was wrong. He caught Soohyuk and Hwihyun's expressions turn a little gloomy when the song ended.

He gathered his courage and said, "Hwihyun, can you go ask if they can play that song again?"

Why hadn't he thought of this back then? Why had he just thought of it as his sons fooling around?

Getting up from his seat, Hwihyun said, "Okay, I'm going to ask him to play it just five, five more times. So, really think about it, Father. Seriously. Don't let me down."

"All right, all right. I won't," said Professor Cho.

He was right. His sons wanted to hear him say it. The song started playing again as Hwihyun came walking back to his seat. He didn't miss it this time.

As the song was about to end, he awkwardly rapped along with Will Smith's voice, "Daddy loves you, daddy loves you."

Both Soohyuk and Hwihyun burst into laughter at the same time. He could suddenly see why Ms. Seo was so certain about Soohyuk. Soohyuk's smile was very much like his own. Surprisingly so.

Every time the song repeated, he jumped in to rap those lines. That was a moment he would never forget in his life.

Ms. Seo couldn't fall asleep late into the night, knowing that Professor Cho and Hwihyun were having drinks with Soohyuk. Hwihyun was late. He had come back around midnight last time, but now the clock had struck one in the morning and he still wasn't home. So, she kept waiting.

When it was well past three o' clock in the morning, she finally heard a knock at the door. She scurried to the door, thinking that he must be so drunk he couldn't even open the door himself. But upon opening the door, she found that Hwihyun wasn't alone.

"I asked Father to take me home. Thank you, Father. I'm so drunk. I'm gonna go to sleep," mumbled Hwihyun, then disappeared inside after clumsily taking off his shoes.

Ms. Seo said with a smile, "Thank you for staying with Hwihyun until now."

While she was debating whether or not she should ask what he thought of Soohyuk after seeing him tonight, Professor Cho said, "Yoonkyung."

Her heartbeat picked up speed right away. His eyes started to water.

He said with certainty, "Hwiyin's back. I know it's him. He is our boy."

Ms. Seo couldn't help but jump into his embrace.

Soohyuk watched the Saturday morning light creep in as he lay there with Yuna in his arms. He hadn't been able to sleep a wink because he'd felt like he was walking on clouds all night. He kept repeating what had happened at the bar in his head. Hwihyun's eyes revealing his anger and his sadness when he said that he was still it. The subtle change in Professor Cho's way of addressing and looking at him. And the song.

Filling his lungs with as much air as he could, he tightened his arms around Yuna. She pressed into his chest with a long sigh. Soohyuk rested his chin on the crown of her head for a moment and started to organize his scattered thoughts. Hwihyun, the crybaby Hwihyun was always smiling. He'd thought that Hwihyun had grown into a well-adjusted adult, but from what he saw last night, he was wrong. And Professor Cho… He was acting as if he knew who Soohyuk was. They'd listened to "Just the Two of Us" at least twenty times last night, thanks to Hwihyun's drunken habit of repeating himself. Every time Professor Cho sang along with the chorus, he'd looked at Hwihyun once, then Soohyuk once.

A gentle breeze of joy swept over his face. His smile slowly widened. *Yes, now I see.* He had no idea how he'd found out, but Professor Cho was sure of who he was. Soohyuk silently laughed, even throwing his head back in joy. He relished that moment of glee. It was as if a great weight had been lifted off his shoulders. It was all thanks to Hwihyun telling him about his family.

"I have to make him stop playing hide-and-seek now..." he mumbled.

He didn't want Hwihyun to have to force himself to smile anymore. He didn't want Professor Cho to quit his job either. He wanted to keep seeing everyone in the same space like he was now.

Soohyuk leaned his head back to look at Yuna peacefully sleeping. She was cute even when she was asleep. Her regular breaths coming out of her slightly parted lips were adorable as well.

"It's all thanks to you," he whispered.

It was indeed all thanks to her. He never would have found out about all this had he avoided them like his natural instincts told him to. He would have avoided and avoided them until he hurt himself again. She was right to push him. He felt so much better now, and happier too.

He leaned forward to kiss her bare shoulder. "I love you," he murmured to the sleeping Yuna.

He gently ran his hand along her spine. His fingertips brushed against her skin, and her warmth seeped into his frozen heart. He kissed her ear this time. *If I hadn't met you...*

If he hadn't met Yuna, if he hadn't fallen in love with Yuna, he would have lived the rest of his life a prisoner to his own restrictions. He would have lived drunk with the cold aloofness he put on to mask the resentment and hatred. Thinking that, his love for Yuna deepened even more.

Soohyuk rubbed his scruffy chin against her neck affectionately. When she raised her face in sleepy protest, he lightly kissed her lips. Once, twice, thrice… Every time his lips touched hers, he stayed longer before he broke off.

Yuna raised her hands to fumble along his shoulders with her eyes still closed, then soon found his tousled hair and dug her fingers in it. Soohyuk leaned forward to kiss her more properly this time. He stacked his body on top of hers. Her lips arched in a smile against his.

Leaning his forehead against hers, he whispered, "You changed my world for the better." He caressed her body as if it were the most precious treasure in the world. "You made me feel what it's like to have a family." His voice trembled. "You…"

Yuna opened her eyes and looked at him. Their touching hearts started to beat as one. Soohyuk's eyes watered. He'd hid his tears from her before, but not anymore.

Letting the tear fall on her cheek, he confessed, "You gave my life meaning."

Yuna raised her hand to pull his face toward her. He closed his eyes. Her lips lovingly stamped his wet eyelid.

Hwihyun looked at himself in the mirror as he brushed his teeth. He'd blacked out again. He couldn't even remember how he got home last night. His mother had told him a little bit ago that his father had brought him all the way home.

This was the second time he'd blacked out like that. And both times, he'd been drinking with Soohyuk.

"There's something about him," he mumbled.

He'd called Professor Cho as soon as he woke up that morning to check how he was doing. His voice was lively and bright, which was a relief. *The heaviest of the heavyweights,* thought Hwihyun after the call.

He raised a hand to scratch his tousled hair, and cracked a

smile. It reminded him of the way Soohyuk brushed his hair, telling him that he was sorry.

"He's kind at the weirdest moments," said Hwihyun.

But for some reason, he couldn't stop smiling. After finishing brushing his teeth, he started washing his face. He suddenly looked up. He could hear the song he'd sung last night in his ears like a faint echo. And Professor Cho's answer. He snatched the towel to dry his face and walked out of the bathroom.

"Are you done? Breakfast is ready," called Ms. Seo.

Hwihyun walked over to her straightaway. But he couldn't help hesitating for a second. He'd driven her into a panic the day he told her that his missing brother was playing hide-and-seek and that he was it. Ms. Seo had gone half mad because of him. So, he wasn't sure if he should tell her or not. How would she react if he told her that he thought Soohyuk was Hwiyin?

"You have some soap left here." Ms. Seo grinned as she wiped it away from his face.

Hwihyun looked at his reflection in her eyes. He then remembered what he had told Soohyuk last night. He'd said that Ms. Seo had changed since Soohyuk came to the hospital. *What if she felt something even before I did? What if...*

"I'll go rinse my face again. I guess I was too hungry," said Hwihyun.

When he returned to the bathroom, he calmly looked at himself in the mirror this time. Ms. Seo looking at ease, Professor Cho's voice all lively and bright... How long had it been since he last saw them like this? These changes had all happened after Soohyuk Cha came into their lives. He was the beginning of all of this.

"You know what? Let's do it just this once. Just this once," he said to himself.

He had a certain feeling that things would turn out all right even if his hunch was wrong.

After washing his face again, he went to the kitchen and ate the soup Ms. Seo had been making. He started to feel more and more confident in his feeling that everything would turn out all right even if he did what he was debating if he should do. While Hwihyun finished his breakfast at last and got up to do the dishes, Ms. Seo changed out of her loungewear and came into the kitchen.

"Are you going somewhere?" he asked.

"Yes, I'll be back in a little bit," she answered.

"All right."

He watched her walk out of the kitchen. Her steps seemed light with excitement for some reason. It almost seemed like she was gleeful, like a child who'd just heard good news. Hwihyun finished doing the dishes with a smile and went into his room.

He sat on his bed and grabbed his phone right away. Then, without hesitance, he dialed Soohyuk's number. After a couple rings, Soohyuk picked up.

"Soohyuk Cha speaking."

"This is Hwihyun Cho. How are you feeling? We drank a lot last night," said Hwihyun.

"I'm doing fine. How are you? And Professor Cho?"

Hwihyun's brows slightly narrowed as he listened to Soohyuk's ever cold voice. Then something occurred to him. If Soohyuk were Hwiyin, and he was aware of that too, why hadn't he come to them? There probably was a reason for it. Hwihyun quickly examined all the possible reasons he could think of. Soohyuk might have forgotten everything from the shock since it happened when he was so young, or maybe he'd gone through some kind of accident. There was no other possible explanation. Hwiyin loved Ms. Seo, Professor Cho, and his brother way too much.

Then, he gravely shook his head. No, it was none of that. Soohyuk had sang the lyrics he and Hwiyin had made up perfectly to the letter. His memory was sound. Then why…

It hit him that Soohyuk had been abused as a child. He had to protect himself under extreme conditions. Perhaps he…

Hwihyun changed his mind at once and said, "I feel much better after getting some soup in my system. And Professor Cho is, as you know, exceptionally gifted in processing alcohol, so he's fine."

"I'm glad to hear that."

"Thank you for putting up with me last night," said Hwihyun.

"No problem. I had fun."

"I had a lot of fun as well. So much so that I'd love to drink with just the three of us again," he said.

"I'm sure we could if we worked out our schedules. Let's do that."

Hwihyun smiled.

"If what I'm about to say offends you in any way," said Soohyuk, "I'll let you punch me as revenge later."

"Whoa, that's a scary disclaimer. What on earth could you be leading up to?" said Hwihyun.

"It might feel like it's a little late, but you should live your life now. Stop playing hide-and-seek."

He slightly frowned again, feeling touched. Though Soohyuk wasn't revealing himself for whatever reason, he was his brother. So, he was going to wait until Soohyuk came to him on his own time.

"I'm not sure if I could. What if my brother suddenly shows up one day and yells at me for it?" asked Hwihyun.

"Then bring him to me. I'll take care of him for you."

Hwihyun's eyes watered as he said, "That's a relief."

"And stop forcing yourself to smile."

"Hyung," said Hwihyun. Soohyuk fell silent. "Can I call you 'Hyung' in private from now on, Dr. Cha?"

Soohyuk was almost whispering now. "I thought there was only one person you called 'Hyung'?"

"I'm sure he'll understand too, when he meets you," said Hwihyun.

"Maybe."

Wiping the tears trickling down his cheek with the back of his hand, he said, "By the way, until when do I have to decide if I do want to punch you or not?"

"Are you actually going to?" asked Soohyuk.

"You're the one who offered, Hyung."

"We'll talk more about this later. Do you want to have lunch with me on Monday?"

Hwihyun grinned from ear to ear and said, "Sure. The weather's been very nice."

"I'll see you on the terrace."

"Okay, Hyung," answered Hwihyun.

"That's cheesy."

"Hyung," teased Hwihyun.

"Goodbye."

"Bye," said Hwihyun before going on a frenzy of jumping up and down and screaming in excitement. He couldn't have been more grateful he was alone in the apartment.

———

Professor Cho and Ms. Seo sat down at a table by the sunny window and savored the taste of their coffee. It was the exact same setup as last time, but something was different this time. Their hands seemed much more relaxed as they reached for their cups, and there was a barely visible smile in the lips that sipped the coffee. They were sitting in utter serenity.

When they were about halfway through their coffees, Professor Cho said, "Something's telling me that Hwiyin knows who we are."

"Yes, I had that same feeling. I think he's pretending like he doesn't know us on purpose," said Ms. Seo.

Professor Cho hesitated for a moment. Hwihyun had told only him that Soohyuk was abused as a child. He knew for sure that Ms. Seo would feel guilty if he told her that. There was no way she wouldn't. After spending all morning pondering the matter, he had made the decision to tell her, since she had to know in order to fully understand where Soohyuk was coming from. But now that he was actually seeing her in person, he couldn't bring himself to say it.

"If you know something, tell me," said Ms. Seo. "Hwiyin never used to tell me the bad things even when he was young. So, I never realized that I was a bad mom. Don't let me be a bad mom out of ignorance again. Help me. Please."

Encouraged by her plea, Professor Cho said, "I heard that Hwiyin…was abused by his adoptive family as a child. He was beaten a lot, I heard. And that's apparently the reason he became a doctor."

Ms. Seo's face turned ghost white. Her fingernails dug into her palms.

"I've been trying to figure out how a kid as smart as Hwiyin could disappear like that. You know how he doesn't eat anything a stranger gives him?" asked Professor Cho.

Ms. Seo answered as her voice trembled, "They drugged him to take him away from us."

"That's what I think too. But how did Hwiyin get out of sight in the first place? Why did he take whatever they offered? We both know he's not someone who would be that gullible," mumbled Professor Cho.

Oh... Ms. Seo suddenly recalled the day he'd disappeared. It had happened in a matter of five minutes. Back then, she was on medication for her severe depression, but she had to fight unreasonable urges every day. That was what happened that day too. She was fighting the urge to just leave everything behind and kill herself. That was why she didn't notice that Hwiyin was gone.

"It's all my fault. I made him like that. I...I..." muttered Ms. Seo.

Reaching out to take her hand, Professor Cho said, "No, it wasn't your fault. You know how much he loved you, right? Whatever thought went through his head, I think he did it for you. He did it out of love."

Tears rolled down her cheeks. Hearing that didn't fix her broken heart. It was still because his parents hadn't given him enough love and protection that Hwiyin had been forced to live such a cruel life. Her tears wouldn't stop.

Professor Cho quietly watched her. When she finally calmed down a little, he said, "Hwiyin has changed so much. To the point that you couldn't recognize him at first either. Why do you think that is? I think it was because he was trying to survive somehow. But when he smiled, it was just like you said. He looked just like me."

Ms. Seo looked at him with watery eyes and said, "Because he's in love. There's a very nice young lady he's with."

"Yes, he told me that he's living with someone he referred to as his fiancée," replied Professor Cho.

The two looked at each other for a moment, smiling.

"I see," she said. "That's why he's been changing little by little. He used to be so cold and reclusive. Things are brightening up at the emergency room. I think it'll only get better from here."

He then quietly replied, "So, we should probably wait, right?"

"Yes, I think we should. We just need to keep waiting by his side like this," said Ms. Seo.

"Yes, you're right. But it won't be a meaningless wait anymore. We're going to cherish every day that is to come now. If that only means that I can apologize to Hwiyin for what I did... if he could let go of at least a little bit of what he must have had to hold in for so long, then I really..." Professor Cho's voice trailed off.

She quietly replied, "I feel the same way. I have done something to him I could never atone for, even with death. If Hwiyin ends up even a tiny bit happier, at whatever cost... that's all I could ever ask for. I'd be fine if I never heard him call me his mother again."

"Yoonkyung," called Professor Cho.

Gently smiling, she said, "I get to see my son again. What more could I ask for? That would be being too greedy. From now on, whatever Hwiyin does will be a miracle to me, no, us."

Professor Cho chuckled. Ms. Seo silently laughed as well, sharing his joy. When they looked at each other after that moment of glee, they felt as if they were much closer to each other than earlier today. Before, it had felt as if they'd crossed the point of no return, but now, all of a sudden, they were back.

"I'm really glad I have you," said Ms. Seo sincerely.

Professor Cho hesitated for a moment. He'd been planning to quit his job at the hospital once Soohyuk decided whether or not he was going to stay. He was worried his obsession would drive his beloved family to hell again. But now, Hwiyin was back. His son he'd been searching for all over for all those years was back. He didn't want to quit anymore. He wanted to stay by their sides.

"We should probably tell Hwihyun, right?" asked Ms. Seo.

"Yes, he deserves to know," replied Professor Cho.

Smiling, she asked, "Do you want to come home with me, then?"

"I would love to," he answered.

As he was getting up, he suddenly realized that his wish was going to get in the way of his family's happiness again. A heart-wrenching pain hit him, but he hid his sadness with a smile.

CHAPTER 26

Soohyuk got off the train with Yuna. They were at Daehakro to catch a musical.

"I never thought I'd come somewhere like this," mumbled Yuna as they walked through Marronnier Park.

"This is the first time I've come here, too," said Soohyuk.

Yuna looked askance at him for a moment, then burst into laughter. She'd come out to see a musical for the first time, thanks to Soohyuk. After hearing that she'd never seen a musical, Soohyuk had looked up the most popular show that was playing right now and booked two tickets.

Yuna curiously looked at the small theaters lined up on either side of the street. She wouldn't have batted an eye if someone made fun of her for looking around like a country bumpkin visiting a big city for the first time. Daehakro was a place of mystery and curiosity for her.

Soohyuk walked alongside her, holding her hand. This was the first time he was stepping outside of his usual neighborhood. He'd always stayed around the apartment and the hospital, so this felt like some sort of brave adventure.

Suddenly, Yuna stopped. She'd spotted a dancer dressed in

traditional attire dancing on one side of the park. It looked as if the dancer was guarding the park alone in the dark. Their wide sleeves and white hat cut through the moonlight and ruled the air.

She watched the dance without budging an inch. Her lips started to twitch as if she were holding back tears. Soohyuk quietly wrapped his arm around her shoulder and pulled her toward him. She looked up at him and sheepishly smiled.

Tightening his arm around her, he leaned his head down to kiss the crown of her head. Her arm wrapped around his waist. The two stood as one and watched the dance for a little longer. When they were getting close to the time the show would start, they finally started walking again.

The theater where the musical was playing was a fairly large one. Yuna's eyes twinkled with anticipation. They followed the crowd down to the basement. The seats Soohyuk had booked were in the mezzanine.

"They said it would be easier to see the stage from here," said Soohyuk.

Yuna thanked him for being considerate of her short height. It felt like it took forever for the lights to dim and the show to start. She kept staring at the dark stage.

The wait ended at last. The stage lights turned on, and the curtains opened. Yuna slightly gaped. It had only just begun, and she was already buzzing with excitement.

Soohyuk stared at Yuna all through the first act. He didn't want to miss a second of her eyes gazing at the stage. He sat in his tiny seat with his arms crossed and his eyes fixed on Yuna. He'd never met someone who could enjoy the moment as fully as Yuna. Most people, in his experience, didn't even realize that most moments had already passed and were never going to return because they were too weighed down by their own baggage.

His lips gently smiled as well. The numbers were joyful, it had a good enough plot, and the orchestra was pleasing. But they weren't the reason he was smiling. The real reason was Yuna.

During the intermission, Yuna held Soohyuk's hand tightly and said, "I want to tell you something before I forget."

"Tell me," said Soohyuk.

"I love you," she said.

He smiled mischievously and said, "Tell me again."

"I love you."

Pretending to get up from his seat, he said, "Let's go home, then."

Yuna realized what he meant by that immediately. Blushing red like an apple, she held him back, saying, "No, not yet. I want to watch the whole thing."

"If we do, will you do everything I ask of you tonight?" asked Soohyuk.

Yuna blushed even harder. Seeing that she was not answering, Soohyuk supposed that she was getting a little scared.

When he pretended to get up from his seat again, Yuna finally said, "Fine. But under one condition."

"What is it?" asked Soohyuk.

"I'll tell you only if you promise that you'll say yes," said Yuna.

"I promise."

"Give me three vetoes," said Yuna.

Soohyuk frowned. *She got me.* He had no choice but to give up three of the things he wanted to do to Yuna.

"Thank you for your kind offer." Yuna laughed.

Soohyuk crossed his arms and sighed. She'd played him again.

The second act started. Soohyuk found it a little tedious because it was mostly about the characters explaining what had happened in the first act. He had to force down a yawn. But Yuna was still just as focused as she was during the first act. Soohyuk fixed his eyes on Yuna again. The boredom immediately subsided. He was wide awake again.

When the show finally ended and he thought that they could

leave, the cast ran out on stage, yelling, "On your feet, everyone! Let's have some fun!"

"Is it not over yet?" asked Yuna, confused.

Soohyuk nodded and said, "I hope it doesn't take too long. We need to get you home."

Pretending she hadn't heard him say that, Yuna got up on her feet like everyone else. But she just stood there, awkwardly fidgeting with her clothes. The music started again and the people started to bounce in their place as one. A wide smile appeared on Yuna's face. This was truly an experience. She'd never been to a show like this. She started bouncing as well. She didn't know much about music, but she knew more about having fun than anyone else.

Soohyuk proudly watched her bounce up and down next to him, enjoying the show. *She really is having fun,* he thought. *I just want to grab her and take her back home, but I'm going to have to wait. Yes, I'll wait.*

The show ended at last. She yelled till she became hoarse, and jumped till she would regret it tomorrow. Coming outside couldn't have felt more refreshing. It almost felt as if she'd come out for the first time after being locked inside for years. Not hiding her joy, she grinned from ear to ear as they walked.

Soohyuk couldn't help but pause. "Come here," he said.

When she went to him without hesitating, he cradled her face with both hands and pressed his lips again hers. Yuna wrapped her arms around his waist and returned his kiss.

Darkness enveloped them in the empty street. The ring on his hand that was wrapped around her face shined under the lamp light. The ring on Yuna's hand wrapped around his waist twinkled as well.

CHAPTER 27

It was the beginning of a new week. Standing in the morning sunlight pouring in from the windows, Soohyuk was checking the charts one last time with his gown hung over the chair behind him. He was just coming out of a night shift.

His keen eyes scanned the chart, which held the record of the night's battle of life and death. A family returning home from visiting a relative's grave had been caught in a horrible car accident. The child in the car had even suffered from terrible burns because their car's engine caught on fire. Soohyuk clamped his mouth shut. A burn injury was a sort of monster that followed you around for the rest of your life, incessantly reminding you of the pain. Moreover, considering that the child with the burns was in seventh grade and he was soon going to go through puberty, Soohyuk knew that he would have to bear far more than any other child his age would. He didn't know what kind of a life was ahead for this kid, but he only hoped that he would not give up until the end.

He heard someone approaching him from behind. He could

tell who it was without even looking up by the warm smell. It was Ms. Seo.

"Good morning," she said.

"Morning," replied Soohyuk.

It was still as short a reply as ever, but hearing even that made her happy. She opened the thermos she'd brought from home and poured a cup of coffee.

"Have some coffee, Dr. Cha," she offered as she pushed the steaming cup of coffee toward him.

Soohyuk didn't decline, but he didn't gladly accept it and start drinking it either. The people around them started to glance at Ms. Seo. They were tensing up as they watched Soohyuk once again not accept Ms. Seo's kind gesture. But she didn't care. She would have been fine if he tossed the cup of coffee straight into the bin.

"Have a good day, then," she said to Soohyuk, who still had his eyes fixed on the chart, then lightly trotted along to find something to do.

She maintained her usual gentle expression. She'd been waiting for this moment all morning long, just staring at the clock to count the time till she could see Soohyuk again. A warm smile appeared on her lips.

When she and Professor Cho had gone to talk to Hwihyun, they'd found Hwihyun already certain that Soohyuk was Hwiyin, as well, to their surprise.

"I'm sure he wouldn't keep us waiting for another twenty-seven years," Hwihyun had said half-jokingly. "He's already acting like a big brother to me."

That made Ms. Seo and Professor Cho realize that it was Hwihyun who'd helped them the most in their search for Hwiyin until now. Thanks to Hwihyun being so supportive and reliable, they'd been able to go look for Hwiyin all over the country and could find the courage to get out there again when they came home to their younger son after a long day of no success. Seeing

Hwihyun act all grown-up made their hearts ache with sympathy and love.

Now, Ms. Seo glanced back at Soohyuk and beamed with delight. He was drinking the coffee she'd given him.

———

Days and weeks passed. The sunlight became warmer by the day, and the trees started to put on their green summer clothes. One afternoon, Hwihyun was eating lunch with Soohyuk on the rooftop garden.

"So, when are you going to introduce us?" asked Hwihyun.

"Who's 'us'?" asked Soohyuk, pretending not to know what he was talking about.

"Yuna, of course," said Hwihyun.

"Later," said Soohyuk.

"God, it's like she's made of gold or something," complained Hwihyun.

"She is made of gold."

Hwihyun nimbly moved his chopsticks to grab a bite of Soohyuk's food, and shoved it into his mouth before he could protest. He had taken one of the pork cabbage wraps.

"Hey!" shouted Soohyuk.

"You were eating really slow, so I thought I might help you out a little." Hwihyun shrugged, chewing the food very slowly on purpose, as if he were trying to savor every part of it. He had a habit of finishing off his favorite dish first, and Soohyuk had a habit of saving it until the end.

Soohyuk glared at Hwihyun with his cold eyes, then muttered, "Yes, keep that up. See where that takes you."

"Come on, Hyung. What, do you want this back?" said Hwihyun as he mischievously opened his mouth.

"God, no," said Soohyuk, leaning far back.

Hwihyun cracked a smile, then swallowed. It was fun to tease him from time to time like this.

When they were drinking coffee as dessert after finishing their lunches, Soohyuk asked, "Where's Professor Cho?"

"He's gone to a seminar in Hong Kong. He'll come back in a week or so."

"Is he really going to quit?" asked Soohyuk.

He'd already added a new condition to his contract while negotiating the terms with Dr. Jin. He'd said that he was only going to sign with them if Professor Cho stayed at S University Hospital with him. He didn't want to send his father far away when they'd finally been reunited after all these years.

Hwihyun looked off into the distance for a moment, then said, "I'm sorry, Hyung, but I think that's out of our hands. I think it's something only Mother could fix."

"But she doesn't seem to know," said Soohyuk.

"Of course she doesn't, because no one's told her."

"Then tell her. Tell her and make the two of them deal with it on their own," said Soohyuk.

Hwihyun faintly smiled. *What about the witch? No one could ever win against that old woman,* he thought.

Soohyuk had a feeling he knew what his brother was thinking. He crossed his arms. "It's none of your concern what happens next. It's between them. So, tell her, and step aside. Don't intervene even if they end up fighting."

"But how would I do that?" asked Hwihyun.

"By looking away. Go on some dates. You're not going to find any if you just stay put in the same spot, so make yourself get out there. You'll find your match eventually."

"You think?"

"Try. Try something, whatever it may be. No one's going to do the work for you. You need to do it yourself," said Soohyuk.

Hwihyun thought for a moment, then finally replied, "I will. I'll take ownership of my own life and all that."

"Good idea," said Soohyuk.

"By the way, Hyung, I'd love to have some grilled pork tomorrow," said Hwihyun.

"Ask Ms. Seo to make it for you. Yuna does enough work already," said Soohyuk.

"You're being so stingy."

"Go find yourself a cook, then."

The warm summer breeze brushed past the two squabbling brothers.

Ms. Seo waited for Professor Cho to come down to the hospital lobby. He'd returned only yesterday from a seminar overseas. The reason she was waiting for him was because of something Hwihyun had told her earlier.

"Father said that he's going to quit his job here," Hwihyun had said.

"What do you mean? Now? But Hwiyin is here."

"I think that's actually why. He doesn't want to make the three of us suffer again."

Now, she was sitting on the chair, just waiting for Professor Cho to arrive.

He walked into the lobby at last with a smile on his face. As soon as he was close enough to her, he asked, "What would you like? Iced coffee?"

Ms. Seo was at a loss of words. She couldn't believe what she was seeing. *What on earth...*

"Are you all right? Why have you lost so much weight?" she asked bluntly.

Forcing a smile, he changed the subject. "I'm thirsty. Why don't we first have some coffee?"

While she was too shocked to speak, he went to the cashier and returned with two cups of iced coffee.

Sitting across from her seat, he took a sip of coffee and said, "This is very good coffee."

Ms. Seo quietly said, "You're not eating. You can't even swallow the food, can you?"

She'd lived many years with him as his wife. There was no way she couldn't see through what was happening. Professor Cho was a very sensitive person. To the point that he couldn't swallow food when he was under extreme stress. And when that happened, he lost a lot of weight, just like now.

"How long has this been going on?" asked Ms. Seo.

"It's just that I couldn't eat much while I was in Hong Kong because the food wasn't to my liking. No need to be concerned," said Professor Cho, trying to brush it off.

"Is it true that you're quitting?" she asked.

He closed his eyes tightly, then opened them again and answered, "It is. Hwiyin is finally back, so I…"

"Do you really think you'd be able to leave while we all stay behind?"

Looking at her with sorrowful eyes, he said, "I'm sorry I put you through so much over the years. I'm so sorry."

"Forget your apologies. If you really thought that we could ever be happy without you, you really are a fool," she said sternly.

His eyes started to water. But he wasn't going to change his decision. This was the only way he could free them from Ms. Jung's obsession. So, he just quietly sipped his coffee.

Ms. Seo looked at his bony face. She thought back on all the years tainted by her love-hate relationship with him. She had loved him. And she still loved him. They needed him.

"Honey," she called.

Tears welled up in Professor Cho's eyes.

"Don't leave us. You don't need to force yourself into loneliness like that," she continued.

He bit his trembling lower lip.

"Remember what I said before? We should start living our own lives now," said Ms. Seo.

"I do. And this is my way of making that happen," said Professor Cho.

Sensing the deep sorrow hidden inside his calm voice, she faintly smiled. "Do you think I would believe that when you look so thin?"

"Yoonkyung…"

"If it's truly for me, if it's truly for us, don't go. Let's not run away anymore. Look what running away from your mother brought. Our lives, and our children's lives, were completely ruined," she pleaded.

He clamped his mouth shut again.

"Is this really what you want to do with the chance to try again after twenty-seven years?" asked Ms. Seo.

"No, of course I want to stay too. Seeing you all like this every day… I…" His voice trailed off as the truth slipped out of his lips. He raised his bony hand to rub his forehead.

"Then stay. Stay with us. But in order to do that, you do need to do one thing," she said. Professor Cho gazed at her. She continued, "I'm not saying that you need to choose between your mother and us. I'm not going to ask you to let go of your family. But you do need to persuade your mother. You know your mother best. Only you can do this. Persuade your mother."

His hand reached out before he could stop it to tightly grasp her hand. "Are you giving me another chance?"

"If you do it right this time. I've never even been on a proper date. So, you're going to make it worth my while. If you can, I'll give you another chance." She smiled.

He lowered his head to lean his forehead on the back of her hand and whispered, "Anything, if it means that I can stay by your side and the kids'."

But he didn't know how he was supposed to persuade Ms. Jung. They were here in the first place because none of the things he'd tried had worked. Was his death really the only way to end this? His chest started to tighten at that thought.

Ms. Seo whispered, "I'll wait. I'll wait until you come back. I'll be waiting right here, however long it takes, so please just come back."

He raised his head to look at her. She gently smiled as if she could read his mind. Her smile… His two sons' laughter…

I want to be happy now, too.

"I'll come back," he firmly stated. "I'll come back as soon as I can."

"And I'll be waiting," replied Ms. Seo. Then, glancing at something behind him, she added with a mischievous smile, "Boy, are you in trouble, though. How do you plan on dealing with Hwihyun's lectures on the state you are in right now?"

"I'll have to hide," said Professor Cho with a chuckle.

Her smile widened. "Too late. There's your youngest coming right now. I'll go ahead and give you two some privacy. Good luck." She got up from her seat with her cup of coffee in her hand and said, "Thank you for the coffee."

When she'd only taken a couple steps in the opposite direction, she heard Hwihyun's voice from behind. He was giving his father a lecture on taking care of himself, as she'd expected. Feeling full of joy, she smiled. Little things like this made her happy.

She spotted Soohyuk stepping into the lobby. *He must be coming to work now,* she thought. She started to speed up. People and plants and such swooshed past her at a much higher speed than usual. It almost felt like the world was turning faster all of a sudden.

Her world indeed was changing. By her own choice, this time, not anyone else's. So, she strode across the lobby.

The house was silent. So silent that Ms. Jung could hear the water droplets drop from the faucet that wasn't turned all the way off. She got to her scrawny feet and stood in front of the faucet, which was sending ripples of sound throughout the house. Her petite body seemed even smaller when she stood in front of the big sink. She returned to her seat after turning the faucet all the way off. Perfect silence enveloped her at last. She looked at the table with expressionless eyes. The food she had laid out for her son's breakfast was still there, untouched. Cold rice, bone broth soup with spots of oil floating on the surface, perfectly ripe pickled peppers, lightly salted bean sprouts, an omelet, and kimchi.

"You really didn't even touch it," she mumbled to herself.

Professor Cho had left this morning without having any breakfast again.

"You're going to hit your limit one day, Professor Cho," she muttered, shaking her head.

He had lost a preposterous amount of weight while he was in Hong Kong, like he had suddenly fallen ill. Words couldn't describe how shocked she'd been when she saw him the previous night. She was already worried about him because he was alone now, and now his health was another thing she had to worry about. So, she'd stayed up all night, making that bone broth. She'd watched the broth simmer for hours, hoping he'd at least have a spoonful. But he'd gone off to work without even touching it, no matter how hard his mother worked to make it.

"What good would this do?" she muttered.

She, of course, knew what he was going through. Her son was a very sensitive and kindhearted man. He only became like this when there was something serious on his mind. Something that took up all his energy. She also knew what it was. She could see him starting to wither, as if he were reaching his limit of missing his family.

"I did all that for you," she said.

And she still believed that was true. She only wanted him to make a better choice because she knew him so well. She wanted him to reach for a higher place where he could soar. She didn't think there was anything wrong with that.

"Are you really going to leave this house? Where would you go if you did?"

Professor Cho had stopped talking to her a long time ago. So, she didn't know if he was really quitting his job and leaving Seoul. Born and raised in Seoul, she'd spent her entire adulthood there as well. This was their home, and he was saying that he wanted to leave.

Ms. Jung clenched her thin hands, thinking of the way he was losing his weight. He meant it. He was letting go of everything. And that was eating him away from the inside. She was sure he was going to end up in the hospital as a patient this time if he kept going on like this.

As she looked around the large house, her eyes were as devoid of life as the browned leaves on the ground in the fall. "Was it always this quiet?"

This silence suddenly felt unreal. The stillness was suffocating.

She buried her face in her hands. Her fingers were swollen from all the hardships she'd been forced to face in her younger days. She was only barely able to use her hands now because her doctor son had tried everything he could to fix them.

"Can't you just let us keep on living this way? Is that not an option to you?" Questions no one was answering escaped her lips. "We've come so far already."

Knowing how much she'd gone through for him, her grateful son had tried his best to only show her the good things. But she didn't want him doing that if it came at the expense of his health and his life. He was her only son… *Son. Child.*

Cold shivers ran down her spine. It was too quiet. Frighteningly so.

Letting her hands covering her face fall down, she mumbled, "Where have all of you gone?"

She recalled the time when this house used to be filled with the noise of two mischievous children running around. They used to stomp on the staircase so much that she would shout at them that the house was going to crumble down if they kept at it. She screamed at them, asking why they were so loud and reckless. She'd hated Ms. Seo so much that she never cared for her grandsons. They just never seemed that loveable to her. She couldn't stand the thought of who half the blood coursing through their veins was from. But at least Professor Cho wasn't as thin as he was now when they were here. It wasn't this quiet in the house either.

A couple days passed by like that. A few mornings later, Ms. Jung watched Professor Cho get ready to leave the house without having anything for breakfast once again. His hair was graying. He was losing so much weight that the clothes he had on were visibly larger than his body. He really seemed like he was sick now. There was no other reason he would be losing that much weight.

"Professor Cho, please, have at least one bite of breakfast..." she pleaded.

"I'm all right, Mother," replied Professor Cho.

"You're going to seriously hurt yourself if you keep going like this," she said.

"I'll only have myself to blame."

"Are you thinking of leaving me all alone, Professor Cho?"

He straightened his back, then quietly said, "No one knows what the future holds, Mother."

"I told you not to say things like that!" she screeched. "You don't say things like that to your mother! There's barely enough time left to speak only of the good things, and yet, you…"

"Have a nice day, Mother," interrupted Professor Cho. With that, he opened the front door and left.

Ms. Jung stared at the closed door like she was lost, then stubbornly clamped her lips shut. She went to the table and starting clearing everything. She threw all the rice, soup, and side dishes he hadn't even touched into the trash. She was going to make new ones. Her son was going to realize how devoted his mother was to him one day.

Clang!

A plate escaped her old, withered hands and shattered on the floor. She froze in her position with her eyes fixed on the shattered plate for a moment, then eventually crouched down to pick up the pieces.

Tears started rolling down her cheeks. She'd thought her tears were all dried now because she'd cried so much in her earlier days, but she was crying once more. Hot drops of tears dropped onto her veiny hands as she cleared the pieces. They reminded her of her shattered son. Was it too late to save him now?

Ms. Jung collapsed on the floor in a fit of sobs.

The phone rang, making her heart skip a beat. Wiping her eyes, she managed to get back on her feet in time to answer it.

"Hello?" she said, suppressing her sobs.

"Is this Mr. Sanghyung Cho's residence?"

"It is." She then asked in a piercing voice, "What is your business?"

"This is the emergency room at M Hospital. Mr. Sanghyung Cho was found collapsed on the streets, so he…"

Ms. Jung dropped the phone, screaming, "No!"

CHAPTER 28

$\mathcal{M}$s. Jung hurriedly ran to the M Hospital emergency room. It was not that far from home, but it felt farther than anywhere in the world right now.

As soon as she was inside the hospital, she rushed to the reception desk. "Where is my Professor Cho—"

"It's all right, Mother," said her son from behind her.

Spinning around, she found him in one of the seats in the waiting room. He stood up like he'd been waiting for her.

"What—what happened?" she mumbled.

Bowing his head as if to express his regret, he said, "I sat down for a moment because I was feeling lightheaded, and the passerby mistook it for me collapsing. There's nothing to be worried about. I'm completely fine."

At a loss for words, Ms. Jung stared at his face. She didn't know what she could do for her son anymore.

"I'm sorry, but I'm running a little late, so I'm going to have to head straight to work. I'll get you a cab," he said. But Ms. Jung didn't move an inch, her eyes still fixed on his thin body and tired face. "I'm fine, Mother. Let's go, now. We're in an emergency room, so the faster we make space, the better."

Swallowing down her tears, she said, "You should perhaps call Hwihyun and…"

"I have no right to do that, Mother," answered Professor Cho.

Right? What more does a father need to do to have the right to call his son? He was only born thanks to his father. Isn't that enough? she thought, but she decided against arguing with Professor Cho right now. He looked too pale. If he lost consciousness again…

"Fine." She pressed her lips together. "I'll find my own way home from here, so you go on to work."

Professor Cho looked back and forth between his mother and his watch with a slight frown. "Are you sure?"

She nodded. "I'll leave after taking a short break, so don't worry about me. Go on."

He got up to his feet at last and said, "Please excuse me, then. I have a patient coming in very soon."

"You're really going to be all right?" she asked one last time.

"Yes," he answered.

She waved at him to say no more and go. When he left the waiting room, Ms. Jung moved to a corner where she would not get in the way of others. She then looked around at the emergency room, feeling the weight of what had almost happened here, in this place where life and death were only seconds apart.

That night, when she heard the front door open, Ms. Jung straightened her back in her seat on the couch. Professor Cho had come home past ten again today, even after the event in the morning.

"Welcome home," she warmly greeted her son.

But she couldn't bring herself to look into his eyes. The shattered plate, the emergency room. Her heart kept aching as she thought of how his collapse on the street could have led to a much worse outcome.

"Have you had dinner yet?" she asked. "Do you want me to fix you something?"

Professor Cho looked at Ms. Jung, who was strangely not meeting his gaze. He silently bowed and walked past her.

"Tell me what you want me to do," she said, and he paused in his step. "Enough with the silence now. I don't want to see you like this anymore."

Professor Cho slowly turned around to face her. She still had her eyes fixed elsewhere in an effort to avoid looking at him.

"So, you're willing to talk?" he quietly asked.

Ms. Jung realized for the first time that he'd been waiting for her to say this all along. Tears welled up in her eyes, then trickled down her wrinkled face.

"Yes, let's talk," she said. "It would be better than losing a son."

Professor Cho sat down on the sofa across from her. His mother still refused to look him in the eyes, like she was afraid of what she would see.

"Mother." His voice rang through the house that had been so silent all day long.

Her lips quivered as though she were shaking.

"Thank you for letting me talk to you," he said.

Tears kept streaming down her face. That made his heart wrench, but he continued in a composed manner, "Growing up, at times I was proud, and other times I felt guilty for being your son. I thought there was nothing I could do to fully repay all that you had to go through because of me. I know you love me. I also know that your world revolves around me. And because of that, I was proud to be your son."

Ms. Jung stubbornly kept her eyes away from him.

"Then one day, I found myself wanting to be a parent like you. I wanted my sons to be proud of having me and my wife as their parents. Do you understand what I'm saying?"

Ms. Jung didn't nod. She just let the tears obscure her view.

She'd sat in the emergency room's waiting room all morning. No one there had come alone. They'd all had at least one family member with them, whether it be a wife, a child, or a parent. But Professor Cho had been alone. That was not what she wanted for him. It never was and never would be. What kind of a mother would want to see their child like that? She'd only wished that someone a little bit better would be by his side, and look what that had led to.

"It was because of me that you could bear your way through all those difficult years, right?" he continued. "I am the same way. I wanted to die when I lost Hwiyin, but...I gritted my teeth through it all because my wife and Hwihyun were there."

Ms. Jung didn't say a word. Hwiyin. How she hated that boy. She couldn't help but think of what could have been if it hadn't been for Hwiyin.

"I love my wife. I love Hwiyin, and I love Hwihyun more than anything in the world. And I love you too, Mother," he said.

Ms. Jung's voice shook as she said, "So, did that girl say she'll take you back, then?"

That girl... She was talking about Ms. Seo.

"No," he answered.

Ms. Jung raised her brows in an instant. Seeing that, he stood up from the sofa and kneeled on the floor.

"Yoonkyung and I are going to start over, starting with the two of us. We've come back all the way to the beginning after going down the wrong road, so this time, we're going to make sure we take the first step the right way. It took me a long time, but I finally realized that first step should be our relationship with each other." Watching his mother's lips clamp shut, he continued, "So, I'm sorry, Mother, but I'd like to go back to my wife now. I want to be with my sons even for just a little bit."

"Then what do you want from me?" she said.

"Please decide for us how that should happen," he said.

Ms. Jung got to her feet. She couldn't say anything anymore without bursting into sobs. She looked down at the crown of Professor Cho's head. It had specks of white on it, like he'd been caught in the snow outside. *Where did all the time go...* His shoulders looked so bony from losing all that weight. *My son has been alone...*

She took a deep breath and lightly nodded. Turning, she walked out of the living room.

The next morning, Professor Cho came out of his room to find a suitcase by the front door. When he looked back, hoping it wasn't what he thought it was, he found Ms. Jung.

"Don't worry, it's you who is leaving," she said. "You said you wanted to start over. I'm sure she wouldn't want to see you if you were still with me. So, go. I...I will take good care of this house so I can give it back to you someday."

Professor Cho took big steps toward her and pulled her into his arms.

"Thank you, Mother," he whispered.

"I want you to be happy now. But don't ever think of leaving the place you spent your whole life in. And more than anything, you have to take care of yourself. Don't starve yourself like this. And don't let yourself end up in the emergency room ever again," she said as she tried to mask her turbulent emotions.

"Yes, Mother. I will take care of myself," he replied.

"All right... All right... Now go. You're going to be late for work," she said.

He pulled away from her and looked at her for a long moment. "Goodbye, Mother," he said.

Ms. Jung silently nodded.

Soohyuk was standing in the lobby. His shift had ended and he'd changed out of his work clothes. He was waiting for Yuna. They were going to show Minjoon to Professor Cho. And once the examination was done, they would go camping on Mount Yumyeong like they'd planned a couple days ago.

When he saw Yuna, he strode toward her at once. He was sure it was Yuna.

Yuna beamed at Soohyuk as he approached her. She was getting a wheelchair for Minjoon with the staff's help.

"Hello." She waved at him.

Soohyuk cracked a smile. She was just as cute today as any other day. "Let me help you with that," he said.

"Thank you," she said.

Soohyuk pushed the wheelchair out to where Minjoon was waiting with his parents.

"Hello," said Kyungjo brightly.

Soohyuk nodded to Kyungjo and Yoonjae as a hello.

"Hi, Uncle Soohyuk!" Minjoon shouted in a booming voice. When he pulled up the wheelchair in front of him, Minjoon collapsed down on it, exclaiming, "Oh, that was hard."

"Was it that hard?" he asked.

"Oh, yeah, very hard." Minjoon giggled.

The boy's laughter was no longer heart-wrenchingly exaggerated. It was just comfortable and genuine. Soohyuk pushed the wheelchair with Minjoon sitting on it.

"We're going to have a barbeque today, right, Aunt Yuna?" asked Minjoon. His mind was completely focused on camping and had no space for who he was here to meet.

"Of course. What would camping be without a barbeque?" she answered.

"I can't wait to see the doctor, because I can't wait to go camping afterwards," exclaimed Minjoon.

"Okay, okay." She chuckled.

They'd made an appointment with Professor Cho beforehand, so when they got to the exam room, he was waiting for them. But he wasn't alone. Ms. Seo and Hwihyun were there as well. Soohyuk hesitated for a moment, but he soon nodded at them, then introduced them to Yuna's family.

After they all exchanged greetings, Professor Cho took Minjoon into his arms and set him down on the bed. Soohyuk had already told him about Minjoon's condition. There was no cure for his condition as of now. The only way to go about it was to deal with the symptoms as they came. But a medicine was going to come out soon, they were certain. He and Hwihyun were going to help Minjoon persist until then, along with his family.

"You seem like a bright young man," said Professor Cho.

"Yup, I'd say I'm pretty bright," answered Minjoon. Grinning, Professor Cho carefully examined him.

"How's your walking?" asked Hwihyun from the side.

"It's hard, but I still like it. I like the massages Mom gives me every day too," said Minjoon.

Professor Cho couldn't help but be touched by his answers. This boy had managed to stay this bright even with his sickness. He glanced at the people who were raising this child. He couldn't help but admire them.

Professor Cho asked Minjoon again, "And is it hard to breathe at all?"

"Nope, not at all," said Minjoon. "By the way, can you speed this up at all? We're supposed to go camping after this."

Professor Cho and Ms. Seo grinned. *What a confident boy he is.*

"All right, I'll try to speed it up," answered Professor Cho.

After he was done, Hwihyun stepped forward to check his legs. He managed to check everything meticulously, as he'd planned, even with Minjoon pestering him the whole time.

When the examination was over at last, Minjoon started to

become cranky. He was getting bored. His parents and Yuna tried to keep him occupied while the doctors discussed their observations.

After checking the chart, Professor Cho suggested, "Let's do this. The rehabilitation department is doing the best they can, but let's double check on the progress ourselves. I think Dr. Cho could be a lot of help since he's pretty well known in the neurosurgical field."

Putting both his hands in the pockets of his gown, Hwihyun said, "I'll contact Professor Shin at the rehabilitation department myself and ask for help."

"Yes, that sounds like a good idea," said Professor Cho.

"Minjoon is such a positive child, so I'm sure we'll have great results," said Hwihyun.

Yoonjae was a little stunned. Yuna had briefly caught him up, but he'd still had no idea Soohyuk's long-lost family was made up of such amazing people.

But Yuna had told him plainly, "Don't look at them. Look at Soohyuk. Just keep your focus on my man, Soohyuk Cha."

Yoonjae glanced over at Yuna. He would have understood if she still looked a little intimidated, but she didn't seem intimidated at all in the way she was listening to them while holding Soohyuk's hand.

"Mr. Lee," called Professor Cho. When Yoonjae turned his gaze to him, he continued, "You have an amazing son. I truly admire you. Also, thank you for taking in Dr. Cha."

"I should be the one thanking you for looking out for our boy like this. And I don't think there's any more to say about Dr. Cha. We're already family."

Ms. Seo grinned and reached out to hold Yuna's hand. She squeezed it tight.

Riding in the convertible car with Soohyuk, Yuna threw her head back to look up at the sky, clear and blue overhead.

"You're going to hurt your neck," said Soohyuk.

"No, I'm not," said Yuna.

But Soohyuk still reached out a hand to bring Yuna's head back upright like he was worried. Yuna pouted, but his hand pushing her head back up was so gentle that she let him.

"Your face has changed a lot recently. Have you noticed?" asked Yuna.

"I have," admitted Soohyuk as he kept his eyes on the road.

"It was even clearer when you were standing next to Hwihyun earlier. Well, to me, at least. It might have been because I already know everything, but you two looked kind of similar," said Yuna.

"You think?" answered Soohyuk.

"Mhmm. I think you two might look completely like each other by the time December comes. Everyone will know at a glance that you're siblings." Yuna smiled.

Soohyuk faintly smiled as well. The changed environment must be changing him again. He was making different expressions now, bringing out the side of him that had been hidden until now. He remembered there was a question he hadn't asked Yuna yet.

When they stopped at a light, Soohyuk asked, "Who do you want to marry, Yuna? Soohyuk Cha, or Hwiyin Cho?"

"You," she answered cheerfully.

It was a wise answer to a foolish question.

She then asked, "What about you? What name do you want to use when you marry me?"

"Soohyuk Cha. When Kate called me that, I became her son," he answered as Yuna smiled brightly. He added, "I wouldn't have come this far if it weren't for Kate. I wouldn't have met you either. She is my mother."

"Mhmm."

"I'm sorry for making you marry a thirty-five-year-old grand-pa," he jokingly said.

Yuna burst into joyful laughter. They'd both thought he was two years older than he actually was until recently.

"I'm sure they'll understand. You're going to invite them to the wedding, right?" asked Yuna.

"Of course," he said.

"I'm glad you seem comfortable with them now."

"It's all thanks to you. I think by December…I'll have a chance to call them my father and mother," he said.

"Do you have an idea how that'll happen?" asked Yuna.

"I do," said Soohyuk.

"How?"

"I'm thinking of just asking them straight out if they want to come to the wedding," he answered, and Yuna giggled.

Her giggle continued for a while, then she held his hand and said, "That sounds like something you would do. That's why it makes it even more awesome."

Soohyuk laughed as well. As she observed, he was feeling a lot more comfortable than before. He was finding ways to continue to spend time with Hwihyun, Professor Cho, and Ms. Seo, though they didn't explicitly call themselves a family. Thus, they were learning to be around each other little by little.

Before December was over, before the wedding, he would tell them.

That night, he and Yuna shared a slow dance under the stars, while Yoonjae and Kyungjo danced nearby. Then Yuna called Minjoon over for a dance as well. Yuna danced with Minjoon's feet on hers, like Soohyuk always did with her, and the sight touched all their hearts. Minjoon ended up dancing with all four of them. His laughter echoed across the camp on the mountain.

It was another memory they would cherish for the rest of their lives.

CHAPTER 29

When December came, an enormous Christmas tree was set up in S University Hospital's main lobby. On the small desk next to the tree were cards and pens, so anyone who wanted could write down their wish for Santa Claus. As they were in a hospital, most of the cards held wishes for someone to get better.

A small but extravagantly decorated Christmas tree was set up in front of the pediatric emergency room as well, for the first time ever. It was Soohyuk's doing. He'd found it unimaginable for a pediatric emergency room to not have a Christmas tree, so he'd bought one and brought it to the hospital himself. The staff helped him decorate the tree. Children who came to the emergency room, running a high fever, forgot about their pain for a moment as they looked at the twinkling Christmas tree, and every child in a wheelchair with an IV sticking out of their little arm smiled in glee as they reached out their hands to touch the stuffed animals on the tree.

"Who knew Dr. Cha liked Christmas trees that much? Seriously," whispered one of the nurses.

The head nurse quietly replied, "Come on, now, you should know a little better after working with him for a year."

"What?" she whispered back.

"Do you really think he's someone who would like Christmas trees?"

"Right? You think it's weird too, right?"

The head nurse mischievously said, "Dr. Cha actually likes kids, you know. That's why he set it up here out of his own pocket."

Pouting, the other nurse said, "Really? You always give him special treatment. You always take his side. I believed you when you said that you cared about us too, but it was a lie."

The head nurse grinned. "Fine, I'm sorry. I like Dr. Cha the best, I admit it."

I must be taking after Dr. Cha, she thought.

Suddenly, the doors leading out to the waiting room opened and Soohyuk came into the exam area. The head nurse was a bit surprised. This was his day off. The emergency room wasn't all that busy today.

"Did someone call Dr. Cha?" she asked.

"Not that I know of. Umm...I don't think he's here alone," the other nurse whispered.

Indeed, Soohyuk hadn't come alone. He'd brought Kate here for a brief visit, after taking various measures to prevent accidental infection. Kate had come to Korea for Soohyuk and Yuna's wedding in a few weeks. The date was set for the twenty-fourth of December at a renowned hotel's banquet room here in Seoul.

"So, you're saying that you'll continue working here?" said Kate.

"That's right. This is my workplace," answered Soohyuk.

Kate looked around with a warm expression. "I'm glad it looks a little less busy than H Hospital. Although, that's not necessarily a good thing for business."

Soohyuk cracked a smile and led her back out to the waiting room.

"I'll go inside and say hello for a second, Mother. Wait here," said Soohyuk.

"Yes, of course," she answered.

She proudly watched Soohyuk disappear inside again with a warm smile, then mumbled to herself, "This right here was the place you were meant to be."

Kate was happy with everything she was seeing. H Hospital had been packed with patients at all times, forcing Soohyuk to spend many nights there working overtime. What used to make her heart ache even more than anything was Soohyuk's coldness. The way he never let down his guard to anyone broke her heart. But from what she could see in his face, a lot had changed.

"You're finally happy," she mumbled, fixing her watery eyes on the Christmas tree at the doorway of the emergency room.

The head nurse greeted Soohyuk as he walked toward her. "Hello, Dr. Cha."

"I apologize for bringing a visitor without warning," he said.

"No, nothing to apologize for. May I ask who she is?" she asked.

Soohyuk answered with a smile, "She is my mother."

Everyone except the head nurse looked visibly surprised. *That blonde American is his mother? Then that means...*

"She came here for the wedding," he added.

"I see. She seems like a very kind lady," the head nurse said, smiling. "Congratulations again on the wedding. While we're on the subject, Dr. Cha," she added.

"Yes?"

"Are you really not going to invite us?" She frowned. "I'm very sad. You should be doing this the Korean way. Why are you doing it the American way?"

"Because that's all I've known all my life," said Soohyuk.

"All right, I guess that's it then. May I at least step outside for a moment to say hello to your mother?"

"Yes," said Soohyuk.

She followed Soohyuk outside.

"Mother, this is the head nurse of the emergency room. She helps me out a lot," he said.

When he was about to introduce Kate to her, the head nurse started speaking in perfectly fluent English. "Hello, I am Sangoak Jeon, the head nurse of this emergency room. It's been an honor to work with Dr. Cha."

Dumbfounded, Soohyuk couldn't help but crack a smile. He remembered her making him speak in Korean before, saying that her English was bad. *My, my, this place is packed with players.*

After Kate chatted with the head nurse for a few minutes, Soohyuk continued to show his mother around the hospital.

"This place is huge," said Kate.

"The pediatric emergency room is going to expand too. We've started the construction behind the building to move to a larger space," said Soohyuk.

"Oh, where that big hole was on the ground?"

"Yes."

Kate brought his hand into hers and patted it as she said, "Ms. Jeon said earlier that S University's pediatric emergency room has gotten much better thanks to you."

Faintly smiling, Soohyuk took Kate to the café as she held on to his arm.

"Let's have a cup of tea here while we wait for them," he said.

"I'm getting nervous. I'm not sure if I'm even qualified to see them," she said.

Soohyuk had told her that his family was here. The main reason she'd come here today was to meet them.

"Qualified? You're already my mother. What more qualifications would you need? There's nothing to worry about," he reassured her.

Placing her hand on her beating heart, she said, "Yes, all right. Yuna is adorable, by the way. I can't believe she's thirty-one when she looks that young! It's truly unbelievable."

"I know how adorable she is. What do you want to drink?" answered Soohyuk.

After Kate told him what she wanted to drink, he headed to the cashier. He found Ms. Seo walking toward them from the other side of the café, as he'd thought she would. Judging by the way she was hurrying toward him when he knew it was still her lunchtime, it seemed like Ms. Jeon had notified her about Kate.

"Dr. Cha, I heard your mother is here," she was, slightly panting. "I couldn't wait, so I had to come. Professor Cho will be joining us in a little bit."

"You have lunch together now? That's a lot of progress," he said. Watching her blush, he added, "Aren't you scared the witch might come chasing after you?"

Ms. Seo laughed. "Not at all. I'm too old to be scared of things like that. I've had scarier things happen to me. My mother-in-law is nothing compared to those."

"Really? What changed her mind?" asked Soohyuk.

Ms. Seo's smile disappeared. She'd asked Professor Cho again and again for the same exact reason. That's how she'd learned he'd been sent to the emergency room. And that he was alone when it happened. Thinking of that, her heart had started racing and tears had started streaming down her cheeks. *He couldn't call anyone...* She supposed that Ms. Jung had also realized what it meant to be alone. But both Ms. Seo and Professor Cho had decided not to say anything about that to their sons.

"I was so embarrassed because I finally realized what I'd done to you and our boys," he'd told her.

"No. You—" she'd started to say something, but was interrupted.

"The thing you said before, about not being able to call ourselves a parent, remember that? I finally realized what you meant by that. I'm sorry, Yoonkyung. I truly am. I've done some unspeakable things to you and to our sons."

"All right. I accept your apology."

"Yoonkyung," he'd called.

She'd interrupted, "I said, all right. And if something like that happens again, you call me right away, okay? If I find out after it happens like this again, we're actually over this time. And show your decision through your actions to Hwiyin and Hwihyun. They're not interested in hearing what we say anymore."

"Yoonkyung, do you really mean that?"

"Yes. I gladly accept your apology, and I'm still waiting. So, just hurry up and come on back."

She recalled his thin hand tightly squeezing hers.

"Ms. Seo?" called Soohyuk.

Sounding exaggeratedly cheerful, she said, "She was afraid she might lose her son. Ms. Jung apparently said when he went on a hunger strike at home that age doesn't matter when it comes to death."

"Professor Cho went on a hunger strike? That kind, soft man? I thought he'd never change," said Soohyuk.

"He's a wise man," said Ms. Seo.

"Please." Soohyuk scoffed.

Lightly patting his back, she said, "People who learn to change are wise. Ms. Jung is wise in that sense as well. She only gave in once, and she gave in at the most crucial moment on purpose." Her face returned to its regular color as she said, "Can you introduce us?"

"After I order. What would you like, Ms. Seo?" he asked.

Ms. Seo... Her heart ached for a moment. When would she be able to hear him call her "Mother"?

But she soon put on a smile and said, "I'll take a café mocha, and the professor will want a vanilla latte, and Hwihyun will take yuzu tea."

"Yuzu tea?" asked Soohyuk.

"He has a bad cold," she explained.

"Ah, that's why he hasn't been asking me to go drinking with him."

After paying for the order, he brought Ms. Seo to his table and said, "Ms. Seo, please meet my mother."

Kate got up from her seat, smiling, and offered her hand for a handshake. Ms. Seo grabbed her hand with both hands. This was the generous lady who had raised Soohyuk to be such a great man. Her eyes started to water.

"I'm so glad to finally meet you," said Ms. Seo. "You must be proud to have such a talented doctor as your son."

Frowning as if she were trying hard not to burst into tears, Kate said, "This is all thanks to his hard work. I haven't done anything."

"You should be proud. He's someone S University Hospital could not go on without now," said Ms. Seo.

Professor Cho belatedly showed up at the café, panting. "I'm sorry. The card reader suddenly broke down so it took longer than usual to pay."

"Mother, this is Professor Sanghyung Cho," said Soohyuk.

"Hello," said Professor Cho. "It's an honor to make your acquaintance."

Kate's eyes started to water. She could tell that Ms. Seo and Professor Cho were both being genuinely grateful. *But Soohyuk really did all this on his own... I haven't done anything for him...*

"No, it's my honor, and I should be the one thanking you both," said Kate. "I wouldn't have had a son if it weren't for you."

None of them had acknowledged their family connection outright until now. But they'd all understood for some time that they all knew.

"Why don't we all sit down? I'll go get the drinks," said Soohyuk.

As he picked up the drinks at the cashier, Hwihyun trotted toward him with a mask on.

"Hyung," he called.

"Hello. I heard you're sick," said Soohyuk.

"I'm doing much better now. Here, let me help you," said Hwihyun.

"It's fine. I'm not horrible enough to make you carry things for me when you're sick. We got yuzu tea for you."

"Thank you," said Hwihyun as he followed Soohyuk back to the table.

"Hello, I'm Hwihyun Cho, his brother," he said to Kate. Kate beamed.

"Here are your drinks." Soohyuk passed the drinks to the right person, pretending not to have heard Hwihyun. And so, they started talking again.

The next day, Soohyuk was working as usual. There was an endless line of sick children. Most of their patients this week were coming in because of the flu. The head nurse was introducing a new nurse to everyone in the midst of the hustle and bustle.

"This is Dr. Kim, a third-year resident," she told the new nurse as they passed by one of the doctors. "Let me also introduce you to the tyrant of this pediatric emergency room, Dr. Soohyuk Cha. He's gotten a lot softer recently, but he definitely will make you cry if you make a mistake, so be prepared. You have been warned."

Soohyuk cracked a smile at the new nurse, who looked a tad nervous, and moved to the next patient.

Ms. Seo quietly watched Soohyuk. It felt as if her heart had bruised the moment she'd heard him call Kate "Mother," the day before at the café. She'd been trying so hard until then to not get ahead of herself, but everything she'd been suppressing had all burst out the moment she'd heard that. She felt like she was going to fall ill on her bed like Hwihyun. She wanted to hear him call her that at least once before the year ended. At least once.

Her thoughts were interrupted by a guardian who needed her help. She hurried over to assist them.

Soohyuk glanced at Ms. Seo as she rushed over to help the parent of a child who'd just finished getting treatment. She looked much more tired than yesterday, and rather distraught. It was probably because he'd called Kate "Mother." Every time he referred to Kate as his mother when they were all talking together, Ms. Seo winced. The time had come for him to put everything out in the open.

On his break, he went over to the Christmas tree, waiting for Ms. Seo to be free. Christmas was still two weeks away, but there was a fair amount of presents under the tree already. They'd all been brought in by the staff. He reached out to take one of the gingerbread cookies hanging on the tree and took a bite. It was Yuna's. She was baking batches of cookies every day. They were very popular, so whoever wanted one had to come and get one early.

Soohyuk checked on Ms. Seo while eating the cookie. She was finally free.

He walked over to her and said, "Could you come here for a second, Ms. Seo?"

Ms. Seo curiously followed him to the Christmas tree.

"Was there anything special you wanted for Christmas as a child?" asked Soohyuk.

"I'm not sure. I've never thought about it," answered Ms. Seo.

"Then you should. I, on the other hand, do have something I'd like for Christmas," said Soohyuk.

Her heart started beating fast. She was starting to realize what he was doing.

"What is it?" asked Ms. Seo.

"A childhood memory." He grinned and added, "No worries if they're all gone. I'll leave you to it, then."

Ms. Seo forgot to even say goodbye because she was too

preoccupied with searching her memories. *A childhood memory. A childhood memory of Hwiyin's.*

Ms. Seo headed straight home as soon as her shift ended and took out all the boxes she'd piled neatly to one side. They were all Hwiyin's. She'd packed all his things, but hadn't thrown out any of them. In truth, she couldn't. They were all things Hwiyin used every day. She looked for the thing he was most attached to. She rummaged through every box.

She finally found it in the last box. It was a tattered, old, gray stuffed bear with only one ear. She picked up the bear with trembling hands. One of its ears had ripped off when Ms. Jung had tried to take it away from him, shouting that boys shouldn't play with stuffed animals, and he'd clung to that ear. Hwiyin would surely recognize this memento of his childhood memory.

It was time to write the card now. It was probably their genuine apology that he truly wanted. That evening, Ms. Seo wrote the card with Professor Cho.

Wherever you were, we always missed you and wished that you were happy. We have many things we'd like to wish for, but the direst wish of all of them is your happiness. We miss you every day. We know we will never be able to pay for everything we've done to you, but we love you very much, and wish we could see you on Christmas. From your remorseful parents.

After finishing writing, she read it again with a serious expression. She didn't like it. It didn't fully convey all that they wanted to say.

"I think we have to write it again," she said.

Professor Cho scratched his head, looking awkward. He'd moved into the apartment next door. They'd started dating again, but they weren't quick to sign the marriage license a second time.

He wanted to present her with the sweetest romance he was capable of.

"What should we write, then?" he asked.

"Umm…I'm not sure. I'm just anxious, is all. It definitely seems like Hwiyin's trying to say something to us. You think he is too, right?"

"Yes, I think so too. Boy, this is hard. I don't often write sentimental cards," mumbled Professor Cho.

"Hurry, think," said Ms. Seo.

Before the professor replied, the door of the apartment opened and Hwihyun came in.

"I'm back," he said as he took off his shoes.

"Hi, Hwihyun. Did you have dinner yet?" asked Ms. Seo.

"I did. What are you two up to over there?" asked Hwihyun.

"We're writing a card to your brother," said Ms. Seo.

"Really? Did he ask for something?"

"He said that he wanted a childhood memory for Christmas," she answered.

"I see." He saw the gray bear and smiled. "You got it right on the nose. That was his favorite."

Feeling relieved to hear that, Ms. Seo showed him the card she'd written and said, "Can you take a look at this, Hwihyun? What do you think we should write?"

Hwihyun read the card, then added a line, laughing.

You owe me a punch. Love, your brother.

Ms. Seo and Professor Cho burst into laughter as well.

Soohyuk came to work half an hour early as usual. The heavy-looking clouds seemed ready to shower them with snow at any moment. Kate and Yuna were going shopping together today. Kate had been thrilled since the moment she met Yuna and had been wanting to give her a present. He wasn't really worried about how the two would get along. They didn't speak the same language, but Yuna's physical communication skills were top-notch, so they could very easily communicate with one another.

"I wonder which childhood memory I'm going to get today," he mumbled as he strode into the lobby.

His dark gray coat ruffled behind him from the current that his quick steps created. When he finally arrived at the pediatric emergency room, he first checked the Christmas tree. There was a large mound of gifts at the bottom for the patients to take today. This was an ongoing event until the twenty-fifth of December. Soohyuk was willing to spend however much it took from his own pocket to buy the presents, and the other staff members were enthusiastically helping out.

Standing in front of the tree, Soohyuk opened the bag he was holding. Inside were Yuna's handmade cookies. As he carefully started hanging the beautifully packaged cookies, his eyes narrowed. His heart started pounding. His gaze had fallen on a gift tag on one of the presents beneath the tree.

To: Dr. Cha

A cheerful smile appeared on his face. The tag was attached to the gray stuffed bear. That tattered old bear had comforted him for many nights during in his childhood. And here it was again, waiting for him.

Soohyuk reached out and lifted the bear up. A note was tucked into its hand. He quickly glanced around. No one was looking. Not even Ms. Seo was watching him. He shoved the bear inside his coat and moved away from the tree.

Ms. Seo was frowning with concern. The stuffed bear she'd left under the Christmas tree was gone, but there was no answer. Had she interpreted Soohyuk's message wrong? She was getting nervous. Her heart started anxiously pounding.

"Ms. Seo," someone called.

She jumped. It was Soohyuk.

"Yes, Dr. Cha?" Her voice trembled with excitement.

"Have you thought about it yet? What you'd like for Christmas?" asked Soohyuk.

Brightly smiling, she answered, "A Barbie doll. I wanted one so much, but it was too expensive at the time."

"All right," said Soohyuk before he turned around and disappeared.

It was past lunchtime when Ms. Seo finally got her answer. She couldn't swallow one bite of her lunch because she was too nervous, but she finally ate a little after both Professor Cho and Hwihyun kept urging her to. Upon her return to the emergency room, she looked around for Soohyuk. He was in the intensive care unit.

But on her way to him, her eyes caught something. She scurried over to the Christmas tree. The next moment, she was cackling like a madwoman. Written on a rectangular box beneath the tree were the words:

Ms. Seo's. DO NOT TOUCH.

Smiling, she took the box in her hands. She then contacted Professor Cho and Hwihyun, wanting to open it with them.

"Should I open it?" suggested Hwihyun when no one dared to touch the box. They were all too nervous as they sat around the table at the café.

"Yes, I think you should," said Ms. Seo.

Hwihyun carefully opened the box, revealing a Barbie doll inside.

Ms. Seo smiled warmly. "He asked me what I wanted for Christmas," she explained.

"I see," said Professor Cho.

"There's a note here. Should I read it?" asked Hwihyun.

Holding Professor Cho's hand, Ms. Seo said, "Please do. I'm just so nervous right now…"

Ahem, hem. Hwihyun cleared his throat and read the short note aloud. "No need to feel so guilty about it. It's all in the past. I was well enough. I'm all grown-up now. I've become a good doctor, and I have a woman I love. We're getting married soon. I would be honored if you, Mother, and Father and Hwihyun would all come and bless our marriage."

Ms. Seo's face was already drenched in tears. Professor Cho's eyes were watery as well. Hwihyun clenched his fist around the note and leapt to his feet. It was a long time coming.

"I think I need to go deliver that punch he owes me," he said.

⁂

After stepping out of the intensive care unit, Soohyuk was on his way to organize the patient charts when he found Hwihyun fiercely barging into the pediatric emergency room.

He came straight up to Soohyuk and said, "You owe me a punch."

"I don't think so," said Soohyuk. "How about a hug instead?"

Hwihyun's heart was racing a mile a minute.

"Damn you," he mumbled as he violently hugged Soohyuk. "Thank you for coming back."

"Thank you for waiting."

"I hated you so much I wanted to kill you," mumbled Hwihyun.

"Why don't we all just die of natural causes at an old age?" suggested Soohyuk with a chuckle.

"I'm definitely going to kill you if you disappear again," said Hwihyun.

"Okay, all right." Patting Hwihyun's back as he kept hugging the life out of him, Soohyuk said, "Thank you for seeking me all these years. I'm sorry, I never meant to take this long to come back. If you really want to punch me, you can. But lightly."

"No…I can't. Because you're going to get back at me with two punches if I punch you once," said Hwihyun.

Soohyuk grinned. "Of course I am."

"Stupid Hyung," mumbled Hwihyun.

"I'm sorry. I'm especially sorry to you," said Soohyuk.

Hwihyun hugged Soohyuk even more tightly. His eyes started to water and his sight soon became blurry.

The doctors and nurses nearby were staring at them with wide eyes. Smiling, Soohyuk said, "My brother and I have been reunited after twenty-seven years." When the doors opened and Ms. Seo and Professor Cho walked in, he added, "And those are my parents."

Screams of excitement and joy burst out from everywhere.

With his arms crossed, Hwihyun watched Soohyuk and Yuna recite their marriage vows. He'd personally thought until now that people who got married on Christmas were cheesy, childish people who were a little too much into fairytales. But now that he was at a wedding happening on Christmas Eve…

"I admit, it's not half bad," he mumbled.

Soohyuk and Yuna were glowing. To be precise, they were glowing because of all the makeup and hair products they had on, but they also seemed to be glowing on their own somehow. Like they were literally radiating happiness. Hwihyun's lips loosened into a slight smile. His brother and sister-in-law looked nice. So nice that he felt the urge to actually meet someone now.

A humble reception started after the ceremony was concluded. The dance between the groom and the bride marked its beginning. Wearing a blindingly white wedding dress, Yuna smiled brightly and let Soohyuk take her hand.

"You look so adorable today," said Soohyuk.

He couldn't take his eyes off her. His whole heart seemed to be beating for Yuna now. Her hair and the white dress she'd specially picked out for today were simply stunning. But what he liked the most about her today was the way her eyes twinkled whenever she looked at him.

Soohyuk used his arm wrapped around her waist to pull her closer to him.

"You've gotten good at this," he whispered.

"Yes, because I had a lot of practice with you," laughed Yuna.

He thought of their first slow dance. He was not going to forget that moment until he died. Or the kiss, the love, and the hug they'd shared. All of those moments were now engraved in his very soul.

Soohyuk lifted her chin with his hand, then leaned down to kiss her lips. They tasted sweet. One kiss wasn't enough. He kissed her again, then again. He could feel Yuna smiling. He smiled as well, and their lips lined up perfectly against each other. They were so focused on each other that they didn't even notice when the music ended.

"I want to dance with Aunt Yuna," said Minjoon as he pushed his wheelchair in between them, all dressed up like a little gentleman.

Soohyuk laughed and gladly stepped aside for the two to dance. Smiling brightly, Yuna took the handles of Minjoon's wheelchair. They then started spinning and dancing to the music.

At the side of the dancefloor, Soohyuk offered his hand to Kate. "Dance with me, Mother."

Kate, who had been blotting her eyes with a handkerchief since the ceremony, took Soohyuk's hand and got up from her seat.

Hwihyun approached Ms. Seo. "Wouldn't you rather dance with me than Father on a day like this?"

"Of course. You're better-looking, too," said Ms. Seo with a grin.

Hwihyun laughed and led her to the dancefloor.

When the music changed, Soohyuk went up to Ms. Seo this time, saying, "Why don't you take this round with me?" Then he added, "Mother."

CHAPTER 31

Today was another busy day for Soohyuk.

After listening to all the symptoms a mother listed for her son's illness, he looked at the boy and said, "Now, let's take a look at you."

The head nurse was still standing by his side with her usual kind smile. Soohyuk was being so kind to the patient right now that it was hard to believe he'd been angrily yelling at the production team just a couple minutes ago.

A documentary production team was visiting them today to film a "Twenty-four Hours in a Pediatric Emergency Room" special. Bursting with the desire to let the entire world know of the amazing doctor Soohyuk Cha, Dr. Jin had thought this would be a good opportunity to show that Soohyuk belonged to S University Hospital.

Some of the staff at the pediatric emergency room who liked showing off welcomed this, such as Professor Park. But others did not. Soohyuk was among the latter. He was extremely annoyed by the production team shoving the camera in his face and chasing him around, asking for an interview. He didn't make any effort to hide it either. Still, they did not give up, and ceaselessly moved around to find the best angle. In that process, they inevitably caused an inconvenience to the patients.

A few minutes ago, an incident had happened. A needle in a child's arm had gotten pulled out, and blood had splattered all over the floor. That instant, Soohyuk had snatched the camera.

He'd marched out of the emergency room and thrown it on the ground as hard as he could, saying, "No one is more important than the patients here." He gestured and formed a circle with his fingers. "This is my personal space. If you invade my personal space, I will not hold back on you."

No one had dared to say anything, for they all knew the infamous temper of Dr. Cha.

"I will pay you back for the camera, but only after you let your audience know why it broke in the first place," said Soohyuk.

Letting the audience know why the camera broke would've cost them much more than the cost of the camera itself. They also couldn't have the people know that they were bothering the sick children just to shoot a documentary. It was the production team who'd ended up apologizing. They apologized to the patients as well. They then dared not to come close to Soohyuk at all. They had no choice but to film at a safe distance.

After Soohyuk put in the order for the boy's tests, he took a short break. The phone rang.

A nurse came running toward him and said, "An infant of six months with cardiac arrest is on the way. Estimated time of arrival is in three minutes."

Soohyuk ordered, "Clear room one in the intensive care unit and get ready."

He went outside to wait for the ambulance. When it arrived, the little girl inside was blue and the paramedic was performing CPR. Soohyuk took over as they brought the girl to the intensive care unit. Soohyuk focused on the child and the child alone once again.

Soohyuk was organizing the charts with an expressionless face. A new year had come, but he'd still never been able to get off work at the designated time.

"Well done again, son," said Ms. Seo. Soohyuk turned his gaze to look at her.

With a warm smile, she asked, "Would you like a cup of coffee?"

Rubbing his scruffy chin, he said, "Fill her up all the way, please."

She poured the coffee into the cup she'd brought. "Is everything all right? You usually only drink half a cup." She handed him the cup.

Drinking the warm coffee, Soohyuk mumbled, "I have to go pick up the wife, so I'm trying to wake up a little."

"Yuna? Is something wrong with her? Is she sick? Do you want me to stop by later?" asked the concerned Ms. Seo.

Soohyuk thought her affectionate worry was sweet. With a quick smile, he said, "No, she's not sick. We just have something we need to check."

Something about his smile made her heart pound. *Does this mean...*

"I'm going to be a grandma, aren't I?" asked Ms. Seo.

Soohyuk nodded. Yuna hadn't been feeling well the past couple weeks. Her periods were very regular, and she'd skipped the last cycle, so it was clear at once that she was pregnant. But they'd had to wait a few more weeks to actually see the baby and hear the heartbeat. Today was the day they were going to go in for the first ultrasound.

"I'd love to go too, but I just started my shift," said Ms. Seo, looking disappointed.

Soohyuk said, "Don't worry about it. I'm sure we'll bother you with the baby more than you'd like in the months to come. We're completely inexperienced parents, you know. We're going to need a lot of help from grandma."

"Well, of course. I'd love to help." Ms. Seo grinned.

Soohyuk's baby, she thought. Even just thinking about it made her shudder with glee.

"I heard Hwihyun's going on blind dates," said Soohyuk, taking another sip of coffee.

"Yes, he was so insistent on not doing any of that, but thank god he changed his mind. I'm sure learning that he's going to be an uncle soon would only motivate him to try harder," said Ms. Seo with a chuckle.

"I'm sure it would." Soohyuk turned his focus back on the charts.

When he had meticulously looked through everything and finished the coffee, he finally got up from his seat.

"You'll call me later?" said Ms. Seo.

"I will," said Soohyuk.

"Thank you."

Soohyuk cracked a smile. He gave her a light hug and brushed her back.

"How are the dates going?" he asked, referring to her and his father.

"We had a fight last night," she grunted.

Soohyuk looked at Ms. Seo with curious eyes. "What happened?"

"It's nothing," she mumbled.

He had a hunch what it had been about, judging by her blushing face, but he still said impishly, "Just dump him if you don't like him. No reason you should live with the same man again when there are so many good men out there."

"You're saying the exact same thing as Hwihyun." Ms. Seo smiled.

"We're brothers, remember? Goodbye, then," he grinned.

She waved as Soohyuk hurriedly disappeared.

Yuna sat beside Soohyuk in the waiting room at her doctor's office, holding his hand. This was taking too long.

"Are you nervous?" he whispered in her ear.

"Mhmm." She nodded as usual.

A wide smile appeared on his face. "But you're not scared?"

"I'm a little scared too. I can't help but wonder if I'll be a good mom," said Yuna.

Reaching to pull her into her embrace, he whispered, "You're going to be the best mom ever. Like you are the best wife ever. And I'll always be there by your side."

"Mhmm." She nodded again.

Oh, she's cute. She's so cute. What am I going to do with her? He usually pulled her into the bedroom whenever he couldn't handle her cuteness, but now he had to restrain himself. *Still...* Soohyuk hugged her so tight that she could barely breathe. Still, he'd love to have a child between them. The little world they shared that Yuna had built for them was now safe and stable. And in that world they'd created by themselves, a new life was beginning. Just thinking of that filled him with joy.

Their names were finally called. Soohyuk followed her into the ultrasound room. And together, they heard the strong heartbeat of their child as their hearts pounded along with it.

The day their child was born, Soohyuk learned what complete happiness was, being surrounded by family who were congratulating them like it was their own child. Minjoon was more enthusiastic about his new baby cousin than anyone. This was happiness.

Soohyuk watched Yuna gaze at their baby with a smile. He couldn't help but smile proudly as well. This was a happiness he would never have experienced had Yuna not started it for him. He reached out to brush her hair. No word in the whole world could've possibly described his love for her. He still wanted to try.

"I love you," he whispered.

Yuna looked at him with a smile. *Just the two of us.*

"I love you," whispered Soohyuk again.

Five years later, Professor Shin from the rehabilitation department carefully took off Minjoon's ventilator as everyone watched.

"All right, now slowly start to breathe," he instructed.

Minjoon did as he was told. He coughed because he hadn't breathed on his own for a while, but his breath soon started to sound regular.

Soohyuk listened to his lungs using his stethoscope. "Try breathing a little slower."

Minjoon had been relying on the ventilator to breathe for a year now. And it had been a month since they'd started administering the new medicine to him. Professor Cho and Hwihyun were also here, to see how much he'd progressed.

After listening to his nephew breathe some more, Soohyuk took off the stethoscope and said to Yoonjae and Kyungjo, "It's definitely working."

Yoonjae and Kyungjo ran up to him and hugged him as hard as they could. They watched Minjoon breathe on his own with tearful eyes. It had been a long and hard fight. They had been looking forward to this day for so long now. Modern medicine kept making progress and finally, new therapeutics were available for general DMD treatment.

"What do you think, Minjoon?" asked Soohyuk.

Minjoon, who'd started using braces created specifically for him two years ago, straightened his body and said, "It feels like I'm on top of Mt. Everest and looking down at the world, breathing without a ventilator."

He then gave them a thumbs-up.

When everyone was joyfully laughing, Soohyuk said, "Look at you, acting all cool now."

Minjoon playfully replied, "Don't forget that it was thanks to me that Aunt Yuna came to live with you, Uncle Soohyuk."

"Oh, is that right?"

"Oh, yeah, I basically saved you." Minjoon gave him an impish smile.

Soohyuk said with a snort, "Oh, of course you did. My gratitude to you."

"In honor of that, I'd like to have some kalbi patties for dinner tonight," said Minjoon.

Soohyuk looked at him with an air of arrogance and said coldly, "Better luck knocking on someone else's door, kid. We're going on a date tonight."

"Oh, come on," grunted Minjoon.

"That's enough of that, then. Good day, everyone," he said.

Hwihyun turned to look at him and asked, "You're leaving already? You're not going to have lunch with us?"

"Yuna's waiting for me at home. She really wanted to come too, but two little rascals kept her back," said Soohyuk.

"Ah, I see," said Hwihyun.

Professor Cho jumped in, revealing his side as a grandpa who was madly in love with his grandsons: "As a reward for coming all the way out here on your day off, we'd be glad to take those two little rascals. You said it was date night tonight."

"I'll keep that offer in mind," said Soohyuk.

"We'll be waiting, then, *hem, hem*. We'll always be waiting, *ahem*. All right?" said Professor Cho.

Soohyuk cracked a smile and nodded. He couldn't help but feel touched when he saw Professor Cho cherish his children so much. Yuna was even happier about it than he was, for her two sons were getting the love of their grandparents, something she couldn't remember getting. She liked it even more than getting all the attention from her in-laws.

"I'll see you again in a couple days, Yoonjae," said Soohyuk.

"Thank you so much, Soohyuk," said Yoonjae and Kyungjo together.

They reached out and held his hand tight for a moment to express their gratitude. He nodded to them and walked out to the hallway. He couldn't wait to see his wife's face beam with glee when he finally came to rescue her from their sons and gave her the news. He knew she must be exercising extreme control to stop herself from calling him or her brother, so he could only imagine how thrilled she would be.

When he hurried home and opened the front door, he couldn't help but smile ear to ear as he heard the upbeat music flowing out into hallway. Yuna must have used the best move she had to tire out their sons and relieve her fears.

He took out his phone to film a video, and then carefully peeked into the living room.

It was what he'd expected to see, but he still gaped in awe. Seeing Yuna dance with their two sons always made him happy. And excited. Juhwan, who looked more like Soohyuk, and Jeeho, who looked more like Yuna, both jumped up and down in glee. *Oh...why do you have to be so cute? What am I supposed to do if you just keep getting cuter by the year?* Soohyuk followed Yuna around with his camera so he wouldn't miss a single thing she did. When she started shaking her hips, he gave up on filming. She was so adorable and loveable that he couldn't bear it any longer. He had to go give her a hug.

"Dad!"

"Dada!"

Both of his sons came running to him and clung on to each leg. Soohyuk walked over to Yuna with the boys on his legs like koalas and kissed her.

"Minjoon succeeded in breathing on his own," he said.

Yuna stared at him like she was too in shock to have a reaction.

"I'm sure a lot of the patients are going to get better too, now. Minjoon's progress shows that the medicine is very effective," added Soohyuk.

Screaming in joy, she jumped into his arms. He wrapped his arms around her waist. He was still standing tall and strong with his wife and two sons clinging to him. He just smiled, enjoying the gleeful kisses Yuna was showering him with.

But the more she kissed him, the more he started to feel a certain hunger.

"In celebration of that news, let's send these two away to Mother and Father and go break the bed," he said.

Her face blushed a beautiful red.

The End

I suddenly had a thought one day. In what ways does love leave its mark? Love starts with two lovers, who form a family through marriage, and expand that family by bringing forth a child, the ultimate culmination of *love*. So, perhaps love leaves its mark through the creation of a healthy family.

Reaching that conclusion, my thoughts naturally led to a story I wanted to write. A story of Soohyuk Cha, who might seem like an ill-adjusted individual but actually has more love for people than anyone deep inside his heart, and Yuna Lee, who gives her best to everything life throws at her, "just the two of them." But these two have family members who love them more than anything in the world: Soohyuk has his adoptive mother, Kate, and Yuna has her brother, Yoonjae. Because they have them, these two characters have managed to fight through all the hardships they've faced in life rather than succumbing.

I believe that love creates family, not the other way around. I wanted to depict that in the format of a sitcom, but I wanted something healthy that is not riddled with toxic messages and could be read by the audience. That was how I came up with the central theme, "empathy."

I personally think that a strong, healthy community is one that empathizes with its members. In order to create that, I had to incorporate a lot of the things I experienced in my own life.

As I said while this was serialized, most of the episodes that took place at the hospital were things I saw and experienced firsthand, as my son and I frequently visited the emergency room since he was young. A small portion of them were inspired by stories I saw on the news, and the car accident episode was constructed based on what I heard from a reader while this was serialized in *Romantique*. And all the complaints and grievances I had against the staff from my experiences with them were so gratifyingly addressed by Soohyuk. As I heard you all react, empathize, and sympathize with the characters, I experienced the greatest joy an author ever can experience.

This could not have happened without all of you.

My most sincere gratitude to all my readers for gifting me with the happiest moment of my life.

Thank you,

Ryu Hyang
    May 2017

ABOUT THE AUTHOR

Ryu Hyang was born in Seoul. She wishes to be a writer who brings joy to everyone who reads her stories and is always in their memories. She is a romance buff to the core who always dreams of happy endings. Her published works in Korea include *Light and Shadow, Golden Time, Glory, The Gift, Ryuhyang, Dear My Rose, The Good Man, Creep, An Ocean of Light, Summer, The Beauty and the Beast, To the One Who Loves Me, Candle in a Storm, One Fine Day, The Night Wind, The Fair Wind, Colors of the Wind, The Sound of the Wind, N.I.G. (Now is Good), The Vow, Just the Two of Us, River Flow, Sally Says,* and *The Nights Under the Moonlight.*

9 781952 787102